Killer in the Mirror

Myriah Saulnier

Visit the author's website at www.myriahsaulnier.com

ISBN 978-1-7383987-0-6 (print)
ISBN 978-1-7383987-1-3 (e-book)

Book Cover by Myriah Saulnier & Noor Fatima

Illustrations by Free Stock Media through Canva

First edition 2024

To Cody, you finally get to read it. Thanks for being my biggest cheerleader through everything. I'll love you forever.

"Everybody tells me it's 'bout time that I moved on
And I need to learn to lighten up and learn how to be young
But my heart is a valley, it's so shallow and man made
I'm scared to death if I let you in that you'll see I'm just a fake
Sometimes I feel lonely in the arms of your touch
But I know that's just me, 'cause nothing ever is enough
When I was a child I grew up by the River Lea
There was something in the water, now that something's in me
Oh I can't go back, but the reeds are growing out of my fingertips
I can't go back to the river
But it's in my roots, in my veins
In my blood and I stain every heart that I use to heal the pain"

River Lea by Adele

CHAPTER 1 - JANE

So many have died because of me. At first, I thought it was my personal curse; one which followed me from town to town ripping out anything that was beautiful. It began when I lost my best friend and then my father in the span of one year when I was 17. Then a few months later, I learned what true evil was. I thought I had bounced back from this wretched town of hate and loneliness and loss; I made myself a new and better person since I left it all behind. But now that I'm back here, I realize that I never changed. My surroundings and my life did, but my soul didn't. It's in my blood. There's something evil in this town and whenever I am here, I feel it linger in me too. I heard a singer once describe the darkness inside her and how it originated from her small town's water supply. It ran through her veins forevermore, she said, regardless of where she fled to. I feel the town of Isinbury has the same effect. There are people here who are truly good, don't get me wrong. Some I consider my only family left in the world. But those people have secrets too. And I have lost my ability to trust anything or anyone at all anymore. Including myself.

I stop these thoughts and focus on the task at hand. It's pitch black out here but I make my way to the cabin door. With my gun in one hand and my flashlight in the other, I turn the door knob. It's unlocked. I hesitate, knowing it isn't just my life that might be on the line here. I crouch and enter the place as quietly as possible. As I do, I hear a muffled sound to my left. Just as my flashlight turns to shine on a pale, wet, distorted face, I feel a hard thump on the back of my head. Did I hear the thump first or did I feel it smash into my head first? The delirium has started. I smell the iron of my bloodied head wound as I fall to my hands and knees and quickly lose the battle to fight for my life... My body drops to the cold wooden floor and my eyes close. The killer has me unconscious.

FOUR WEEKS EARLIER - JANE

Someone is breaking into my apartment to make good on those death threats I've been receiving. I heard them try the handle. It's locked. Now they are pounding on the door, making me jump in tune with every thud.

I used to get the threats scrawled on loose scraps of paper or dirty napkins, stuffed in the drawers of my desk at work or stuck proudly via sticky note on my computer screen for everyone walking by to see. A sympathetic colleague eventually reported the harassment to HR, and now I mostly get the threats in the mail, my email, and even stuck to my front door. Whoever reported it, I'm sure they were trying to help, but now the rest of them just think it was me who complained, and so they have added the word "snitch" to their list of nicknames for me, along with *loner bitch, cop killer, liar* and *traitor,* to name a few.

My cellphone rang a few minutes ago, a high-pitched ringtone waking me from a deep sleep. I feel disoriented, sprawled out on the dirty floor of my apartment. I feel the heap of half-drawn duvet covers still cocooned around my sweaty body. I must've taken them with me from the couch to the ground, undoubtedly during another fitful sleep. I adjust myself onto my back and take a deep breath to calm my nerves. The television is still on from the night before. It often runs silent in the background as a distraction to my thoughts, a way to feel less alone.

The firm pounding knocks on the door have stopped. They're now kicking near the lock, the weakest part of the door. It won't be long before the door falls down and they're inside. I've rented in an old building that's seen better days and more useful landlords.

The door breaks apart with a splitting sound, probably sideways off its hinges, the rest of the fragments falling to the ground in pieces. I wince on impulse, then lie completely still. Eyes closed. Waiting.

Normally, I would've grabbed my nearest weapon, either my personally licensed gun or the few knives kept hidden throughout every room of this tiny apartment, but I don't care anymore.

I'm a good person. Smart. Hard-working. Generous. And it took this one thing–Marcus flipping my world upside down–to make any sort of life I had completely fall apart.

I wonder if my neighbours have called the police, not knowing that it's my fellow officers that have been sending the death threats, the ones probably entering my apartment right now. The same ones breaking in when I'm not home and moving things around to scare me.

Fine. Have at me, asshole. It's not like I want to live with this guilt weighing on me for the rest of my life...or this new and chronic inflammatory disease that's left me disabled. A fiery burning pain coursing through my entire body: a constant reminder of that night.

Trust me. I hate myself even more than you hate me. You'll be doing me a favour.

The intruder makes their way into the middle of my tiny place and stops about five feet away from me. My ears focus on the heavy, sure-footed steps walking past all the garbage and mess on the floor, the steadiness of their breathing, anything verifiable at all that will help me identify them before I let it all go.

But as I'm making my peace with leaving this cruel, lonely world, I smell the aftershave. It's a mix of woodsy and vanilla. A few hours old but recognizable all the same. And I hear a murmured, tired sigh. One that I have known for all my life.

And I realize, with a shock that feels like a shiver shooting down my back, I am not dying today. At least not by the hands of this man.

Bobby.

He gives me a soft kick in the ass which makes me yelp in surprise and I open my eyes to him standing directly above me.

"So you aren't dead," he says in his familiar baritone. "Good to fucking know."

Now it's my turn to sigh. "You better replace that door before the landlord gives me shit about it."

"He'll only care if he notices, so you probably have a few months before then." Bobby looks around at the dozen takeout containers with strange rotting meat and dried-up noodles scattered on the hardwood floors and side tables and I know immediately what he's thinking. This general dirt and grime is evidence of a person who has given up. He exhales slowly.

"Jane Beckett." My name comes out of his mouth the way a scolding mother would say it. "Why did you let it get this bad?" He hesitates and adjusts his tone. "I know you've been dealing with shit lately...but haven't you been seeing the therapist the force issued to get that all off your chest?"

"A lot of good she does," I say thick with sarcasm. "She mostly wants to talk about my childhood as if she learned how to be a therapist from watching soap operas. And she ties her hair up so tight she looks surprised all the time. It's distracting." I soften a little as my eyes meet his. I'm one of those people who uses sarcasm or comedy to mask my pain or discomfort. He continues to give me a stern look that says there's nothing funny about the situation I've put myself in.

"Okay, in all seriousness, she just doesn't help me. She just brings up a lot of crap that has nothing to do with what happened."

"You were supposed to give it an honest try, Jane. God, you're so much like your father." He rubs the stubble growing on his chin. "Stubborn as hell," Bobby adds, almost smirking before getting serious again.

Bobby and my dad were best friends growing up and family after that. When I was born, Bobby was named my godfather, even though I grew up calling him my uncle. It wasn't until I was eight that I figured out we weren't even related by blood but that didn't make any difference to us. He was my Uncle Bobby; the one who gave me the best presents on my birthday and let me stay up late watching scary movies with him when he came to babysit; he let me have my first sip of beer and taught me how to shoot a gun when I was 10.

"Why are you ignoring my calls?" He grunts as he reaches down and picks up my cell phone. "I heard it ring before I knocked down the door. For a second, I actually thought you might be dead."

The colour is slowly coming back to his face. I must've actually scared him. He sits down on the couch behind me, his bones too creaky and old to join me on the floor. I sit up, with slight difficulty, and bring myself up next to him on the couch. My left hip and leg are completely numb and riddled with pins and needles. I wince as I try to move my left ankle and toes.

I'm wearing only boxer shorts and a loose T-shirt, so I pull the blanket up with me and around my shoulders. The processed dinners and couch-potato behaviour of the last six months have not been kind to my once fit body. I close my eyes and round my left shoulder slowly, feeling the cracks and pulls of my healing muscles respond. I breathe deeply to fight off the burning ache.

It smells bad. It's either the dishes I've left for over two weeks now, which are piled up like a daring game of Jenga on my kitchen counter, the trash which is overflowing, or it's me.

I lean into Bobby and rest my head on his shoulder. Even in his company, I feel defeated. He reaches out and envelops my relatively small hands in his giant rough ones.

"I'll e-transfer you some money to cover the door repair. Sorry about that. I guess I panicked." The silence grows. "This place isn't as nice as your apartment in Vancouver. Do you miss it there?"

I shrug. I loathe it here but I don't want to give him any more reasons to worry.

"Jeez, looking at this place reminds me of your bedroom as a teenager. You're almost 30, Jane. Time to learn how to clean up after yourself."

"Hey now, I still have almost a year until I turn 30. Plus...you know I *usually* keep things squeaky clean." I've just had other priorities lately...

As if reading my thoughts, he says, "I'm not sure what your excuse is. Don't tell me it's because you've been busy. I know you're bored out of your mind with desk duty. And your landlord told me he hasn't seen you leave your apartment in weeks."

I notice his hands have more wrinkles than normal, so I study his face which reveals it too has added lines to the corner of his eyes and mouth. His hair is shorter, a fresh haircut I presume, but still just as grey and flat as when he last visited me at Christmas. It's been three months since then.

"It's been quiet at the station. I told them I'd take some vacation."

He rolls his eyes. "Yeah, eh. Did you go anywhere?" He folds his arms, waiting.

"Yeah, I did." He stares at me, waiting for an answer. I stare blankly back. "To the bathroom. Then back to the living room. And sometimes to the front door for takeout."

I feel a smirk break through. Surprisingly, he doesn't laugh or smile. Tough and serious, as always.

He usually visits a lot more but before this vacation...or, um, mental health break, I was actually busier than normal. I had constant physiotherapy, psychotherapy and legal meetings with the police force...and I guess he must've been dealing with his own stuff too since he hasn't been calling for our usual check-ins. I wonder what's been keeping him so busy. Or maybe I've been letting his calls go to voicemail. I can't really be sure. The last six months since what happened with Marcus has been mostly a blur. I remember Bobby visiting me in the hospital and staying with me a few weeks afterward, then a few months later with his visit during the holidays. But then, after he left and I switched divisions and cities, after things settled down somewhat...the loneliness and the heaviness of my situation really became apparent to me and I started to let myself go. I began smoking a lot of pot. First to deal with the chronic pain and then to deal with the depressive episodes...and all of a sudden, it's been 3 weeks since I left my apartment.

Although Bobby seems to have lost about 10 pounds, he still carries the extra weight around his waist. I know him well enough to tell he's visibly aged a few years in the span of three months though. Something is wrong.

But before I can ask what that is, he turns to me and gives me a serious look.

"Want to talk about it?"

My mind switches gears instantly and then all I can think about is Marcus and how I killed him.

"No. Not really."

He shrugs, pulling up my T-shirt sleeve without permission and giving my shoulder a good inspection. It's fatherly instead of patronising, in a way only Bobby can get away with, and too sentimental for me to handle right now. I shrug him off.

"I know it's been hard on you," he says quietly.

"I'm a big girl, Bob. I can take care of myself." His eyes avoid mine, instead choosing to look around my apartment again, taking it all in. I look away. I don't want to see disappointment there.

He pulls me in close to him now, letting me go limp in his embrace. "Janey," he says softly, "it's not your fault. He didn't just fool you. He fooled the entire force *and* his family at home."

"Rachel won't take my calls, Bob. She won't even answer her front door. She's in denial of what Marcus was involved in, even though Internal Affairs raided her home and found the evidence they needed. She blames me...which is fair. I can accept that," I manage in a low, defeated voice.

I think of 4-year-old Javier smashing his dinosaurs together and roaring loudly, completely distracted from everyone else in the room; Maggie, only seven, so precise and concentrated during her living room dance performances when I'd come to visit.

I love those kids. They're like family.

My heart physically hurts for them now. I can't imagine them not understanding where their dad has gone or why he was taken so early. I can feel my eyes starting to well up. I clear my throat to try and stop the ache. I miss them so much but Rachel probably won't ever let me see them again.

Bobby gives me another big squeeze and gets up from the couch making his way into the kitchen. "I'm gonna make some coffee."

He makes his way to the kitchen and shakes the empty coffee tin, disappointed. "Okay...I'll make you some tea then. That would help your nerves even more." I've never seen him make tea in his life. He must be really worried. Or maybe his longtime partner Judie is rubbing off on him. He rummages through the cabinet until he finds a packet he approves of. "Your shoulder seems to be healed up but how's the recovery besides that? Still having that burning pain through the arm and abnormal swelling?"

"Yeah. It pretty much burns 24/7. Turns blue, on and off swelling and is stiffer than rigor mortis."

He nods as he fiddles with the two dozen or so empty liquor bottles that I had managed to keep stacked in one corner, while the water boils. "You need to keep up with physiotherapy. They can help you manage your complex regional pain syndrome. If you don't keep it up, it can actually get worse."

I don't remind him that the only thing that can cure this terrible disease is for the injured nerves to regrow, which the specialists said will still take years. Years of being disabled. And if they don't regrow properly, or if my body continues to mix up my fight or flight responses through my central nervous system? I could be disabled forever.

He cleans off the counters in silence, placing dirty dishes in the washer. He gathers up the full garbage bags, ties them and leaves them by the door. I don't have the energy to tell him to stop.

Despite my internal spiral, I feel better now that he's here; a sense of calm and warmth only heightened by the presence of family. I'm reminded that I'm not so alone in the world, after all.

Why had I not answered his calls? The guilt rises in my throat as if I'm being strangled by it.

He comes back to the living room to sit across from me this time and he fiddles with his hands. He's nervous.

"What's wrong, Bob? Are you here to check in on me or is there something else?"

He clears his throat. "I wanted to see you. Check in on you. It's my job, you know." He's smiling but I can tell it's forced.

"Out with it," I say. The suspense is killing me. My mind wanders to the worst case scenarios: someone I love back home has passed away, or Judie fell on the stairs and is in the hospital. *Please*, not Judie.

"There's been two murders back home," he says abruptly. He means in Isinbury, the small, isolated British Columbia town near the Northern Rocky Mountains, populated with about nine hundred souls; the place I grew up with my parents and where Bobby is now Staff Sergeant RCMP Detachment Commander. Basically, the town's sheriff.

He sees my eyes widen and quickly says, "Not anyone close to us, honey. Two girls a few years younger than you. Twenty-three and twenty-four." His head drops. "Megan Kline and Lilyann Richardson."

I know their families. This explains the visible ageing and weight loss. There hasn't been a suspicious death in that town in over a decade at least. Being RCMP Detachment Commander in Isinbury is mostly a retired cop job, even Bobby would admit that. Mostly small theft, drugs and drunks, domestic disturbances, like any other small town. You take this kind of job not for the glory, but to be close to the mountains and the wilderness, to slow down and make a family. Certainly not to handle a murder case.

"Have you called in the major crimes team?"

He waits another long minute.

When Isinbury's previous Detachment Commander retired, my dad Henry got promoted in his place. Bobby followed him, both transferring from Vancouver to Isinbury which was somewhere more quiet. More calm.

After my father passed, Bobby took over the job. He took over a lot of jobs for my father after he passed. The most important one, being my guardian.

"I need your help, kiddo," he says sharply. "Simple as that." He looks me in the eyes, sternly, his smile disappearing. He takes a big breath. "You have the homicide experience, the time on your hands and the necessary background knowledge of Isinbury. I'm afraid I'm too close to the residents that I'm not seeing things clearly and to be honest we are too small of a deal for the province to send in the big guns yet. I need you." He repeats.

I swallow hard. The excitement of working once again on a murder case, not just investigating simple B&E's or speeding charges, makes my heart skip a beat. Then I think of Marcus. "You know how I feel about that town, Bob. I'm not going to be any less biased than you."

"You're the smartest investigator I know, Jane. It wasn't because I knew a few pals in the force that you were promoted so quickly. The men in your unit might tell you that to make themselves feel better, but it's nonsense." He watches me look out the window, avoiding his gaze. "It's because you were made for this job. You see things that others don't and you follow your instincts. You're just like your dad that way. Those are rare finds nowadays." He hesitates, looking down at his hands.

"I'm basically the lowest of the low these days. I'm back from admin leave, because I'm keeping up with therapy once a week, but I've technically been demoted. Not *officially*, but they aren't giving me my usual shift work until another three months at least, based on advice from my trauma therapist *Teresa*."

"Listen, you acted as you should have and the force is just covering their ass. I thank God that you made it out of that alive and if the city's too stupid not to beg you to come back to MCU, then it's their loss."

KILLER IN THE MIRROR

The Major Crimes Unit. The highlight of my still-early career for the better part of four years. I was lucky to make it there in such a short time. I was the youngest one on the team. The squad always teased me about it. Not Marcus though. He always saw a talent in me that I had trouble seeing. He would build me up and challenge me always, trying to help me grow in my role there. He was more than my partner; he was my mentor.

Bobby is still rambling on. I catch the end of it.

"...Now I'll be damned if I let you rot away here, especially when I have a bloody nightmare on my hands back home. You know you can help me." He eyes me, his voice rising.

I've never seen Bobby raise his voice to anyone.

"Maybe you aren't the police officer–" he pauses for emphasis, "the *woman,* I thought I helped raise you to be." He looks away from me and lets that sting. It does. I still don't respond. I get my stubbornness from my father, like he said. My mind is racing with excuses, both reasons to go and reasons to stay.

"The Jane I know wouldn't have let her life become this..." He motions around the apartment and then to me, before continuing. "She wouldn't pass up the opportunity to solve a case and put someone away who deserves it." He looks at me again, softening. This time his mouth raises in one corner, like a peace offering.

"I'm not going to try and convince you further or continue to build up your ego. If you're not interested, then I'll see you at our next visit. Which at this point, might be Christmas."

I take a deep breath to try and calm my nerves. "I don't know if I will pass the fitness test if they push for it, which they probably will."

"They won't demand a fitness test for this position, I already inquired about it."

13

"Really?"

"Yes. Let me know what you decide to do. I've cleared it with the agency and the head of your detachment..." he trails off, not sure how much to say about their willingness to let me go.

"What did they say?"

This news sparks a new hopefulness inside of my gut that I almost don't recognize. But it is soon squashed with Bobby's next words.

"They're willing to put you in for a temporary transfer...a trial of sorts. It's still a desk post, but I've managed to have you seconded to the case, primarily in an advisory and liaison capacity. Of course, I'll use you for other tasks too, but we don't need to share that with them."

I close my eyes, trying not to let the frustrated tears escape. This is my life now. It also means I'm still not cleared to receive my RCMP-issued firearm back.

"They're aware you already know the geography, culture and community, so you're perfect for the job."

He means they were more than happy to get rid of me, though he'll never admit it. The "E" Division that I serve, is the largest Division in the agency, accounting for about one-third of the entire force and located here in British Columbia. After graduating from the 26-week training program at Depot, the RCMP Training Academy in Regina, I was lucky enough to be placed relatively close to where I grew up. Most graduates are sent to any location, in any part of Canada, which has the greatest need for police services. Pretty sure Bobby pulled in one of his favours, although he's never admitted that to me. Favours, of which he seems to have an endless supply, after ten years working in Vancouver when he was a young Mountie alongside my father. I spent my first five years in general duty assignments in the North District at Prince George, before being promoted as Corporal to major crimes investigations in Vancouver for the past four years. After what happened with Marcus though, my colleagues made sure I felt their distaste every single day and it was suggested that I transfer. Even my closest friend and colleague, Lena, stopped talking to me once I became a pariah. Distanced herself from me, stopped answering my texts and avoided me in the office. The Prince George branch was my best option as I already had some connections here. But it's mostly a desk job, and I hate it.

I look around my apartment for an answer and for a moment, I think I find one. But my self-doubt creeps in and my mouth stays firmly shut.

"I leave for Isinbury tomorrow at 7 a.m. sharp," Bobby says, before passing me the cup of Chamomile and heading for the door.

I put down the cup of dirty water–I never did take to tea–and stand for the first time today, my head a little dizzy. I feel my hands shake as I say my next words.

"I guess I'll be coming with you then," I say, trying to sound more assertive than I feel.

Bobby stops, still facing the other direction. "Good," He manages gruffly, reaching into the side pocket of his jacket with his right hand, setting down my badge on the table. He must've gotten it at the station before coming here. Since I'm on desk duty, I've been keeping it in my office desk. Not carrying it around with me is another constant reminder of what I had and lost. It's strange how emptiness can feel so heavy.

He walks out of my place then, not saying anything further, stepping past the fallen, broken door.

CHAPTER 2 - JANE

We take turns driving and stopping for things like fast food, coffee and gas. We make our stops quick because the drive up is a little over 9 hours from Prince George taking the main highways and we're both nursing migraines from lack of sleep. I leave my heated seat cranked up for the entire drive to help with the back ache and make sure to stretch my stiff joints at every stop.

I'm used to B.C.'s beauty, but sometimes you take it for granted in the city. Being out here, it's all they have, so it's harder to ignore. I like it that way. The scenery is what makes this drive bearable.

We have a super small airport in Isinbury, but it's mostly chartered flights or for emergencies, linking the rest of the world to the Northern Rockies.

We take the Trans-Canada Highway as far as we can, heading towards Jasper, then the roundabout exit onto BC-5 N which we will cruise for a few hours still, before our last big exit. Bobby insists on taking the last leg of the trip because I can hardly keep my eyes open anymore. I don't argue. We're still four hours away, but as soon as he gets on "the deserted highway" as the locals like to call it, he can usually go at a steady pace of 120 km per hour, wildlife permitting.

This winding back road highway is closed in by rocky hills on its sides, with tiny spurts of water and the occasional bursting waterfall sneaking through the rocks and shining in the sunlight. This used to be my favourite part of the drive home, but I doubt I'll be able to stay awake for it. My eyelids are burning, they're so tired, and my mouth tastes stale from all the coffee.

I spent all of yesterday after Bobby left my apartment getting my shit together. I patched up the door, sent the landlord an apology email and the e-transfer from Bobby, did my four loads of laundry essentials and took a much-needed hot bath with epsom salts to ease my full body aches. I cleaned up every inch of my place, horrified and embarrassed at the dirt, the grime and the general stink. I used to be one of those anxiety cleaners, though I know now once you hit the amount of stress that I did, no amount of scrubbing your home raw will make the problem go away.

After all of that, I had thrown open the drawers of the dresser and packed my newly cleaned clothes, my overnight bag and a few essentials of the job including my recorder, my notepad and my laptop. I hesitated at my old patrol uniform, unsure of how formal I wanted to get in Isinbury, especially if I'm only *an adviser*.

I decided on some smart-looking polos and dress shirts with dark jeans or work pants. This is what I feel most confident in, even though it reminded me of the homicide investigations department that I miss. I always threw on my best suit to make an impression with the particularly hard cases and suspects. But it was effective with the average witness, suspect or victim too as they usually found it easier to talk to us with a softer appearance. It also worked better with the department's low budget for uniform allowance.

I picked up the neatly-folded uniform and hung it back up in the closet. Instead, I squeezed into my olive-green puffer jacket and dark wash jeans. I threw on my army-style black boots for the first time in nearly a year. I forgot how good it felt to wear these ass-kickers.

"Tiny but mighty," Marcus used to tease when I would wear these. The memory made me smile first before feeling like someone pulled my heart from my chest.

I felt a rush of emotions take over me then, a tickle forming at the small of my back, making its way up to my ears and through my eyes in the form of tears. My knees felt weak so I sat on the bed letting myself feel helpless and stupid...why did I think going back to Isinbury was going to help my situation? There are people and memories there I want to avoid too. I might as well keep going past Isinbury and make my final destination the Yukon so I can disappear altogether, somewhere new. Somewhere without my haunted past looking me in the face like a challenge.

I caught my eyes in the full length mirror in the corner of the bedroom and forced myself not to look away. I looked pale and washed out. My shoulder-length bob doesn't turn out like those beach waves some women are blessed with, but a weird mix of straight and curly at the same time. I noticed a small belly pouch around my waist too. I suppose sitting on your ass and eating crappy food while indulging in a game of self-pity will do that to a person.

When did I become this? The type of person who can't look themselves in the mirror for fear of what they find there?

On top of everything else, these new health problems have really tested me these past few months. I can't believe I ever took for granted waking up every morning feeling fine, not in full-body pain.

This is my new normal.

Try to focus on the really good stuff, especially when it all seems impossible, Bobby's voice says in my head. Like he's tried to tell me so many times this year. So I try to.

I still feel a nervous ball in my chest and a sort of emptiness, but it's a good start. Nothing like a new case to work on to bring me back to reality and to distract me from my thoughts. I relax into the old dusty car seat and enjoy the radio silence, letting myself drift into sleep.

~~~

My eyes shoot open a while later. Another nightmare. I can't bear to replay it all in my head anymore; those final moments with Marcus. My therapist says it's normal to replay situations when you have PTSD. It's our mind's way of coping with an unbelievable situation. But when will I stop torturing myself about this?

I struggle to get my breathing under control as Bobby looks over at me, concerned, but not wanting to pry. I nod as if answering him that I am fine and when my eyes finally adjust to the light, I notice we are about 15 kilometres away from Isinbury.

I feel my heartbeat kick into overdrive.

I can see where the mountains dip to the ground on each side, a small entry between them, a road taking you to town. Almost like a dare to every person who enters past them; an entrance for a price. I imagine the mountains, forming back into one and closing the gap once we're through, swallowing us whole in one large gulp. Keeping us hostage in this strange town where everyone keeps secrets, half have substance abuse problems and where nothing good ever happens.

CHAPTER 3 - JANE

Not counting my brief visit for my mother's funeral eight years ago, or the two times I've come to visit at Bobby's for the holidays, it has been 11 years since I've been here. Really been here.

There's not much reason to come out this far. It isn't close enough to any city to commute. You come here for a quiet life. It's mostly a fly-in community, and on any map, it's labelled as a pit stop.

"Isinbury, County of Caribou," the sign reads, "Population 900. Next stop: Toad River, 188 km away".

It's late evening when we finally make it into town which looks almost the same as I remember, although definitely showing its age even in the twilight. A few things have changed since my last visit, but it's still a community connected by the forest and the mountains, the two bars in town and the Tim Horton's near the highway.

We have two gas stations, two grocery stores, the liquor store, the beer store, the laundromat, the Town Hall connected to the post office, and some mom-and-pop shops on the main drag. For a small rural town, I spot only one shuttered *for lease* sign. The red brick on Main Street looks a bit dusty and worn, but proper maintenance of the trees and shrubs in front makes it look almost charming.

"I can't believe The Raven is still standing," I say to Bobby. I look over to it and notice several people out front smoking or with drinks in hand. Some wave at us. Bobby waves back.

He shrugs. "It's probably the only booming business we have left in town, these days. Everyone and their cousin go there." He smirks my way and raises a brow. "Makes for some interesting stories the next day."

"Oh God." I shake my head, but I'm smirking. "So it's still the go-to place then?"

"Yep. We have another bar in town now, but mostly just old farts like me go there to get away from the craziness of the young people at the Raven."

I look at the buildings clustered together at the end of the street. The Music and Movie Shack, Sally's Convenience and Grocery, two second-hand stores and a new clothing shop called The Red Dress. They all share the same cement-build, white-painted exterior, that show their decay with the mould and ivy growing at their corners. They look a little worse for wear, but I'm happy to see them still in business.

"You guys still have movie rentals?" I say, not hiding the shock in my voice.

Bobby gives me his hearty laugh. "Yes, we do. We still have shitty internet connections out here so Netflix isn't always the number one choice."

"Netflix is overrated anyway." The smile is evident in my voice. "Those were some of my favourite memories as a kid. Going to *The Shack* with my parents on the weekend to pick out the movies we would watch. Then heading over to *Sally's* to load up on movie snacks."

The nostalgia is overwhelming. And heart-crushing. My hand moves instinctively toward my chest which feels tight.

"I remember those nights." Bobby says, leaning over to rub a comforting palm on my shoulder. "We can definitely squeeze in a movie night soon."

The tightness in my chest releases a bit, feeling more like a dam that's overflowed. I've missed him.

There's a new bakery with fresh renovations in the middle of the street that I've only seen in Facebook photos, but the police station next door looks just how I remember. I imagine my dad walking out of the front door right now, dressed in his work suit and tie, greeting me after school, lifting me into his arms and growling in my ear as I giggle. A few pedestrians walk by it absentmindedly.

The community hall part of the building is tucked away in the back, with its garages for rescue services facing outward onto a side road for firefighters to easily manoeuvre out.

The police station section is facing main street, in the heart of everything. It's a one-floor, relatively small structure of mixed red and brown bricks. There's a 6-inch-tall strip of sky-blue panelling visibly separating the building and the roof, and a proud Canadian flag pole to the left, in-between the station and the bakery. The side facing the street is mostly made of full-length windows, with large orange letters to the right of the double see-through doors stating "TOWN OF ISINBURY - ROYAL CANADIAN MOUNTED POLICE DETACHMENT FOR COUNTY OF CARIBOU." This is the public's entrance. The side entrance to the right of the building, next to the parking lot, is for staff. I know from Bobby's Facebook updates that in April, tulips and other brightly coloured flowers take the spotlight in these dreary looking gardens on either side of the public's entrance. A few weeks to go, and I'll see the tulips in person this year. Kind of a crazy realization.

Tulips used to be my mom's favourite flowers, and when my dad was the RCMP station commander sergeant, he let her plant a whole garden of them in the front to remind him of her often. Naturally, Bobby kept the tradition going with his partner Judie's help, who is responsible for all the town's decorative vegetation. If Mom was still alive, she would have kissed Bobby for it.

I think of her kind and gentle spirit as we pass the nursing home connected to the hospital where she lived for so many years before her heart finally gave out. Research over the past twenty years has finally determined a link between depression and heart disease. People who have a history of depression are apparently four times more likely to suffer a heart attack in the following years. Or so I learned on the internet after she died. Her medical examiner (now retired) tried to explain to me it was due to her "chronically elevated levels of stress hormones" and the "activation of her fight or flight response" which had lethal effects on her heart. If you ask anyone in town however, they'll tell you it was because her heart broke when my father died. It's a romantic notion.

I remember around that time, Bobby always saying, "You girls are my family and I'll always take care of you." Over and over. Especially when it got tough. I always thought it was like, if he kept saying it out loud, God would take pity on us and lift some of the burden we were on him.

I watch the town speed by on the way home. It has definitely become a bit poorer, older and neglected since I was a kid. Or maybe I'm just spoiled by the city and its constant need for appearing fresh and new. I do notice more housing developments and fast-food places on the edge of town, including a new Dairy Queen.

We pass some other cars on the road, people who recognize Bobby's truck and stick their hand out the window to wave. Bobby returns the gesture every time.

Bobby owns a modest size log home at the edge of town, but has a lot of private property which makes it costly. He isn't rich by any means, but has always saved up and spent only what he had to, so affording it was never a hardship.

I roll down the window when we're almost there to inhale the pine that weighs heavy in the air. Something about it calms me.

"Man, I missed that smell." I say, catching scents of wet bark and the dirt road too. Bobby doesn't have any neighbours–just how he likes it–and his house is surrounded by a small forest. He has a long, bumpy driveway covered by trees on each side and I scan the forests for signs of wildlife but only see a few deer.

"Will Judie be home?" I ask, hopeful. Bobby's partner, Judie, lives in her own separate place in town, but they've been together for over 15 years. She's like a loving stepmother or fun aunt to me, one that I've always considered family. Before Bobby, she was my mom's best friend. We've been through a lot together, the three of us.

"Not tonight honey, sorry," he says with a small frown. "She's visiting her sister in the hospital and will probably crash at home afterward. Her sister Ruth is draining...but she'll be here the rest of the week, I suspect. She hasn't stopped talking about your arrival."

"I miss her so much."

"The feeling is mutual, I promise."

The truck pulls up outside the log home and Bobby leans over to pass me the house keys.

"Someone's impatiently waiting for you," he says, as a smile spreads wide on my face.

I take the keys and run up to the door. As soon as I have it open, I'm jumped by Bear, Bobby's seven-year-old black Newfoundland who is so tall his head touches my waist when he's on all fours. I fall backward with a laugh as he jumps around me excitedly. My big newfie boy is covered with drool but I nuzzle my head against his anyway and give him all the love he deserves. He weighs around 150 pounds yet that's never stopped him from being a lap dog. Although Newfoundlands are often used as working dogs for their tremendous strength, intelligence and strong swimming abilities, Bobby keeps Bear around mostly for company. Newfies' calm dispositions and loyalty to their owners are also a plus, and is what allows Bobby to bring him to the station most days. I have always wanted a dog myself but I work too much and I'd never have time for one. Now that I've been demoted to desk duty for the foreseeable future, it might be a good time to rethink that.

I sit up and use Bear as leverage to get me back to my feet. My back aches something fierce and I long for my heating pad that I pretty much live on, most days.

"Someone missed his girl," Bobby says, referring to Bear and I rolling and playing in the dirt driveway together.

"Yeah, I can tell. I bet Bear missed me too though…" I quip.

It takes a minute but Bobby gets it and lets out that special chuckle of his that I love.

Feels good to be home.

We step inside and Bobby brings my bags to the spare room. It's a strange feeling for me because after being away for so long, it feels only *familiar* rather than *like home*.

Other than a new red couch in the open-spaced living room, everything looks exactly the same. All the same stuff – brown leather armchair peeling at the edges, light wooden side tables, same red and yellow mosaic lamps – and all in the same place. The soft, grey, worn blanket still folded neatly on the back of the couch.

"Wow, it's like I've been transported back in time."

"We did upgrade the couch since you were here last and there's a new widescreen TV in the basement," he hollers from down the hall.

He comes out of his office now with a pile of notes in his arms, which he lays on the kitchen table.

"Working through dinner?" I suggest.

"Let's start in the morning. I'm burnt out," he says. "I've got some tuna casserole leftovers here from Judie. We can heat it up if you're hungry. Sorry it's not more." He takes the covered dish out of the fridge and starts scooping himself some onto a plate. I do the same.

"I love Judie's cooking. This is perfect," I say. "Haven't had a home cooked meal in a long time either. Especially not anything this good."

My stomach growls in anticipation. That doughnut was the only thing I ate today other than cups of coffee, a bag of chips and a convenience store sandwich, which I'm told doesn't count as food.

"I'm going to change into something a little cozier now that we're staying in for the night. Be right back."

I bring my last suitcase and walk through the open-spaced living room and kitchen area, appreciating its large windows and beautiful high ceilings. I pad down the hallway to the first door on the left which is now the spare bedroom. Before entering, I peek into the room opposite and am happy to see it's still Bobby's home office. It's decorated with all sorts of man-memorabilia and a beer fridge in the corner, with a large oak desk in the middle and a safe underneath. Bobby isn't really sentimental, but the wall is covered with picture frames. Most notably: one of me at my police college graduation, me with my parents and Bobby when I was little during a backyard BBQ, another of me shooting my first gun in Bobby's backyard, and a photo of Bear and I one Christmas under the tree. There are others without me too: one of Bobby fishing with his friend Kenny, my dad and some other guys I don't know up at a cabin, and a stunning younger portrait of a twenty-something Judie in black and white. I'm going to have to ask him about how he got that last one. I smile. More than half of these feature me.

Maybe he's sentimental after all.

I turn on my heel and enter the spare room. There are a few taped-up boxes in the corner and faded rectangular spaces on the wall from where I took posters with me. Other than that, there's hardly any evidence of this being my old room. It's still the same pale purple colour I had when this was mine, but the room itself is missing character. My mother's family heirloom, a giant dark wood dresser, now sits opposite the bed with a tiny T.V. on the top right, both of which were hers when she was in the residence. I empty most of my clothes into the dresser, leaving a few in the suitcase to hide my personally-licensed firearm I brought in case of an emergency. Bobby wouldn't approve. I *know* I should have left it locked up in my apartment, but I feel better with it. So I keep it in the suitcase, with a pile of clothes on top of it and push the whole thing under the bed with my foot. Another framed photo of me with my parents when I was young is on the dresser, also from my mother's belongings. I used to have the same framed photograph at my apartment...but it went missing along with some other photos I swear I had. I've been so distracted lately.

The bed seems different too. I walk over and hesitantly collapse on it to test its comfort. It's even comfier than my own back home. I probably have Judie to thank for picking out this mattress, since Bob is clueless about those things.

I climb into my stretchy pants and a loose, comfy T-shirt and when I make it back to the kitchen, my plate is steaming. It smells cheesy and comforting, and like home.

He brings the food over to the table and I grab some utensils and extra napkins. We devour it all, feed Bear his grub, then get ready for bed.

Bobby gives me a big hug after making sure I'm all set for the night.

"Was gonna give you a hug when I first saw you yesterday, but you stank."

"Gee thanks, Bob."

"Hey, thanks for showering." He snickers, then his face gets softer. "Nice to have you home darlin'."

"Feels good to be home. Goodnight." I watch him until he rounds the corner and closes his door softly. Then I head into my own bedroom with the dog, and we both climb into bed. After about an hour of scrolling news sites and social media–my typical bedtime routine–Bear whines to go outside.

I can hear the crickets and toads singing their nightly lullaby as I sit on the steps of the deck and look up at the stars which take over the dark sky in a pattern of twinkling lights. Bear sniffs around for a good spot to squat. I forgot how fresh and pure the air is out here. I can smell the grass, the pine, the dirt and the boggy water nearby. I love it all. It's better than the city that mostly smells of fumes, cement and garbage.

It's a little chilly for a spring night, but I grabbed one of Bobby's winter coats from the front closet and it's wrapped around my shoulders. It smells faintly of my mother's perfume but maybe I'm just imagining things. It could be Judie's perfume as well. It probably is. I take in the smell slowly, anyway.

God I really miss my mom. I almost can't remember what she used to be like and realizing that I hardly even think about her anymore makes me feel like the worst daughter in the world. All I know for sure is that when she was alive, when she was still herself, that is, I felt seen and understood and like I was less alone in the world. And since she passed, I've hardly been able to feel those feelings with other people no matter how hard they or I try. It's that feeling of complete peace, happiness and belonging... and I've been chasing that feeling my entire life since.

I try to do what Teresa the therapist taught me and push out all negative thoughts and feelings, and just be present. Bear comes to sit next to me and eventually lets his limbs spread out on the frosted grass. Being close to him helps with my stress. My mind wanders to how lucky I am to be here right now. Working a case. Having a job to do. But also, to be in the presence of family. I should've just packed my things and came straight to Bobby's instead of taking that desk job in Prince George, wallowing in my apartment being self-destructive.

Bear looks up as a twig snaps in the woods and I tense. Is someone out there?

It's after dusk, so there's still some low light casting down its glare at us from behind the house and across Bobby's yard that is surrounded by pine trees. I never used to be intimidated by the thick brush, but I suppose being a homicide cop changes your perspective.

I remember then that my gun is under the bed and my pocket knife is in my backpack.

Bear growls a warning. Then pulls himself up into a crouch, and I do the same.

A few seconds later, a skinny raccoon dashes its escape from the tree line to the left side of the yard where the forest is thicker. I sit back down and soothe Bear. He stays watchful.

"Thanks for freaking me out, you big scaredy cat." I pat his head, but he hardly notices. "Come on inside."

He usually has great recall, but he stays in a crouch with his tail straight, on high alert, still facing the bushes where the raccoon has disappeared into.

"Inside. Bear, inside."

He lets out a low growl again and my heart beats faster. "The raccoon left, Dummy. Come on." I tug on his collar, trying not to panic.

He gives a frustrated grunt, then turns slowly for the door. He's sulking and mad at me.

I close the door after him and flick the locks. I look briefly out the window but all I see is darkness. I'm being paranoid.

I grab myself a cup of water from the tap and take my nightly medicine to help with the nerve pain and insomnia. I check my phone and realize I've been using my data. I find the password for the Wi-Fi on the side of the fridge, scribbled on a piece of scrap paper under a magnet. The password is something like: B5HjfL678MyB4. It takes me three tries to punch it in correctly. I should probably remind Bobby network passwords don't need to be top secret if they are literally posted to the fridge.

When I make it back to my room, I'm wide awake again, so I take a peek inside some of the boxes in the corner. I open the one labelled BOOKS, and sift through it. These belonged to my parents, but some of them are favourites of mine from when I was a child.

I'm looking for something that will help put me to sleep when I come across my dad's favourite book, The Murder of Roger Ackroyd by Agatha Christie. I smile big. He loved this one. I thumb the pages, imagining him curled up on the couch with it, when I notice a folded photograph tucked into the middle. I pluck it out and study it, confused.

It's a baby portrait, done professionally, but it's not me. It's of a young boy with orange curls on top of his head, toothless and wearing an ugly puke-coloured sweater. I don't have any cousins. And no one in my family has red hair.

I turn the photo around but there is no writing on the back of it to explain who this child is or why my dad had a photo of him. It was probably given to him by a friend and he used it as a bookmark. I chuck the photo back into the box and take the book into bed with me.

Bear seems to have forgotten earlier and he climbs in after me. I'm grateful to have his warm body next to mine. For a second, I think having him next to me might actually help me sleep better.

But then I toss and turn, restless and sweaty, and have nightmares the entire night.

CHAPTER 4 – JANE

"We have another promising police officer in the making," Bobby says, breaking me out of my thoughts. We're already almost at the station. I was up at 5 a.m. restless and ready to start the case. I fixed up some scrambled eggs, bacon and toast for us this morning which we ate quickly and took our coffees to go.

Bobby continues, peeking at me from the corner of his eye, expectantly. "A young lad named Adam, doing his co-op placement. Remember when that was you?" He chuckles.

"Yeah, I remember you forcing me to do long, boring, admin work during those hours. Almost made me not want to go into policing, 'cause I thought half the job was paperwork." I hesitate. "I guess that part was pretty accurate."

"Hey, it helped you lose those bad influences you called friends. I'm hoping being around cops half the day works the same for Adam too."

I was rebelling against the grief I felt losing my dad and what was left of my mom in such a short amount of time. We both know this. Neither of us mention it.

I had made some bad choices back then. He bailed me out every time, but not without consequences.

"What's Adam's story?" I ask and Bobby side-eyes me. "You have a soft spot for *projects*."

I wave my hand over myself as an example. He shakes his head but his smile reaches his eyes. It quickly fades.

"His sister was the second victim."

"Ah."

"And his father asked me to keep an eye on him or at least keep him busy, which I don't mind doing. Gets him out of school so he doesn't have to face any bullying either."

I remember what it was like after both my best friend Abby and my father were gone. It was like I had a giant red bullseye painted on my back: the best friend of the popular girl who ran away and the daughter of the cop who died mysteriously in the Rockies. Grief–especially during high school–alienates you. I feel bad for the kid, having been exactly where he was once.

I try to change the mood by doing my best voice impression of Bobby, which is just me puffing out my chest and speaking as deep as possible: "You gonna give him the ol' 'spend time in the woods, read these second-hand crime novels, work hard at the station and you just might make something of yourself kid' talk?"

His eyebrows raise a little in surprise, then his brows furrow. "It worked for you."

He's right. As much as I tease him about it, volunteering here straightened me out. It also made me feel closer to my dad who was gone by then. It gave me a sense of purpose, and eventually paved the way for the rest of my career.

It also made for some interesting work placement reports. It's still a small town and there were definitely some endless days of pencil-sharpening and filing–and therefore long sighs and glares from me to anyone who would notice–but there were also days where I got to witness Bobby and Kenny overseeing minor drug busts, breaking up fights, arresting domestic violence offenders, and helping several people into the back cell to sleep off the night before. They wanted to show me the excitement of working in this industry and all the good you can do, while also keeping a close eye on me and keeping me under their wing.

We drop off my prescription renewals at the pharmacy in town first then pull up to the station detachment as the sky turns the town a darkish yellow. People are starting their day. Residents are in bulky coats and warm hats chatting on busy sidewalks and waving to each other, opening shops or grabbing their morning coffees.

Because we're located so far north, our climate switches between subarctic and humid continental. What that really means is that the citizens here have to be ready for any possibility. Isinbury and its surrounding area is actually colder than anywhere else in British Columbia from November through February. I remember it well. It's freezing, dry and dreary. And unlike the rest of the province, we regularly get a few feet of snow. Still, our summers are usually warmer than even Vancouver.

I'm happy to have missed the majority of winter up here and although I can still feel a cold dry breeze while I make my way into the station, the end of March has brought with it some sun.

We park behind the station in Bobby's spot, and he motions for me to follow him through the side entrance. I pull on my toque and shove my bare hands in my jacket to keep warm.

As we hop out of the car, a couple walking by stops to stare at us. The man comes over to Bobby and shakes his hand.

"Hey Bob, how's the investigation going? People are starting to get...fussy, you know."

Bobby leans on his right hip and crosses his arms. He's closed off.

I decide to give them some space and peek in the front windows of the police station instead. It looks mostly like it did a decade ago, except cleaner and more modern. The waiting area is empty and the walls are the same aged yellow they were when I was doing my co-op placement here.

I hear the end of Bobby's sentence as I turn back towards them.

"–letting me know Jim, what people have been saying, but it doesn't change the fact they don't know what the hell they're talking about and we are doing a very thorough job. We brought in the Major Crimes unit, for God's sake."

That's pretty polite for Bobby. What he really means is: *mind your own fucking business.*

Jim leans in to him and says under his breath but loud enough for me to hear, "This *girl* isn't going to give any of us here any comfort that things are being handled correctly." His eyes flash to me and I give him a hard stare back.

Bobby is already walking away, effectively ending the conversation. I follow. Bobby yells back at him, "If you have a real complaint with some sort of validity, you can talk to someone at the front desk, other than that, piss off and let us do our jobs."

I wonder if the rest of the town is unhappy with how this has been handled so far and what I've gotten myself into. To them, I'm still Liz and Henry's kid. Not a 29-year-old Corporal detective in major crimes, with city experience. Or maybe they've read the news, and think I'm not to be trusted.

"Well, that was unpleasant," I mumble under my breath.

"Sorry about that," he says gruffly. "We've had a little uproar here and there, from the townsfolk. They think we're taking too long to solve the case, as if this is some damn television show instead of real life." He walks ahead of me and uses his electronic badge to unlock the side door.

I turn my face toward the sky to feel the light on my face before stepping inside. Who knows if the sun will be up the next time I'm outside?

There are two offices on either side of the door we just came through. I know for a fact one of them belongs to Bobby.

There are two desks facing each other in an open main area in front of us. One looks completely bare and the other has papers strewn everywhere and a few used mugs scattered about. Old-looking computers, phones and equipment litter the station's interior, set up as the detachment's informal incident room.

We relieve a red-eyed Kenny from the night shift, who saunters over to me with a huge smile and open arms, before enveloping me into a giant bear hug.

Kenny is Bobby's second in command: ranking as Station Sergeant and Deputy Chief. He's in full uniform and sporting a long brown bushy beard I haven't seen before. He has definitely put on some weight in the last year since their Vancouver visit. Perhaps that explains the beard.

Bobby, who has known him for decades, has always described Kenny as the typical "rough around the edges" type. A bit brutish but mostly harmless when you get to know him.

He was a friend of my father's too, so I grew up with him. Perhaps this is why I've never found him particularly threatening, but I know some of the town's residents would say otherwise.

Now that I think of it, Kenny's "bad cop" is a good compliment to Bobby's "good cop." I wonder where I fit in, on the scale.

"It's so good to see you darlin', but I'm tuckered right out. We'll catch up in a few hours after my nap," he says sleepily. "Quiet night last night other than a bar brawl that had to be broken up. See you two later."

We follow him out into the front reception area so Bobby can introduce me to the civilian administration clerk Hilary. Her mousy brown hair is tied up into a ponytail and she's wearing bright pink lipstick and leopard glasses while chewing gum theatrically.

"Nice to meet you, dear," she says, flashing me her best tired smile. I nod and return a polite grin.

The front door desk has been updated with bullet proof glass and a waiting area to the right.

"Everyone needs to be buzzed in by Hilary here to get beyond this point," Bobby points out.

There are two people waiting in reception and one of them stands as he sees us, raising a hand in greeting, but Bobby turns quickly on his heel, bringing me with him as a loud buzzer sounds overhead, helping us elude more unhappy civilians.

"That was a close call," he says, smirking as he leans in conspiratorially.

The door leads us into the main incident room again and Bobby gives me a quick tour since it's been over a decade since I was last here. Beyond these offices and toward the back are the change rooms, the two jail cells and the small meeting room. The filing room is downstairs.

"Not much has changed," I say out loud, as he holds a plate of doughnuts out to me. I choose the powdery one and take a giant satisfying bite.

"They're from Sara's bakery next door," Bobby points out, searching my face for clues while grabbing a chocolate glazed one for himself.

I make a non-committal noise, but remind myself I really should pop over and say hello to an old friend.

The doughnut's white powder spreads over my fingers and I lick it off discreetly, while taking a peek at "the murder board" which is one of those visual layouts crime TV loves to make fun of. I read some of Bobby's notes on the ride up so I know most of this already. I recognize a few names up there as potential suspects and that worries me. One name in particular makes me want to vomit.

I grab Bobby's case notes again, and bring them over to the case board so I have the full visual. I want to see if there is anything I might have missed the first time around.

The first victim, I already know from Bobby's case notes, is 24-year-old Lilyann Richardson. She was murdered walking home at night, after a blow to the head then strangled, on February 10th. Very public and risky. Her shirt was pulled open and her bra pulled down to reveal her breasts. The rest of her clothes were untouched. Bobby's thought process is laid out clearly in his notes: "Likely, he did this post-mortem because if she had struggled, a button would've come loose or we would've found a tear in her shirt. What is the source of his sexual frustration? No sign of sexual trauma other than the breast exposure...was this to embarrass her or send a message?"

Lilyann was found by early morning commuters on a wooded path downtown and the scene was called in by the local bar's owner Laryssa Lynn, who also used to be friends with my parents.

The second victim is 23-year-old Megan Kline, originally thought to have died of an overdose, later deemed suspicious, on

February 20th. Only 10 days after the first murder. First assumed an accidental death or suicide, until later evidence suggested she may have witnessed the first murder, deeming her a liability. Her toxicology revealed high levels of heroin but her autopsy proved suffocation as the true cause of death.

Her naked body was found in her bed by the 14-year-old babysitter 24 hours later. The pillows and blankets had been pulled to the floor, either by the perpetrator or her children. She was a single mother of two, a toddler aged four and a 10-month-old baby. That's the worst part. They were in the house all day, left unattended, with their dead mother in the bedroom.

Whoever killed Megan walked past the toddler's room and seemingly took the baby out of the crib before leaving the mother's bedroom open for them to find her in the morning...dead, naked, cold and eyes wide open. It's horrifying and cruel.

He's pretty cocky and not worried about being caught by DNA evidence. So far, he's been lucky. He seems to have an idea of what he's doing to cover his tracks. But that streak won't last forever. Soon, he will leave a part of himself at the scene and we will nail him to the wall with it.

"Sexually assaulted?" I ask, still facing the murder board.

"Autopsies say no," Bobby replies from a desk behind me.

I turn to face him. "But why was Megan naked? It seems like the murderer took off her clothes like he did with the first victim, or otherwise found her like that. It's likely someone she knew as there was no sign of forced entry. She either let them inside or they knew where a spare key was." I'm mostly talking my thoughts out loud.

"The only spare key we know of is from the babysitter who let herself in, figuring it was like any other night Megan had a work shift and was running late," he says. "The door had been locked. And before you ask, the babysitter has since been cleared of any suspicion because she has a solid alibi of co-starring in a school play the night before, seen by 50 plus attendees and fellow students."

"Mm-hmm," I mumble, reading down the page in my hands that holds Megan's murder file.

The father or fathers (as some relatives have implied) of Megan's children are unknown. Birth certificates have been left blank. Neighbours only saw the babysitter coming and going and occasionally Megan's brother or sister visiting. There has been some speculation of her sneaking in various boyfriends through her window at night but none of this has been confirmed. All we know is she was a very private person who mostly kept to herself.

"If the neighbours are correct and she was letting boyfriends in through the window, that's probably also how the murderer left if the door was locked, right? But he would've had to know about the window beforehand? Or decided to go through it at the last minute?"

"We've picked up a few prints from the window. None of them are in the system."

"And I'm guessing no one wants to come in to disqualify themselves from the suspect pool by providing their prints?"

"Correct."

I'm finishing my second cup of coffee when the buzzer at the front door alerts me to the admin clerk Hilary who's walking toward us, sandwiches in hand. She leaves one on each of our desks.

"Oh my god, thank you so much," I say, unwrapping the delicious smelling paper. It's curry chicken salad, my favourite. How did she know? My stomach rumbles loudly in response.

She seems to read my mind and gives me a more genuine smirk than this morning as she heads back out to the front.

I steal a glance at Bobby who's already scarfing down his food. He's eating while standing, staring at the murder board. A dribble of filling lands on his chest and he grumpily wipes it away. I stifle a laugh.

"Not to ruin your appetite but what is the sexual element here? The first murder, he was risky enough to do in public. Why take a chance and expose her like that unless it means something to him?"

He nods and chews. Unphased. "I thought so too. There isn't any sexual trauma to the victims, only exposure. He's sending a message. He's sexually frustrated or wants to embarrass a woman in his life, something like that. His M.O. seems to be asphyxiation so far and that often does have a sexual element to it."

"Ex-wife? Friend zoned? Mother issues?" I shake my head. "History of sexual offences? Let's go ahead and flag anyone who fits that criteria for now."

"Already did. But in this town? That's a lot..."

"I'll want to look at the results, anyway. He's the smart, careful, planning type. Cross-check it with those in the victims' inner circles. I want to go through the list of family, friends, neighbours, work colleagues and see what we can find."

"Yes boss," he grins a little as he says it and I feel my cheeks go hot.

"Sorry, I didn't mean to under–"

"No, it's good. I want to hear your input and have your fresh eyes on this. It's just a bit strange flipping from you being my little girl to you being the capable detective I know you are, working a case like this with you."

He's right. It is weird.

"I'll get used to it," he adds. "Anything else you want or need to get started?"

He jams the rest of his sandwich, the size of a fist, into his mouth. He wipes his hands together then goes into his office. He comes back with a small binder, still chewing, and leaves it on the table for me, taking a seat at the messy desk across from me.

The front door buzzes, alerting us to someone at the door.

CHAPTER 5 - JANE

It's Kenny again, red-eyed and pale, but smiling. "Hey again. I might've said this before, but it's nice to have you here with us, Jane."

"Thanks Kenny. You look awful though." I point to his eyes even though I noticed his untucked shirt and loose shoelace first.

"Oh, it's not usually my shift. I had to cover Jackson's on-call. His wife is in the hospital about to have their first born."

"Any news on that?" Bobby asks, frowning as he takes in Kenny's dishevelment.

Kenny shrugs, unphased. "I've been sleeping. Thought you'd know."

Bobby massages his temples with his right hand. "I'll text Jackson now. Ask for an update."

Behind Kenny, the door buzzes again and his husband Glen enters, smiling ear to ear, with arms open wide. An excited squeal comes out of me and I rush into Glen's open arms. He staggers back with a laugh.

"Oh my god, Glen!" I say excitedly, pulling back to take him in. Glen is small framed and soft-spoken as always, smartly dressed in khaki pants and a soft mahogany coloured cardigan that compliments his light brown skin. Smooth face, shiny bald head. Kenny steps forward, slings an arm over him and gives him a peck on the side of his head.

"I didn't get an excited greeting like that," Kenny chides. "I guess you're the favourite."

"Aww, Kenny, I'm sorry," I manage, pulling him in for a hug as well. "I think I was just so full of nerves this morning I wasn't myself."

"Plus, I'm the favourite," Glen whispers, smirking.

"Plus, he's my favourite." I add.

They're a perfect example of opposites attracting. While in Glen's company though, Kenny's softer side effortlessly comes to the forefront.

"We have so much to catch up on since our last Facetime call, but we'll get time to do that on the weekend," Glen says. He notices my confusion and quickly fills in the blanks. "Ah, Judie and I just decided this morning that we're going to have a little family dinner at Bobby's on Saturday, with the whole gang."

"Oh, that's great," I say, a little nervous to see everyone again.

"Anyway, I just wanted to come and surprise you but I'm heading out to a meeting so I'll let you get back to work. Call me if you even just want to talk, okay?" He reaches out and squeezes my hand, gently leaning into my shoulder. "I'm here for you, if you need me."

I feel a tightness in my throat so I nod a thanks and he smiles back kindly, understanding. He gives Kenny a goodbye kiss and heads out the door. I pull myself together and pretend to be interested in a pen on the desk in front of me.

Kenny coughs uncomfortably in the silence that follows.

"How many officers do you have these days, Bob?" I ask, my voice still hoarse.

"We've got three mounties: myself, Kenny and Jackson full time. Plus, the civilian clerk you met, Hilary. Four staff to police a population of 900, in a jurisdiction that covers 17,500 square miles. Jackson typically mans the station from 6 p.m. onwards. We typically lock up from 2am to 6am, and any emergency calls outside of regular office hours are routed through the police dispatch operator. You know how it goes."

"I forgot how small towns run their detachments."

"Yeah, the emergency dispatch response will call your cell if you're needed, so keep your ringer on."

"Will do. What about fire rescue services around here?"

"That would be SAR. You know, Search and Rescue." Bobby says.

Kenny chimes in. "Jimmy Slovak is in charge of SAR, which includes fire rescue services. He has a small team of volunteers with specialized training on call, including me, and a retired paramedic who helps him and us out from time to time as well."

"Slovak's office is in the community centre next door, and we often share some emergency equipment," Bobby adds.

"Cool," I say. "I've worked closely with SAR before. It's certainly not an easy job. Do you guys get much action out here?"

"We have a few wildlife disturbances every year," Bobby says. "Bears, moose or bison usually...sometimes wolves disturbing the peace. Mostly cases involving hikers or campers in the forests by the edge of town who were lucky enough to walk away pretty much unharmed."

Kenny adds, "Yeah, we get a lot of emergency calls from backcountry campers or hikers in the mountains. Several of them, especially the locals, are emergency-prepared but just unlucky. Others are the tourists that think they're indestructible and their situations would've been totally avoidable if they'd had the right background or forethought. Luckily for them, our services are free and we don't charge extra for *stupid*."

Bobby and I don't laugh like Kenny thought we would. Instead, the room goes deadly quiet as we all think about how my father died, and all three of our faces flush deep red.

"Oh God, Jane." Kenny says, tripping on his words. "I'm such an idiot. I wasn't thinking. Please forgive me."

I clear my throat. "It's fine. Of course. Let's just move on."

Another thought pops up which darkens my features. Bobby notices right away. "Are you okay?"

"Yeah, it's not that."

I glance nervously at Kenny who responds to my hesitation by sighing. "Please, spit it out."

"Not to make things awkward for anyone, but can I please have a list of those SAR volunteers and their alibis for the nights Lilyann and Megan were murdered?"

I try to use their names instead of the placeholder, victim. Marcus taught me that.

Kenny grunts, but Bobby nods his head, siding with me.

"If I was a serial murderer in a small town, who was capable of killing a woman quickly and quietly in a public main square and knowledgeable enough about how to avoid DNA detection...I could be one of these SAR volunteers. Were any of them close with Lilyann or Megan? 'Cause those people would be at the top of my suspect list."

Both of their faces suddenly go blank, the smiles wiped off so quick you might not even realize they were ever there. Kenny coughs and nods toward my left.

"Hey guys...I was just dropping off some coffee. Sorry to interrupt."

The voice is husky yet smooth, but the tone of annoyance is not missed by me. I turn and notice a giant bear of a man standing behind me. He's wearing light jeans and a soft grey Mountain Man sweater, with his long blond hair pulled back into a ponytail. He's probably 6'4 and a little over 200 pounds; built like an ox, which is what my dad would've said. It's hard to think that such a large person could come through the front door and none of us would hear him being buzzed in.

"Let me guess...you're on the SAR team?" I try with my most polite, yet authoritative voice, trying to hide my burning frustration, even though I know my cheeks are giving me away. He's smiling politely, but I can tell he already doesn't like me.

"Yeah, I'm on the SAR team. Liam Hennessey. Nice to meet you."

"I'm Jane. Bobby's...family." I say awkwardly. I've never known what to call myself: God daughter? That sounds so formal.

Liam seems to relax a little at this. Linking myself with Bobby was a good idea then. I've reached out my hand for a well-meaning handshake, but his hands are full of coffee and he just shrugs lightly. My hand falls to my side awkwardly.

"No hard feelings," he says, still being polite about it. "I can come in for an official statement, if you'd like." He walks over to the guys and drops a coffee next to each of them. Then he turns to me, and now he seems embarrassed.

"Oh sorry. I didn't bring a coffee for you." He looks to Bobby for rescue, but Bobby just smirks.

"That's okay, I've already had two or three today," I manage, adding, "plus you didn't know I was here." His stare is intense and it's making me uncomfortable. I try to avoid his gaze.

He nods, no doubt happy I've smoothed this one over for him. But then he says, jokingly, "I guess we had that in common." And as soon as he says it, my face flushes red again. I look up but he's smirking now. And so are Kenny and Bob.

"Anyways, I'm gonna go stop by the home and check in on my mom," Liam says, giving a farewell wave. "Have a good day guys." He turns toward the door taking a few steps, then turns back, as if he's forgotten something. "And nice meeting you Jane." He smiles at me then, a grin implying he's been humoured by the whole scenario, and leaves.

"Fuck's sake." I say under my breath when he's gone. The guys are chuckling in response. But I'm annoyed. First off, this case should be kept confidential and second off, I might have to work with Liam and I've just acted like a complete arse. "You could've told me he was there."

"I didn't notice—" Bobby starts.

Kenny interrupts, smirking, "But that wouldn't have been as funny."

I shake my head, feeling my anger rising and trying not to let it get to me. "This isn't a game, Kenny. We need to keep this case confidential and maybe Liam is going to go blab to the SAR team now and give them a heads up about what I said."

"He won't say anything," Bobby interrupts. "I trust him."

"Me too," Kenny says, a bit annoyed with me now.

"But I agree, we should check out their alibis. Kenny? Maybe you should lead here, since they're more likely to trust you."

"Sure, fine," he says, jotting down notes in a tired looking notepad he's grabbed from his back pocket.

"I mean...now that I think of it, Liam was considered a bit of a ladies' man around town when he first got here, so he could very well be connected to one or both of our victims." Bobby says.

I throw up my hands. "Exactly what I was trying to say. Why do you trust him so much? Do you even know him?" I ask, flustered.

"I dunno. He's a good lad. He's from Vancouver. Recently came to town because his mom has some sort of disease that affects her lungs. One of our doctors here is doing a community-based clinical trial about it," Bobby says, leaning back in his chair, hands behind his head.

"Worked out for us," Kenny says. "He came here for his ma but we had put feelers out that we were in need of more paramedics for years now and he was the first good candidate we found. It's been great because we only have one full-time paramedic and I used to fill in for her when she couldn't be there, as part of the SAR team. I know the basics but Liam knows it all."

"Sounds like a really capable guy. I can see his mom needing to move out here for better medical treatment, but why would *he* leave Vancouver permanently?" I say, not trying to be a dick about it, but of course that's how it comes across.

Bobby weighs in now. "He hinted to me that he has some sort of PTSD he's working through and that's part of the reason why he moved. I wouldn't be so judgmental about it, Jane." He gives me a knowing look.

"Okay. Sorry. I just didn't get it." I look down, pretending to shuffle papers on my desk. Hearing Liam has PTSD doesn't soften my suspicions like Bobby expects it to. I might have PTSD too, but from my experience, it's only made me more unreliable and brazen. Liam's probably the same way. And there's something about him that instantly throws my guard up. I also don't like people sneaking up on me or making me look like an idiot.

I don't care if I look like a dog with a bone, so I press on.

"*Did* you look into his alibi for the nights in question?"

Bobby sighs, but looks up from his notes and smiles sympathetically. "His neighbour Kim Jenkins, the town doctor, saw him and his younger sister at home, both nights. Plus, he's not the only newcomer here. We've looked into them all and so far, they all have pretty reliable alibis. I hate to say it, but it looks like this is someone more local, someone we know."

"My best guess is these are unrelated cases of domestic violence which led to accidental murder," says Kenny. "It's the majority of what we see up here. And we still haven't identified the father of Megan's children."

I sigh. "Do we have a man connecting the two? Were these girls close at all?"

"Complete opposites." Bobby says. "And no real link other than the fact they both worked at the Raven, Lilyann as a waitress and Megan as a dishwasher. One was a complete socialite while the other was a single mom who was a bit of a recluse."

"We have witnesses saying these two rarely spoke," Kenny chimes in. "They wouldn't even walk together on the same route home."

"Were they unfriendly?" I ask.

"Not more unfriendly than regular women at that age," Kenny says, with a shrug.

"There's also a possible drugs link," Bobby says, exchanging a glance with Kenny. "As you know, there was heroin in Megan's system. She was a user from time to time. And Lilyann's ex-boyfriend is one of the dealers in town we have identified."

"Great. That's probably our lead suspect, right?" I ask, trying to keep the eagerness out of my voice.

"Yes, he's one of them," Bobby continues slowly, "but there are others that are equally worth looking into." He hands me their notes.

Based on the two murder victim reports, they have already begun a loose criminal profile.

Isinbury's adult population consists of about 462 males to 233 females. The rest are youth. The women here seem to handle the deficit just fine. They are a strong, resilient bunch.

What this means for our criminal profile, however, is that we started with around 462 adult males as initial suspects. We cut that number down by taking out men over 70 years old and under fourteen, and those with critical illnesses or disabilities who are unlikely to be able to hold down a grown woman fighting for her life, while strangling the life out of her, then dragging her deadweight to a more secluded path.

All of this brings our number down to around 320. Even then, a good one hundred of those men are of thick build, physically strong and mentally capable of carrying out these murders. We have about 100 or so adult women who fit this profile as well. We're keeping our options open. Most of the men and the women on these lists hold down manual labour jobs in Isinbury or a little out of town, frequent the gym or are outdoor sports enthusiasts.

It's not surprising that a lot of them will fit our physical profile. And everybody knows everybody. Social circles don't really apply to a town this small.

At the top of the suspect list, is that name again. The one that makes my anger flare and my body want to throw up. I push it aside for now.

"Can I see their houses?" I ask. I mean where Lilyann and Megan lived. "I like to see everything in person. I'm a visual thinker."

"Yes, sure. We'll take my truck." Bobby says as he grabs the keys. I make myself another coffee for the road.

CHAPTER 6 - JANE

The people of Isinbury tend to choose their friends based on how much they frequent the Raven, but also on what area of town they live in. Retirees, farmers and working professionals or even just those with a lot of inherited money, tend to live on the outskirts of town in the large log homes. The low-income housing is close to the schools, and the three other main residential areas hold the average joes who live a middle-class life.

The first house we arrive at is Megan's, who lives in low-income housing and is a few blocks away from downtown where she used to work at the Raven. Bobby points to the house directly behind. It's my friend Sara's. I haven't actually been to her home since she's been an adult and moved out of her parents'. We usually just skype. But it's in the bad part of town, which makes me worry about how she's doing financially. I wonder if Sara knew Megan before she died, since they lived beside each other.

Bobby hands me my protective gear and we glove up and put on our paper foot covers over our shoes.

It's a tiny shack of a house, which is arguably messier than my apartment had been just a day ago. There is no sign of cleanliness or order. There is grime on the baseboards, walls and countertops. Toys are sprawled everywhere yet there is a rectangle sized hole in the middle of the floor. Bobby sees me staring at it.

"It was a bin of toys. We checked it thoroughly and nothing came of it, so we decided to let Megan's mom take it. She has the kids now." His voice breaks a little on the last word. This case reached him deep and it still hurts him.

"A bin of toys in the middle of the room," I say quietly. "This place isn't big so you would be tripping on this every time you walked to the kitchen."

We make our way to her bedroom. I check the photos Bobby took before they searched the place and touched anything. The drawers were already left open and clothes were strewn about. This isn't due to a messy forensics search. This is how she lived.

As if reading my thoughts, Bobby says, "she struggled with mental illness. The drug habit didn't help. She ended up losing her job at the Raven after Lilyann died because she refused to show up anymore and Child Protective Services were called because the neighbours were worried. That's why Megan had started having the babysitter come again. But the babysitter said most nights Megan was still at the house, just in her bedroom with the door locked. Megan's mother was going to fight for custody. Originally, all signs pointed to a legitimate overdose or suicide even though we technically didn't find a note. The only thing we found that was odd, was *that*."

He points to another photo in the evidence folder I have in my hands. These photos were taken from a notebook they found in her bed, filled with pencil drawings of demon-looking creatures. Each one features a tall figure in a hooded robe, with very detailed eyes and skinny arms that reach off the page to my hands that are holding it. The autopsy said her fingertips were silvery black, stained with lead. I trace the drawing with the tips of my fingers, imagining her doing the same only hours before her life was taken.

She was terrified, not suicidal. Bobby's notes reflect the possibility before my mind jumped to it: did she accidentally witness Lilyann's death, as they both walked home from their shifts at the Raven? Detailed pay stubs as well as eye witness reports confirm they both walked home in the same direction that night, where they lived only streets apart.

Even though they were both women walking home alone after midnight, Lilyann apparently actively avoided Megan. I guess she felt superior in some way to the young mother of two?

"We interviewed everyone who left the bar around 2:30 a.m. the night Lilyann was killed, and they all said they saw nothing out of the ordinary. Including Megan, who we now believe to have been lying." Bobby says, while taking a seat on the couch. "No one spoke up. Most of them were walking the other way. Megan said she took the long way home because the weather was so nice...There's no way to prove which direction she really took." He goes on, "We also interviewed everyone who works there and all the Raven's regulars, multiple times, and nothing suspicious...We know, if it's connected, which it seems to me it is, the killer is calculated and patient enough to wait for his opportune moment when no one will see him. Maybe he even watched Lilyann for a bit first or knew her schedule personally. But how did he find out that Megan saw what happened and why didn't he take care of it that night?"

"Maybe he noticed her a little too late or saw someone else coming and panicked." I point to his notes in my hands. "According to several of your witnesses here, they knew Megan as a quiet girl, who often blended into her surroundings. She most likely froze when it happened, and hid behind something until she was sure he had left and she was safe."

I remember Bobby's words: the socialite versus the quiet single mom. I pull out the photos of them, given to us from the families and I'm not surprised by what I see there.

"Plus, she wouldn't have fit into his fantasy, if that's what this is about." I mumble, out loud.

The photo of Lilyann shows a smiling skinny blonde with nice skin and perfect teeth, in a blue sunflower dress with her straightened hair perfectly combed to each side of her head. Megan's photo shows her tiredness and comes off a little darker, though she's attempting a slight smile towards the camera. She has dark circles under her sad eyes, her hair is thrown up in a messy bun and she's wearing a baggy sweatshirt.

I get a slight tickle up my spine as I see myself reflected in this photo. I push the thought out of my mind and refocus.

The photo shows the top of a blond child's head near the bottom–the child likely propped up on her lap–but has since been cropped to show only Megan. I wouldn't say she looked any different than any other new mom I've met, though.

The difference between these two women however is striking.

"As for how he found out, I'm not sure," Bobby says, continuing to fill me in. "But he somehow does, then he follows her, and starts biding time. Like you said, he's patient."

I go to her bedroom window and look out. "This wooded trail would have given him cover to spy on her," I yell down the hall. "Maybe she also figured that out and that was why she was holed up in here. Keeping an eye out." Goosebumps surface on my arms and neck, thinking of Megan by the window, watching the killer look in, her kids in the next room. "Why didn't she call the police?"

"Maybe she thought he would leave her alone if she proved she could keep her mouth shut," he hollers back.

The first kill feels like more of an opportunist kill to me. He would have been too occupied with keeping Lilyann quiet and getting it done fast, than checking his surroundings once he managed the initial blow to the head. This second kill was much more calculated than the first. He took his time with this one. He enjoyed putting her through days of agony and fear before finally coming for her.

I find Bobby on the couch, his head in his hands.

"He seems too smart to let a witness go, even if she promised to stay quiet. The only exception would be if he personally knew Megan and cared enough about her *not* to want her dead." I take a deep breath. We both know what I mean by that. It could be one of her children's fathers, one of her parents, or her brother Adam. "Adam, he's the one volunteering at the station right?"

"Yes. But he's a skinny lad. Doesn't fit the profile."

"Can we get a forensics ident team out in the woods to scan for footprints? Especially ones that are facing the window in Megan's bedroom. And flag anyone who fits the profile?"

"Sure, sure," he says, already calling the phone number.

"And take me to Lilyann's house," I interrupt. "I think I'm done here for now."

When I ask Bobby what other information he has about Lilyann, he tells me other than working, she took a free photography class at the library with her best friend, and had a few regular-ish boyfriends whom she would see throughout the week but nothing serious.

"What about the boyfriend you mentioned? The drug dealer?" I ask, confused.

He obviously balks. I stare at him. He's driving so he keeps his eyes forward. Not meeting my eyes.

"What is it?"

I can handle a lot of stuff, but lying or withholding...it's harder to forgive. Especially now, after Marcus.

"Remember what I taught ya, and don't let your prejudices get the better of you."

That makes me worry. Then I remember the name on the murder board and the top of the suspect list. The one that made me take a second look and flipped my stomach upside down. I was so shocked to see the name, that I didn't even look for the connection to the case. I swallow; a hard pill of dread.

He pauses for a long second more, sighs, then reaches over into his bag and pulls out another binder labelled *Lilyann Richardson*.

My eyes scroll down the list of suspects he's spoken to, mostly statements from Lilyann's loved ones. When I come to the boyfriend list, I see a few names. I'm pulled out of my hunt to see Kenny and his husband Glen's son Brian on the list. I was pretty sure he was married...The others are mostly construction guys who were one-time-flings. So I'm confused what Bobby means until I see the serious boyfriend's name, who she dated on and off for two years. Harrison Blake.

I glance at Bobby, frustrated that I forgot to ask him about this and that I was avoiding his name on the board. Also annoyed that he thought I needed to be told this lightly.

"I saw his name earlier. I forgot to ask you about it." I say, almost gritting my teeth. "You and I know he is capable of hurting someone. Why don't you think he's involved with this?" I hear my voice rising in anger but I can't stop it. "Of course, he's fucking involved in this, Bobby! He's her *boyfriend* and has a *record* of sexual violence."

He's trying to stay firm and calm but I see it in his eyes. He's holding back anger too. "I'm not saying he's *not* involved. I'm just saying, he's only one lead we are pursuing." He pauses, unsure if he should go on. "Miranda was his alibi. They were at her house in her basement *watching movies.*"

I mock-laugh at that. "Of course. Could they prove that actually happened?"

"Her parents saw them going into the basement around 8 p.m. and they didn't come back up until morning."

"She still lives with her parents?"

"That's what you're focusing on?"

"Sorry, back on track now. Their basement has a large window big enough to crawl through. I should know. I've done it!" I try to calm myself but my hands are shaking. "Plus, her parents are a bunch of wackos. They've been drunk off their asses every time I've seen them. Not exactly reliable..."

"Jane, trust me on this one. I understand it's a loose alibi but he seemed to really care for the girl. He's very upset about her death."

"Don't make me laugh, Bob. You know he's a great actor when he needs to be."

That ends the conversation pretty quick. We stay quiet for the remainder of the drive.

I consider the likelihood of Harrison or Miranda being involved in murdering these women. They were always very manipulative and cruel. They had a sinister nature to the way they lived their lives; they learned from their parents firsthand. I suppose that is why they always stuck around each other. They had a shared interest of befriending innocent souls, finding out what their weaknesses were and using whatever those were to exploit them for personal gain. They are assholes, no doubt, but killers?

I realize now that I won't be able to avoid them upon my return. They're persons of interest in this case.

I'm torn between needing more hours in my day and feeling like it should be midnight already.

CHAPTER 7 - JANE, 17 YEARS OLD

I've pretty much just chugged a twenty-sixer of blueberry vodka with Abby and am about to smoke a joint. I know I'm being reckless but Abby asked me to come to Miranda's tonight, and she has been really distant lately. We used to be so close. Without her, I'd be a complete loner. I need her. And she knows it.

Also Harrison is here. We've been sort of seeing each other, then breaking up, then getting back together. Typical teenage whirlwind romance.

We spend most of our weekends this way, drinking whatever we can find in our parents' liquor cabinets or giving creepy older guys our cash to buy us something at the liquor store. Sometimes because we're friends with Miranda and Harrison, we get invited to the older kids' pit parties, bonfires near the beach or in the woods next to the caves. But nothing is going on tonight and it's summer. We're bored out of our minds so we're having our own party in Miranda's backyard, inviting anyone who wants to have a good time. So far, everyone has had excuses. Only Harrison's drug dealer *Big Danny* said he will show up later if he has nothing better to do. Personally, he gives me the creeps. I also know Dad would totally kill me if he knew I was hanging out with him.

Miranda's parents have a sort of vehicle graveyard behind their house; scraps sold for parts. It makes for a fun, almost spooky weekend scene. We usually hang out, party and sleep in the broken-down RV in the backyard, and take joy rides in the decrepit, once-red van with no doors.

Abby asks, "So your parents really don't care what we're up to? They won't say anything to our parents?"

Miranda laughs heartily at this and takes a big inhale of a joint before responding. "They never know what the fuck they're doing themselves let alone what I'm up to! They're blasted out of their minds on drugs." She shrugs. "It's whatever." She goes over to the radio and blasts a song really loud. She's moving her hips slowly and provocatively in front of Harrison, giving her best pouting face and moving her hands up and down her bony body as she does. He's shaking his head as if he doesn't approve but his smile says differently.

"I'm just glad we have our own place to go to on the weekends. Thanks M," he says. They're just friends apparently but there's some sort of bond between them that makes me feel jealous but also weirded out. We always fight about their relationship because I don't trust either of them. He takes a large sip of his beer, his eyes still watching Miranda.

The room is starting to spin and I'm suddenly not feeling very well. I try to tell Abby who's next to me but she shrugs me off and goes to dance with Miranda. They're putting on a show for Harrison. I don't know why I came because this is stupid and no one here is even paying attention to me.

I drank too much, all because I wanted Abby to be my best friend again and for Harrison to want to get back with me. He and Miranda are two years older than us, and for some reason that means a lot to Abby. I never cared about them until Harrison started showing an interest in me. His deep brown eyes and long skater boy hair is so different from any boy I've ever known. He's bad but mysterious, and that made me like him instantly. It's exciting when his attention is strictly on me. When he calls me his girlfriend. I feel important.

He twirls my hair sometimes or holds my face in his hands and calls me pretty. I know he's a bit of a player but I've never seen him act this way with Abby before, even though she's 100 times prettier than me. I think it sort of pisses her off. She's your typical blonde-curls-skinny-but-with-big-boobs chick who can dress edgy one day and then preppy the next. I don't know why he didn't go for her instead. Or maybe they've gotten together and did it behind my back.

The girls start playfully kissing each other to get a rise out of Harrison but he just laughs. His face is red so I think he likes it but I can't be sure. I take another hit of the joint and stare out the window pissed off.

Miranda seems frustrated all of a sudden so she grabs Abby and tells us we're going driving.

"I can't drive now," I manage to say. My words aren't coming out quite right.

Harrison hears me and puts his arm around me, following the girls to the red van. He's sort of helping me walk as I can't feel my feet.

"Looks like someone drank and smoked way too much this time. Mrs. Goody Two Shoes is becoming more of a bad ass every day. Must be my influence." I think he's flirting with me. I can't quite see him but I can hear it in his voice.

Suddenly, I feel something grasp my left breast hard. It hurts.

"Owww."

"Oh come on, you like it. I was just making sure you were still awake there, cutie."

My mind can't process things right now. But I know I'm in pain. We've made it to the van.

"Here, Abby, take your friend, she's loaded." Harrison says, clumsily handing me over to her. I think I bang my elbow and my knee trying to climb in. I feel myself slump downward, uncomfortably.

I hear her sigh. "She's *your* girlfriend."

"Not anymore. We're on a break, remember?"

I think I'm in the backseat of the van. As long as I'm not in the middle, I won't fall out of the doors that are no longer attached.

"Shotgun!" I hear someone yell. I think they're talking about the passenger seat. Or maybe someone has brought a gun.

One of them starts driving the van in what feels like circles and the dizziness becomes too much and I start puking violently. I ignore their protests and lean my head back to stop the nausea.

Then it all goes black until the next day when I wake up around 2 p.m. in front of the caves, my hands covered in blood and my best friend missing.

CHAPTER 8 - JANE, PRESENT DAY

We've arrived at Lilyann's, which is a few blocks down from the station. It's one of two flats above the grocery store and according to a for lease sign, the other has been empty for over a year. Her house is a one bedroom with a galley kitchen and a bathroom so tiny your knees touch the wall opposite when sitting on the toilet. Travel and lifestyle magazines with their corners folded, not by choice but rather with use, are stacked beside the sink. This girl had bigger plans. Even if they were mostly made while sitting on a dirty porcelain throne.

The whole thing is a bust. There is nothing helpful that Bobby and Kenny haven't already noted or brought back to the station, and I'm too distracted to focus. We stop at Sara's bakery for some treats before she closes, and after crushing me with a bear hug, she begs me for a girls night out at the Raven. Bobby catches my expression over her shoulder. He raises his eyebrows and smirks at me, relaying a message in our secret language only we know: he's telling me to behave.

"I'm going to check in with forensics about Megan's house," he says, sending a wave to Sara and making a quick exit out the front door.

I roll my eyes playfully. "I'm not really here for a vacation Sara. I'm here to help out with the case."

Her head hangs sideways and she gives me a spirited glare. "When did you get so un-fun?"

"Murders aren't very *fun*." I meet her worried eyes as I reach over and snack on one of the pastries we just bought. I savour the treat as I try to muster up some more positive energy. I feel like my emotions have been turned off since the situation with Marcus. Like I'm stuck in survival mode and even faking a smile takes all the energy I have. "Sorry. I'm just tired." Her back is turned to me now and she fixes me a black coffee. Just the way I like it. The heat feels good in my hands and I gulp it down.

"Decaf by the way, 'cause I know you've probably had ten cups already today," she says warmly.

"Hah! You're not wrong."

When I meet her eyes again, there's something dark there that gives me pause. Something different from our last video chat. She's slim as always, wearing faded skinny jeans and a black V-neck, but the bones in her cheeks are more pronounced and her blonde hair that's usually perfectly curled in ringlets, rests straight and limp on her shoulders. I notice her running shoes too, thick with mud.

"Okay, fine." I force my voice to sound lighter than I feel. "We can go to the Raven later tonight, if that works? I *could* use a break. And a drink. I can definitely use a drink."

She rounds the corner of the counter and quickly pulls me in for another fierce hug. "Thank you Jane. I really need a night out and we haven't done anything like this in over 2 years!"

"Has it really been that long?"

"Yep. But we're fixing that now. How's 8pm for the Raven? Dinner and drinks?"

"Sure, sounds good." I lean over to grab the treats from the counter and notice a bottle of antidepressants hanging out of her purse. Right now doesn't feel like the right time to ask, so I'll try to see if there's a way to bring it up casually later. I do care about her and I know I've been a really shitty friend lately. I make a silent promise to her to do better. "See you at 8!"

I head out the door into the cold wind and take a deep breath in. I try to suck the negativity inside me into a tight ball and shoot it out in a powerful breath, as instructed by my therapist. It doesn't work. My heart still feels like a giant is crushing it between its forefinger and thumb.

When I'm working like this, I carry the case notes in my bones until it's solved. I fall back into a chair once I make it back to the station.

I wake up to the phone ringing. At first, the lights above are blinding and I forget where I am. Then it all comes back into focus and I realize I'm at the station. I must've just nodded off to sleep. There are papers on my lap still, some have fallen to the floor. I look at the clock on my right and it reads 7:43 p.m. I wipe the drool from the corner of my mouth.

Bobby answers the phone. I hear only his side of things.

"Yep, I'll check that out in the morning. Property damage can wait, we have a murder case on our hands. What's the other thing?"

A pause.

"*Mmhmm*. Okay. What's the address again?"

Silence.

"Alright no worries, we'll head there now, Kenny and I."

Pause.

"Yeah, you too."

He hangs up and sighs. He turns to me and nods a greeting.

"Hey there sleeping beauty. How was your nap?" His smile turns up at the corner of his mouth.

"How long was I out for?"

"Just an hour or so. You needed it."

"What's the call about? Should I come along?"

"Just a domestic dispute. *A regular*, if you catch my drift. I'd ask you to come but the guy is a real piece of work and Kenny seems to have a knack for getting under his skin."

My eyebrows lift instinctively.

"Yeah, the wife is too scared to press charges, but I just know one of these days he's going to take a swing at Ken and then we can put him away for assaulting a police officer."

I grin. "Well good luck."

He phones Kenny who's in the basement filing room, then asks if I need a lift home.

"Actually, I'm off to The Raven to meet Sara and catch up. I shouldn't be out late. Is Buddy's taxi still in service?"

He pulls out his wallet and takes a business card out and hands it to me.

"Here's the number for Buddy's, but if you get in any trouble, just call me and I'll come get you."

He says it as if I'm a rebellious teenager again, instead of a 29-year-old homicide cop. Somehow it doesn't sound condescending from him, instead it makes me feel warm inside.

A smile spreads across my face. Feels like old times.

"Thanks Bob. I really appreciate it."

"What, no sarcastic comment?"

"Nah. It feels good to have you look out for me. Have a good night."

"Always kiddo." I see the smile reach the corners of his eyes as he nods and leaves.

Kenny is just a step behind. "Are you coming along?"

"Nah, I'm heading out soon. Or should I stay and man the station?" I realize there's a few hours left before they close up.

"You don't have to. I've let the dispatcher know we're out on scene. Jackson had his baby by the way, so he needs a few days but I'm sure he'll be back before he's supposed to. Very eager, that one."

"Okay. I'll wait a bit anyway."

He thumbs toward the door, where Bobby has honked from his truck. "What is it?" His face looks pale as he turns to me. I wonder if he thinks it's another murder.

"Domestic dispute. Apparently, you have a special touch with this guy."

His face brightens, and I just make out what he says before the door closes behind him. "I'm gonna get him this time."

Ten minutes later, I close up and send the admin clerk home. When I'm locking up, I bump into a retired mountie walking by who seems thrilled to see me. Obviously, he knew my dad and worked beside him for years. He remembers me when I was young. We exchange a bit of awkward small talk, me mostly listening to his best stories of my father, before I politely excuse myself.

This town sure is filled with memories. And people who *do not* forget.

I make my way on foot to The Raven. The cool night air is hitting my face and it must be going to storm soon because my joints are sore as hell. I make a mental note that I need to follow up with my family doctor on that one. I seem to be getting more sore instead of less. I pull my jacket tighter and throw on my gloves. It's a five-minute stroll from the station if I really take my time, which I do. Most of the main street shops were closed by 5:30 p.m., with the exception of a few restaurants, the pizza place and the bars. The grocery store at the end of the street, opposite the police station, also stays open until nine.

The sun has set and turned everything in town pink. The mountains are taking cover under the shadows and the nocturnal animals are waking up from the day's rest. The Raven opens at 3 p.m. now instead of its previous noon, a suggestion made by the mayor to discourage day-drinking. Laryssa, being the businesswoman she is, agreed to his proposal on the terms she could stay open until at least 2 a.m. which is the by-law. If you ask me, she got the better deal. She wouldn't have had many customers during the day anyways, and more time open at night means more sales for her.

The streets are pretty quiet except for a few stragglers and cars. On my way to the bar, I check out the centre of town and how it has changed since I was here last. Beside Sara's bakery, which is on the corner, is The Clothing Shop, a little removed from the actual main street but which seems to have doubled in size to accommodate the town's high demand. In front of The Clothing Shop and beside the bakery is a tiny spa advertising manicures and pedicures for prices unheard of to me being a city girl. My eyes continue to follow the right side of the street, where I notice Langdon Walker's Construction, Building and Real Estate Services, beside the spa, which must be the boyfriend Sara keeps mentioning. Then there's Town Hall and the post office, and "The Family Restaurant" which has survived and thrived my entire existence, even though it has had multiple owners. I turn away from Town Hall and to my left which is the main bar The

Raven. A group of teens are smoking outside, their cigarette tips flaring orange in the dark. On the left side of the street, there's now an International Restaurant and a financial centre with a bank, separating the Raven from the lonely police station at the end.

I open The Raven's heavy front door, the noisy chaos of the bar instantly breaking the peaceful silence of dinner time on main street. The Raven has a mainly wooden interior with thick stained-glass windows on the walls and clear plastic dividers separating the booths to enhance privacy. It's very Irish. The place feels hot and reeks of stale beer, alcohol and body odour. The floors are that permanent kind of sticky and I peel my squeaking boots off it with each step, the sound announcing my presence further. All dozen or so patrons look my way and stare, shameless and judging, as I take my seat at the bar to order a drink. A few women around my age look me up and down. I stare firmly back at them. Laryssa waves them off, which seems to get them talking amongst themselves again. Although a few continue to stare, the room returns to its regular volume.

I scan the room again, hoping to see a familiar face but I don't see it. I used to be close with Abby's younger brother Jake, but we lost touch when I moved to Vancouver. I decide to look him up on socials and reach out. Maybe he's still in town?

"Nice to see you honey," Laryssa says. "Even under these terrible circumstances."

Her red hair has thinned over the years, but it's still dyed a bright red giving off The Little Mermaid vibes. She's in her late fifties but still looks like she could pass for forties, especially the way she's dressed: tight plaid shirt, tight blue jeans and some cowboy boots. "Sorry about that. New blood in town always gets them talking, especially when they're as cute as you."

"I'm hardly new blood," I mumble. "Just haven't been here in a few years."

There's a darkness to her eyes that I remember and new wrinkles at the corners, but a lot of her is exactly the same: bright red lipstick to match her hair, easy to laugh and flirty with the men seated at the bar, and no ring on her wedding finger.

"Oh, they recognize you alright. I'm afraid that makes it even worse."

I don't have a response to that.

"Rum and coke, please. Diet if you have it."

She winks at me as she fills the glass a little stronger than usual. Sara still hasn't shown up when I ask for a second. I decide to also order water to slow me down.

"Lots of gossip going around," she says to me. "Biggest thing to happen here in a decade." Her eyes catch mine and I look away. I think she means since my father's death. Or my best friend's disappearance.

"Hear anything helpful?" I pry, picking at my cuticles.

"Nothing too much about the case. I usually text Bob about anything that might be valuable." She smiles brightly, as if we're friends. I remember my mom despised Laryssa for some reason, and I never warmed to her either. She was more a friend of my dad and Bobby's.

"I was close with those girls," she says suddenly, leaning on the counter towards me. A deep frown forms and a single tear falls before she quickly flicks it away. "I took them under my wing. I saw them almost every single day. I still can't believe it."

"I'm sorry. It must've been quite a shock."

74

"It was." She leans back then, wipes the counter and avoids eye-contact. But her body language has shrunk and I notice the black circles underneath her eyes. She attempts a smile before heading to the other side of the bar to cut lemons.

Being back in this town makes me feel uneasy. It brings back so many unwanted memories and I carry them all on my shoulders and feel the weight of them constantly pulling me down.

I was dealing with so much back then that I actually didn't deal with anything at all. I pushed out all of my grief and vulnerability and ignored it by drinking myself until the point where I would puke or pass out. At *every* party.

It was my way of pretending I was fine. I was so freaking stupid.

Jake would often pick me up and take me home when I got blackout drunk, sneaking me in through the back door and staying beside my bed while I slept it off. Sneaking in and out of the house was easy then, because my mother was too depressed to do anything but sleep and watch television.

Jake hardly ever came with me to parties and I never called him at the end of the night, yet he always knew where to find me and save me. I wonder now if Sara called him, watching me from a distance and still looking out for me even though we were no longer friends.

After the blackout night with the van, I mostly became a hermit until just five months after my father died, when Sara and I became friends again on my eighteenth birthday.

I was at a bush party that someone had invited me to. I didn't know that many people at that party, so when Harrison started flirting with me, and kissing me soon after, I was relieved to not be alone. We had broken up for good earlier that year, but it felt good to think about something other than my fucking parents. Or Abby who had disappeared. I thought it was simple, and the distraction I needed. I was wrong.

Sara might have ignored me when I first went up to her at that party, but I know now that she kept her eye on me all the same. She didn't approve of my coping habits, so she kept her distance, but she still cared.

She was the one who pulled Harrison off of me when he wouldn't stop and I was too drunk to do anything about it. He had stripped me of some of my clothes and had pulled his own pants down. Although Sara stopped him before anything else happened, his intentions were clear. Even though I was saved before I could've been raped, something of mine was taken that night; call it innocence or naiveté, it still haunts me to this day.

That's just one of the many reasons I have a really hard time opening up to people. Trusting other people is even harder for me.

Although Sara didn't plan on being friends with me again, we ended up leaving that party together, all of our sins forgiven and forgotten.

And I never got blackout drunk again. Even now, I know my limit with alcohol and stick to it.

Sara helped me through a lot back then, and after I proved to her I had changed and wanted to make my life better, she never left my side. Sara and Bobby were my biggest supporters, cheering me on and encouraging me to follow my dreams and pursue a career in the city and in the RCMP. Without them, I might have ended up like my mother.

The bar entrance opens and a few people I sort of recognize but can't name enter, with a frazzled Sara behind them.

When I look at her, two emotions always overcome me. The first? A soft sisterly tenderness. But the second, is a shameful envy of how easy her life has always been compared to mine. I can't help it.

I understand people with hard, messy pasts. They make me feel less like an anomaly. I'm comfortable around them, much more than people who do everything right and who have lived an easy, happy life. As much as I crave that for myself, I'll never be one of those people and I find it difficult to connect with them.

"I'm so sorry I'm so late," she sighs. Her blonde hair is in a messy bun on top of her head, one of her shirt's buttons is undone and her lipstick is partly on her chin. I reach over and help fix her up, as she slouches on the bar stool. I've never seen her like this before. She's meticulous about these things.

As I'm telling her not to worry about it, she continues on in a rush. "One of the teachers at the elementary school reminded me, a little too late, that I had agreed to bake cupcakes for a special fundraiser the day after tomorrow. I thought I still had a day to prepare. I had to run to the grocery store down the street, but of course they were all out of sour cream, so I had to go to the more expensive one on the edge of town, and well, I needed to make about five batches of 24. Half chocolate and half vanilla too. Anyways, it's been an insane couple of hours."

I raise my eyebrows at her and try not to laugh. I would've just told them to be happy with what the bakery had on hand, but Sara is too nice to suggest something so wild. Laryssa is already walking over to us with Sara's red wine, and hands her a food menu.

"Sounds like it's a good night to drink then." I lean in and give her a hug.

The bar has filled up quickly but we manage to grab a small two-person booth in the back.

"I'm starving, how about you?" she says excitedly. I forgot she's like this in person. Very twitchy and hyper when she's nervous. It's been a while since we've hung out and sometimes it's uncomfortable breaking back into friendship. She gulps down half of her wine. "Also, it looks like you will meet Langdon on Saturday."

"Great! I've only heard...everything about him already," I tease.

"Yeah, yeah. Shut up. The naan pizza and chicken wraps truly are the best items on the menu by the way." She orders a grilled chicken wrap with a salad, balsamic dressing on the side.

I trust her opinion and order the meaty naan pizza with garlic dip. I could use some carbs to comfort me after my first full day in Isinbury. People have not been welcoming.

As if she knows, she asks me how my first day was. Knowing I can't tell her much, I mostly just tell her it was stressful and busy. I also tell her my brain is a little fried and I could use some irresponsible fun. Even as I say this, I know I have a reputation to uphold.

"As much as people want the killer to be caught, I know they don't want me to succeed," I say as quietly as I can.

She nods. "Sorry it's like that Jane."

I'm not being self-conscious or spiteful–Bobby and I understand the way people think in this town and have already discussed this same topic. The fact I made it into news headlines recently only adds to their distrust.

I try to take a deep breath. Stress only aggravates my chronic pain symptoms and I don't want another reason to fail at this job.

Especially when so many people seemingly want to see me do just that: fail.

I don't remember when it started, but I have always had this underlying anger that will be dormant one second and full-blazed the next. They told me when I started training to become a Mountie that my temper was an issue, something I'd have to consciously work on...deep breaths, meditation, pausing before acting, that sort of thing. I've taken a few anger management courses of my own volition, to try and combat it and get it under control, but never found anything that stuck. In a world where there is so much to be angry about, how do you find a balance between caring and the self-preservation of one's mind?

"...Hello? Earth to Jane," Sara says between giggles. My cheeks get hot and I apologize. I was completely zoned out of our conversation that had something to do about the school's fundraiser. It's a homemade art and bake sale to raise funds for the nursing home. I return my attention to Sara smiling in front of me who this matters a great deal to. Sara gives my hand a pat to reassure me it's fine and asks if Isinbury's finest will be showing up to contribute.

"Of course. I'll drag Bobby and Kenny along and make them empty out their wallets. You know how I feel about the nursing home. I'll be there."

Our food arrives and we take a few minutes of silence to enjoy it while it's hot. My pizza hits the spot.

We exhaust a few topics of town gossip, the windy weather and the new jewellery store opening up on main street, before I excuse myself to use the loo. I'm not working right now, but I'm always listening. Always saving up questions to ask later, always hearing the inflection in people's voices in the room around me and studying their small body language details. My mind is a library.

I notice I'm a little tipsy when I get off from my bar stool, but I make my way into the ladies' bathroom without issue. I'm finished peeing when I hear the door swing open then closed, and the lock set in place. I carefully and quietly lift my legs to avoid being seen from the space between the door and the ground, and I listen. The person walks the length of the bathroom and pounds on my locked door. I freeze. They hesitate a second longer and it looks like they are about to check under the door, but their cell phone rings, distracting them. I listen to the click clack of their heels continue on to the sink, and hope they believe this stall is empty. You never know what people will reveal when they think they're alone. The woman, presumably, is sorting through a bag in front of the mirrors. I hear the bag drop on the counter and then the ringing stops.

"Hey, yeah, she's here. Sitting at the bar. Looking all top shit too," the whiny voice says then scoffs. A pause. "What should I do? Do you think she's here for us?" Another pause. "Okay, okay. I'll see you then." I hear her hang up then snort twice, in quick succession, followed by a satisfied sigh. I swing open the door.

Miranda's eyes fly open as wide as I've ever seen them, her reflection in the mirror giving away her panic. She quickly uses the back of her hand to wipe off any trace of what she just snorted off the bathroom sink. I don't know why she bothers really, because I obviously know what she did and that her cryptic phone conversation was probably about me.

"What the fuck do you want?" she says, still facing away from me but stealing glances in the mirror. "And why were you hiding in that stall like a fucking psycho?"

I look at her face, in her reflection. "The better question would be, why did you lock yourself in this bathroom to make a sketchy phone call and snort what I can only guess is coke?"

She sneers at me in the mirror and then turns her attention to her bag on the counter. She grabs a bright red lipstick and puts it on slowly, ignoring my accusation. The colour looks terrible against her extremely pale skin tone. Her blonde hair is greasy and orange-yellow, and she looks terribly thin. She reeks of cigarettes and cheap perfume. What the hell has she been up to these past years? By the look of her, nothing good.

"What I do is none of your damn business," she goes on, "and I don't care if you were some hot shot cop in the city for a little bit, you're still a nobody in this town. We all know you got fired from your job there and came running back to Bobby–"

"–I wasn't–" I try to interrupt but she keeps talking over me.

"–You're as pathetic now as you were back then Jane. Also, you got fat." She snorts.

I clench my teeth together. Obviously, nothing between us has changed.

I manage in a low voice, "You don't know anything about me Miranda. Not anymore. And if you piss me off, I *will* arrest you for having illegal narcotic substances in your possession and for being publicly intoxicated and causing a disturbance."

This seems to shut her up, so she passes me angrily, hitting my shoulder with hers as she unlocks the door and leaves, because she can't help but be childish.

"Really mature," I yell after her as the door closes. She hit my bad shoulder. I wonder if she knows that or if it's just coincidence.

My fingernails dig into the palms of my fists. My head feels like it's going to explode. I walk over to the sink and let cold water from the tap engulf my wrists. It's something I do to calm myself down in moments like these. The cold is a welcome distraction on my hot, sweaty skin.

I have no idea what I did to make her hate me so much. I could always tell her niceness to me was fake; that she had a different, darker reason to invite me around. I know she would steal some of my clothes and feign innocence when I asked her about it; spread rumours about me sleeping around or being pregnant. I should've clocked her a hard one to show her she couldn't push me around, but back then I was like a scared mouse.

I check myself in the mirror and try to figure out which one I am more of now. Tiger or mouse? Lately, I feel like a mouse painted orange with black stripes.

"Fuck."

I release my hair from its tight ponytail and use my fingers to tousle the curls out from hiding. I wipe the makeup that has melted from under my eyes and reapply some eyeliner and mascara. I don't want to make it too obvious that I just cleaned myself up in here so I throw on some lip balm and leave it at that.

On my way back to the bar, I notice a few heads turn but my eyes focus on Laryssa. I order some tequila shots. I'm not feeling tipsy anymore after that *delightful* conversation in the bathroom but if that changes, I will switch to water.

As I turn away from the bar, shots in hands, I collide with a tall and bulky man and the liquid goes flying into his face and all over his plaid shirt.

"Oh my God. Where the hell did you come from?" I gasp, as he swears under his breath.

I look up and it's Liam. Of fucking course it is.

"I came from over there." He points with one hand to Sara who looks horrified, the other hand wiping the tequila from his face. "I was coming to help you carry these. I'd say it was nice to see you again but I'm starting to get worried for the next time we meet..."

What I didn't quite notice the first time was that the man standing in front of me is very handsome. His wavy blonde ponytail is peeking out from behind his head and his olive-green eyes are alight with something I'd guess is humour. Thank God he seems to have a good sense of one.

"Shit I'm sorry." I turn to the bar helplessly looking for a solution and see Laryssa stifling a laugh but at least handing me some paper towel. I start to wipe this stranger off but this annoys him slightly and he gently takes the towels from my hands, the dryness and intimacy of his rough fingers touching mine, making me step back.

"It's fine. It happens." And just like that, his demeanour softens. He catches my eyes for the first real time. The bar is quieter, people staring and I'm suddenly very aware of my cheeks and chest feeling hot.

He puts a heavy hand on my shoulder. "Really, it's okay. Are you good? You look like you might pass out."

"Sorry I think I'm just embarrassed. I've certainly never thrown drinks on anyone. At least not by accident." A nervous laugh escapes me. This seems to bring a hearty chuckle out of this man.

"You're not exactly what I expected."

"What did you expect?"

"I've been hearing all day how we have a new, too-serious, super moody detective." He's still smiling but what he said unnerves me. Is that what people think of me?

He notices. "Sorry, I meant that's not the impression I get of you at all. You actually seem a lot more down to Earth." He leans over the bar and orders three tequila shots to be put on his tab.

Does this man have a short memory? He just called me down to Earth, even though the only thing he knows about me is that I want to interrogate him as a murder suspect because he volunteers his free time saving people and now I've thrown tequila in his face. The thought of it almost makes me laugh out loud again. He grins at me, as if reading my thoughts.

He has his plaid shirt slung around his arm now, damp, and he's just in his black undershirt now. He's not a body-builder but he looks strong.

"I should really be buying you a drink," I say quickly. "I mean, or at least offer to wash your shirt."

This makes him laugh. "Do people still offer to do laundry for spilling something on them? It seems old fashioned. Everyone has a washer and dryer."

"Yeah...I guess that was stupid. Saw it on T.V. once. How about that drink then?"

"How about a drink another time to make up for it?"

I blush and hate myself for being so readable. I feel a small smile gather at the corner of my mouth anyways.

Laryssa hands over the shots then and she eyes me as she says, "Liam, you better take these over for her." She gives me a cheeky grin.

We get back to Sara and there's two empty wine glasses in front of her now, and she twirls my loose locks between her fingers when I'm back beside her. "Don't worry about that. Hardly anyone saw." She lies.

"Pretty sure there's probably a video of it on Facebook by now, but thanks," I say.

Liam pulls a chair over to our booth. The bar is in full swing now, with loud rock music blasting and the lights turned down low to accommodate those who want to let loose on the makeshift dance floor in the corner. The floor is half full with drunk people laughing and partying it up. Many of them are tugging on each other's arms and bodies in some sort of dance move, and a few couples are holding each other close and kissing wildly.

We down our tequila shots, which I take quickly then shove a lemon in my mouth to counter the sting.

"I can't get shitfaced Sar," I yell to Sara over the music. "And you should slow–"

"I know. I know, you have a case to solve Jane," she leans in and says to me. "But I haven't seen you in two years! So, let's have some more fun, then I promise we can call it a night!"

At that, she takes my arm and yanks me on to the dance floor with her. I stand there, shaking my head until I can tell she won't let me leave. I try relax even though I feel like I've never been so embarrassed or vulnerable in my life. I try to let the music pump through me, slowly swaying my body from side to side. My eyes are closed shut and I still feel the burning liquid in my throat from the shot. Liam is holding our booth for us but I can feel his eyes watching us too. I look over and he smiles, giving me a single loose wave. I feel so awkward and out of my element right now I could scream. But Sara has had a hard year too and I haven't really been there for her so I try my best to lighten my mood and relax.

I fall back into the booth after just one song. Sara looks disappointed. Liam has gone somewhere. He's not at the bar so probably the bathroom.

"I can't really be dancing and drinking shots right now, Sara. You understand that, right?" I lean into her ear so I don't have to yell over the music. "I have a reputation to uphold. They won't respect me or take me seriously if I fool around here."

She crosses her arms but her face is relaxed. "That's not true. I think if you hang around the locals and act like the locals, they'll feel like you're more one of them. And may even open up to you more."

She sort of has a point. My dad was a Detachment Commander like that. One you could always find in the local diner or grabbing a pint here at the Raven. He was constantly signing up for baseball beer leagues and helping charities during his off hours. People trusted him *and* liked him. They like Bobby just fine but he has a very different approach to being Detachment Commander and how he handles local relationships. It's all business.

I'm a lot like Bob in that way. So is Kenny.

Maybe it would help to change things up a bit and approach this town like my father would. More open and friendly.

Sara's been watching me think this over. I tilt my head and smile at her. "Fine, I'll give it a try."

As if on cue, Laryssa comes up to us with more shots, this time some sort of sweet-smelling liquor. She points to a table of four 30-something construction men sitting in a booth to our left, still in their work boots and grinning at us. I look at Sara who just shrugs, picks up the two shot glasses and puts one of them in my fingers carefully. We down the shots and she turns to the group of men and gives them the thumbs up. I shake my head. Even shitfaced, she's just so dorky and cute. She heads in the direction of the dance floor when a new song comes on and I follow. She waves a hesitant Liam over who has just come from the bar. He downs the liquid from his whisky tumbler, still on his first of the evening, and walks steadily over to us.

I haven't seen Miranda since the bathroom, which was over an hour ago, and I hope she left.

I close my eyes again and let myself feel the music. After a few songs, I realize I'm having fun.

I sneak peeks of the room but mostly I focus on Sara and Liam. His hips are moving slowly back and forth with the rhythm of the song, and he brushes his hand through his hair, now down and swaying with his body. It's a fast song next, and he's stepping side to side, almost in a diagonal motion, with his arms swinging back and forth and in different directions. It's almost like the cha cha but he pulls it off somehow. Every time his head resurfaces in front of me, I notice he's smiling. Maybe even laughing. He's a great dancer and when I sneak a look at the booth of construction guys, they look pissed to see him with us.

I also notice the way women look at Liam. There's a hunger and an eagerness in the way they look at him, talk to him and behave around him. It makes me want him too. It sets a fire in me I haven't felt in a while. It would make me instantly dislike him if he wasn't so damn humble about it. But maybe he's not? I've only known this guy for a few hours.

I'm having one hell of a time and so is Sara. Liam orders another round of drinks on him—whatever we want, he says—so Sara gets some sort of sour college girl shot (despite me telling her again to take it easy), while I order a diet coke. The room is already spinning, so I stick with something more manageable.

I coast with my drink for the remainder of the evening which mostly consists of watching Sara dance her heart out with some of her other friends, and more yelling over the bar's impossible noise to try and have a conversation with Liam in the booth.

I look at my watch and decide to call it quits a little after midnight. Liam and Sara seem disappointed, but I know they both understand. Liam offers to drive us home since he only had one drink. Sara takes him up on his offer, but I remember him telling me he lives on the opposite side of town than Bobby, which is almost a half hour drive from the centre of town. If he dropped me off as well, I would be adding a whole hour to his trip home. I explain that I'll be fine and I don't want him to go out of his way. Liam gives me a sideways glance and asks me how I plan on getting home.

"Buddy's taxi." I say more confidently than I feel.

"You can try calling him, but he rarely answers after midnight." Liam says, leaning back with his fist held up to his mouth as if he's holding in a laugh. It's understandable. Main Street is in Isinbury's centre, with about 90 per cent of the residential areas surrounding it. Most people just walk or bike home.

"What about an Uber then?" That sends them both into a fit of rumbling laughter. I hold back my own chuckle as I realize how ridiculous it is.

Isinbury is a town, untouched by the outside world. They have never had Uber.

I think about all the locals walking home, with a killer on the loose, and wonder if maybe Uber is missing out on a good business opportunity.

Liam insists on driving me home and because it's so late and I truly don't have another option, I obey. I'll have to make it up to him in some way...but I don't say that out loud in case he gets the wrong impression.

He just needs a pee break first, so Sara and I head outside to wait for him and get some fresh air. That's when I bump into Harrison.

When I realize who it is, I start to whole-body panic. I squirm away from his skinny, sweaty body but he stays in my way. He's not worth the trouble so I shove past him.

"Where do you think you're going?" he says to me, following my quickened steps. "Nice to see you too, *Jane*."

I can feel the sweat beginning to form behind my neck and under my bangs. Sara crosses her arms while stomping away from him, and does her best to look unfriendly.

"Heard you were being a real slut in there," he spits at us. "Came to see for myself how much of a fool you've been making of yourself." I know he's looking for a reaction from me, and I'm trying my best not to give it to him.

I continue walking away when he grabs my left wrist in a firm hold and yanks me backwards toward him, almost making me trip. Pain sears through my wrist, arm and shoulder as I start to see black dots in my vision. I stay very still.

"Let go of me. *Now*." I growl.

He says very quietly, and quickly, "Once a tease, always a tease, eh?"

Even when the words aren't fully out, I start to see red. I turn to face him, shocked at his words, and I think I see him trying to aggressively kiss me, half-joking, half trying to prove his dominance over me. I can't hold back. I've drunk a little too much and am not thinking straight anymore. My emotions are bubbling to the surface and although he doesn't scare me anymore, I feel it a part of my duty to show him he can't treat women this way.

I twist my left arm up in the air to bring it backward and down in a full swing, which should make him lose his grip...but I've lost a lot of strength in that arm since the gunshot wound and instead my arm seizes with pain, mid-swing. It makes me cry out a little in pain and I hate myself for showing weakness in front of this man. He laughs bitterly at my reaction and while still holding on to my arm, he tugs me toward him in one violent jerk backward, whispering, "I own this town now, bitch."

I can hear Sara yelling at him and I feel her trying to pull me from this messed up human being who she knows has damaged me before. He's still laughing at my unsuccessful self-defense. So, instead, I shift my body to the right, shake Sara off, and steady my knees. In one quick, continued movement, my right foot smashes into his groin area then my right fist makes hard contact with his face, breaking his nose with a snap. He cries out in pain this time, letting go of my wrist and falling to the ground, muttering something that I couldn't care less to hear. I notice a black Honda with tinted windows pull away from the parking lot suddenly, and a couple of men smoking in the bar's patio whistle at me. Sara and the rest of the locals outside look on in shock.

"Don't ever fucking touch me again or I'll break more than your nose."

~~~

Liam arrived in the crowd sometime between Harrison grabbing my arm and me breaking his nose. He rushed over to me and Sara afterward, avoiding Harrison who was trying to duck inside the bar, holding his bloody face. I'm already a block away heading towards the police station, away from the bar and from everyone there, when Liam catches up to me. I'm hunched over a street trash can throwing up everything in my stomach. I feel more than sober now, but the adrenaline has worn off and the emotions feel raw and bubbly inside my stomach. At first, I couldn't feel how cold it was outside because of the adrenaline pumping through my body, but now I have a slight shiver.

"Hey, are you okay? I sort of saw what happened," he says, hesitantly making his way over to me. "I have to say, nice job."

"Yeah, well, he had that one coming for a long time," I say, almost under my breath, bringing myself back up to a standing position and spitting one last time in the trash. I wipe my mouth with the back of my hand. "That wasn't smart. I could be suspended or face charges for that."

"What can I do to help?"

"Nothing. I'll have to warn Bobby as soon as I see him. Come clean."

"It was self-defense. Anyone could see that, Jane."

"Fuck, it felt good to punch that smugness off his face. So damn good."

"Felt good to watch it too." He hands me a pack of spearmint gum and I take one gratefully.

He asks me again if I'm alright. I wave him off and keep walking. I can hardly feel my fingers now, they're so cold.

"Wait, where are you going?"

"Please drive Sara home for me," I yell, not turning in his direction. "I'm just going to sleep this off at the station." I can feel the anger pulsing through my veins as if I'm on fire. I can hardly hear what Liam is saying to me.

"Jane! Jane!" I hear Sara calling after me. "Jane, come back!"

I try to keep walking but she trips and falls against the pavement, screaming out as she lands. I turn on my heel and run to her. Any residual anger has evaporated in that second. Instead, I feel a different kind of sweat, a cold one that is brought on by worry. She has scraped her bare knees and the palms of her hands pretty bad, but she's alright. I apologize to her over and over, until she waves me off, telling me in a slur of words that I don't have to say sorry. I look up at Liam and ask if she might have hit her head. He says she didn't. I hold her face in my hands and look her over, as she starts to shake. I think she's cold until tears come rolling down and spotting her shirt.

"He's such an asshole, Jane. I can't believe what just happened." She wails. I try to shush her but she goes on. "What he did to you back then... I... I should have... I should have been there for you more. We should've gone to the police," she says this between sobs and I hold her close to my chest, patting her head and peeking up at Liam to see if he understands any of what she is saying. He's looking away from us, trying to give us some privacy.

"Shush, it's okay. Everything is alright."

Liam and I help Sara back to a bench outside the bar and mostly people are giving us our space, with occasional glances our way. They're loving the drama, I know. I'm just hoping Harrison doesn't come back out to finish what he started.

Sara pulls out a smoke and lights it–something she only does when she drinks–so we make our way to the side of the building which is the smoking side. I'm shaking with adrenaline so I grab the cigarette from her hands and take a big pull. I cough a little but the rush goes straight to my head and I feel a little better. Liam has gone to his car to grab some of his first aid supplies.

There is only a couple on this side, keeping to themselves, and Sara and I. I notice one woman walking from the tree-lined path 10 metres away, looking a little distraught and walking fast. No one is behind her; I've checked. Sara is talking to me about something, but I'm not really listening. I feel uneasy. I wonder what's taking Liam so long. I drag from her cigarette again. My hands are still shaking uncontrollably and I can feel the bruising start to form on my right knuckles.

The distraught woman is closing the gap between us quickly and her dark eyes seem to be set on me. She has messy dark hair being thrown by the wind and a long black coat zipped to her chin. Five feet away. She isn't veering off. Maybe I am imagining things. She's two feet from me now and even though I step back out of her way, she darts faster, blocking me from Sara. I turn toward her, startled, thinking she might need my help–maybe I've read the situation wrong–when her cold angry eyes make me stop. She looks like she hasn't slept in days. She looks familiar. I probably went to school with her, as I have most people in this town. She leans towards me, voice lowered, but threatening, "I know what you did."

I lean away from her and she stumbles forward a little but catches herself, annoyance clear on her face.

"What the hell, Brandi?" Sara says, slurring her words.

I level myself with this woman. "Look, my partner Marcus was–"

"Not your partner. Your friend. Abby." She interrupts. "Twelve years ago. Harrison, he told us–"

Then, the left side of the woman's face explodes. Blood, bone and brain matter spraying against my face. It's slow moving at first, people are in shock, but then they start to run. And they start to scream.

I feel my arm being tugged again, hard enough to pull me straight to the ground. It's Sara. She's yelling for me to get down. My hearing hasn't adjusted, it still sounds like I'm underwater. It takes me another minute to come to my senses and then I'm up and running toward where the shot came from. Without a gun for protection.

It's the hardest part of the job. When every bone in your body is screaming to do the opposite; to protect yourself, to run the other way. We run toward.

The ideal place, based on the angle of the shot, would be the tree-lined path in the centre of town three to four blocks away. It's the only place I can think of with enough cover for someone not to notice a gunman. It's also provided him near-successful cover before, if it is the same man.

I run fast and note every person I see on the way there. I enter at the closest entrance and make my way to the end. No one is here. The ground has been disturbed along the tree-lined path too many times to make out any obvious tracks from our shooter. I look for the spot I would choose, the part at the farthest end with the thickest bush and the three giant boulders. A risky move, because I know kids used to like to smoke or fool around here. I use the flashlight function on my phone and think I make out an imprint of something unnatural on the ground next to the tallest boulder. Possibly the butt of a rifle laid against the boulder waiting for an opportunity. They must've been here just seconds ago. I look around through gaps in the bush, but the town square is near empty. I hear people in the direction of the bar and that's it. I look above the boulder and although there are thick trees surrounding me, if you lie pressed up against the rock, you have an untainted view of the bar. And with a scope, I imagine you'd be able to see faces clearly. They'd have to be experienced with rifles to correctly hit their target from this distance, which doesn't do us any good because hunting is a huge sport around here. I look around me for other possibilities. There are no other spots that would provide cover with a perfect beeline shot to the bar and that woman. Oh my god. What was her name? Brandi? And what she said before she died.... Harrison told her something. About Abby. And about me.

I see Kenny running down the street from the police station, headed my way.

"Radio for the coroner's office and get forensics moving," I yell to him.

Liam arrives a minute after I've already processed the situation. His hands are covered in blood, likely having checked on the woman. I saw the life go out of her eyes as the bullet struck, but if I didn't, his face right now would prove to me she's dead.

CHAPTER 9 - JANE

I wake to the smell of fresh coffee, vomit and blood. I panic before remembering the events of last night and where I am. Sara is beside me in my bed at Bobby's. She's pretty shaken up. Judie brought her here while the guys and I were out processing the scene. SAR sent their *ident* team, which included forensics.

We have more than two bodies now. Bobby reached out to the Chief Superintendent for the North District RCMP and they're sending two detectives from Major Crimes in Vancouver out here to close this. Two people from my old team. I'm beyond stressed and extremely curious about who they're going to send.

I climbed in next to Sara for a quick nap after being up for almost 40 hours. She has apparently been puking most of the day. Partly due to a hangover and partly due to her nerves.

I climb out of bed and see the bowl I left out for her filled with bile. I doubt she has anything left in her stomach.

I lift the sheets up to peek at the wounds on her knee and see that she bled through her bandages. The sheets did not make it unscathed. I check her forehead for a fever, but she's fine. She opens her eyes to my touch and squints. I reach over and close the curtains to make it darker.

"Did I dream it?" she asks sadly. I shake my head. She groans and rolls over in bed, turning away from me and facing the wall.

"Sorry. I know that was really hard to see. Give me one second before you go back to sleep, okay? I want to fix those bandages."

She lifts the covers up and groans again. "I'm so sorry. I'll get you new sheets I promise."

"It's fine. I'm a homicide cop. I know how to get blood stains out of things."

Cold water and hydrogen peroxide.

She turns a bit pale.

"Oh, right. Sorry. I'll shut up."

I grab the bowl and make it to the bathroom for the first aid supplies. When I'm there, I catch my reflection in the mirror and flinch. Other than looking like the walking dead, there's a small brown spot of blood near my ear that I missed in my shower last night. I grab a face cloth and wet it, rubbing it harshly all over my face and especially near my ear.

I go back to Sara and fix her bandages for her and let her go back to sleep. I change into my work clothes even though the bedside clock reads about 9 p.m. I follow the smell of coffee into the kitchen where Bobby is standing in the dark. He's fully dressed but with his house slippers on, his gaze out the window even though it's dark and he can't see anything outside. His right hand is limp, loosely holding his coffee cup that remains on the counter. He is a statue of stress.

We both haven't slept much. I'm so damn tired.

I walk over to my pill organizer case and stare at the day markers. I think I missed this morning's medication. And last night's. My body definitely feels like I did. I decide to take the night-time pills, skipping my sleeping meds and popping two extra strength Tylenols on top of my twice daily NSAIDs; nonsteroidal anti-inflammatory drugs. This should help with the pain radiating through my shoulder and back that's quickly becoming unbearable.

Bobby watches me with sympathetic eyes but doesn't move or say a word.

We know the imprint near the boulder was indeed a rifle butt. Likely a Remington or a Savage Arms bolt action rifle with scope. Both brands are quite popular around here and we've already interviewed anyone with a licence for those in town and made sure all guns were accounted for. It took all day and nothing came of it.

Two men that Bobby is close with came forward with grandfathered guns without papers. They aren't suspects. We believe there are more grandfathered and unregistered guns in town that we've missed, but we have no real way of proving that and we are not able to get a warrant on a hunch. The shooter likely has an unregistered rifle. He's smart. And with the 3x9 scope, most people can easily make a 300-yard shot.

"Did you get any sleep?" he asks, half-heartedly.

I shrug my shoulders. "According to the clock I got about 3 hours of sleep but I think it made me more exhausted not less."

He mumbles, "Yes, I feel the same."

I grab a tall mug from the cabinet and pour myself a coffee. Then I make my way over to the dog bowl and fill it up with Bear's breakfast. The house is silent except for his munching. I go sit in one of the stools on the kitchen island, facing Bobby. His face quickly changes into a stern scowl.

"Harrison is trying to press charges for your little fist fight."

I close my eyes in shame. In the chaos of what happened, I had forgotten to tell him about this first. He's learned from someone else. I blow out breath in an attempt to alleviate some of the tightness in my chest.

"Fuck," I say, trying to avoid his disappointed eyes. "I didn't do it on purpose. My body just reacted."

"That's a problem, Jane. It means you're probably not capable of being here right now with a clear mind. I think you should call the therapist and see what she thinks."

It stings. But he's right.

"I have a video appointment with her Sunday afternoon. I can wait until then."

"You promise?"

"Yes, I promise." Even as I say these words, I'm afraid I don't mean them and I feel my cheeks redden at the thought.

"Do you think the charges will hold?" I manage.

"Doubtful," he says as relief floods through me. "A young lady caught a phone video of what happened between you two and turned it in. It reads as self-defense and worse for Harrison, it looks like assault and battery against a police officer. His lawyer knows it too. They didn't seem very serious when they came in. I think they just wanted to scare you a bit."

"Are you sure?" The ball in my chest tightens again. I press my hand on it trying to get my emotions under control. If this video gets released to the media, I might lose my job for good.

"Yes. The video depicts you giving him a warning to back off and let go, and even though he was unarmed, it can be argued he posed a threat to you. Especially since he had a firm grasp on your disabled arm."

It's the first time I've heard him talk about me as disabled. I don't know how to feel about that, yet. I feel a hot blanket of shame, confusion and fear roll over me. He continues talking.

"A police officer punching someone in the face is always bad, but it helps that you're a woman and a foot shorter than him."

For once, I'm thankful for my smaller stature.

He walks over to me, his hands hesitantly hovering over my arm. "May I take a look?"

"Sure, I guess." I don't really know what he's looking for until I pull my sleeve up and he gasps. It's quickly followed by angry swearing, which has Judie peek out from their bedroom door at the end of the hall and ask if everything is alright.

I look down to see the purple-yellow fingertip bruising around my arm. Harrison, you fucker.

"Nothing, dearest, go back to bed," Bobby hollers in his most polite and calming voice.

Her brows furrow, studying him, but then she calls softly, "Okay, I love you two. Be safe."

"Love you too," Bobby and I say in unison as she closes the door.

"We need to get Kenny to take photos of this at the station – to protect you but also if you want to press charges yourself."

"Fine to photos. I'll think about the charges." I take a long sip of coffee. "How did the rest of it go?"

"We took Harrison's statement, lawyer by his side. Several people saw him at the bar with a bloody nose at the time of the shooting."

"What about Miranda? She would've done this if he asked her to."

"That's a little harder to pinpoint. People say they saw her at the bar with him when he had a bloody nose...but no one can tell if she was there exactly when the shooting started."

I sigh.

"Brandi was Lilyann's best friend. This could link her to the deaths of the first two. Harrison claims he doesn't know what Brandi was talking about, though said she blamed him for breaking up her and Lilyann's friendship, and later, for her death. We found these messages in her Facebook inbox to him." He reaches over and grabs a folder and slides it my way. "It proves he's telling the truth about her harassing him, though he went pale white when he saw these messages and knew we had 'em. His lawyer quickly called it quits after that, so we didn't manage to get a clear answer about the reason for the messages."

Most of it is angry capital lettered threats from Brandi. Things like: WHY DID YOU TELL HER, SHE'S DEAD BECAUSE OF YOU, YOU RUIN EVERYTHING YOU TOUCH. And one in particular that catches my attention: I'M GOING TO TALK UNLESS YOU PAY UP.

A tickle forms at the back of my neck and I try not to panic.

The messages show a read receipt, so Harrison saw these, he just chose to ignore her.

"What is it that Brandi knew? Do we have any idea?" I ask, avoiding eye contact, trying to keep my voice even.

"No and do you see that first message? It looks like Lilyann might have known something as well. Something that got her killed. I have no idea what the hell would be worth murdering someone about in this town."

"Drugs maybe?"

"Maybe. Harrison has been involved with that crap ever since you knew him. It's rumoured he runs the show now. Took over from Daniel Briggs after he...well you know."

"No...I don't know. Who's Daniel Briggs?"

I notice Bobby's shoulders tighten and he starts clearing the counter and doing the dishes. He does this when he's stressed: avoids eye contact and keeps his hands busy. Whatever this is about, he doesn't like it.

"Briggs was a drug dealer who ended up dying in the back cell of the station. Do you remember that? It was shortly after...well, shortly after Abby went missing, and then, a month later your dad died, so you probably never heard of it 'cause you were dealing with so much back then." His voice softens. "We brought Daniel in as part of a police-led anti-drug measure, connecting him to the majority of drug operations going on in town at the time. We locked him up in the back cell for two days to await transfer to the city. Twelve hours later though, we found him dead in the cell, covered in spit-up, apparently dead from a heart attack."

"A heart attack?" I say, bewildered.

"Yes, that's what it looked like at first. But I thought it could be poison, you know, either in his food or by someone who snuck in the side door. We didn't have a door buzzer entry system at the front or the keycard entry to the side door, back then. The medical examiner, Dr. Bruce Jenkins, did an autopsy though and said everything was normal except for evidence of some prescription drugs."

"Could he have taken something ahead of time to cause a reaction 12 hours later?"

"He wasn't the type to go down with the ship. He was going to strike a deal with the Crown Attorney for a smaller sentence."

He's still avoiding eye contact. This topic clearly makes him uncomfortable.

We both understand the implication of the second possibility.

"The ruling was that he must have gotten his meds mixed up somehow and it caused a heart attack."

"Were you working that night, Bob?"

He hesitates, brows tightening together. I know that look. He's contemplating what his next words are.

"Your dad was on duty that night but had fallen asleep."

My eyebrows raise and my mouth goes slack in shock. I think I remember now...but my memory is pretty hazy during that time because of the depression.

"He hadn't been feeling too well, your dad, and I had offered to cover the shift for him. You know what he was like. Didn't want to owe anyone anything. Anyways, the side entrance hadn't been locked properly I guess, so any bugger could have wandered in and done it to keep Daniel quiet," Bobby explains, tapping his fingers on the desk. "Your dad woke to hear him heaving right before he died. Henry tried CPR, but it really didn't make a difference."

I process this information and feel myself start to sweat. My dad was the detachment's commander sergeant, my hero, my best friend. After this incident, he started treating us coldly, working late and coming home either pissed off, drunk or both. And then he died.

Bobby continues. "We thoroughly interviewed everyone involved or anyone who had access to him in that cell, but came up blank. I think we were just relieved to have it over with. Your dad was devastated that this had happened on his watch. He wanted the guy to go to prison and hopefully take a few of his buddies with him. He wanted them out of the town where they were doing a lot of damage to the at-risk youth who made them rich," Bobby manages that last part in somewhat of a snarl.

I think of the town now and the drug problem it still seems to have and cringe. At least Dad isn't around to see that none of that mattered.

I keep Daniel's name circled in my mind, something to check into later, but not likely related to our case. I take out my pain relief rub and apply it on both shoulders. Bobby gives me a funny look.

I shrug. "I smell like a mint, but it really helps."

"Can I give it a try?" He asks sheepishly. I chuckle and hand it over. He applies it to his lower back.

"Look at us, old folks," I joke.

"I'm sor–"

"So Harrison took over from Briggs?" I ask, interrupting him, changing the subject. Bobby nods, seeming to understand. He refills his coffee cup.

"Yeah he did, but we've never been able to do much about it. He has a decent, expensive lawyer. We might be able to bring him in again in the next few days but I doubt they will tell us anything productive."

"I hate the guy, and yet, something about this doesn't seem right."

"Go on," he presses.

"If this is all related...this is an extreme criminal escalation. He goes from strangling the women quietly to almost getting caught during a public shooting..." I pause, thinking it over.

"It fits in with the assumption he stalks his victims first, though. He must have been watching Brandi and knew she was about to tell you something he didn't want getting out."

"Either that...or he was aiming for me instead."

Bobby looks down at his mug. "That also crossed my mind."

An uneasy silence grows. We look up at each other quietly, before I shake my head and move on.

"Anyway, the killer doesn't try to hide or dispose of the bodies. He leaves them to be found. What's the purpose of that...If it was Harrison, I would think he would want everything to be taken care of quickly and quietly, especially if he's hiding something...unless he's sending a message to others, a sort of 'look at what happens to people who stand against me?' Does that make sense?"

"It sort of does. Though it sounds like you just thought yourself in a circle." He thinks it over. "But then, why only women? And we haven't found any bodies directly connected to his drug business."

"Yes, I realize. Maybe I'm overthinking things." My mind is on the caves.

Bobby sighs. "That video Jane. It made me see red."

"I'm sorry, Bob."

"No, I mean, I saw the way he grabbed your wrist and tried to kiss you. I imagined strangling him myself." I watch his eyes grow wide and then he swears. "Stupid bastard."

I finish my coffee. "What about Laryssa?" I try to change the subject.

"What about her?" He seems surprised.

"She owns the Raven. Two of her employees are dead and another woman was just shot outside of her bar."

"Sure, but we've interviewed her several times already. You know the Raven is the hot spot for the town. *Everything* happens there."

"Are you saying this just because you grew up with her?"

"No. People saw her at the bar last night, though no one can really pinpoint an exact time she was behind the bar. She often works in the back. And she has an alibi for one of the two nights."

"Right...who was her alibi again?"

"The town's young new doctor. Kim Jenkins."

"...Jenkins? Why do I recognize that name?"

"Her father was the medical examiner when you were growing up here. The one I just mentioned, the coroner for Daniel Briggs. He was a close friend of your dad's too. Do you remember him?"

I shake my head. "I don't think so...Plus everyone here seems to know Dad. Knew him, I mean."

"His wife ran the funeral home too, before they sold the place, picked up and moved to Calgary."

"And Kim Jenkins is their daughter?"

"Yes."

"What's she like?"

"Kim? She's lovely. I mean, definitely a beauty on the outside, but she's a laidback and bright young woman on the inside. Very kind. A bit quiet and reserved, but her patients adore her. She's close with Laryssa."

"How old is Kim?"

"Around your age I think."

"So Laryssa is twice her age?"

"You sound pretty *judgey* for someone who hangs around with an old fart like me all the time," he says, his tone light.

"I'm not judging, I just find it weird. Is it possible they're dating or are they just friends?"

He laughs at this. I cock an eyebrow.

"I have gotten the impression their relationship is a lot like ours. Laryssa was close with Kim's parents and I think every time they came to visit, Laryssa would play the part of "fun aunt" and bring her camping, skiing–you know, sort of like I did with you." He's thinking of something now, but not sharing.

"I've never pictured Laryssa as the kid-loving type, but I suppose 'fun aunt' describes her to a tee."

A flash of a memory passes through my mind before quickly disappearing. Laryssa in her car, a red-haired teenager in the backseat with headphones in.

Bobby interrupts my thoughts and I realize I didn't hear most of what he just said.

"...a way of always taking people under her wing." He thinks this over. "Loner and misfit types." He shrugs. "Figured it was because she had a tough go herself during her teenage years."

"Hmm," I reply, lost in thought now. I used to be one of those misfits and loners in Isinbury. I still am 10 years later.

Maybe I can use this to get closer to Laryssa. There's something about her I don't trust.

"Why so curious about Laryssa all of a sudden?" He asks.

"I'm not sure. Just trying to follow all the leads." I wait only a second before diving into what's really bothering me. "Are we going to search the caves?" I can't hold it in anymore.

"I'm not sure it's a good use of our time. Harrison knows we saw those messages and we grilled him about the caves after what Brandi said before she died. But he's probably already sent someone to grab the drugs or whatever he has buried in those caves."

"You're just gonna let it slide?"

He gives me an annoyed look. "We sort of had our hands full last night and today, as you know, so we didn't have time to send SAR down in the cave system in the middle of the night for some drugs that may or may not be there. Either way, the major crimes team should be here in a few hours and it's their call now."

He downs the rest of his coffee and turns back down the hallway without another word, heading toward his office.

Laryssa. The Caves. Harrison.

I know what I have to do.

CHAPTER 10 - JANE

Bobby reminds me of the school fundraiser on our way to the station. That would explain why Sara got picked up by Langdon before dawn this morning.

I drive Bobby's truck because he has a really bad migraine. Bear's in the back.

We arrive early enough that there's still stuff left for sale on the tables. The event was moved to the public recreation building last minute, because no one wants to really hang around town square right now. It's much warmer here anyway. I unzip my coat and put my toque and mitts in my pockets. I have Bear on his leash and go to buy a few white macadamia nut cookies, but the mean-looking woman behind the table sneers as I walk up. I pretend not to notice and keep walking to the next table.

There's the Walker family showcasing modernized Indigenous desserts, like Bannock doughnuts and several puddings. Their table is obviously the most popular today, with a huge line waiting to be served. When I get to the front of the line, Jacob Walker and his wife Emilie seem pleased to see me. They're both wearing Métis capotes, a long wrap-style wool coat with hoods. Hers is a bright blue with the hood pulled up and his is red and white stripes, hood down and coat left open.

Jacob kneels down to pet Bear, who seems thrilled to see him.

"You're so grown up," says Emilie warmly. "It's strange getting older, because you still feel the same age but everyone you know keeps ageing."

"I get that," I say, smiling.

Her brown eyes are kind, her cheeks rosy and her hands weathered. I remember her from when I was younger. She worked at the school in the Principal's office as an admin clerk but she also led an outdoor physical education program I was in called the Forest School. She taught us survival and foraging skills, as well as about the different Indigenous communities nearby such as the Dene, Cree, Dunne Tsaa, Tsáá? Ché Ne Dane, Dene Tha' and Kaska peoples, many of whom are connected through kinship networks, and the enduring presence of the Métis community. It was my favourite class I ever took.

"We're happy to have you back in the community with us, Jane," she adds.

"Thank you, it means a lot," I say, thankful to have some allies. "How have you been?"

She shares an intimate, knowing look with her husband, before answering. "We've been doing well. We have lots of grandkids now so we're very busy."

"Are they all yours?" I nod toward the young boys and girls behind them, serving desserts and wrapping handmade gifts.

Both of their smiles reach their eyes. I feel my face mirror the same.

Jacob leans in and says, "Yes, they are, and we have about 11 more grandkids elsewhere, if you can believe it."

"That's amazing. A full soccer team," I joke.

They laugh politely. Another patron grabs Jacob's attention and he nods politely to me, before reaching out to shake this other guy's hand animatedly.

"Can I interest you in a blueberry cookie and cream bannock doughnut? It has homemade blueberry jam in the middle," she says, beaming with pride.

"There's only one left," I say, though my mouth begins to water at the sight of it.

"Then it was meant to be yours," she says, phrased as a question.

"Okay, well, manners aside, I'd love that last doughnut."

She chuckles, carefully placing the doughnut in parchment paper, as I check out the rest of the table which is filled with handmade artwork and jewellery. I pick out a beaded bracelet for Judie and a brightly coloured painting of a lone wolf for myself; the wolf is painted in bright blues, purples and white, with a striking orange moon behind. Something about it makes my heart sing, so I buy it and Emilie smiles at me, kindly, as she wraps it.

"This is very you," she says, as if we've been friends for years.

"Do you think so?" I ask genuinely. I haven't been much of an art person ever. I don't even paint my place or hang anything up.

"Sit with it awhile, and you'll see what I mean," she says.

"I will," I say, "thank you, for everything." I place the objects carefully in my backpack but keep the doughnut in hand.

"Anytime," she says, but pauses. "Take care of yourself, Jane."

I smile and give a wave, although the tone sounded more serious than she likely intended it to and I feel myself shiver.

I head toward Sara's table, finally. She's talking to someone but she gives me a little wave of hello. Her bouncy blonde curls are perfect and her face is painted on with her best business-owner smile. She looks so much better than when I last saw her. She's one of those natural beauties who's a bit nuts about maintaining her health regime and going on daily runs. Seeing her transformation though, I might have to start following her lead.

I buy half a dozen of Sara's blue icing cupcakes. I take out my phone and snap a selfie of us with one of the cupcakes and send it to Bobby, with a text saying: *Come find me, otherwise I am stuffing my face with all of these.*

I take a big bite out of the bannock doughnut and moan. Sara laughs.

"That's one of the Walkers' bannock doughnuts, isn't it?"

"Guilty," I say, mouth full.

"Can't blame you, I made sure I got one before the fundraiser even opened."

"I guess they're sort of your in-laws, right?"

"Yeah, they're all great. I love being part of a big family." Her voice falters. I pretend not to notice. It's something we have in common. Not a lot of family left.

I stuff a twenty-dollar bill in the donation box, just as Liam comes into view a few feet to my right, whistling at me.

"Damn, they must be paying you the big bucks down south," he jokes loudly. I look around quickly to see if anyone else heard. I don't want to make a big show of donating, especially if the residents already think I believe I'm better than everyone else. Liam notices my hesitation, but misreads it. As he closes the distance between us, he steps back with his arms in a surrender and grins. "Sorry, I just wanted to properly announce my presence this time, as I was concerned for my safety."

I shake my head at him in good humour with my mouth full, licking the corner where the icing has smeared.

"Don't worry, I think I've gotten all my tequila-throwing and martial arts out of my system." I pause. "For now."

He grins and bends over to give Bear some love. Most people are doing the same as they pass. He's like the perfect emotional support dog and that's exactly why we brought him.

"Whoever made up the saying 'you punch like a girl,' must've never met one like you."

"Yeah, well that wasn't a real smart move on my part," I admit sheepishly.

"I've never gotten a good vibe from him," he admits.

"Yeah, well, doesn't mean I should be breaking his nose," I grumble. "Even though it felt really good to do so."

"I'll say it again, it felt really good to watch you do it."

We share a laugh. He might be quiet as a cat, but he has a goofy, subtly flirtatious side that reminds me of the best parts of my father. My dad always said, the way to a woman's heart isn't diamonds but laughter. My mom would tease him by saying a smart man would offer both.

Liam catches me mid-thought. "We're getting some disapproving looks. I guess we shouldn't be laughing at a time like this," he says seriously.

"They're probably right. For a split second, I actually forgot." I shake my head. Part of being a cop is desensitization to the job...still, I feel a wave of shame, laughing only a few days after someone's head exploded on me. Probably something I should talk to the therapist about... "Want a cupcake?"

He reaches for one in the box I offer to him, and I notice his nails are painted all different colours and done horribly, the polish reaching past the nail like someone did it with their eyes closed. I'm about to ask him about it when he stuffs the whole cupcake in his mouth in one bite. I can't help but smirk, and when he notices, he flashes me a huge dorky smile, blue icing dying his teeth. My lips cave inwards trying my best not to laugh.

Sara comes over handing him some napkins. "Well look at you two. Brightening the spirits."

My face goes instantly red. "I think Bear is the one bringing smiles to people's faces. I still feel a heaviness in the air, but this fundraiser came at a perfect time: brings the community together and helps them focus on more light-hearted moments."

Sara pulls an eyebrow up and turns to Liam. "You might not believe me, but that's the most anti-Jane thing I've ever heard. She is the *queen* of doom and gloom."

I roll my eyes. Liam grins.

Just as an awkward silence starts to arise, a small figure crashes into Liam's side at full force. He catches her mid-flight and tosses her over his right shoulder. A burst of giggles erupts from his back.

"Hey Julia! I didn't know you were visiting." Sara calls over Liam's shoulder.

Liam turns his back toward us so Julia can answer, upside down, "I'm leaving now. My sister is over there. I've just come to say goodbye to Liam."

Liam tosses her back over and helps her to stand. She caves herself into his embrace, shyly. "Julia meet Jane. Jane, this is my younger sister Julia," Liam says.

The tiny human pulls herself up as best she can, moves her long blonde locks aside with a small arm and holds out a dainty hand, her nails covered in the same rainbow polish as Liam's. His crazy manicure is starting to make more sense. I shake Julia's hand. Despite her size, she has an impressively firm handshake.

Her eyes shrink when she smiles, just like Liam.

"It's nice to meet you," she says politely. Liam crouches down and picks up her small frame, spinning her around in a hug and bringing her back on her feet. She stumbles a little from dizziness, but giggles as she dramatically falls to the ground, jumps up, and stumbles again. She reminds me of a little girl I used to know with blonde locks and boundless energy, with the ability to hold the attention of everyone in the room.

Abby.

My thoughts wander back to the caves.

"Behave this week, you little snot," Liam says jokingly. He pulls out a fiver which seems to make her still for a moment as he waves it around. "Be good for our sis and there will be more of these in your future."

She grins at it greedily, nodding enthusiastically and shoving the money into her little pocket. She's wearing a pretty blue and yellow floral dress with white tights and white running shoes.

"Can I pet Bear?" she asks me.

"Of course. He's very friendly. He even likes hugs if you're gentle."

"I *know*," she says boastfully. She's obviously met him before. She leans in to give Bear a hug and then eyes her brother before jumping into his side again. "Bye, Liam. Make Spaghetti next time. It's why I come to visit."

She skips off towards the bake sale, money in hand and flicks us back a peace sign.

"Love you!" Liam yells in her direction. He shakes his head as if he's unimpressed but I can tell this encounter has softened him. He even looks a little sad.

"Sorry about that. My sister can be a bit bossy. And flamboyant." He chuckles and looks after her in a way I've only seen parents do.

"I really like her. She's hilarious." There's an easy silence between us. I decide to echo my thoughts out loud. "She reminds me of a friend I used to have when I was younger. Looks like her too with all that blonde hair."

Sara gives me a worried look before turning back to her bakery sale. Liam doesn't seem to notice.

"Yeah, I tell her we should cut it soon but she's determined to grow it to her butt. I can't really tell her otherwise, as I'd be a hypocrite." He shakes his head, showing off his own blonde locks reaching down to his shrugging shoulders.

"You have good genes to be able to grow it so thick and long. I think the last time mine felt like that was before high school." He smiles and his eye contact is brazen and intimate as always.

I catch Bobby and Kenny out of the corner of my eye surrounded by a small crowd. People are asking about the case and last night's shooting, and if we are even capable of doing our jobs. I see Jacob Walker making his way over to support Bobby. They're very close.

Liam follows my gaze. "Should we intervene?" He suggests.

I feel Bobby's truck keys in my pocket. "You go ahead, I just remembered I have a small work emergency." The cupcakes are still in my hands and so is Bear's leash. "Wait, can you hold these for me until I get back?"

"Of course, no problem." He grabs the treats and leash from me and I thank him.

Then I exit the building quickly and hop into the truck. My mind and heart are racing.

I stop by the station to grab a helmet with a built-in headlamp, extra batteries, a flashlight, some rope, an extra fleece sweater and a rain jacket. I'm already wearing my hiking boots which have good tread and are rain resistant.

Now that the guys have their hands full, I head towards the caves.

As I do, I have a chilling thought. Those caves would provide the perfect cover for someone to sneak up and take us out. A picture of Bobby's lifeless body, sprawled out in the pitch black of the caves, his head bashed in and blood oozing down his face appears in my mind. It makes me emotional. How do I risk putting their lives in danger, if this is a trap?

It's a difficult part of the job, I hear Bobby's raspy voice saying in the back of my mind. *Putting yourself and your partners in danger to protect the lives of your neighbours and strangers. But you'll see soon that it's a great honour.* I'm thinking back to my graduation day after the ceremony. We're huddled in a crowd of graduates and their loved ones in the grass. Judie, Glen and Kenny are making their way over to us from the seating area. Bobby was allowed to be the one to hand me my certificate, which wasn't really allowed, but because he was friends with a lot of higher ups, they made it happen. I held my shit together, closing the gap between us across the stage with heavy-booted steps, in my red suit, him in his, my posture perfect and my face composed...until I saw his face crumple, a few silent tears running down his face as I approached him and saluted. I shook his hand with a smile, my own tears running down then, and he pulled me into a hug. *Definitely* not allowed. But there were a few cheers in the crowd. It was an emotional scene. My dad would've been the one to do it, and Bobby stood in for him, like he always has.

I even thought I saw my dad in the crowd for a moment - a split second, at the very back, covered by the shadow of a tree. But when I looked back over, he wasn't there of course. A trick of the imagination. Or my mind saw what my heart wanted to see.

Feels like forever ago now. So much has happened in my life since then. My feelings about life and loss and family have shifted with the stress and growth of working in such an emotionally demanding field. I see the world in whole new eyes, the eyes of someone who must push feelings aside to tackle any given day and whatever it decides to throw at me. I might be emotionally stunted sometimes, but it's a way to protect myself. It's what I do to survive.

My phone vibrates in my pocket, bringing me back to the present. I check the screen. Bobby is asking me where I am.

I've decided, against better judgement, to check out the caves by myself first. This way, the only person I am putting in danger is me. Besides, the killer doesn't necessarily know what we know. Unless it's Harrison. But I think I can handle him myself; sober, clear-headed and ready.

Bobby isn't even that interested in searching the caves. I'm following a hunch.

I left a detailed note in Bobby's office, explaining where I am and my suspicions about the caves. He's going to be pissed, but I left it anyway so they can find me after I make sure the cave is clear, or well, if something happens and I can't be found.

There are three large cave systems in Isinbury, all huddled together near the campground and about a kilometre from the beach. But I already know which one I am going to. My gut tells me if Harrison really is involved, there's only one cave it can be.

I'm almost there. I haven't been to those caves since I woke up that July morning by myself. The day I was found after blacking out at Miranda's and missing for 12 hours.

I'm facing my demons. I can't ignore this any longer.

CHAPTER 11 - JANE

The mountain range dips into the tepid Isinbury river, which leads to a small beach area by the forest's edge. The campsite and hiker's parking lot is located here so I park my car and head into one of the trails. The only other car here is a black Honda with tinted windows. It reminds me of the one that peeled out of the bar's parking lot two nights ago. It's a common vehicle, I remind myself.

The air is cold but the ground is moist, and a thick fog has come in with the wind. Wet forest debris is one of my favourite smells in the world. Something about it is so comforting. Wet leaves and Judie's homemade cocoa, the wooden smell of Bobby's house and spring tulips, that remind me of my mother.

I can see about 20 feet around me before the rest of the world disappears into a white, hazy unknown. The trees that pass my line of sight, enveloped by the fog, appear more like tall, dark shadows leaning in to get a closer look at me as I arrive at the entrance of the cave.

My pounding heart pulls me forward, step by step.

It was a half hour walk through the foggy forest from the parking lot and I have about four hours of daylight left. That won't matter once I'm in the cave though, which is why I have at least two light sources with me.

I check the path leading to the caves for fresh footprints but because this is such a busy area, especially for the local teens, the path is mostly worn and blended together. I do make out a couple of small footprints near the front but never going farther than the lip at the top and too small to be those of an adult. As I'm finished with those, I catch one large set of footprints, maybe a size 13, near the entrance to the right. It goes in until the rock where I lose it.

Fuck. I might not be alone out here. It could be Harrison trying to cover up whatever he's involved in, or one of his goons. Or simply a lone man is coming out here to do strange business in a cave which is creepy but totally possible...or it might be our killer.

It starts raining pretty hard, its rhythm beating against my body in tempo with my heart. I was hoping to be in better shape to tackle this but the rain makes every joint in my body ache and it's extremely distracting. I silently curse Marcus for turning me into such a vulnerable person. A disabled person, as Bobby pointed out.

I try to focus. I'll have to watch my step inside as an opening at the top allows the rainwater to pour through and soak everything in its path. I'm thankful for the rain jacket and my hardy boots, but I'm very much missing my weapon. Everyone knows guns are useless in a cave system so I've left it behind. It can take the whole thing down on top of you. I secure my helmet and switch on the headlamp. Then I enter the cave.

This particular cave has a fairly large opening, probably the size of my apartment back home, with a roof that sticks out ten feet from the opening. There are empty beer cans and trash left in here on the grassy rock surface from parties long finished, and something that looks like a small fire pit in its centre. This was an ideal party spot even when I was a teenager, but no one in their right mind would go farther in than the opening because it's so dangerous in the dark. Not only are there wild critters running around in here, but there are sharp mineral deposits sticking out from the rock and spontaneous drops near the path that lead you even farther under the Earth. Bobby has had to come rescue a few idiots down here before, so he's told me all about the dangers awaiting me now. Without the proper tools, you could be stuck, hurt or even killed. But I have come prepared.

At the back of the opening to the right, there's a crevice in the wall about two feet wide. I throw my backpack down first. I don't really need to suck in, but I do it anyway and squeeze through it carefully, watching my head as I do so. My right shoulder scrapes against something sharp and I let out a curse. So far, not off to a great start. I think about Bobby and realize that he probably wouldn't even be able to fit in here with his beer belly.

I'm through the crevice and the only way to go is down a steep decline, almost a drop, which leads to a pitch-black underground, extending beyond the zone of light but large enough to permit entry. I bring myself down on my butt and crawl down the slope like a spider, bracing myself by digging my gloved hands and rubber-soled boots into tiny fissures in the rock wall. The vertical shaft is about six feet long, but I keep my balance and gracefully land on its stony bottom that expands itself into three horizontal cave passages. I listen for any sound of an intruder other than me.

It's quiet except for the sound of water dripping and the occasional squeak from a mouse. Or is that a bat?

It instantly drops 10 degrees. My body throbs angrily in response. I take a look around me with my flashlight and notice mostly rodent droppings and clusters of what looks like rocky popcorn that I believe are described as cave coral, to the immediate right of the vertical shaft where a steady spray of rainwater falls. It smells earthy and damp down here.

I take my time, the tiny rocks underfoot twisting my ankle one way after another, and enter through the first passage to my left. But it quickly leads to a small room, which means a dead end. I back up and try the second. After an hour of jumping, climbing, ducking and squeezing through the path on my belly–my body protesting every damn movement–I find my way to a small hole leading out of the cave hidden behind a wall of thick ivy. I'm thankful for the fresh air but only briefly. I turn around and make my way back which takes even longer because I have to use the rope to lower myself down the walls I just crawled up. I do the mental math and it is probably around 6 p.m. The guys will have made their way back to the station and found my note by now. I need to hurry.

I suddenly hear a downpour of rock, coming from the crevice I first entered to make it down here to these three branches of pathways. I crouch in the corner and take out my pocket knife, pointing it towards the crevice with my arm bent and ready. But instead of human legs which I'm expecting to see, it's a fox. And we just scared the shit out of each other. I fall back in shock and it hisses at me and hurries down the first passageway. I relax a little, fold the knife closed, but keep it in my hand, just in case. These wild animals are really making me jumpy. I feel more like a city girl than ever, and I hate it.

I turn to the last branch of this cave system. I take out the fleece from my tiny backpack and put it on, under my rain jacket. My body feels numb. I think proactively and take two extra strength Tylenol, daydreaming about a hot epsom salt bath to soothe the damage I've done to my body today.

About ten minutes in, the third branch opens into a sloping, boulder strewn cavern. I step past a vertical pit in the floor which looks more like a sliver. There are a few windows through the rock wall which I check out one by one. The last window is large enough to crawl through and will lead me further down into the cave. I take out my flashlight and point it slowly across the cavern. Some pieces of bone fragments are in the corner. Likely animal and from scavengers. I take a photo with flash, in case I'm wrong. I think I hear an echo of a voice but it could be my imagination. A shiver runs itself up my back and I get a chill. Still shaking, I take another look around me suddenly. I'm alone except for a few bats.

Relax Jane. Try not to think of the size 13 footprint.

I have checked the entire cave system except for this hole. I'm not one for half-assing things, so I gather up some small amount of courage and pull myself up and into the black hole. But as I'm doing so, a bat screeches and flies past, startling me and sending me tumbling down the tunnel in fear. I lose my knife trying to unsuccessfully grab on to a fissure in the wall while I'm sliding down this bumpy, bruise-inducing shaft. I bang my head, luckily secured in the helmet, but it breaks my only steady light source. I continue to fall down in the dark, seconds feeling like minutes, scraping my chin, my elbows and my legs until I finally land in a pit of freezing cold groundwater with a splash. I scramble to the surface and am relieved to find out the water only reaches to my shoulders. That murky smell has definitely been coming from this standing water.

I can safely stand, but my headlamp is broken and my foot is caught in some sort of wooden crate that is under the water.

Strange place for a crate, don't you think?

The crate's sides are sharp and I wince as I unsuccessfully try to pull my ankle towards my body from its tight hold, scraping the area above my ankle and most likely drawing blood.

Great, I'm going to give myself some sort of funky cave-water infection.

I feel around the cave's wall with my hands, completely blinded by darkness and try to find my flashlight. But I stop moving when I think I hear someone walking around in the cavern just outside where I am trapped. My heart is beating out of my chest and it throbs in my ears as I strain to listen. I try to quiet my breathing and my racing mind by picturing the fox. I freeze when the intruder makes an audible noise. Foxes definitely don't cough like that. Whatever is out there is unquestionably human. And there's only one reason they would bother coming through this far.

I unbuckle my belt as quickly as I can. If I need to, I can use this as a weapon or at least for self-defense.

"Jane! Are you here?" the voice calls out. I can't place it.

"Jane! We got your note. Are you here? Can you hear me?" A strong sense of relief washes over me from head to toe. It's Liam.

I call out to him and explain where I am and he finds me right away. The other windows are too small to allow human visitors, so I'm not hard to find. I tell him I'm stuck and there's water down here and he tells me to wait for a minute while he calls out for Bobby and Kenny who are checking the other passages. When he returns, he lowers himself down carefully using his strong arms and legs, then literally *plops* into the water beside me. His headlamp is working and I'm thankful for the light. I'm not claustrophobic but I've always been a little afraid of the dark.

He adjusts his lamp so it's not blinding me. A rope is securely fastened to his waist with a second rope in his left hand.

"Are you okay?" He asks softly.

"Yes, but my ankle is caught in something and whatever it's caught in, it's stuck. I can lift my leg but it's really stuck in there."

"Did you try going under the water to free it?" He asks.

"Not yet. Have you *smelled* this water?" I ask defiantly.

He stifles a laugh, I'm sure of it, but then he sounds wounded as he says, "Work emergency, huh?"

"Sorry," I whisper. "It wasn't personal."

He moves on. "Close your eyes for a second, I want to check your injuries. There's blood pouring down your face that has me concerned."

I do as I'm told and feel the light blind me anyway. I jump at his touch even though it's feather-light. "Sorry. You have a pretty nasty cut on your chin, but you'll live. Does anything else hurt? Your neck? Your back?"

"Yeah, literally my entire body." I answer, annoyance evident. I try to soften my tone. "Sorry. I fell down the shaft and feel pretty stupid about it. And I was already hurting before that...neck and back seem fine though, nothing seems broken, if that's what you mean?"

"Do you mind if I quickly do a medical assessment so we know it's safe to move you?"

"Um, sure."

He asks me to move my neck around slowly, checking for any neck injuries. Luckily everything there is intact.

"Take off your helmet and turn around, please."

"I can't. My foot is stuck, remember?"

"Do your best. I'll meet you halfway."

I cooperate. He carefully makes his way around me and aims his headlamp to check my head for wounds. Easy to do, since I'm a foot shorter than him. Then he firmly checks down my spine, pressing against each vertebrae and insisting I tell him if something feels wrong.

"I need to check your SI joints, since you had a nasty fall. That's your–"

"Yes, that's fine. I know what SI joints are. You have my permission but hurry up."

He breathes in an impatient sigh, as he inspects my SI joints, which are just above my butt, with his fingers. I feel extremely embarrassed but only for a fleeting second, and then he's done.

"I think you're good to go, but there's definitely some inflammation in your lumbar region that has me a bit concerned."

I turn to face him again. "Probably normal. Normal for me, anyway. I have complex regional pain syndrome but my doctor said there's a possibility of a secondary autoimmune disease."

"Ah, okay. Well, let's get you out of here first and then we can take a better look at you when we're out."

Liam reaches down into the stinky water to push the box from my foot, his chin barely above water and freezes. He stays like that for a few seconds, then stands up straight and gives me a weird look. I stare back at him, confused.

As I impatiently reach down into the water to help myself out, his arm reaches out to stop me.

"Don't," he says.

I give him a look before reaching again, pulling my leg up with the box as far as I can. I can't avoid going underneath the water, so I take a deep breath and go under up to my forehead. My fingers are wrapping around my ankle, feeling their way from the sharp ends across the skinny, smooth legs of the crate that have a weaker texture than wood.

But as I move my fingers outward along the oddly shaped crate legs, I feel what I can only guess is some sort of fabric material wrapped around parts of it. I suddenly understand Liam's expression.

My foot is stuck in what feels like a rib cage.

I pull myself back up and inhale air greedily, as if I was under much longer. Liam sees my face and he dives back down. As carefully and quickly as possible, I feel him snap one of the bones with both of his hands, the movement ricocheting against my leg and freeing my boot.

Bobby has apparently arrived but I can't make out his words. I think I'm in shock. My foot was stuck in someone's rib cage. I have been standing in this cloudy water with a dead body. A decomposing, rotting body of someone I probably know.

No, wait. It's all bones. That means it's probably not decomposing and has actually been here a long time. Right?

The bile returns and this time I can't help but release it. I throw up right in the water. I try to apologize to Liam who only shakes his head and says he might do the same. He wraps the second rope around my body in some sort of rescue knot and helps lift me up easily into the tunnel to Bobby, who has me by the elbows and is bringing me out of the cave's window with care. I realize when he pulls me into a hug that I can feel my body spasming.

Kenny and Liam are dealing with the body situation, as I test my ankle and see how much weight I can put on it. I'm fine, but I have a bloody, *definitely* infected, gash on my ankle...from a fucking rib cage...how is everyone else being so calm about this?

I've seen over half a dozen dead bodies in my career, but this time is different. I was having a bath with a fucking corpse.

As Bobby starts to guide me out of the cavern, I turn my head just in time to see Kenny pull out piles of separated bones from the tunnel. There is no way to tell, before the autopsy, who these bones belong to, as the head is not even a real shape anymore and the torso is broken apart from my stupid foot. But I'm frozen in place as I notice the body looks smaller than an adult's.

I keep watching as Kenny grabs something small and shiny from Liam who is still retrieving items from the water. My eyes focus on the only thing that might identify this body right now. Everything around me becomes really still and focused, as I recognize the silver charm bracelet in Kenny's palm. The bracelet looks worse for wear, but I can make out two distinct charms on it: a mountain peak and a champagne glass. I was the one who gifted that champagne glass charm to the person who owned this bracelet. The same woman who these bones probably belong to.

CHAPTER 12 - JANE

I groggily start to head towards the cave exit and am completely and utterly in shock. Someone is mumbling and making strange sounds. I realize after a few minutes it's me, although I have no idea what I am saying. I keep a firm grip on Bobby's shoulder as my knees feel extremely weak. Jackson, the other RCMP officer in Isinbury, as well as SAR team leader Jimmy Slovak meet us halfway through the caves. Slovak goes to meet Liam and Kenny, while Jackson helps us make it out and to the truck.

We pass two large vans of tech and equipment and a flurry of Search and Rescue volunteers. They're about to perform a full grid and cave system search for any remains that have been scattered due to scavengers. Seeing them like this, a rush of officials in what was just a peaceful forest, reminds me so much of when they searched for Dad. The similarities are like a mirror image; past and present colliding and hitting me like a bullet to the heart. I reach my hand out to stabilize myself for a moment on the truck, focusing on my breathing. Breathe in and hold for five seconds. Breathe out and exhale for five seconds. Bobby helps me into the truck and I let myself silently cry in the passenger seat, with my knees tucked into my body, as he drives me to the hospital. He tells me he called ahead and told Dr. Jenkins to meet us there and that the boys will follow us in a separate car once they're done processing the scene. He doesn't say it out loud, but I know we won't need a transportation service; The SAR team will bag and then transport the remains of my childhood friend Abby to the hospital morgue once they're ready.

I never once put any real thought into the possibility that she hadn't just ran away. She was always going on about how she wanted to make it to Vancouver, get a job as a bartender and save up to travel the world. Her first charm on her bracelet was the globe, and she had saved up for a month to buy it.

Her love of Vancouver was sort of the reason I think I ended up there. In case I ever ran into her.

Nothing was terribly suspect about her disappearance. She left a note on her pillow, using her favourite purple pen, saying "Don't follow me. I've gone to start a new glamourous life, away from all of you." It was exactly something she would have done. She was known for her dramatic flair. There was a small investigation of course, but short-lived, as she was 18 years old and seemed to have left of her own will. There was no body or eyewitness to say otherwise. She was labelled *endangered: missing* and that's the extent of what the police could do.

She was impulsive and stir-crazy, stuck in this town with her parents who didn't understand her and who didn't care to. She was one of seven siblings, and they were hardly phased when she had left for a new life. *One less mouth to feed*, I imagine her father saying with a shrug. I think of her stuff that was gone, along with her beloved suitcase, and wonder who would've gone to the trouble of picking it up and making her seem like she had left. Obviously, the same person who put her in that cave.

I continue to sob and berate myself in my head for not doing more for her, not asking more questions about her sudden disappearance, or not merely finding it curious that she didn't show up in any of my frequent internet or database searches for her in the years to follow.

I was too focused on the fact she didn't bother to say goodbye; the way she distanced herself from me weeks *before* her disappearance. I was pissed at her. And that prevented me from seeing the truth.

The sky is dark now. The sun made its final retreat past the west mountain about a half hour ago. Bobby tries to help me out of the truck and I push him away. I need to snap out of this. I force myself to focus and enter the small-town hospital where Dr. Jenkins is waiting for us in the main corridor.

She looks uncomfortable. Her red hair is tightly wound in a bun which reminds me of Teresa, my therapist. And she's wearing the same pale, worried expression. Maybe it's a mandatory look for women in the medical field; stressed out and overworked. We have that in common.

"Hi Jane. My name is Dr. Jenkins. You can call me Kim if you'd like." She's about five inches taller than me so she hunches down a bit to peer at my face with a large pitiful smile. Her eyes are bright and kind, but she looks too young to be in charge of the ER.

I remind myself small towns provide bigger opportunities for younger people.

I mumble a hello in response, then I'm brought into the closest room where she performs her initial examination and checks my vital signs. Dr. Jenkins mentions something about shock and points to a needle, but I can't quite make sense of her words. Bobby nods to her. She injects me with something that calms me down instantly. Makes me feel warm and fuzzy but also a little more focused. I stare at the blank wall while she cleans and bandages my cuts, dressing my entire chin. The room is quiet as she works.

She wants to send me for an X-ray and a possible CT scan for the lower back inflammation. She's also nervous about my ankle after Bobby explains the condition of the water it was cut in. I try again not to think of it. She cleans it with a sterilized cotton ball then hunts in a drawer on a trolley next to the bed until she finds a white plastic tube and screws the top open. She puts a hefty amount on the bright red cut before wrapping it in gauze, and slides the tube in my backpack for future use. When our eyes meet, Bobby gives me his best attempt at a smile.

Once I'm all taken care of, Dr. Jenkins turns to Bobby and starts lifting his shirt up to inspect his stomach. He turns away from me, embarrassed or wanting privacy. I stare anyway.

For the first time, I realize blood has soaked through his white undershirt, revealing long horizontal lines of red as if Bobby got clawed by Freddy Krueger himself.

"What happened?" I ask, worried, my voice dry and hoarse. Once the shirt is off, I get a better look of what seems like a bad case of road rash.

"I cut it by squeezing through that damn hole to get to you," he grunts at me. "It's nothing."

The guilt covers my body, like a hot shower.

"I'm sorry," I say, to which he just shakes his head.

After Dr. Jenkins is done with us, she says someone will be by shortly to send me for those tests. She starts to excuse herself to look after other patients in the ER but I hold out my arm awkwardly to stop her from doing so.

We study each other for a moment. "It's not really my expertise," I say, "but how much information can you get from a pile of bones?"

"Jane." Bobby's words sound like a scolding.

"No, it's a fair question." Dr. Jenkins says. "It's not ideal, obviously, but I was told we still have bones, hair, teeth and nails which means we can still find answers. This will be important in proving the conclusion that this was a homicide."

I flinch.

"I'm sorry Jane. I'm told you knew her."

I nod slowly. "I heard you will be overseeing the autopsy. Do you have experience doing that?"

"Yes," she answers wearily. "I have some pathology training from school but my father was also the medical examiner here for years so he has taught me a few things which have been helpful for when I get in a pinch. But—"

"You get in a lot of *pinches* around here, *Kim*?" I ask, thick with sarcasm.

She stands straighter. Her blue eyes stare me down. "Although my specialty is general and emergency medicine, I do have some experience that may be valuable to the medical examiner this time around. I have complete confidence in his ability, but Bobby has asked that I also weigh in. So that's what I'm doing." She pauses. "I will send a nurse shortly to make sure your scans are done and that you're good to go. But please stay here for as long as you want." The curtness in her voice is not missed by me. She leaves the room quickly after that.

Bobby sits on the side of my bed and holds my left hand between his big palms. "Was that really necessary? She came in from her night off to help us, Jane. She didn't deserve that."

"I think I'm starting to spiral out of control."

"You should rest a bit," he says firmly.

"Bobby, I might feel exhausted but there's no way I'm sleeping right now. I want to see the..." I falter on the next words, "the ME's examination of the...of the body."

"Jane, I don't think that's a good idea. Plus, you didn't exactly foster any goodwill with Dr. Jenkins just now."

"She's just so clinical about things. I can hardly stand it."

"You two are a lot alike that way."

I shake my head.

"Jane...explain to me how you knew it was *that* cave. You wrote on your note that you would be checking out the cave the farthest to the left. Even though the larger, more popular cave is the one in the middle. That would've been my first guess." He hesitates and this time, he eyes me straight on. "How did you know it was that one?"

I hear myself swallow and hope he doesn't notice. I am probably one of the last people to see Abby alive. I woke up in front of that cave the same day she went missing. Do I tell him that?

"I just had a feeling, Bobby."

"Bullshit. What aren't you telling me? You know people are going to be asking a lot of hard questions."

"Can you fucking drop it, Bob? I just found out my childhood best friend has been rotting away in this town for years and I will never, ever see her again."

He opens his mouth to speak and then shuts it. I don't quite make out what he says under his breath but it's probably a curse. After a few minutes of silence, he gets up from the bed and wanders over to the door.

"This is somehow connected to the others. Lilyann and Brandi knew something and were killed for it. Megan was unfortunately in the wrong place at the wrong time." He massages the stubble on his chin with his right hand, deep in thought. "I'm not sure how Harrison, or how even you, are involved with this but it will soon be out of my hands. The major crimes team is going to want to be involved in this moving forward. There's four bodies now and we both know what they will say. You are too close to this case now. You need to step back." He whips his hand up in the air to fend off my objections already making their way out of my mouth. "Let me and Kenny handle them."

I grit my teeth together and look away, trying to fight the tears spilling out of the corners of my eyes. I'm being pushed out *again*.

"I'm sorry, but it's how it should be. Get some rest, okay?"

I almost say nothing. But I need this, so I soften my voice. "Bob?"

"Yeah?"

"Promise me you'll wake me up with the results?"

He nods once and stalks out the door; one heavy footstep after another, down the quiet hallway reeking of antiseptic and death.

~~~

Because Abby went missing over 10 years ago, the body we retrieved was just bones. The flesh had rotted off and been picked by small scavengers, a decade ago. The patches of clothing still loosely attached to the body, or recovered at the scene, were green and filthy. But I could make out enough of the pink shirt and what looked to be a converse shoe to know it was the clothing she was wearing the night I saw her last. The night I don't remember. The night I don't mention.

Bobby wakes me up around two hours later. I notice two blankets placed over me, probably by one of the nurses. I pull them up to my chin now, fighting off a chill.

The autopsy was relatively quick as there is hardly anything left, and the condition of the bones makes it difficult to be certain of anything. We end up with a presumptive identification rather than a positive identification. Not ideal for a police investigation but the best anyone can expect from the state of the body.

I have a copy of the autopsy report in my hands. Bobby is beside me watching me read it. It's confirmed the bones belong to a 5'1, 18-year-old female with a petite build, and with evidence of a healed fracture in the right knee. Abby's only identifiable injury was a broken knee from an eighth grade soccer match gone wrong. This, along with her dental records, leads the medical examiner to presume these bones belong to Abby Nichols.

This isn't any real surprise to anyone. Not anymore.

Lower down on the page, it says the skull showed signs of extreme trauma and was most likely crushed in some matter *"perimortem"*, which means the injury took place at or near the time of death without any evidence of healing. This is likely what killed her. I feel my free hand pull itself into a fist.

It is undetermined if the other broken bones occurred before or after death. Our best guess points to post-mortem: by the killer throwing her body down the tunnel, crushed by larger scavengers, and by my foot's accidental entry into her ribcage.

After reading the results of the autopsy, I feel nauseous enough to puke so I go to the bathroom in case I do. But my exhaustion takes over and I just shiver instead.

"Are you okay?" Bobby asks gently from the doorway.

I'm wrapped around the toilet still, wiping my mouth off. "Am I allowed to visit with her remains a bit before they contact her family?"

"Yes, if you think you're up for it. I can arrange that."

I'm brought downstairs to the morgue area with Bobby and a medical worker I don't recognize.

I hold my breath before lifting up the sheet. It's not a complete skeleton, but the bones are arranged where they should be. They're a dark beige colour and look a bit rotted. I try to imagine the body that once contained these bones. The gorgeous young woman whose soul was taken from this Earth too soon.

I collapse back into a chair and hold in my sobs, silent tears overflowing. My body feels heavy and my head and vision are fuzzy from crying.

Her bones remind me of my father. How we never had any of him to bury at his funeral.

He was a very experienced hiker and outdoorsman. But he had not been feeling like himself lately, so he had taken a week to go backcountry camping with Bobby. Or so we thought.

When the week went by and he hadn't phoned or returned like he promised, we figured he just needed a little more time away. It wasn't unlike him to show up late and ask for forgiveness instead of permission. But when we saw Bobby in town alone, without my dad... that was when things started to feel wrong, at least for my mom and I. Mom interrogated Bobby, and he confessed that my dad had asked him not to say anything to us and that he just needed some time to think things through. He had covered for him.

When our phone calls kept going straight to voicemail, Bobby and a few others went to go find him, not wanting to believe anything was wrong yet. But they found his campsite abandoned and destroyed, picked through by a bear. No sign of my dad, except a trail of blood leading nowhere and a couple of fingers that were later confirmed his. Bobby officially called in search and rescue which led the manhunt, a week and a half after Dad had left for his so-called "soul-searching vacation."

It took an entire two weeks for the SAR team and the police force to search what they could of the Northern Rockies, come up with absolutely no leads, then deem the case unresolved. And just like that, my dad became one of the 500 or so cases a year that are left with no answers and no closure, just never-ending questions.

It was deemed an accident where he likely wandered off, got in trouble with wildlife or took one wrong step, and then couldn't get help or back to his campsite where his satellite phone was left. This was the part of the investigation that truly haunted Bobby and later, myself. Why would Dad leave his only link to help in case of an emergency, while out in the wilderness completely by himself?

He knew how easily accidents could happen out here. He'd saved countless people with the SAR team over the years who weren't prepared properly when they came out here looking for adventure. It didn't make any sense. Unless it was a conscious decision: he didn't need the lifeline because he didn't plan on making it out alive.

His car was left abandoned in the Snake River parking lot, one of the public entrances to the large expanse of Northern Rockies that could be explored. His backpack was left at the campsite as well. It had his water bottle, a walkie talkie and his wallet with a photo of Mom and I in it. The photo is still in our evidence room.

So the case was left unresolved - Henry Beckett was officially deemed "missing, in circumstances of peril," which was enough for the court to allow my mom and I to claim his life insurance policy. We went ahead with his funeral and tried to move on as best we could. Then, after seven years, he was legally declared dead.

We thought he was going through a midlife crisis and desired a break.

We buried a casket full of his memorabilia while his corpse likely got picked over by scavengers.

Abby's body had a different afterlife. The report is very thorough. They managed to look up the weather patterns the month and year she died, which helps to give us a better understanding of the condition of her final resting place. We had been experiencing a dry summer, so her body most likely hit a cold, hard ground as she was tossed through the cave window. Rain came later, and would have continued to mostly drain or dry out during dry periods over the last decade, then reappear for weeks through the winter and spring. The body that remained, completely skeletonized after three to five months. On the report, the medical examiner explains the decomposing process, in painful detail:

"...once the body was floating in the water for a few weeks, the tissues would have turned into a soapy fatty acid halting bacterial growth. The skin would've blistered and turned greenish black..."

I stopped reading after that.

Once we're back at Bobby's, I think of my dad and I think of Abby. They were both beer drinkers, burger eaters and big dreamers, who made me laugh and made me envious of their power to demand a room's attention just by walking in it. Their spirits were full of boundless energy. I think of everything they could have accomplished if given the chance to live a normal life, not cut short by whatever choices they made or circumstances they were thrown into, that led to their gruesome deaths.

I think of the piles of bones I have already accumulated in my life, at only 29 years old: my father, my friend, my mother, my partner on the force, and the countless victims I was not able to save in my career. It's too much to handle so I sob myself to sleep and stay in bed the entirety of the next two days.

CHAPTER 13 - JANE

I'm in the woods, somewhere between the beach and the caves, running frantically in the dark from whoever is chasing me. It's the middle of the night and even the moonlight is not on my side. I can hardly see a thing and I keep tripping on branches and rocks, bloodying my knees and palms. But I keep going. One foot after the other, with my hands sprawled out in front of me to help me find my way. Twigs scratch my face but I don't feel them. I am numb with fear. I can hear them calling out my name. They think I don't know they brought me here to kill me. I ignore them and keep running. I'm not surprised the others are chasing me, but she and I used to be the best of friends. I thought of her like a sister. I trip on something else and land face first against a rock. I roll over on my back in excruciating pain and try to get my head to focus so I can get back up and keep running. I must keep running. But my head is pounding and I wonder if I'm already dead. I look up just in time to see a flashlight above me. One of them has found me. I try to focus on the face which is revealed when they take off their hood. It's her. I might have a chance. I beg for my life. *We used to be like sisters*, I beg. She adjusts the flashlight to shine on her face and I gasp. It is me. The face is mine. The angle shifts and I am now looking down at who I thought I was. I am the hunter, and the hunted is Abby. I take her head between my hands and smash it against the rock beneath her, finishing her off.

I wake up in a sweat-filled panic. I jump from the bed, and ready myself for a fight. My eyes adjust and my memory returns when I see a worried Judie round the corner with a lunch tray.

"Everything okay sweetie?" she asks, concern in her eyes.

I let my arms rest by my side and straighten my stance. "Bad nightmare."

Judie pats the bed, summoning me back into it, but I'm rigid like a piece of wood.

"Do you wanna talk about it?"

"Not really."

She's made me an egg salad sandwich and some homemade French fries. She was here yesterday and the day before too, but I only managed to sleep, stare at the wall for hours, and eat the soup she brought me in at lunch.

Judie is wearing her favourite white floral top, comfy black leggings and sensible sneakers. Her white hair is cut short and meticulously styled with curlers and hairspray, and she has bright pink lipstick that stands out from her more modest makeup. Beyond the makeup and the hair though, I notice her back looks worse than the last time I saw her. It's slightly arched from over 20 years of misuse and strain as a gardener. I haven't checked in with her in a while and the guilt of that just about strangles me on the spot.

She notices the tears forming in the corners of my eyes. She gives me a sympathetic, small smile and lightly brushes her fingers through the hair on the top of my head. I realize that this is what moms do with their children. This is how it's supposed to be. Gentle, soft, loving and kind. My eyes tear up as I think of how much I love Judie for always being there for me, being my surrogate mother. The tears continue to pour out as I also remember moments like these with my own mom, before everything happened. Moments where she too would rub my scalp, and kiss my forehead, make my favourite foods and tell me that everything works itself out in the end.

"There, there love," Judie whispers. "You'll get through this. We're all here for you."

I squeeze her hand and sit up in bed. She adjusts my heating pad for me to help with the incredible body pain and stiffness that I've been coping with that has also left me bed-bound. My bloodwork came back positive for inflammation but the other tests weren't significant enough for a positive diagnosis. I'm told this is normal and am being referred to a rheumatologist who specializes in autoimmune diseases. Extreme mental and physical stress like I've been going through apparently can exacerbate my symptoms, Dr. Jenkins had explained. Having CRPS might have weakened my immune system and made me susceptible to more autoimmune diseases.

Like I need more reasons to be depressed right now.

Once I'm finished eating, she reminds me today is the rescheduled family dinner and asks if we should cancel.

"How many hours until dinner, if we go ahead with it?" I ask weakly. I remember everyone so excited to be together again, and the guilt feels like a lead jacket.

"Five, but everyone will understand if you want to postpone it again, honey."

"Might be good to have some distraction for a while."

Her smile lights up the room. "Alright then. I'll tell people to keep it casual." She gives me a hug before she leaves with the dishes. Bobby comes in shortly after with some fresh coffees. The heat feels good on my sore throat and I hold it near my face to take in the smell and the steam.

"I don't need a babysitter, you know," I manage, my voice raspy from crying.

He rolls his eyes. "We know that. We're just happy to have you back home and are making the most of it."

He turns on the television and gets comfy beside me as we watch some cable comedy show for a bit in silence.

"How's your belly?" I ask.

"Whatever Kim has in that tube works way better than anything you can buy in the stores." His palm lightly rubs against the rolls of his stomach as if testing the accuracy of his words. "It's a bit itchy but it isn't painful. How's...your ankle?"

I wiggle it around under the covers and it's fine. "Physically I'm okay Bob."

"Your chin looks pretty scabby. Is that normal?"

"Yup."

"Have you been putting the cream on it, like Dr. Jenkins told you to do?"

"Yup."

We go back to being quiet. I see him sneaking glances at me so I decide to start a conversation. But not about anything that happened in the past few days or about my ability to just shut off sometimes. Or about how I might be involved in the murder of one of my closest childhood friends and I don't remember a damn thing. No. We aren't talking about me. I decide to bring up Judie.

"Why haven't you moved Judie in yet? What are you waiting for?"

"Right to business, huh?"

I nod.

"It's complicated."

"She basically lives here, anyway."

He knows I'm trying to deflect my own feelings and problems and focus on his instead. He lets me.

"I know," he finally says in a whisper. "I love her. I'm committed and she knows that. I just don't want to move her in here and then have her realize that I'm boring old Bob and want to leave. It's happened before." He's referring to his other serious girlfriend, Clementine, who he moved in with after six months of dating each other. I suppose she didn't realize how much time and effort Bobby puts into his job every day, or how hard it is to get him to talk about his feelings. She left after only living with him for two months. She married soon after. He was pretty sad about it, but in typical Bobby fashion, he just put in more hours at work and spent more time with his old man pals.

But he never cared about Clementine the way he cares about Judie. This is something else.

"Judie isn't Clem. She knows you work too much and that you're a grumpy old man. She even knows you don't have a clue how to cook a proper meal. But she sticks around anyways. You're lucky to have her."

He nods as I'm talking, pretending not to take me seriously but I see him feeling what I say. I sip my coffee and try not to focus on the heaviness in my chest. After a few minutes of silence, he continues. "We've had our own homes, our own spaces to go to, for the entirety of our relationship. Don't you think the sudden change will make her feel claustrophobic?"

I'm shocked at how insecure he is about this topic. My whole life I've never seen him scared of anything.

"There's a killer on the loose in this town, and you're afraid that she will feel overwhelmed by your presence in this safe and beautiful home that is basically hers anyway?" I manage it all in one breath. I may raise an eyebrow for good measure.

"Well, when you put it like that...I feel like a complete idiot." Then his face gets serious. "I'm surprised she hasn't left me already, if we're being honest." He fiddles with a throw pillow. "I'm not sure if we're ready to admit this might be for the long haul. That's a scary thought when you're old, you know, because it either means you will be with this person until one of you dies, or they will leave you and you will die alone."

I hear the sadness in his voice as he talks about some of his deepest fears. I wonder if this is his first time saying them out loud. We aren't usually the kind of people who talk about our feelings. We generally have our walls up that protect us from our pain. But every once in a while, we let it all out. The conversation and feelings and pain are always safe in each other's company. We share the load. Even if it hurts. He continues talking.

"I love having her around. She makes me laugh and takes care of me and she's the first person I want to see every day. I know these things. But I guess I got scared of asking her because it became such a big deal and it was easier to leave things the way they were instead of trying to make a big change that might have her running to the hills."

I rest my head on his shoulder and try to process before answering. "Maybe it's time to ask her and see what she says, Bob.

147

Tell her everything you just told me. I think you have a pretty good shot."

We watch the rest of our show before getting ready for the big dinner. I take a really long hot bath, filled with some special CBD epsom salts Judie got for me at the pharmacy. I try not to think of anything at all. I mostly succeed.

I don't really feel like changing out of my pyjamas so I compromise by putting on some black comfy jeggings and a royal blue cozy sweater. I don't wear any makeup but I wash my face and clean the bandage on my chin, and leave my hair down for once.

I try to force my mood to shift in a better direction. Two extra strength Tylenol again and a large glass of merlot seems to help. Glen and Kenny arrive first to help us prepare the feast, even though Judie has it covered. It's an hour later before Sara and her boyfriend Langdon show up along with Liam. They all come in the same vehicle. For some reason, I'm in charge of greeting the guests and getting them something to drink. Sara steps out of the truck first and runs over to me and envelops me in a strong hug. It's almost too much to handle.

"I'm always here for you, you know that," she whispers in my ear then pulls back. She turns to invite Langdon into our conversation and to introduce us. We all went to school together when we were younger but hung out in different crowds. He was popular; us not so much. He looks older now and more charming than Sara's Facebook photos would suggest. He's a tall man with light brown skin, short spiked black hair and a small angular beard. He's wearing a silver wolf and raven pendant necklace, probably from his sister's shop, the only First Nations artist with a physical store in town, called Walker's Indigenous Creations. The same family with those awesome bannock doughnuts from the fundraiser.

Being from one of the founding families of Isinbury, he has done quite well in this town: owning a booming home-building business and proving himself an authoritative and respected figure in the community. There's rumours he's going to run for Mayor this year, and Sara told me that as a tribute to his heritage, he mostly employs First Nations residents.

I see the self-confidence radiate off of him as he walks over to me. I try my best to be friendly.

I offer my hand to him, but Langdon avoids it and comes in for a bear hug instead.

"Sorry Jane, I'm a hugger just like my lady."

He lets me go and puts an arm around Sara, who's beaming with smiles. Other than the fact his dark brown eyes are a little too close together, he's handsome.

I'm relieved to see Liam emerging into view, giving me a nod and his timid smile that reaches his warm eyes.

When standing side by side, Langdon is the clean-cut, freshly shaven and well-dressed version of Liam. They're both the same broad, tall build, but Liam's hair is lighter, wavier and longer, as well as untamed. And although Liam's clothes are always clean and crisp looking, they're just a tad too casual, as if he just threw on whatever he grabbed from the closet without giving it much thought. Right now, he's wearing an essential white T-shirt and a soft cardigan, with some brown khakis and a pair of loafers.

"You look nice Jane." Liam says softly. "Perfect evening for an outdoor dinner too. Though we brought the heaters just in case."

"Perfect, it's still a bit chilly for my liking," I say, rubbing my arms.

I get everyone to follow me through to the kitchen where the noise level immediately rises a few notches. As everyone is greeting, Sara grabs two beers for herself and Langdon.

I turn to Liam, reaching for one. "Want a beer?"

"Oh, no thanks," he says bashfully. "I would love some of that Shiraz Glen brought in though."

I return the beer to the ice bucket and pour two glasses of red wine.

I circle my finger around my wine glass as the guys continue to tease each other playfully. I can tell they've been good friends for a while. When I ask about it, Liam tells me they became close a week after he moved here and didn't know a single soul.

"He was the only one to introduce himself to me right away," Liam says. "I thought he was trying to sell me something at first because no way could someone be that annoyingly charming. But that's just who he is. And because we share the same sense of dorky humour, we stayed friends."

Langdon playfully awes out loud. "That and because he's my only competition for best looking dude in town. You know that saying...keep your friends close, and your enemies closer?" He winks.

Liam shakes his head and laughs. "Too bad you're so ugly," he quips. Sara tells them to act like adults. Her tone is lighthearted.

"Good thing I found the only girl that matters, and she thinks I'm sexy as–" Sara leans into Langdon and gives him a deep peck on the lips, essentially shutting him up. He pulls her in closer to him flirtatiously and I notice the genuine happiness on her face. I'm staring at them, invading their private happiness bubble, as he brings her palms to his mouth and kisses them.

Liam leans in to me and says, "Cute in a sickening way, aren't they?"

I nod. "I didn't know it was even possible to still be so smitten with someone after a year being together." I try to keep my tone light.

"Well, technically it's been a year and a half. But yeah, it's definitely possible. Just look at Glen and Kenny. And Judie and Bob." I turn to follow his gaze and notice Bobby clumsily wrapped around Judie who is busy stirring something on the stove and reaching in all directions with her free hands. Although she looks frantic, there's a sort of peace on her face as Bobby holds her from behind for that quick moment, then he releases her and takes a swig from his beer on the counter.

Glen is sitting on Kenny's lap, wrapped in his arms, as he talks to Judie about the new members of his youth group.

So much PDA. Sara and Langdon have stepped a few feet back so Liam and I are having more of a private conversation. I try to pretend I'm not as lonely as I feel.

"I feel like an intruder looking in," I say quietly.

"Yes, there is definitely something in the air tonight." He takes another sip of his wine. "This is...so good. Where's it from?"

"Oh, from Spain I think?"

"I like it. A little smoky."

"Yes, I'm not a connoisseur or anything, but it's easy to drink and that's good enough for me." He eyes me for a second, considering, then seems to forget it.

I empty my glass with another swig, and ask if he wants a refill. We walk over to the island in search of another bottle. He opens one with ease and pours us both a generous amount. "So, when was the last time you had a family get together like this?"

"We visit around Christmas, usually at my place in Vancouver, but we haven't had everyone over like this to Bobby's in forever. I admit, I haven't been the best at keeping in touch with everybody." We walk outside and into the gazebo, wines in hand. I turn the dial to light the electric fireplace inside and instantly warm up my hands.

"Oh, why not?"

I study his face to see what he knows but I can't read him.

"You really haven't heard any rumours about me in town?" I ask, trying not to sound too confrontational. I feel myself tighten with stress and anticipation.

"Sorry," He says, his face getting red. "I was trying to...well, yes. Everyone in town has been talking about what happened to you in Vancouver. The dirty-cop-partner thing. I don't normally listen to rumours unless it's someone I'm curious about." He shrugs. "I was trying to let you tell me if you wanted to."

"What are they saying?"

"Stupid stuff. Not worth repeating."

I sigh heavily. "I don't even want to know. I find it all exhausting." I turn my head and stare into the lightbulb at the top of the gazebo, a trick I learned from my mom when I was small, how to stop yourself from tearing up. "I've already dealt with rumours and shit-talk from my colleagues after it happened. I would get sticky notes that said 'killer' stuck on my computer screen."

"That's intense." He takes another sip of his drink. I can feel his eyes on mine. He rests his head on his left palm, listening as I continue.

"Immature if you ask me." I sigh. "It's well known in the force, if something happens and you're forced into a situation where you take out your partner like that...even if they're a dirty cop and it's self-defense and you're fully cleared...your career is over. Done. Plateaus or plummets. Doesn't matter if it was a good shot. Desk duty for the rest of your life."

"Why though? That makes no sense."

"No partner will ever trust me again to have their back. I become a stain that no one can get rid of. It's stupid and wrong, but it's just how it is."

"Is that why you're here now? To get back into the action?"

I raise a brow.

"Sorry, you don't have to answer that if you don't want to," he says, waving me off, sounding a bit embarrassed. "Sorry to even bring it up. I'm sure it's something you're trying hard to move past and I know it's been a hard enough week for you."

"It's okay...I didn't want to come at first...This town holds a lot of bad memories for me...but I just needed to get out of there, you know? To be surrounded by people who love me, that's what I needed. And yes, I guess the distraction of a case helps too." A chill works its way up my spine then, and I shrink inward in response. Liam seems to notice, as he stands up and shrugs off his navy cardigan, extending it to me.

"Oh no, it's okay–"

"It's the gentlemanly thing to do. Plus, I'm like a small heater, I don't need the extra layer."

I grab the cardigan and shrug it on. It smells of his cologne, a woodsy citrus scent. It's so nice and warm that I'm immediately grateful.

"Thank you. Remind me to grab a sweater when we go back in."

"No need. The cardigan suits you." His smile reaches his eyes again, crinkling the corners.

I pause, a small smile escaping me. He's so disarming and comfortable to be around. A passiveness that somehow makes me feel stronger around him.

But the look in Liam's eyes, that stare that makes me soften, also makes me decide to tell him what happened with Marcus.

~~~

My mind wanders to the last moments I spent with Marcus. It often does in quiet moments like this. No matter how hard I try to push it out or control it, the memories still come rushing in, as if I'm being tortured by my own mind.

Marcus and I had been investigating a highly publicized case of a murdered young woman who was the daughter of one of the wealthiest men in the city. The investment banker. Her body and her friend's body both washed ashore after being missing for more than 48 hours; naked, bruised, and both stabbed over fifteen times.

Phone records indicated she was meeting her uncle who had promised to take her on one last boat ride through the Harbour before driving her to Seattle with her friend.

They never made it.

Marcus and I headed to an abandoned Shipping and Receiving warehouse in one of Vancouver's industrial wastelands, after a reliable witness passed on a tip to me about it doubling as a hideout for white collar criminals who didn't want to be found; a sort of Airbnb for the criminal underworld. The uncle had paid a lot of money to get out of town and was supposedly hiding out there.

Marcus didn't think it was worth checking out—I found that strange—but I insisted, following my gut. He eventually agreed but said he wanted to check it out just the two of us first and call for backup later if the uncle was there. He admitted he had been under scrutiny lately and didn't want to waste anyone's time and have it come back to bite him in the ass. I followed his lead, like I always did.

We separated to cover more ground. I covered the first floor, he tackled the basement, both of us promising to call first if we needed backup. But I heard two echoing shots go off from the direction of the basement and when I arrived at the scene, my partner was unharmed but two men's bodies were crumpled on the floor, a bullet in the middle of each man's forehead. Execution style.

I'm embarrassed now because it's obvious to me, months later what was going on.

One body was the uncle, the other an unidentified person. An accomplice maybe, or a guard perhaps, while the uncle waited to be picked up and taken out of the country from the warehouse.

I watched Marcus wander over to the bodies pleading self-defense.

"This man had a gun," he said, as if reading my thoughts about only hearing two shots. A handgun lay a few feet away from the second body. "He drew on me."

It made sense to me at the time. I wanted to believe him so badly.

While I was trying to take in the scene though, he stepped in front of a small bag by his feet that I hadn't noticed before. Almost...hiding it from my view. That was the first sign my gut felt something was wrong.

He was asking me to go upstairs and call it in because there was better service up there. He caught my eyes curiously looking at the bag behind him and he laughed, strangely sounding unlike himself, telling me there was nothing in there.

"Let me just check," I had said foolishly, walking toward him. I don't know what I was thinking. I guess I wasn't. He immediately got defensive.

"You don't trust me, Jane?" He asked, his voice strong and steady.

But I couldn't ignore the feeling that something was off. And I remembered then, picking him up down the street from the office of the RCMP Internal Division a month before. He was in a foul mood that day, and since then, he'd often go places by himself to check things out and ask me to cover for him, which was unusual.

His eyes were scanning the room, looking for a way out or another sort of threat maybe, and then they locked on mine... just in time to see the realization pour across my face, my body tensing and reacting slowly.

"What's going on here?" I asked him, stepping backwards and reaching my hand back for my gun on impulse.

It was like most stand-offs with suspects, when your life or the lives of others are hanging in the balance of the outcome; when the universe switches to slow motion, and sometimes, like this time, it was as if I was watching us from someone else's perspective.

I raised mine first, but our guns met in the air.

I was pleading with him to put down the gun while he continued to claim his innocence. I remember vividly how much I was sweating at that moment. The dank smell of the basement filling my nostrils and my ears tuned to full attention. It wasn't until I mentioned his family that he switched tactics and tried to bargain with me.

He told me, exasperated, that it was a bag of cash. A few million at least.

He said one of his kids was sick, that he couldn't afford the treatment and this could help her. I was her godmother. He was playing my weaknesses, but I had remembered him telling me she hadn't been keeping up with her soccer because she had been under the weather. For a moment, I froze. I didn't know what to do. "A one-time thing, Jane, I promise." He was saying. "We could split the money 50/50 if you want."

But why was he meeting with the Internal Division if his kid was sick? Had he done this before? And why didn't he come and ask me for financial help? I would've given him whatever he needed, no hesitation.

And that's when the pieces came together for me.

Because when taking in the scene, I had a jolt of recognition that I had ignored until now. I looked back at the second body that laid lifeless on the ground in this cold dark basement. The guard, not the uncle. It was a man I recognized from Marcus' wedding.

It was one of his childhood friends who occasionally got mixed up with bad people and who often called Marcus to bail him out of the situation he put himself in. Sometimes, he was a reliable informant. But Marcus stopped taking his calls years ago and didn't bother with him anymore. Or so I had thought.

This friend of his had given Marcus the tip about the uncle. I know that now. And I knew at that moment that they had planned to kill the uncle and split the bag of money that was supposed to help get him out of the country; Marcus looking like a hero for catching the bad guy and no one was the wiser about the cash.

But I had ruined his plans. I had gotten the tip about the warehouse and pressured him to follow it up with me before he had time to work out another solution. He panicked when we arrived, not knowing how to explain his friend being here or the money.

In the end, I guess he gambled that I would look the other way; let him take the money and get away with it all. I was his loyal follower after all.

Maybe I would have. I never got the chance to think it over.

The corners of Marcus' mouth faced down and his brows knit together in a painful grimace, as he watched me recognize the second body. His eyelids closed slowly, his emotions caught in his throat for a second too long before he pulled the trigger.

But as my mentor, and my partner, I had studied his every movement and decision for years. I knew he said his silent goodbye a split second before he shot me. My body reacted before my mind was able to catch up. We were both wearing our police issued bullet-resistant vests. But I jumped to the right, the bullet entering my shoulder just underneath my collarbone and beside my armpit, as I released my own trigger, carefully catching Marcus in his strong, tanned throat.

I ran to him as his body fell to the floor.

It is the most gruesome thing I've ever seen, even as a homicide detective. The blood spurting out of the man I once loved like family. The man I saw every Sunday when I would go over for dinner, or to watch the game with and down a couple of beers after work, letting off a little steam. I was the godmother of his second child, for fuck sakes. Maggie. The one who wasn't sick after all. Another lie.

The warm blood thrashed out of him and onto my clothes, my face, my hands, as I held him in my lap, trying to stop the bleeding. Angry, frustrated tears pooled my eyes and ran down my cheeks, falling on his face. I looked into his panicked eyes, feeling helpless and betrayed, as the backup I had called for when I first heard those shots finally arrived. But it was too late. He died within minutes.

~~~

Liam listens intently and afterward, we exhale an audible breath at the same time and we both notice it, which somehow lightens the mood.

"Anyways..." I close my eyes as I say it, almost as if to shield myself from the memories. "I may play it cool but I'm on real thin ice right now. Any fuck up and I could end up needing to choose a different career altogether. I'm on strict orders to check in with my therapist weekly and I'm not even allowed to carry my gun."

Liam slowly wipes down his face with his right hand as if he can wipe the stress right off. His hand lingers on his chin, his palm holding it in place.

"You're not a killer, Jane. You did what you had to." Liam says softly, trying to pull me back to the present.

I notice myself shaking. I put the empty glass down on the table in front of me and sit on my hands to still them.

"Still. Everyone loved Marcus and no one wanted to admit he was a bad cop in the end." I pause. "Even though the RCMP's Internal Division had a whole case file on him and were about to press charges, and my body cam proved everything."

"Yeah, I did read something in the news saying you were cleared following extensive interviews and evidence. Did your colleagues change their opinions then?"

So he did read the news. I swallow. "They stopped leaving me notes but I never received an apology. I even moved to a different city and department to get away from it all."

I push the mental image from my mind as Liam struggles to find an appropriate response.

"I'm sorry Jane. I don't even know what to say, other than I'm sorry you went through that." He seems sincere.

"I still have tissue damage in my left shoulder where he shot me." I pull my sweater to the side and show him the scar. His eyebrows lift in response. "Shattered my shoulder blade. Had to put it back together with pins and screws."

"So, you're setting off metal detectors for the rest of your life, huh?"

I laugh. "Like you wouldn't believe."

"Did you go to physiotherapy afterwards?"

"Sure I did. But I developed complex regional pain syndrome which feels like my arm is on fire most days, and now I'm being referred to a specialist because I probably have some sort of secondary inflammatory autoimmune disease."

"Fuck, I'm so sorry Jane."

"I survived a gunshot wound that I'm pretty sure was meant for my chest, just to become chronically sick now. Disabled even." It's my first time saying it out loud, and it finally seems to fit. *Disabled*. It's my new reality and I might as well get used to it.

I'd like to blame the wine for my honesty, and maybe that's part of it, but in truth, it just feels good to talk to someone about it. Someone who isn't judging me. Someone I'm not tasked with speaking to about this, like Teresa the therapist. Someone who didn't know me before all this happened, and is constantly comparing me between the *Before Jane* and the *Now Jane*.

Getting this off my chest is a relief. And maybe, in a way, I felt the need to explain this to Liam because I want him to know my baggage, and the real story, so he can differentiate truth from rumour and make his own opinion of me. I also wanted to see if he still looked at me the same after knowing all of this.

To my surprise, he does.

For now.

"If there's anything I can do for you Jane...if you need me to yell at someone, buy you a drink or just be angry for you, let me know. I'm here. I'm also a medical professional so if you ever need tips for coping with your symptoms, I can help."

Sara and Langdon are a few feet away now, on their way to join us, but Judie calls for help bringing everything out.

"You two stay, we will go," Sara hollers, smiling mischievously.

"You've sure had a tough year." Liam continues.

Surprisingly, not my worst one ever. I don't say this out loud.

"Feels good to be around family at least," I say, changing the subject.

"I hope you're happy to be back, even though it's been pretty rocky so far," he says it almost like a question, lightening the tone.

"Yes. For the most part." He nods at this, understanding that things have changed a little in the past couple of days.

The silence spreads as we get up to join the others at the outdoor table full of flowers and vases with tiny lights inside. The plates are some of Judie's good china ones with the pink blossoms on the side. It's a gorgeous setup. Judie has really outdone herself.

Langdon goes around and turns on the heaters. They have his company logo on them so he must've brought them from work.

"Well, Jane," Liam says my name all velvet-like, and I allow myself to look into his hazel eyes this time up close. They make me feel something that I can't quite explain; almost like I'm freefalling in the universe, tethered only to the part of him that makes me feel like my existence in the real world matters. I feel like I've known him my entire life. It's such an insane thought that I almost laugh out loud. I think he's reading my thoughts because he doesn't look away from my stare and is returning a serious, calming gaze of his own.

He breaks the silence.

"Let me know if there's anything I can do to make you happier to be back," he says lightly, with a warm smile. "I mean that." He rests his warm hand on the tip of my good shoulder before making his way to his assigned seat. Bobby comes out carrying dinner to the table. Everyone else is seated so I grab my spot next to Sara and Glen. We're eating in the back garden where the trees block most of the cool breeze. The sun has set, and the tiny lights Judie set out have flicked on, lighting the lawn as if it was the Milky Way.

Liam asks about how Kenny and Glen met during dinner and it genuinely brings a smile to my face and I'm so grateful for happy memories that a small tear escapes and I quickly brush it away.

When those two got together 30 years ago, it was a totally different town. Hell, it was an entirely different *world* then.

Glen talks about how their first few years of dating were done in private. "We were masking as roommates for fifteen years until same-sex marriage became legalized nationwide in 2005. Then we broke the news to everyone that we were going to get married...Though I don't think any of them were surprised." He chuckles.

"We saw the way they looked at each other for years," Judie says, smiling ear to ear and leaning into Bobby who has an arm draped over her chair. "The absent hand resting on the small of the back in stolen moments...the millions of small ways they cared for each other that went beyond friendship..."

Kenny and Glen's hands are held together tightly on the top of the table and I note Kenny's thumb carefully caressing Glen's. Kenny's large worker's jacket is draped over Glen's shoulders for warmth and it dominates his delicate frame.

I surprise myself by joining in. "I remember their intimate wedding that happened when I was in elementary school. Lots of dancing and singing, and a huge pork roast on the lawn." What I don't say out loud is that it was also one of the last moments I remember of my parents being truly happy and visibly in love. Instead, I add, "It was a joyful day for everyone."

"Now here we are, almost 20 years later, and Isinbury now has a Pride Week in June each year and a rainbow crosswalk on main street," Glen says, beaming with a sense of achievement. "It hasn't been easy, but we've been successfully working on building the LGBTQ+ community. Me working as a youth leader and Kenny in a very public and authoritative position, often speaking at the local schools as a sort of ambassador." Glen looks over to him. "My husband...the shy sporty nerd, publicly speaking to the queer community. Never thought I'd see the day." He's teasing, but Kenny leans into his husband's ear and whispers something about not being shy in bed. He says it louder than he intends though and most people giggle in response but Langdon stands up awkwardly drawing attention to himself.

"How about that dessert?" Langdon tries, hoping for a laugh that doesn't come.

"Yes, I'll go get it," Sara says too quickly. Judie jumps up to help and Langdon follows them both into the kitchen.

~~~

After dinner and dessert is done, and the plates are cleared, the conversation turns more serious. They are talking about Abby and the case, all of which became public knowledge yesterday when Bobby spoke to her parents.

The forensics team found some more bone fragments belonging to Abby and some human DNA in the form of hair follicles in the caves and more distinct footprints. However, since it's a public and high-traffic area, none of this would really hold up in court.

Bobby stayed at the station to help walk the case through with the two detective sergeants from the serious crime unit at RCMP North District in Prince George. The same detachment where I was just on desk duty. I actually sort of know one of the Mounties, but only by name and reputation.

"Yes, they've arrived to help us, a total team of *two* people." Bobby says, gruffly. "We aren't a priority. But I prefer it this way. We don't have the room to fit any more than that."

Kenny chimes in. "They aren't bad guys to work with so that's a plus."

"Did they really not arrest Harrison for this yet?" Sara says almost a whisper. "Brandi mentioned him right before her head got shot off!"

A few people flinch at that. I take another long sip of wine. I notice a few glances in my direction. The wine is starting to go to my head.

"He was brought in for questioning and threatened to be arrested on suspicion of murder," Bobby says. "But he lawyered up again and the evidence is pretty insubstantial so they had to let him go. For now."

There are a few angry mumbles from the table.

Bobby doesn't mention that Harrison's bank account showed steady cash withdrawals being made, up until the week Brandi died. This either proves the black mailing theory or has something to do with his drug business.

He also doesn't mention that the major crimes unit wants to talk to myself and Miranda next. Or that Abby's missing person's report states the three of us as some of the last people to see her alive.

I go in to give my statement after the funeral on Monday.

I'm thankful now that my dad never processed a missing person's report for me that morning as well. It already looks bad enough.

Glen rests his hand on mine, giving it a small pat and quickly changes the conversation for my benefit.

I start clearing the table and Liam and Sara lend a hand. They insist on doing the dishes, so I make my way to the couch where Bear is and make sure to get all his favourite spots to be scratched. The wine is helping me relax, maybe even feel a bit more normal, but my chest remains heavy especially after that conversation. Bear groans in satisfaction, and nuzzles his giant head onto my lap. I lean sideways and press my face into his fur.

Sara joins us a few minutes later and we mostly just sit in silence, watching Bear be cute. This soft, unjudging puppy love surrounds me like a warm hug and I feel paralyzed by the feeling of goodness for a small precious moment.

Sara snaps me out of my temporary bliss, by reaching out to touch my arm and grilling me on what I think about Langdon.

"He seems really sweet," I tell her. A sort of lie. Something about the way he looks at me makes me feel uneasy. "You bring out his soft side." At that, she smiles.

She tells me she's dated a few construction guys, here and there, but nothing ever serious. "Once you date one, you've dated them all." But with him, she says, it was different. Sara holds my hand and tells me he asked her to move in with him. I'm a bit nervous for her, as this is a huge step, but she seems happier than ever, so I try to be glad for her.

"I'm glad you're getting your happily ever after. You deserve it," I say, bringing her in for a warm side hug. When I pull back, her smile from a minute ago has vanished and her features are clouded.

"You do too, Jane." She replies. "You deserve a happily ever after more than anyone in this town." She gets teary-eyed, which sets me off and I curse at her under my breath before we start to nervously laugh at ourselves for being so emotional right now. We're wiping away our tears when she changes the subject. "We're moving into a house they're building now in the little subdivision, just down the road from here actually. It should be ready in a month or so."

I know the houses she's talking about. They're two-storey log cabins, with big backyards and quite expensive. Since Langdon owns the company that is building them, I'm not surprised he saved one for himself.

We sip our wine a bit more and reflect on how good it feels to be surrounded by family and friends. The wind is cool through the screen door and it freezes my cheeks. I pull Liam's cardigan tighter around me.

Sara lightly kicks my foot to get my attention. I look over at her grinning. "What?" I croak.

"Him Tarzan, you Jane," she says to me in her best deep voice. I shake my head but a laugh escapes.

"You mean Liam?"

She nods, grinning.

I shrug. "There might be something there but the timing is shit. I don't want to take anything else on right now."

"You'd be surprised how a good man, the right man, can heal certain wounds," she says this as if it's so easy. "You should give him a chance."

I think of my similar conversation with Bobby earlier and realize I'm on the other side of it. "I have known him for over two years, Jane. Always such a nice guy. Takes really good care of his sisters and his mom. He helped Langdon get his business off the ground and he's like part firefighter, part first responder, part carpenter. Doesn't get any hotter than that, but don't tell Langdon I said so."

"He seems a little too good to be true, don't you think?"

She's shaking her head.

"I've been there before," I murmur so lightly, that it's barely audible.

"Oh Jane. Don't be so pessimistic."

"Sar, look at my job. I'm constantly surprised by the worst of humanity, and most of them start off as seemingly regular, even good people."

They bring their kids to the park, have silly fights with their spouse at the grocery store, and order complicated Starbucks drinks like everyone else. They tend to get away with living mostly regular lives before they get caught for doing something unimaginable. Child killers, murderers, rapists; I've seen a lot.

"You don't know what it's like to talk to their loved ones afterward and see the utter confusion and anger and disbelief in their eyes."

They are desperate to believe that we have the wrong person...until all of the evidence comes to light and then they see that they were just blinded. They had no fucking clue that the person they share a bed with every night or who they gave birth to, could be this other deranged person.

"I've been that loved one, Sara. I know how it feels to be that person, desperate for a different outcome. I don't have it in me to survive that again. I'm not saying Liam is a murderer or anything like that, I'm just stating that it seems to me he's hiding something and I don't want to find out when I'm in over my head."

I think back to Harrison; the first one to show me what evils people were capable of if you let down your guard. I think of the few men afterward who I allowed to share my bed with throughout the years, who I never let sleepover and who I never called back. Never getting too drunk, too vulnerable or too close. The only steady men in my life were Bobby and Marcus. Both of whom I considered family. Marcus; the second person to completely fool me, and right under my fucking nose.

"Sure. I understand being wary of it. But you're not going to give Liam a chance because you're suspicious he's too perfect?" She rolls her eyes. "Are you going to keep going for bad guys because you think you know them better?" She raises her hands in frustration. "That's so stupid Jane. I'm sorry but it is."

Sure, I have trust issues. It comes with the job. I'm also just as scared to reveal every part of me to someone else. I get a chill again now, wondering what surprises I have in store for myself. I picture Abby's face. Are there things I'm hiding now from my loved ones, from myself?

Sara sits up a little straighter and turns her body to face me directly. She's giving me her power pose.

"I get that you see a side of people that is messed up, and sometimes they hide it so well, like Marcus did, and that makes you afraid to make connections in the world. I get all of that."

Even after a year of not being close, she still knows me so well, and that too, gives me a cold sweat.

"But if you hide away from the actual *good* in the world too, like these people here, right now, who are genuinely good and so happy that you are back, then you're letting the bad stuff win. You can't let it take over your life Jane." She pauses, softening her voice even more. "Everyone that you have lost: your dad, your mom, Abby, they would want you to live your life. It's the way we honour our dead, Jane. By living for them." She lost her younger brother when they were only six and eight. Drunk driver ran him over when he was biking home one evening. I know she isn't just talking about my dead. She's speaking of her own.

This town; it just takes and takes until there's nothing left.

She gives me a small smile, lifting her hand from her stomach to rub her palm against my back, before walking away and letting me process everything she just said. I wipe the tears threatening to spill from my eyes and rest my head back on the couch. Am I this screwed up because of my trust issues or my fear of loss?

It's the way we honour our dead. By living for them.

I repeat it in my head, over and over like a mantra. Then I get up, splash some water on my face from the bathroom sink, and rejoin the party until the wee hours of the night.

CHAPTER 14 - JANE

The next day the house starts to stir around noon. Glen and Kenny called it a night shortly after midnight, their daughter Helen coming to pick them up and drop by to say hello. Judie and Bobby went to bed soon after. But the four of us stayed up talking and laughing until around 3 a.m. when one of Langdon's friends picked them all up in his van.

There was a moment right before Liam left last night, where he thanked me for opening up to him as we said our goodbyes and gave each other a farewell hug. We had graduated to that point, which wasn't that hard considering there were a lot of goodbye hugs going around and it would be extremely weird if we didn't hug too. It would most certainly draw attention to what I was trying hard to ignore.

But that moment, after the little-too-long embrace in his sweet, warm arms, I had caught myself lingering. I had inched back less than half a foot from him, his arms still loose around mine, and he looked into my eyes to try to understand my next move. I looked into his eyes, searching for my own next move too. I was caught up in that moment that seemed to last a lifetime, trying to gather my courage and then losing it–a battle of drunken wits with my two personalities Confident and Scared–before I awkwardly drew myself back and wished him a goodnight. Scared had outweighed Confident who threw herself angrily and heavily about in my defeated heart.

Even now, I am kicking myself for being so awkward. I just feel like I am leading him on. I'm still wearing his cardigan. I don't know what I'm doing.

I hear a knock on my door before Bobby enters, my cellphone in hand.

"Hey kiddo, you forgot this in the kitchen..." he says, eyeing me with a playful smile.

"Why are you looking at me like that?"

"Like what?" he says, feigning innocence.

"With that stupid grin on your face? Wait, did you read my texts or something?" I try to think of last night and if I had sent out any embarrassing drunk messages to anyone. That doesn't sound like me, so why is he looking at me like that?

"Okay, before you get mad..." he begins. "We have the same phone case and I honestly thought it was mine. Judie thought so too, because she told me my phone was buzzing. Anyways, I checked it out and realized after I had read it, that Sara did not intend to send that to me..." He lets that linger and throws me my phone. I catch it mid-air and read her text:

Hey doll, how are you feeling this AM? I totally caught your almost kiss with Liam before he jumped in the car with us! OMG! He seemed a little bashful in the car on our way home so he must have had a great evening with you despite the no-kiss...PS: Sorry if what I said last night came off the wrong way. You know I love you and only want to help.

My face gets red when I realize that Bobby read all or part of this text. I look at him with my best tough guy face.

"It's not what you think," I say, soft and slow. He erupts in a great belly chuckle, in response, that breaks the quietness of the morning. He finishes laughing and grins at me.

"Honestly, I think it would do you some good to get involved with someone like Liam." His upbeat tone and words surprise me. "He's a great lad. He might even be up for breaking you out of your rock hard shell. As long as it doesn't interfere with your well-being, I'd say go for it."

Although I'm really tired of people telling me "I deserve happiness," I can't help but feel a gleam of hope. I want to join the relationship bandwagon. I do. My life has been a long lonely road so far and I'm tired of it. I crave the comfort of having another person in this life to go to when things are tough. If that possibility exists for me at all.

He gives me a wink and then strides back out to the kitchen.

I text her back and let her know that she just outed me to Bobby, to which she replies "LOL."

I add: *And thank you for the talk. I needed it. I know it couldn't have been easy to say, but I appreciate you caring for me enough to say it, even though I make conversations like that hard.*

Other than my video chat with my therapist, which I keep as short as possible, we spend the Sunday as a family. Judie, Bobby and I, plus Bear, lounge around the house and go for a nature stroll, before heading to the grocery store to pick up some supplies. While at the store, we bump into almost every person we know, including Dr. Jenkins and her father; one of my father's old friends. He's also in that framed photograph of the guys' fishing trip from Bobby's office.

As we tour the store and make small talk with some of the locals, I make note of every person I see.

Isinbury has some seasonal tourists because we are nestled in a wilderness oasis of Northern B.C. with hiking, fishing, hunting, camping and cross-country skiing available nearby. Even though the likelihood of an outsider, a tourist, killing locals is rare, we still keep it in the back of our minds when reviewing the case.

People keep stopping us to chat and it's raising my anxiety so I excuse myself to get some fresh air outside and head around the side of the building to a bench out back. I used to sit here all the time with Abby. My heart hurts at the thought.

My phone buzzes a few minutes later. It's from an unknown number. It says: *How do you go on living like nothing is wrong when so much blood is on your hands?*

I look up quickly to see if this text belongs to someone nearby, but there's no one except a grocery store worker taking out the garbage. My body responds in full panic mode: sweat drips down my back and my ears start to ring.

There's a thick treeline towards the back of the lot, leading into some hiking trails but I can't make out anyone obviously there.

Still, I feel like I'm being watched. My heart is racing and I look back down at my phone; hands shaking.

I begin to type *there's no blood on my hands*, but think of Marcus and delete it. Instead, I answer: *Who is this?*

I watch the dots as they thumb out a reply. *Someone who knows what you did.*

~~~

Abby's funeral takes place Monday morning and more than half the town shows up to pay their respects. While most of the people there don't remember her, I'm sure it would make her smile knowing how many people showed up to celebrate her life. However short it was.

Today is the first real sunny day we've had since I've been here and most people aren't even wearing coats. The sun is warm and bright, and I can't help wondering if it's shining for Abby.

I hardly slept last night. I have concealer under my eyes but I doubt it's fooling anyone. Sara brought me a hot coffee when she met me outside the church. I'm borrowing a black dress from Judie, who stealthily left it on my bed yesterday. I didn't think to bring a black dress, but I'm in Isinbury so it should've been a given for me. I swear I'm cursed.

I keep checking my phone to see if that unknown number will text me again. I tried to trace it, but it's a burner phone. The threat from yesterday...I can't get it out of my head. It makes me paranoid of every single person I see. Even those I'm closest to.

Sara and Bobby stay by my side throughout the ceremony, keeping a close eye on how I'm doing. I know they have good intentions, but being babied drives me nuts.

Having been to a few funerals of people who were close to me, I like to think I am allowed to have an opinion on how cruel they can be. Not only did you just lose someone you loved dearly, but now you have to think about them straight for the next week as you go through the visitations and funeral arrangements. Then you're forced into a social setting where you have to try and have conversations with people, a lot of whom you don't know or would rather not speak with. Funerals are supposed to give you closure or allow you to come to terms with them being gone forever, but how are you supposed to do that when no one is giving you time to think, let alone feel?

It's worse if your loved one died an unnatural death, because you must also answer neverending questions from the police. If the death itself didn't fuck you up, the aftermath of what you must now go through certainly will. I have no clue why more people don't just start shouting at funerals, or pointing fingers at people who didn't even know the deceased and are just there for some sort of show. It makes me sick. I am not even 30 yet and I have been to 14 funerals for people I was close with, half of them fellow police officers. With the exception of my grandparents who died of old age and my mother who died of a heart attack, they have all been unnatural deaths. There wasn't any shouting at them. Though when I look around now, I can't help but wonder if we're all shouting, just inside our heads instead of out. Is that the real reason people are so damn quiet at funerals, because they are just holding in their screams? Or is it because there's literally no way to really comfort someone who has just lost a golden soul in their life with empty words that most often come out sounding cliché?

I head over to the family, with my head bowed to pay my respects. As I reach Abby's mother Irene, she turns in my direction and her face contorts into a snarl. She spits in my face and starts yelling at me, her arms batting against my chest, cursing me for letting her daughter slip away. She does this in front of the entire service. I feel my eyes begin to water but instead of arguing, I take her full wrath. It's what she needs right now and I can't blame her. I *did* let Abby down. I let them all down. She's quickly taken off me. Abby's father is shaking his head and apologizing to me. He's trying to get Irene to stop, pulling her elbows back and away from me. A middle-aged man with short, light brown hair steps between us, successfully calming her down by whispering in her ear. Bobby finally makes his way to us through the crowd, and tries to calm everyone down, before stepping away with the parents towards the reception. He gives me a worried glance over his shoulder so I attempt to wave it off for his benefit, as if I'm not dying inside.

I excuse myself out loud, though no one's listening, and turn in the other direction. Someone catches my elbow and I spin to see the man who calmed down Irene.

"Thank you for that, but I should go," I say quickly. He lets go of my arm but keeps my gaze, smiling as if we share some inside joke.

"Is there something else you need?" I hesitate, unsure now, who this man is and what he wants with me.

"Oh God, Jane," he says thick with mockery. "Don't tell me you've lost your mind along with your ability to laugh shit off."

It's then that I properly look up and place the face. I gasp.

"Holy shit." I erupt. "Jake, is that you?" He nods. He has a sharp haircut that perfectly frames his face and a suit that fits him flawlessly. He's not the muddy, laid back country guy in plaids I used to know right now. I wonder if this is only his professional look or if he just looks like this now. "You grew up."

"Yeah, you too, *detective*." He bumps my shoulder lightly with his fist. I try not to wince. "Nice to see you after all these years."

He grins and pulls me into a hug, which I fall into, a bit startled. He smells of an expensive cologne and his suit is soft. His hug is deep and gentle like the Jake I remember.

Jake is Abby's younger brother by two years. I grew up with him too, and he often tagged along with Abby and I on all of our adventures, because he needed to be looked after and their parents expected us to do it. I never minded, as he would let us gossip, read magazines or do our nails while he did his own thing nearby.

Sometimes he would make us indoor forts, help us climb trees or kill spiders for us. He was quieter than the other boys I knew, and nicer. We got a bit closer after Abby left our lives, and we often walked together on the same route home. We even made out a few times, mostly at parties, but he always stopped kissing me when I drank too much. Nothing ever came of it. I was looking for comfort, that's all.

We look each other over now, smiling and shaking our heads. So much has changed. I come back to the present, and the tears held in from earlier pour out of my eyes.

"I'm so sorry about Abby." He brings me in for another hug, almost tearing up himself. "I looked her up when I first moved to Vancouver but never found anything. I always expected I would hear about her in the news doing something crazy or that she would just show up on my front door one day. But I never heard anything. That should've been a clue, but I–"

"It's alright Jane," he interrupts, saying it softly in my ear, squeezing me tighter. "My mom just needs someone to blame other than herself. It's not anyone's fault but the person who did this to her."

I don't know what to say to that so I just nod. I realize now that part of me didn't want to know if something bad had happened to her.

"I think I always knew something was wrong about her just leaving like that, but I never did anything about it either." He says this to make me feel better or maybe to admit some guilt he has been struggling with, out loud.

"I still can't believe it."

He pulls away. "Seeing you has been the only thing to make this day bearable Jane."

I try to smile. "I feel the same."

"Anyways, I just wanted to re-introduce myself before you slipped away," he says with a slight smile. "I would join you but I really gotta get back to the service. Maybe we can grab a beer or something, sometime soon?"

"I'd love that. Give me your phone for a sec' and I'll put my number in."

He leans his head sideways and sucks his lips in, a nervous gesture I suppose he never shook. "Don't be weird, but I actually have your number already."

I give him a strange look. He just chuckles. "Bobby gave it to me. I stopped by the police station earlier to say hi, but you weren't there. I was hoping we could catch up."

"Oh, yeah, I'm taking a bit of time off right now..."

This doesn't faze him at all as he thumbs something on his phone and a second later my phone buzzes.

"There, I sent you my contact info."

"We should meet up later this week. Can we play it by ear?"

"It's a date." He says grinning, turning toward the church.

My mouth opens to explain it's not actually a date, but I realize he's probably just teasing me as usual.

"See you later Jane," he calls back over his shoulder. His walk is still the same; long laidback strides.

I pass my parents' graves and stop only for a moment, placing a hand tenderly on each stone. Instead of saying anything, I imagine they can feel what I feel, through the palm of my hand. A wordless exchange; a sharing of burdens. That in itself affords me some comfort.

A car crackles through the cemetery's rocky lane, breaking the silence and slowly moving along a few metres from me. Another

Black Honda with tinted windows. I feel a shiver down my spine but I ignore it. I wave to the car, as friendly as possible, even though I can't see who's inside. Probably someone who felt the service was too much. The car speeds up and I watch it leave.

I'm still deep in thought of how Jake has changed, and the embarrassing altercation between Irene and I, when I arrive at the spot, almost on autopilot. It's been years since I came here, yet my body still knows the route: walk past the cemetery, take a left hook into the dense forest, follow the path for about ten minutes, until it opens into a small meadow filled with tall bluebells. This used to be Abby's favourite meeting spot. I take a granola bar out of my purse and nibble on it, remembering how Abby and I would picnic here together many years ago. We started off doing tea and sandwich parties when we were little with my mom, then pizza picnics on school lunch breaks, then just a place where we hung out on a blanket and sometimes shared a bottle of wine from her mother's stash. I think of how Abby was the one who showed me how to do my mascara and how to dress to impress the boys in our class. She was the one who I trusted to ask a boy I liked in a game of telephone if they would hang out with me after school.

My fingers brush against my right forearm as I remember how she would draw a bunch of sunflowers and suns and rainbows on me in art class.

Although she often ditched plans or hid things from me, she meant well. She was a kind-hearted soul who was quick to laugh. She seemed to seek out the loners (myself included), lending her light and courage to them in exchange for her being the centre of everyone's attention. It was a small price to pay. She would invite kids who sat alone at lunch to join us at our table, and would always call people out on their shit. That was why I was so surprised when one day she told me she became friends with a group of older, popular kids. Abby and I were friends long before Miranda and Harrison came along, and because I followed in her footsteps, we jumped into their madness together believing we would both be okay if the other one was close. That's how it always was between us.

I wish we had never met them.

She was like the sister I never had, and even though we were the same age, I looked up to her. She was more confident, outgoing and funny than I ever was. She often called me her little mouse.

I can't believe she is gone.

I lay down in the grass and rest my head on my forearms which are thrown back. The earth is soft and warm. The air smells like wet leaves.

Irene was so upset at the funeral, grabbing on to her remaining children, now all grown up, as if they too would cease to exist. Abby was their oldest, then Jake, then their sister Amanda, their brother Tom, a sister Holly, then the twins. Although Abby's parents were hard on her when she was alive, losing a child really wakes you up to the realities of your own vulnerability and faults as a parent. I think of Irene and the veins in her eyes, bulging from her red face as she let me have it. It was as if I was witnessing her guilt wrapping around her neck and choking her in front me; her desperate arms waving in the air and her fingers extended as if trying to pass it on to someone else so she could breathe again.

We all thought Abby had left. I tell myself this is true. There was even a note.

I always imagined her simply wandering out of town with her favourite suitcase, hitching a ride with a cute boy until she left him at the airport with a spontaneous kiss. Then, bringing herself around the world to experience all the culture, food, art and people she could take in. She had a talent for getting people to do what she wanted them to. That's what I had focused on. Not the fact that she was freshly eighteen and had hardly any savings. She could accomplish anything, and I really thought she did.

The family I have left in Isinbury always understood what the town was for me: a bad omen. Every time I stepped into it, something bad happened. And this time has proven to be no different.

It doesn't make any sense, but I can't help thinking Abby would still be alive if I hadn't come back here. I know she died a decade ago, but to me, she was always alive somewhere else in the world. Now, upon my return, her death was made real.

Maybe I wasn't hiding from Isinbury, but what the town brought out in me. Maybe, I was trying to hide from the truth.

~~~

I'm sitting cross-legged on a patch of grass with my heels kicked off and the sun shining on my skin, still in the meadow. I'm listening to birds sing and tiny creatures nibble at their lunch and create homes for their little families. I smell the pine and the grass and the breeze. I just needed to escape the madness for a bit and remind myself, guiltily, how it feels to be alive.

It's the way we honour our dead. By living for them.

But of course, my mind is stubborn and it will not let me be. Every time I come close to something like closure or peace, it springs awake and reminds me of my demons.

We need to catch our killer and make sure we catch the right one. There's a certain boldness to whoever is behind this. The first murder was rushed and very public; the second involved breaking and entering, passing by children and possible neighbours who could've been witnesses. And the third was when things really escalated: a bullet to the head to silence his third victim, in front of me no less. I must've been so close to catching him there. It worries me what his next move will be. He's getting cockier.

My mind wanders again to Marcus, his bloody face in my hands as the life went out of his eyes.

I can't help but torture myself with the small details of what went down. Him lifting his gun towards me, his expression revealing his next move, and him pulling the trigger. It had entered my shoulder. Was I really that lucky in my leap to avoid getting shot, or did he mean to shoot me there? I had seen him adjust the revolver in his hand and the sorrowful expression pour over his face just seconds before he shot. Did he mean to shoot me in the shoulder or did he mean to shoot me in the head? These are the thoughts that poisoned my mind as I let myself rot in my apartment for months after it happened.

Did he want to injure me enough to be able to run away or did he want to cut his loose ends?

The relationship we had makes me second-guess myself and believe he didn't miss. He meant to hit my shoulder and then go on the run. His eyes...they were full of shock and confusion...before they became the eyes of a dead man. A man, once my family, who I shot in the throat, without hesitation, on the premise that if I didn't shoot, I would be killed.

Am I a killer? More than just a cop who has used her gun to defend herself?

What happened to Abby that night? Why was her body found in the cave that I woke up in front of, the same morning she officially went missing? Could I have something to do with it?

I hold my breath in an attempt to calm myself down. I feel a panic attack coming on. Breathe in, breathe out. Breathe in, breathe out.

I shake my head and my body as if to stir up my buried memories from that night. But it doesn't work. Bobby and Kenny haven't spoken to me about my possible involvement in Abby's death, only that the new Sergeants sent here to help want to interview me...

I pull out my phone quickly and realize I'm going to be late for the interview.

"Fuck!" I yell, jumping up to my feet.

I take the back way by the mountain side and jog over to the station in my bare feet. It's a Monday, but I manage to get myself there without being seen. I slip my heels back on and let myself in the back door–Bobby made me an extra pass–and head straight for the filing room.

I need to do something before–

I hear my name and look up startled. It's Liam. He was providing his own statement of the cave situation while we were at the funeral.

"Hey, sorry, I forgot you were here," I say. My cheeks feel hot. I massage the back of my neck in an effort to relax.

"How are you doing?" He asks. I realize my eyes are probably bloodshot and my face blotchy from crying. I'll work this in my favour.

"Not great. I just needed a break from it all." It's not a total lie.

He nods, accepting this answer. "Do you want some coffee? They just made some. It's pretty quiet here. The new guys, Jamieson and Francis, are just in the bathroom. Jackson is in the front, holding down the fort."

This is it. I need to act fast.

"No thanks, I already had about three cups today." I attempt a laugh. "I just need to grab something from my locker really quick. I'll be back in a minute."

"No problem. Continue on with whatever mission you were on a second ago," he says this flirtatiously. "Seriously, go ahead. We can talk after."

I give a bashful "thanks," and continue on past the lockers in the back to the basement door next to them which leads to the filing room. But before I round the corner, I hear the door opening and I freeze. I'm about to be caught and I can't think of an excuse fast enough.

Then a young and lanky, blonde-haired kid rounds the corner while pushing a key pass back into his pocket. He bumps into me and jolts backward into the wall, swearing.

"What were you doing down there?" I ask, using my accusatory and authoritative police voice. "And who are you?"

His face is in complete shock and turns red as a tomato. "I'm Adam...Kline. The co-op student. Bobby asked me to grab something for him..."

"Where is it then? The thing you were sent down for?"

"Couldn't find it..."

This kid is quick on his feet, but I'm not buying it. I put out my hand, palm up and he places Bobby's key pass in it. I put it in my own pocket then hold out my hand to introduce myself.

"I'm Jane." He shakes my hand awkwardly, not having mastered a firm handshake yet. He looks stricken still, unsure of how to proceed.

"You're not allowed in the filing room as a co-op student, especially where you could access current case information." I pause for a moment, considering and then softening my tone. "Were you looking for updates on your sister's case?"

He nods slowly, looking like a sad puppy. "I'm sorry. Please don't tell Bobby. He's taken a chance on me and I didn't mean to cross the line but I just wanted to make sure you were taking Megan seriously even with her addiction problems and her weird scary notebook drawings and–"

I hold my hand up to stop him. "I promise you, Adam. We're taking her very seriously and doing everything in our power to catch the person responsible. We won't rest until we find Megan some justice."

"Okay...thank you." His shoulders slump a little but he doesn't walk away. Instead, he looks up at me sadly. "Are you going to tell Bobby what I did?"

"How about we keep this between us, as long as you promise not to interfere with the investigation again, okay? It's quite serious, you know. If we found evidence for her case and you handled it or it could be proven you were allowed in the evidence room, it could make that evidence inadmissible in court later. There needs to be degrees of separation not just to protect you but also to protect Megan's case. Understand?"

He nods. Then he brightens a little as a thought seemingly crosses his mind. "I could help in other ways, you know. People don't really notice me and I hear a lot of people talking about what they think happened or telling other people's secrets. Stuff I don't think they're telling Bobby or Kenny about."

I'm so aware of each second passing that I can feel a bead of sweat pouring down my eyebrow, but I try to muster a smile for this poor kid who blends into the background, seemingly has no friends and just lost his sister in a brutal way.

I pull my card out of my wallet and hand it to him. "Here's my card. You can text me anytime and I'll follow up with you if any leads pan out, okay?"

This seems to cheer him up. The colour in his face has returned to normal and his shoulders are more relaxed. "Thanks, I will." He walks away slowly then, looking back at me before I round the corner myself.

Sweet, awkward kid with good intentions but bad decision-making skills. Reminds me of myself at that age.

I finally make it to the basement filing room and it smells like dust and old papers in here. Kind of like a library, but it's cold and dark.

I search in the year 2000 and sort through the files until I find a folder with Abby's name on it. I bring it over to the desk in the middle of the room and take a peek. The front page which usually acts as sort of a table of contents is absent. There is however, one missing person's report, a closed-report summary, and four recorded statements from Harrison, Miranda, me and Laryssa. The closed-report summary mentions I spent the morning on a hike through the woods from Miranda's to the small highway where Laryssa picked me up.

I know this isn't the whole truth. I have no recollection of the time from when I got into the van for the joyride to when I woke up outside of the caves two kilometres away, around 2 p.m the next day. I read through my statement to the part where it says: *I was trying to find a ride 'cause I had lost my phone and Abby had already left and she was my drive.* I check both Harrison and Miranda's statements which say they didn't see where Abby or I went after around midnight because they spent the remainder of the night making out in Miranda's broken-down RV. When asked about Abby and I, they say they assumed we had left together sometime in the early morning.

There is no mention of me waking up next to the caves, it just says I took the forest path in the direction of the highway. Bobby knows I'm involved somehow, ever since I showed him I knew it was that cave, instead of the other two. And no doubt he has taken a look at this file since we found her. This is starting to look really bad for me.

I go over the details of what could tie me to her murder.

They know that I was with her and a group of people, including Harrison, who saw her on what might have been the last night of her life. They know she must have died that night or shortly after, because she was never seen again after that (the missing person's report is hers), and I so helpfully pointed out to Bobby that I thought the scraps of clothing we found in the cave matched the ones I saw her in last.

But they don't know I woke up literally in front of the same cave, possibly a few hours after she was killed, where her body was dumped...hands and sweatshirt covered in blood.

Fuck.

Laryssa's statement says there was nothing out of the ordinary about picking me up on the side of the road. There is no mention of my bloody clothing.

So much about this doesn't make sense. First of all, if I did make my way to the forest completely blacked out, why was I there? Someone would have had to help me get there because I wasn't sober enough to think about directions in the dark. Did we all go together on some sort of drunken adventure? Or was it just Abby and I? If that was true, why would Harrison or Miranda lie about it?

There is only one reason I can think of for their lies, and that would be that they knew Abby was dead or going to be killed that night. By me? By them? I shudder at the possibility.

They could have driven me in the van. I faintly remember getting in for a joyride, but nothing after that. I look through the closed-report summary again. A note at the bottom says the van, a navy 1990 Chevrolet Astro, was presumed stolen that morning as well. Miranda's parents made a claim to their insurance company, but nothing happened after that.

A hopeful part of me makes my heart skip a beat. Did Abby take the van that night to go on an adventure or to meet someone at the caves? Did she maybe just fall, slip, and hit her head? No foul play involved?

It's wishful thinking. There was no van in the forest that I saw. And vehicles don't drive themselves away from a murder scene.

I take photos of the files with my phone to look over later and just as I'm closing the file cabinet, my eyes catch another folder from the same year with a name I recognize. Daniel Briggs. It's the man who died of a mysterious overdose in the back cell. His photograph is in here and I realize I have met this man but knew him by a different name. He was an older friend of Harrison's, a mentor of sorts. They called him "Big Danny." I give the folder a quick glance and notice that the table of contents page is missing here too. Actually, a lot of stuff is missing.

My heart pounds in my chest. I look at about two dozen more folders, which all have their table of contents pages. Bobby, Kenny and my father have always kept a meticulous set of files. So why are these two an exception? Just then, I hear the front door buzz from upstairs, so I shove the cabinet closed and run frantically up the stairs. I make it to my locker just as Bobby pokes his head around the corner.

"I'm glad you're here." Bobby says. He looks around the room, quizzically. "What are you up to?"

"I just wanted to grab my stuff from my locker. Wasn't sure when I would get another chance." It's a flat-out lie, but I look him dead in the eyes and force myself to smile easily. I get my locker open and grab a comfier change of clothes. Bobby always knows when I'm lying, but he seems to buy this or at least let it go.

"Alright, well the guys are ready for your statement now if you're all set?"

"Yes, sure. Sorry I left the reception early. I just needed some space."

He nods, and jerks his thumb behind him. "Come on, let's get this over with."

So much is wrong here. I've never felt suspicious in Bobby's presence. He's my family.

I have a mysterious overdose death in the back cell of the police station, with a lot of paperwork and evidence missing. I have three murders linked together by one unsub, which may or may not be linked to the strange death of my best friend whose body was dumped in the cave where I woke up shortly after she was supposedly killed. I know for a fact I wasn't involved in the first four deaths...but Abby's? I'm not so sure.

I can't remember a damn thing. A total blackout.

If only I could remember something about that night...maybe I could finally know what happened to my best friend and what my involvement was in her death. My thoughts race back to that nightmare of Abby and I in the woods. Me bashing her head in with a rock.

I'm so deep in thought that I almost collide with the major crimes sergeant detectives assigned to help with our crisis, when I get to the main room. I apologize and quickly introduce myself. They couldn't be more opposite. Jamieson is tall, dark-skinned and handsome as the saying goes; obviously the more senior of the two or at least the most front-facing, and although he's very serious, he welcomes me warmly as a colleague rather than a suspect. Francis is a bit wearier and more closed off. He's short, stubby and pale as a ghost, with a permanent displeased look on his face. There is nothing very warm or friendly about him at all.

CHAPTER 15 - JANE

I state my name and today's date for the record. I feel the shift of control as I sit on the opposite side of the interrogation room and try to keep my face neutral and body relaxed.

"I want to first start by letting you know this is not an interrogation, we just need some facts from you and would prefer to have it on the record." This comes from Jamieson. He's taking the lead for now. Francis is sitting in the chair beside him, leaning back with a stern expression and his arms crossed. I have not brought a lawyer.

I nod. "What is it that you want to know?"

"Tell us your theories on what is happening here in Isinbury right now."

They let me lay it all out for them. Jamieson takes a few notes but mostly keeps eye contact, listening. "Our killer has so far targeted only women which he presumably follows and stalks, learning their schedules and habits, before committing highly premeditated murder. He's careful enough not to leave any substantial evidence behind, not to make any loud noises, and escape the scene, mostly without being seen. So, he typically blends in well. The Facebook messages from Brandi suggest our killer could be Harrison." I pause, taking a sip of water and trying to read their expressions. They remain blank. "Possibly blackmail." I don't mention that this meticulous and careful behaviour does not sound like Harrison, at all. Though people change in ten years, I remind myself. Plus, he's been smart enough to avoid the law so far...

Jamieson sees I am waiting for a response or some sort of acknowledgment, so he gives me a small sign of trust.

"Yes, we seem to agree with your working theory that the women found something out about Harrison's illegal dealings or business colleagues which threatened him somehow. According to bank records we received yesterday, both Brandi and Lilyann were receiving large sums of cash deposits monthly, which correlate with dates and amounts of money withdrawn from Harrison's bank account." He opens one of the folders in front of him, searching for further information. "An elderly neighbour has recently come forward claiming she saw Harrison arguing with one of the girls in the weeks before they died. Again, circumstantial at best. Harrison was in a relationship with Lilyann, but the neighbour couldn't correctly identify if it was Lilyann or Brandi that he was arguing with. The description given could match Miranda Flemings as well, a known associate as I'm sure you are aware. If we could get solid proof of an exchange like this, on top of the bank records, it could point to a motive."

"I agree."

"I understand you have a history with him as well. Could you tell us more about that?" I know they've done their research. So, I tell them everything: most importantly his friendship with

Miranda, the attempted sexual assault, and the recently broken nose. Jamieson nods. He knows all of this already. He apologizes for bringing it up, and tells me that they have had two other ex-girlfriends of his come forward with accusations of domestic violence and sexual assault.

"That unfortunately doesn't surprise me." I say, barely above a whisper.

Francis moves his hand up to his mouth, hiding a reaction, and looks away from me to the wall. If I had to guess, he doesn't like me very much. Or maybe he just doesn't like women.

"Are they officially pressing charges?" I ask, surprised by my own question.

"They're talking with their lawyers right now. At the very least, they have agreed to be character witnesses if this moves to trial." Jamieson says, again watching me carefully. He doesn't ask me if I want to press charges or be involved in the trial. Maybe my presence would hurt the case rather than help it.

"You will need to contact your union rep regarding the broken nose incident, and they will be able to help you through the next steps. It will need to go through the proper channels."

"I understand. Of course."

"What do you know about Miranda?" This time, the question comes from Francis.

"She and Harrison have been thick as thieves since high school. They would do anything for each other, I'm sure." Maybe that was pointing the finger too much. I try to rein myself in. "What I mean, is that I don't know for sure if their relationship has ever been romantic or physical, but it goes farther than that. Almost like siblings, though they aren't. She's every bit as cruel as he is."

"So, what you're implying, is that if he is involved, she likely is as well?"

"I would assume so. Yes."

"Have you ever seen them be violent towards each other or to others?"

I flinch. "Sometimes, when we were younger, Miranda would get into pretty serious fist fights with other people our age, and the police would be called, but charges were never pressed." I try to read the room. Something is off. "Harrison is more of a sit and wait fighter, while she prefers an audience." I pause. "That was back then though. I can't speak to anything they did in the last decade."

"It seems like you're unsure if they're capable of murder?" Jamieson implies.

"I honestly don't know. I haven't known them in ten years. And I haven't been able to trust my gut as much as I used to." At this, I see a smirk rise from Francis. I wonder how much he knows about my past.

Jamieson asks me what my relationship is like with Miranda.

I stifle a laugh which they notice. "We've never really gotten along."

Jamieson nods. "Is this because you were dating Harrison?"

"We weren't really dating. And no, I don't think so. At least, not at first. She would sort of bully me in the earlier grades. I made for a good target 'cause I was small and quiet. Then we hung out in the same crowd, and even though she wouldn't make it obvious to everyone else, she would still do small things to make me feel uncomfortable or self-conscious."

"Why did you become friends with her if she had been bullying you before?"

I know this is bait. So, I play it honestly. "My friend Abby wanted to be friends with them for some reason so I tagged along."

"Abby Nichols, whose body was recently found in the cave system here?"

I nod. "Unfortunately, yes."

"Seems you four are tightly connected to all of this somehow."

"I'm not sure what you mean."

Jamieson smirks at me and pierces my eyes with his own. He suddenly looks less friendly and more...like a cat pursuing a mouse.

He continues on. "If I'm correct, *you* were the one to find Abby Nichols' body?"

"Yes." I say as evenly as I can manage.

"Could you tell me about the last night you saw her?"

Those statements are fresh in my mind. It wasn't my initial reason for looking at them but I'm thankful I did.

I tell them we were drinking at Miranda's, and then her and Harrison went off somewhere, and Abby and I fell asleep in one of the vans in the backyard. "When I woke in the morning, Abby had left without me and so I walked through the forest to the highway to find someone to drive me home."

"Do you have any idea why Abby would leave without you when you clearly weren't comfortable at Miranda's?"

He wants to ask me if we had a fight. "No. But she could act like that sometimes. Dramatic, withdrawn, impulsive, emotional. Like any typical teenage girl."

"A centre of attention type." Francis says. I nod slowly. "Why would you want to be friends with someone like that?" He asks.

"I was a teenage girl. And I didn't have many friends. Plus, she also had a way of making you feel like the most important person in the world. You took the good with the bad."

"Understandable." Jamieson says. He sits up in his chair, fidgets a little.

"Do you know anyone who would have wanted to hurt her or was she involved with anyone?"

"She was always very secretive about the boys she was with. Even with me. She might have been seeing someone but she never told me who she was dating. I'd only find out once it was over."

"Was she the kind of girl to meet a boy at a cave in the middle of the night?"

I think it over. A scenario like that had occurred to me earlier so it's surprising hearing the same conclusion come from Jamieson... "Probably, yes," I say with a sigh.

"It seems a bit irresponsible to me."

"That's just the way she was. Ask anyone and they'll tell you the same thing. She was fierce."

"How did you know where to find her body? Too much of a coincidence that you pick the right cave on the first try, don't you think?" Again, I can feel Jamieson's intense stare catching a drip of sweat beading at my brow and it's almost like he can see through the solid desk to my nervous fingers in my lap peeling their hangnails out of pure panic. I stop picking and fist them both instead, trying to steady my breathing but feeling like I'm on stage in front of a million people in my underwear.

"Not really. That cave was one of her favourite places to hangout." It's the truth. I try to stick to it.

"I see. Have you heard that Miranda Flemings is missing?" Francis asks suddenly.

My eyebrows shoot up. "What? Are you sure?"

"Yes." Jamieson answers, sharing a look with Francis. "We've been unable to reach her since Saturday morning." His expression is resigned. "We asked Harrison if he knew where she was but he said he had no idea."

"Did you check his house or her parents' house?" I ask, still in shock.

"She lives with her parents, and they let us check their house since we told them we were concerned for her safety. Which we are. She's involved with this somehow, we're sure. However, she could have become the next victim." He shakes his head a bit theatrically.

"Did you find anything there?"

Francis tries to say something but Jamieson cuts him off intentionally. "They let us search the place without a warrant. Miranda's bedroom is in the garage, and we found enough prescription drugs in there to put her away for possession. She clearly has a heavy hand in Harrison's business. She might even be an equal partner. We also searched the laptop which gave us a long search history of *your* Facebook page, and various Google searches of *your* name and information about *you*." He eyes me.

I'm completely taken aback.

"Looks like you have an admirer," Francis teases when I don't answer.

"Or an angry stalker," I say.

"Whatever the reason, she seems to be long gone and didn't bother hiding anything or packing a bag before she left."

I think before I answer. "Isn't that the morning where Bobby notified Abby's family?"

He nods. "Yes, we came to the same conclusion. Word got out. She must have fled. Why do you think she fled but Harrison stayed put? You said they do everything together."

"They do. It doesn't make sense. She wouldn't leave without him. Not unless she was desperate to save herself for some reason. What has he said about her disappearance?"

"He's pretending to be surprised. We unfortunately don't have enough evidence to convince a judge for a warrant to search his house and he's being uncooperative which is unsurprising. We have eyes on it, but no one has seen her there yet. He's mostly stayed inside."

I wonder who the eyes on his house are. Probably Kenny.

This is a total mess.

"Do you think they are involved with Abby's murder?" Jamieson asks suddenly.

I swallow hard. "No." I lie. "Nothing from that night pointed to something sinister. It was like any other night. *Normal.*"

"Are you sure?" Francis asks me, leaning in.

"Yes. That's why I have spent ten years thinking she just ran away."

"Maybe wishful thinking," he says.

I flinch a little in response. My annoyance clearly shows. "I guess so."

Jamieson gives me a small, sympathetic smile. "Anything else you'd like to tell us, Jane?"

Hell no.

"Not that I can think of." I say evenly.

"Well, you let us know," he says, as he turns off the recorder. "Thanks for your time. I hope it wasn't too much. We appreciate you coming in today of all days." He means the funeral.

"No problem. I'm here to help if you need anything."

I follow their lead as they stand up and Jamieson extends a hand out to me. I shake it firmly. Francis turns and heads out the door without an acknowledgement. Jamieson catches my line of sight but says nothing about it, just cracks the faintest of smiles.

"I really am sorry for your loss Jane." He seems sincere. I thank him. He hands me his business card. "Call me if you come across anything that might be helpful. I know you're on leave, but I know what that really means for a detective." He winks.

I have a feeling he will be watching me closely. I don't buy the whole Good Cop Act.

As I leave through the front door of the station, I see a new poster stuck on the side window, to the right. Although it's facing the other way, the sunlight illuminates through it allowing me to make out the shape of a face. Already, there are a few people gathered in front of it, gossiping. Once outside, I stand away from the crowd and see Miranda's face looking back at me. The photo is cropped, framing her face, likely taken from one of her social media pages. Her bleach blonde hair is newer in this photo, but her eyes still bear her signature dark eyeliner. Big bold, black letters scrolled above the photo request to please call or stop by the station if anyone has information about her whereabouts.

CHAPTER 16 - JANE

I catch Kenny outside The Raven talking to some of the locals. As I make my way over to him, the crowd disperses, giving us our space but still within earshot distance.

"Can I talk to you for a sec?" I ask him, voice lowered. He understands and leads me closer to the tree path and away from any prying ears.

"Bunch of gossipers," he says. "What's up darlin'?"

"Wait, aren't you supposed to be watching Harrison's house?"

"Bobby relieved me so I could grab some lunch. I'm supposed to head right back. Why?"

"Nevermind. I want to know what you think happened to the drug overdose victim, Daniel Briggs, in 2000."

As soon as I mention it, I read it on his face. He's shocked that I've asked. He tries to hide it a second later, but realizes I've already noticed. He presses his lips together firmly, not answering.

"Bobby wouldn't say much about it to me. And I can tell something is off here. Please Kenny." He seems to think it over. Opening his mouth, then closing it, as if changing his mind.

"You really want to know what I think Jane? Are you deadly sure?" He asks, studying my reaction.

"Yes, be straightforward with me."

He pulls me deeper into the path, farther away from everyone.

"I think it might have been your pops."

This catches me off guard. I would've thought Kenny, one of his best pals, would have his back. He notices the surprise on my face and puts his hand on my shoulder firmly. I move away from it like it's on fire.

"I loved your dad Jane, but he could be tough as nails when it came to making sure bad guys got what was coming to them. Briggs was rich with drug money. He could afford the best lawyers and pay whoever he wanted to get out of trouble. He already had a deal in place. It was a grim reality." He stops and studies my eyes, which no doubt are revealing to him my anger and disbelief. "Henry was acting pretty strange for a long while. The job was hard on him. Turned him into a hard man. Do you remember that side of him?"

We tend to glorify our dead, remembering only their best qualities, but of course I remember what kind of man my father could be. I nod, which turns out to be more of an upward shake. I feel a chill in my bones.

"Well, Bob told him he would take the overnight shift with Briggs but Henry *refused*. He ordered Bob home. Anyways, let's just say I wasn't too surprised to get the call that Briggs was found dead in the middle of the night."

I can't seem to find words to say. Kenny's face turns red.

"Sorry I know it's hard to hear, but you wanted the truth. I'm thinking you must've known deep down and that's why you're coming to me instead of Bobby. You're an adult now. I figure you can handle it."

I'm staring blankly ahead, trying to register it all when he leans in close and whispers in my ear. "I'd appreciate it if you didn't tell Bob I told you any of this. He's my best friend but I still think he'd fire me over it."

"Really?"

"I'm not sure. But I took a chance telling you, and I hope you realize that."

I remember the rumours that circulated after my dad's death. Some people said they thought his death wasn't an accident. That it had been suicide instead. I never believed them.

But if this is true...Who knows how my father's mental health was? If he could kill someone in cold blood, maybe he felt suicide was his only way out?

I swallow loudly. "Thank you, Kenny," I say, and before I leave, I add, "We'll keep this conversation between us."

I jangle my keys in my hand as I head to my car. A nervous tick. He catches up to me and places a warm palm on my shoulder.

"He wasn't himself at the end...your dad." Kenny says, looking me straight in the eyes. "But try to remember him as he was before then, and learn from his mistakes." His fingers rub my shoulder gently, still loosely in his grasp. "The past is in the past though, Jane. It does no one any good to start digging it up."

He gives me a hard stare; a silent warning.

"Thank you," I croak. As the car door shuts, I feel eyes on me. Most turn away but Laryssa's doesn't. She's out back smoking a cigarette and is bee-lining it to my car. I pretend not to notice her and start my car, but she's quick. She opens the passenger side and climbs in without an invitation, cigarette still in hand. The door slams behind her.

"Can I help you?" I ask, a little annoyed.

She ignores me at first, opening her window and taking one last long pull of her cigarette, before flicking it outside and pulling the window back up. Silence grows.

"I think we both know what happened to Abby," she says gravely, occupying her hands by patting her red curly locks against her head.

"I don't remember anything at all."

"I think that's a nice lie you're telling to protect yourself Jane." A small vibration in her voice tells me she's scared. She starts snapping a hair elastic tied to her wrist. A nervous habit. "I won't tell anyone if that's what you're worried about."

All I taste is metal in my mouth. I think I have bitten my inner cheek until it bled. "Why are you here then?"

"Well for one, we made a pact that day. You owe me for that and I plan on cashing in soon. And this gives me more leverage now." Her eyes finally meet mine. She has been avoiding them so far. There's defiance there, but also fear. "I'll come to you when I'm ready."

"Is this about you and my dad?" I ask.

She freezes for too long, giving herself away. Then she opens the door, about to leave but hesitates, turning back toward me. "Look after yourself Jane. There are people out there who will kill to keep this secret."

"Including yourself?" I dare to ask.

"No. Believe it or not, I'm on your side." She steps abruptly outside, closing the door and heading back to the bar without another glance in my direction.

~~~

Bobby's house is quiet as I enter except for Bear who seems happy to see me. I crouch down and give him a giant hug. I go through the motions of letting him outside, feeding him and giving him some attention and pets.

But my mind is overwhelmed by a million thoughts; none of them cheerful.

My father could have killed Briggs. Taking another human life, not by means of self-defense. A vigilante. It could have been what made him lose his mind and go off on that camping trip that ended his life. What brought him to such a desperate place?

I think about Marcus again and wonder if being a killer runs in the family.

My mind keeps racing back to what I didn't know about my father; about the police station I work for; about what lengths Bobby and Kenny would take to protect him even when he was in the wrong.

I want to pull the covers over my head and scream at the top of my lungs for my dad to save me from this nightmare. I want to scream and scream until I hear the slapping of his big bare feet in the hallway and his booming voice calling my name in the dark, telling me he's coming, that there's nothing to be afraid of and I'll realize that when I see his sleepy face in my doorway. Safe at last.

But I don't scream. I'm lying in bed, all alone, with my eyes pressed shut, giving myself a stress migraine.

My father is dead. And I might have killed my best friend.

CHAPTER 17 - JANE, 17 YEARS OLD

I wake from a deep sleep and am quickly blinded by piercing light. My right palm shoots to my eyes to cover them. My head pounds and I am shivering.

I suddenly feel so sick that I lean sideways and puke up anything that is left in my stomach. It smells foul and it burns my throat on the way out. Something sharp digs into my left hip. I peek under my hand, still shielding the light, to see where I am.

I am in the forest.

My hand falls and I take in the rest of the scene, not waiting for my eyes to adjust.

"What the hell?" The words come out of my mouth, but they are not to anyone, for I am very much alone. I move a twig from underneath me.

I notice then that my hands are filthy. Tainted brownish red. Whatever this is, it's also on my sweatshirt.

I sit up straight. There are fresh, muddy tire tracks leading up to where I am but there is no car in sight. This is not a road but a small dirt pedestrian path. No one drives up here.

"Hello?" I yell. No one answers. Just the trees that creak in the wind. My hands rub against my arms, trying to warm them. I have an eerie feeling I am not actually alone. "Hello? Is anyone there?" I risk it again.

As I get up slowly, I notice the caves behind me. I'm in front of the third cave, one of the most dangerous ones that hardly anyone enters. I check my pocket for my flip-phone and find it dead.

I don't know what time it is but the sun is above me. I walk towards the highway near town instead of the parking lot. It's about 45 minutes from here if I cut through instead of sticking to the path.

I find a stream on my way and rinse my hands the best I can. The water is freezing and numbs my fingers.

The back of my head feels sore and when I reach behind, I feel a small bump. "Ow." I say out loud. I give it a little rub and look back at my fingers. No blood. That's a good sign. But then, where did this blood come from? *Is it blood*?

Even though the wind is cool, I am sweating by the time I make it to the road. I smell awful, like the liquor I drank the night before mixed with dirt and teenage body odour.

It takes 20 minutes but I finally see a small black car coming towards me. I throw up a thumb and my best attempt at a smile. It passes me without slowing, but then the driver seems to think better of it and stops a few yards ahead.

It helps being the Detachment Commander's daughter sometimes.

I try a light jog toward the car even though it makes me want to puke. I'm afraid if I don't hurry the driver will change their mind again. I take off my stained sweatshirt and bunch it up in a ball.

I look inside the car and it's my dad's friend Laryssa. She looks impatient and upset. She has never liked me. I almost tell her to forget about the drive, that my dad is coming to pick me up, but this road isn't very popular and I could be waiting awhile.

All I want to do is go back home and sleep this off.

There is a young girl in the backseat, a few years younger than me, with iPod headphones in her ears. We wave hello. Laryssa leans over and opens the door for me. I climb in and she looks me over, a slight horrified expression reaching her face. "What happened to you?"

"Bonfire party." I lie, climbing into the passenger seat.

Her eyes focus on my sweater. I pull it closer to me, hoping I'm hiding the stain.

"Who's that?" I ask her, pointing behind us. "Another hitchhiker?" Her face gets serious again. A little flush rising on her neck.

"Just a friend's daughter. I'm watching her for the day." She snaps. "Apparently I have become the town's new babysitter." She glares at me, then pulls the car back in drive. My stomach growls loudly.

I've never seen her with children and I don't know why someone would choose her as a babysitter. I've only seen her overly drunk at my parent's parties or at the bar she owns in town.

"What is your dad going to say about this?" She asks me, breaking the silence.

I notice the time on the clock in the dashboard. It's just after 3p.m. Shit.

"Maybe we don't have to mention it?" She eyes me, considering. She reaches down near my feet and hands me her grey sweater.

"Put this on. You'll look less like you've been rolling around in the mud all night." She hesitates. "And I won't say anything if you don't?" She asks, her tone suddenly lighter, more playful. This surprises me. Out of all my parents' friends, she has always been the most flirtatious and obsessed with my dad. I expected her to want to flaunt her good deed of finding his daughter for him. Maybe I've misunderstood her. I carefully place my dirty sweater near my feet and button up her sweater which smells like fresh laundry.

"Deal." I say, a bit triumphant.

"A pact." She corrects.

I nod but I feel uneasy. I sneak a peek at the girl in the backseat and she gives me a small smile. Her headphones remain intact. Her eyes are brilliant blue like mine, but her hair is a fiery red that takes over her small frame with its bodacious curls.

I don't recognize her from town. I wonder who she really is.

CHAPTER 18 - JANE, PRESENT DAY

I'm on my way to the station on foot from the family restaurant about to surprise Bobby with some dinner and possibly get an update on how things are going. The daily special is warming my hands from its flimsy takeout box, when Kenny bursts out of the station's front door and grabs me, making sauce fly out of the container's leaky sides and spill on the ground. My temper flares, before he yells, "Sorry! Fist fight at the beach, one kid is knocked out cold!"

I yell back, "Do you need help?" but he's off like a bullet.

I enter the station and notice Adam pretending to sweep the floors. He looks bored out of his mind in front of the community tack board, when he looks up and our eyes meet. I walk over to say hi.

"Hey, you staying out of trouble?" I ask.

His face flushes but a mischievous grin spreads across his face.

"Mostly. Though I texted you a few things I overheard outside the bar two nights ago. I only sent you the stuff I thought was super relevant, but I have more notes if you want to see them."

"Yes! Sorry I read your text but haven't had a chance to follow up on anything yet."

"I get it. You think I'm just a dumb kid wasting your time."

That startles me. "No, of course not. Sometimes it's the little things that make or break a case. Keep sending me stuff. I mean it. I'm glad to have a second set of eyes out there."

This returns the smile to his face and it mirrors my own.

"Be careful though. And maybe don't be hanging around a bar on a school night, huh?"

He looks down, embarrassed, and continues sweeping.

"I'll see you later," I say, almost adding the word 'kid' at the end, before thinking better of it.

Jackson is at the front desk talking to the admin clerk Sally, and he gives me a wave as I make my way over. "Bobby's in the back, if you need him. Want us to buzz you through?"

"Yes please. Thanks." I pause, trying a little friendliness. "Oh, and how's the new baby?"

He smiles big, surprised. "He's perfect. We named him Benson. Healthy as can be. Lets us sleep for now."

"That's great." I say awkwardly, with a polite smile. The phone has been ringing off the hook for the last few days. It starts ringing again and Jackson sighs. I'm sure he's kept very busy between a new baby and answering the station's tip line. "Let us know if you need anything," I say softly, as he picks up the phone, answering another *helpful tip* about a neighbour accusing their neighbour.

He mouths a "thank you" as Sally buzzes me in.

I find Bob in his office at the back and although he looks a little suspicious when he first sees me, his eyes light up a little when he sees the food container in my hands. "It's pork schnitzel with sweet potato mash and glazed carrots."

"Awesome, I'm starving."

I let him eat his dinner and tell him I'll leave the second one for Kenny when he gets back.

"Thanks kiddo. Have you eaten already?"

"I'll grab something at home. No worries."

He divides his dinner in half, pretending to not be so hungry after all, waiting for me to dig into my half before piercing a carrot with his fork and plopping it in his mouth. "How are you holding up?"

I shrug. "Fine. Managing. How are things here?"

"Fine."

"No, really. Any progress?"

"Nope. We're sort of at a standstill. No sign of Miranda yet either."

I sigh and lean back in the chair. He tells me he's going to pull another late night with Jamieson and Francis, try to reevaluate and see if there's anything they missed. I try to offer him my help but he cuts me off.

"Jane, I'll let you know if anything new happens, but for now, you should focus on getting your life back on track. Clear your head." Bobby says this to me, without even looking up from his dinner.

He's avoiding my eyes. I feel my throat tighten. He's lost confidence in me. He sees something in me that my unit saw in me back home. They can't trust me. The reason they let me go so easily.

We finish the rest of our meal in uneasy silence. Him sorting through notes, me pretending to scroll through my phone.

After I finish, I wish him good luck then grab my stuff and head out the door.

I hate leaving work when there's so much to be done, but I'm too close to this right now, and they want me to keep my distance. Shutting my mind off for a little bit will help me have fresh eyes in the morning, and maybe I'll think of something that will remind them how helpful I can be.

~~~

The next day I decide to grab a coffee at Sara's before heading out, who knows where. I don't want to talk about anything to do with Abby or the case, but I desperately need caffeine. But before I enter, I see her through the glass door kissing on Langdon.

I enter anyway. The two lovebirds spring apart. Sara apologizes for the PDA and pours me a cup. I hand her a fiver and tell her to keep the change.

"So are you interested in my man Liam or not?" Langdon pries. Sara shakes her head. Langdon notices. "Sorry, am I not allowed to ask about it?"

"I'm not really looking to start anything right now," is all I say.

"Oh come on, why not? You're not a puritan are you?"

"Nope, just focusing on myself at the moment." He's not good at reading signs. I take a sip from my coffee and try to relax. Hoping Sara will intervene and change the subject.

"Maybe it's better this way if you're always this uptight," he says, eyebrows raising.

Sara hits him playfully in the arm. "Langdon. Stop being such a dick."

"You said it yourself, she's wound up tighter than a nun." He laughs. "That he would have to use a chisel to get down to anything worthwhile."

I almost spit out my coffee. I glare up at them from my cup. Sara's face is beet red.

"*Geez*, it was just a joke." Langdon says.

"You should really work on your manners and social cues," I say, then I add, "No idea what she sees in you," as I turn and head out the door, feeling blood red mad.

I look up and realize Jake is leaning on my car, waiting for me. He's wearing pine green cargo pants and a long-sleeved, fitted white T-shirt.

"How'd you know I'd be here?" I ask.

"Don't you practically live at the station right now?" He jokes.

I don't say otherwise. Instead, I head over to him and give him a hug. It's an instinctive habit. "Where are you living these days?" I ask, genuinely curious.

"I travel a lot for work and pleasure, but I own a house here in town, just a couple streets down from Sara actually. And another bachelor-type studio apartment in West Vancouver." He points to my cup. "I see you're still addicted to caffeine."

"I see you're still as observant as ever," I counter.

"Have any plans today? Bobby mentioned you had the day off."

I try to hide my embarrassment. I'm thankful Bobby covered for me. "Yes, I suppose I have the day off. What did you have in mind?"

"You'll see. Can I drive?" He notices my hesitation and winks. "Come on, it'll be like old times."

I ponder that a moment, remembering the time he was seventeen in the driver seat, I was eighteen, a passenger and instructor. We were in a rusty brown Volkswagen, borrowed from one of his friends, and I was teaching him how to drive on the backroads. He was wearing secondhand faded overalls, over a pale T-shirt and his light brown locks were held back by a baseball cap worn backwards. I was in white short shorts and a red plaid shirt, with my hair pulled back in a loose bun so I could concentrate. I remember it like it was yesterday. He ended up putting us in a ditch, having taken a corner too hard, and yet I still climbed back in and taught him for weeks after that. Abby might have left us, but we found something else, in each other, once she did.

Almost a decade later, I shake my head in defeat and climb into the passenger side with Jake, on an adventure once again.

CHAPTER 19 - JANE

Even with my eyes closed, I can tell where he's taking me. I have taken the route so many times in my life that I know it by heart. As a child, I used to be the most annoying backseat driver. Isinbury is a small town, so I used to guess where we were going every time we left the house and would give my dad instructions on whether to turn right or left at the next stop. I even told him to stop at red lights, as if he didn't already know that. I smile thinking of the memory, not so much because it makes me happy but because I remember my father yelling for me to shut up and let him drive, and although at the time I was quite taken aback by his angry annoyance, now I am just thankful for the pristine memory of his loud bellowing voice slicing the air from the front seat; his narrowing light blue eyes glaring at me from the rearview mirror, daring me to object. I don't have many vivid memories of my father when I was growing up, but I have this one. No matter how imperfect it is, it's precious to me.

I smell the mud and the algae on the breeze coursing through the passenger side window, before we hit the bumpy unpaved road to the beach. Jake tells me I can open my eyes now, since the road gives it away. The day is sunny but cold. I pull my jacket tighter to my body and reach into the backseat for my extra sweater from my backpack.

"Do you always bring your backpack around with you?" He asks.

I nod. "It's just more practical for my job. Compact, big enough to carry everything I would need for the day, and it's out of my way if it's on my back as opposed to a purse that slips off the shoulder every minute. I don't know how women do it."

"Men too, nowadays," he objects.

"Fair point."

A bit of awkward silence follows, as the road shifts from paved to bumpy.

"Have you noticed, since you've been back, the way people block you out because you moved away?" He asks.

"Not really," I lie. "Well...maybe a little. But I don't really care to join the inner circle anyways. Never have."

"That's true. Something I've always admired about you."

I change the subject. "I looked you up on the internet, you know. I always knew you were smart as hell, but I'm impressed Jake. Owning your own law practice? That's amazing. And you must be doing well if you can afford to own a place in West Van."

He grins ear to ear. "I bought the law firm from someone I knew in the business who was retiring, so it's not as overachieving as it seems at my age. But, I'm doing alright, that's for sure."

"I've never known you to be modest," I tease. He smirks, but doesn't say anything else. Silence grows. We must be thinking the same thing. So I decide to bring it up.

"You never thought to stop by and see me?"

He hesitates, thinking about something and then letting it go, changing tact. "I wasn't sure how you would react. You kinda just left after you graduated and never looked back."

"I'm sorry, Jake."

I see his grip tighten against the steering wheel, making his knuckles white. "I thought for the longest time both you and her had left me. I had some really low points."

I hold both my hands in my lap and nod. "It's okay if you blame me."

He stares straight ahead. "I blame myself more than anyone. I should've asked more questions."

"Me too," I say, almost a whisper.

He parks the car in the gravel lot now and shuts it off; the world becomes silent.

"Anyways, enough of being sad. I brought you out here because it's one of my favourite places in the world." He attempts a smile and hops out, looking at the sky. It has turned to more of a grey and the sun has seemed to slip behind the heavy clouds.

"Great day for a beach visit," I quip as I get out.

He smiles. "Good thing we aren't heading to the beach then, smartass."

He grabs his raincoat and a smaller backpack than my own, pulling out a pair of women's hiking boots. He hands them to me and I don't get it at first. I turn them around and check the size. Size 7. My size.

"How'd you know?" I ask.

He shrugs. "I remembered."

"Did you buy these just for this trip?" I ask, surprised.

"Yeah, so what. Think of it like a little present and motivation to get you being outdoorsy again. I know you well enough to know you probably never made time for it in Vancouver."

I roll my eyes. He's right of course. "Thanks, I guess."

"Don't be weird about it. I just have a lot of money now and don't know what to do with it," he chuckles, shrugging his shoulders.

He waits for me to put them on then heads towards the trees. I follow hesitantly. We're going in the direction of the forest, which means if we keep heading this way, we will get to the caves where Abby was found.

I'm wondering if spelunking is in his itinerary, when he turns around and says "don't worry, we aren't heading to the caves."

I relax a little and follow his large footsteps through the muddy trail. The trees are bright green and their leaves let down little spurts of warm rainwater which are now gathering on their tops. Chipmunks dart through the path ahead, finding the perfect spots to stay dry while evaluating the forest's new guests.

"God, I love these trees," I say out loud. "The look of them, the smell of them, the way they make you feel when you're engulfed by them. I had forgotten the sort of peace they provide, a quiet spot in the woods to let your worries fall away. I'm kicking myself now for never making time for this kind of stuff in Vancouver."

"I was hoping you'd remember that feeling."

"It's been too long. Thank you."

The caves are just up ahead, but Jake turns right suddenly, off the path and veering behind them. We make our way through what looks like a deer path, with branches tugging at my loose hair and damp clothing. We arrive at a mountain side that appears to be a dead end, when Jake takes out something skinny and long from his bag. He shimmies it, making it longer, or rather, taller, and reaches up to a bundled rope I had not seen previously. He hooks it and it falls to the ground with a thump.

I must be looking at him strangely, because he hesitates before he says, "Are you good to climb up with me?"

I measure the height of the cliff which seems to be about thirty feet off the ground. So about, the regular size of a first-floor building...but also six times the size of me.

"You want me to climb up the side of this cliff, unharnessed, in the slippery rain?"

He shrugs and nods his head; what he deems a reasonable response. He likely doesn't know about my chronic pain disease.

"Are you nuts?"

"Come on, it'll be fun. Or are you not fun anymore?"

He's baiting me and I hesitate. I used to love rock climbing.

"The rock's dry," he says, "but I'll go first and show you how it's done."

He pulls his backpack tighter to his body and readies himself with the rope. I watch him effortlessly climb the rock face, paying close attention to where he rests his foot on the outward pieces of rock in which he pulls himself up to the next step with his thighs. It takes him all of five minutes. Jake is lean and muscular, a total athlete's body. I *might* check out his ass, as he does so. He's a lot more toned than the skinny lanky kid I remember. He still wears his smile easily but the lightness he had when we were younger is lost.

"The view from up here is worth the climb, I promise Jane. Trust me."

He tries to assure me that this manoeuvre is safe and that he has climbed this over a hundred times. He comes here when he needs a break from it all, he says. For some peace and quiet.

I check the laces on my boots and zip up my jacket. My backpack is light enough that it doesn't throw off my weight. I grab hold of the rope, and put my right foot in the first foot hole launching myself upward, the coarseness of it scratching my palms and making them slip slightly. Better do this fast. My hands climb the rope, fingers wrapping around it and straining my knuckles, as my boots find their place among the rock, helping me scale it. My leg muscles are burning, my heart beating out of my chest, but I love it. I haven't rock climbed in ages but I remember its appeal, and it greets me like an old friend.

I just hope it doesn't make me more sore than I already am.

I'm outdoors, with the cooling breeze and the fresh air of the forest surrounding me. I'm almost to the top when I misjudge my grip on a foothold and slip. I scrape my right kneecap on the rock, tearing the skin. I curse. My arms are still wrapped around the rope though and Jake is on the top edge, calmly looping his arms under my armpits, and pulling me up effortlessly, as if I didn't weigh a thing. We tumble to the earthy top of the rock face, and I let out a rush of air. I try to calm my nerves. Out of nowhere, I start to laugh. Uncontrollably. In fact, my entire body is shaking from it and I can't stop. Tears are running down my face.

Jake just stares at me with a slight smile, then takes out a first aid kit from his bag as he inspects my knee. I am laid out on the ground, as a starfish, and he's sitting beside me now. He inches closer, hovering above me and places his hands softly on my shoulders. He's looking me in the eyes and begins to breathe slowly and loudly, exaggerating his breaths. Without him having to say anything, I mirror him and eventually calm down. He wipes the tears that have accumulated on my face.

"Thank you," I murmur. "I thought I would never stop."

"I thought I'd lost you there," he teases. "But then I remembered how we used to do it."

He's talking about the panic attacks I used to have in high school. Abby used to be my person; the one who would help me breathe and focus on the task at hand. After she left, I would call Jake, and he would help me over the phone. Bobby also took over, for times when I felt too embarrassed to call Jake, breathless and mute upon him answering the line.

"That was a fucking close call," I manage finally. "Are you trying to kill me?"

"No Jane. I'm just trying to take you out of your comfort zone and remind you how fun it is to be alive. I know you had it."

I'm a little peeved at how relaxed he is about me almost tumbling to my demise but then I'm distracted by the searing pain coming from my leg. He's pouring alcohol over it and I grunt at him, like a wild animal. He puts a healthy amount of Polysporin on it and a coaster-size brown bandage which covers it perfectly.

"Great. Now I have a knee bandage to match my ankle."

He gives me a curious stare but I wave him off. "Never mind."

"Are you good? Can you stand?"

I roll my eyes and refuse his offering to help me up, gathering myself to my feet with only a minimal amount of pain. "Yup. Now where are you taking me?"

I follow him on mossy rock, taking care not to slip again and make a fool out of myself. The trees from the forest below still reach us up here, but if I cram my neck, I can see above some of them. The trees lead us to an opening, which overlooks the whole town and beyond. Jake pulls aside a large branch which apparently works as a hiding spot for two folding chairs and a few other camping items. I take a seat, farther from the rock's edge than him, and take in the view.

Jake cracks open a couple beers from his bag which I take greedily, feeling the cold liquid pour down my gullet and cool me off. The clouds have parted and the sun is out once again. B.C. weather is always unpredictable.

"How did you find this?" I ask him, watching tiny vehicles peek through the forest below us, on their way to work or town. The town itself looks like one of those miniature crafted cities, where people with way more patience than me, create in their spare time.

"You know I've always loved the forest. It was an escape for me in my childhood, just the same as it is an escape for me now. I found it when I was about 13." He eyes me as he says this, anticipating my next words.

"And why are you only showing me now?" I tease.

"I wanted to have a spot just for myself. Don't take it personally."

I nod. I'm an only child so I always had plenty of time to myself. Jake never had any growing up.

"To be honest," he continues, 'it gets a little lonely up here sometimes. It's so quiet, and it's a great place to think, but then I wonder about why I prefer being alone so much, and then I realize that it's good for a while, but not always. You know?"

"Yeah. I get what you mean. Sometimes even when I'm with others, I feel alone. Do you ever get like that?"

"Yes, but I don't feel that way right now."

I look up at him and meet his eyes, then look down, averting his gaze as I agree with him. "Me neither."

We enjoy easy silence and finish off another beer each. He tells me I'm the second person he has brought up here. The first was Abby. I hesitate at the third beer, because there's no way I can get down that cliff being even slightly intoxicated. That's when Jake tells me there's another route out.

"There's another way out, and you took me the dangerous-as-shit way? Thanks, Jake." My voice remains playful.

He cracks open our beers and we spend the rest of the day catching up on each other's lives, and sometimes talking straight nonsense. I feel extremely guilty about not staying in touch with him when I left, and I say as much. He brushes me off and tells me not to worry about it, but not to do it again. I rest my head on his shoulder after the third beer and tell him about how I'm not sure I am capable of doing my job anymore and how Bobby might have lost faith in me too. His hand rests on my hand, gently holding me in place.

"You can do anything you put your heart into Jane. You've always been like that, even when you were younger. And I must admit, detective work is your calling. I looked you up on the internet when I found you were back in town, and your record is amazing."

I try to mention the Marcus thing, but he stops me, as if he can still read my mind after all these years.

"No one is perfect. But as a detective, you soared." He lays his head down on top of mine. "But, if you really think you can't handle it right now, if you're not just being hard on yourself and having a pity party, then just walk away from it. Everyone will understand."

I take in his words and wonder if I have the courage to walk away from it all. Leave the RCMP and become a gardener like Judie, or a baker like Sara, or even a bartender like Laryssa. Those jobs would be a lot easier on the mind. The opposite to such a dark profession that makes you second-guess the meaning of life and intentions of everyone close to you.

I shake my head. "I wish I could do something else, but I can't. This is my calling. It's in my blood."

So is murder. My inner voice whispers. I push those thoughts out.

I don't say it out loud, but we both know it to be true: the darkness feels like home, and it calls me back every time.

CHAPTER 20 - JANE

Jake led us through a back way, with another rope, but this time the drop was much smaller. Still, he wrapped the rope around my waist and under my butt, and helped me down gradually. We went for a bite to eat at the family restaurant, which became awkward when I noticed Liam was a couple of booths down with another woman. She was pretty and blonde, and wearing a short summer dress with a denim jacket. I immediately got jealous but did notice there was only one plate on the table, in front of him, and they ended up leaving separately. Perhaps she just walked over to say hello.

The whole situation was uncomfortable. Liam walked by our booth on the way out, seeming shocked to see us there, but recovering quickly. I felt my cheeks redden as I realized what this must look like to him. Jake puffed out a bit when Liam froze at our table and for a minute, I worried someone would say something. But no one did and that was almost worse. Liam simply said a polite "Hello," addressing each of us individually, and kept on walking.

"You know him?" Jake asked, curiously.

"Yes, we sort of work together." I said, which was partly true. He didn't grill me on it any further, but he was much more distant through dinner than he had been earlier.

I give Jake a hug goodbye after we eat and thank him for the day. He checks with me that I'm on my way back to Bobby's, which I lie and say that I am, even though I'm not entirely sure yet. He tells me he will see me around.

I walk down to the station, entering from the side entrance, but only Jackson is there so I make a quick exit, still embarrassed about our last exchange. I spend a moment staring at Miranda's photo on the door. My next stop is the Raven and I go inside just to look around and see if anyone I know is here. I catch sight of Langdon in the corner with a bunch of guys surrounding him and the same pretty blonde from Liam's table on his lap. I don't see Sara anywhere and he notices me staring. He pushes the girl off quickly and she stumbles forward, into one of his friend's arms. *Asshole,* I think loudly as if he can hear it. He puts on a fake smile and raises his glass to cheer me but I look away.

Laryssa calls me over from the bar as I'm trying to leave, and asks me who I'm looking for.

"I don't honestly know," I say, barely a whisper, remembering our last exchange and not trusting her one bit.

"It's Wednesday sweetie. No one from your crowd comes here on Wednesday." I try to read her but she's unfailing at this southern charm charade. "Plus, there are a few reporters in here that I'm guessing you're trying to avoid."

I look around the bar but can't differentiate local from outsider. I sigh. "Thanks, I'm going to call it a night." She's called to the other end of the bar and I'm about to turn and walk out until I notice a tiny photo inside of her open wallet on the counter. That catches my complete attention. It's tucked just out of sight near the coffee maker behind the bar. Curiosity makes me change my mind. As she makes her way back over, I ask if she can just grab me a water.

"Of course, darlin'. Are you staying or leaving?"

"About to head out," I reply.

"Okay, I'll grab you a water bottle in the back then." She grins at me and with a swing of the door, she's gone. I lean over the bar to get a closer look. It's a photo of Laryssa a few years ago, with a curly, red-haired teenager that *must* be Kim. I realize with a jolt, that I've met Kim before now, when we were both teenagers. In Laryssa's car. The morning Abby went missing.

The door swings open again, and Laryssa comes back out, extending a cold water bottle my way. I lean backwards suddenly, more of a jump than I had intended, and hope she didn't notice.

I reach into my wallet and put down a five-dollar bill.

"Honey, it's only water. This one's on the house." I don't like owing her anymore than I already do.

I pick up the bill and stick it into the tip jar instead. "Thanks Laryssa. Have a goodnight."

I leave the bar and can feel her eyes burning into my back with every step. I'm thinking of her words from our last conversation: *you owe me, and I'm going to cash in soon.*

I remember back to that day. I wasn't the only one acting like I was hiding a big secret.

I decide to head back to Bobby's and risk running into more reporters. I want somewhere that feels like home. Maybe I'll even catch Bob there and have one of those honest conversations with him, like we always used to. Talk to him about that night and Laryssa blackmailing me and my dad's involvement with Briggs, and the whole lot of it. He would help me work out a solution. Wouldn't he?

The sun has gone down, yet there is still a bit of light in the sky. It's a blanket of dark blue, instead of pure black. I hardly notice I'm driving faster than usual, because I'm anxious to get home and see if Bobby has softened a little. I'm thoroughly checking the sides of the road which is lined with dark forest, for deer and other critters who might decide to cross the road in front of my car. That's when I notice the trees dancing to my right, from the top of the hill to the bottom, like a horror movie starring a man-eating monster or hungry T-rex.

I'm not completely sure what it is that I see. I'm supposed to wear glasses for night driving, but of course I haven't gotten around to it yet. I'd guess it was a grizzly though I don't know what it's running from. I see flashes between the trees of a large black shape tumbling down the hill at an extremely fast pace. I'm so fascinated by it that I don't realize the spike strip on the road's tight corner until the last minute and by the time I press the brake it's too late.

My tires blow out from the strip, and the black shape hurtles towards me from the right and slams into the side of my car, which was still moving over 100km/hour: flipping it on its side and dragging it into the other lane down into the ditch, and finally landing it on its roof. It happens so fast that I can't do anything but close my eyes and hang on for the ride.

The crash is excruciatingly loud. It sounds like I'm stuck in a tin can that is exploding from the inside out. I suppose I am. My body is jolted painfully in one fell swoop and everything goes dark.

I must have passed out at some point, because I wake up with my head hanging in the air, the airbag having deflated, and still dangling from my seat which is now on the roof. I'm hanging upside down.

I'm glad I was wearing my seatbelt, even if I now have a rash above my waist from where it's held me in place as my body battered around the vehicle. My bad shoulder is screaming at me from the force of the seatbelt but I try to ignore it for now. There is a ton of pressure in my head, my vision is cloudy and my ears are ringing, as I try to focus. I must have smashed my head because I can feel the wetness at the base of my forehead, but also because the now-deflated airbag is covered in wet, red smears. I try to focus my attention on the dangers surrounding me: broken glass from my driver's side window, a small fall when I unbuckle my seatbelt. Then I remember the possible bear outside. With all my strength, I reach around for my backpack which was in the passenger seat, but is now behind me. Not very helpful. I crank my shoulder back, reaching desperately, and manage to hook the loop of it with my index finger. I pull it towards me and take out my hunting knife and chuck it out the window for now. I check my limbs, which are all intact (thank God), and straddle the steering wheel, using my thighs to hold me in place, and plant the palm of my left hand on the roof. With my right, I unbuckle the belt and fall in a heap. I rearrange myself, pulling my legs around so that I am on all fours and peek outside the car. I do not see or hear any bear. Although it was a hard hit for the car, it's quite possible the animal survived. I crawl out on my stomach, bag in hand, careful not to snag myself on the glass, and enter the fresh air of the night. I pick up my knife.

It's pitch black now—no streetlights out here in the country—but my flashlight helps me find what knocked into my car. It isn't a grizzly after all. It's a fucking massive tractor tire. Two in fact.

One close to my car, the one that probably hit it, and another farther ahead that must've missed me. They're probably about 500 to 600 pounds each. I feel lightheaded and about to throw up. I leave the tires where they are. I turn to see the damage on my car. It's totalled.

Where the hell did these come from? I cross to the other side and follow some tire tracks up the side of the hill. They're spaced apart, about five metres in-between, as if they bounced down the hill at a fair speed. I know this hill goes upward into the forest, and can be accessed easily by a passing road above. But someone would've had to push the tires to have them gain speed like that and come tumbling down. Could they have been aiming for me or was it an accident? I remember the spike strip. This definitely wasn't a coincidence.

I take out my phone and take a few quick photos of the scene then move the spike strip. I don't want anyone else getting into a crash. Then I dial the station. The operator picks up and quickly transfers me to Kenny who answers on the second ring. I tell him what happened, sitting down on one of the tires, as my head is getting fairly dizzy. He's shouting at Jackson to call Bobby's cellphone.

"Just get yourself safely to the side of the road and we'll be there in a few minutes," he says. "I'm going to send Bobby to the top of the hill to investigate. I'll come down to your level, see if there's anything I can see and pick you up."

But just as he hangs up, I hear a low pitch crack in the air and a metallic ring behind me from my car. I flinch and turn to see a bullet hole in the side bumper, just as another crack sounds in the air. I immediately fall to my stomach and crawl as fast as I can behind my car, which is safer. A bullet whizzes above me, a few feet above my back.

A car's headlights come into view as I'm almost to the other side of my car. I wave frantically from where I am lying down on the road and hope the driver sees me. The jeep pulls over. It's Liam and he's jumping out of the vehicle and running over to me.

"No!" I scream. "Shooter! Get down!"

Another bullet grazes Liam's forearm as he falls on all fours. He leaps up a minute later, running straight for me and pulling me up from the ground and throwing me behind his jeep.

I fall forward but steady myself with my hands. I'm trying to catch my breath when I hear a "Holy shit," from Liam. He's taking in the scene.

He looks at me, his hands lightly brushing aside my sticky hair as he leans over me inspecting my head wound. I haven't looked in a mirror but I'm assuming from his drained face that it doesn't look good.

"Why are you always covered in blood when I see you?" He asks.

I laugh at his comment, but apparently he's dead serious.

My heart is pounding in my ears–*thump thump thump*–then a dull buzzing. I fight to keep myself awake. I stumble a little from my crouch position and he catches me in his big hands.

"I have no idea how you just walked away from that crash." He tries to get me to sit down but I shrug him off and search through my backpack for a small packet of pills which I swallow dry. It should help me focus even though my head is fuzzy.

"What did you just take?" He asks, slightly pissed. "We have to immobilize your head and ice it to reduce the swelling. Let me take a peek and make sure you're alright." His paramedic brain is kicking in.

"Just a couple of Aspirin."

"Shit Jane, that can increase the bleeding. Didn't you take First Aid training?" He lets out an annoyed sigh and then softens, "You probably weren't even thinking straight. What happened?"

I explain the situation quickly and he eyes the forest as I do. So far, the shots have stopped.

"Can you text Kenny and Bobby and let them know there's a shooter in the forest?" I hand him my phone. "I'd do it myself but I sort of am too dizzy, right now." He takes my phone and quickly thumbs out the texts, his eyes focused on the direction of the forest.

"Guess that means the tires weren't an accident," he says, as if seconding my thoughts.

He asks me a series of medical questions to assess me for a concussion. He holds up his finger in front of my face, moving it back and forth but I can't follow it for the life of me. It looks like he has numerous fingers dancing in my face.

He slowly opens the rear door of his jeep and takes out some orange pylons which he throws in the direction of our cars and the glass on the road. It's not perfect but it's the safest we can do for now. My floodlight is hanging off the car so it's no use to us right now. He keeps his own brights on, lighting up our path.

"Jane...Pretty sure you have a concussion. I think whoever was out there might be gone now. I can get you in my jeep, and then I'll run to the other–"

I cut him off. "I have to check the forest. We're wasting time here." I feel myself panting. "Someone just tried to take me out." I pause, reading his expression. His eyes are wide with adrenaline, inspecting every visible part of me, presumably coming to the conclusion I'm insane. "Do you have anything that can be used as a weapon? I don't have my gun."

"Your head is bleeding. You need to stay still. Just let *me* go." he tries.

I shake my head. The dizziness I'm feeling is maybe clouding my thoughts. "The guys are still five or more minutes out and if there is someone in the woods, maybe our killer, they'll be long gone by then. I have the training behind me. Those pills helped. I'm going. You decide if you want to come flank me."

"You're a damn wrecking ball, Jane." He nearly growls.

Marcus used to call me his train wreck. He was my clear head thinker, the one who would call me back from the edge before doing something reckless. He taught me how to be more patient, more thorough, more level-headed on the job. He was cool, calm and collected.

Marcus is dead now.

I bring myself back to the present. Liam gives up and reaches into his jeep again. He has a crowbar in one hand and a fire axe in the other. He holds out the crowbar for me. I glare at him.

He glares back. "I don't want you slicing yourself open with it. A crowbar will be easier for you to use right now. *Safer.*"

I don't even answer him. I grab it and rush into the forest and he follows. Me with my crowbar, my flashlight and my concussion; Liam with his small medical light and fire axe.

We make it to the tree line and hide ourselves behind some large trees. Nothing happens. No shots are fired. I give him the signal to continue. I'm crawling up the hill on all fours and once on steadier ground, I start sprinting towards the right. Liam heads more to the left. There's a light source up above shining toward us, lighting up the forest in dark shadows, and another light coming from the right but facing toward the other vehicle. They look like headlights. I stop to catch my breath, and lean against a tree for support. I can hardly see and every step I take makes me feel nauseous. My body is screaming with pain and I try to tell myself this will be over soon and I'll get them to hook me up to some really good pain meds at the hospital.

I catch movement from my right along with the snap of a twig, and turn in that direction. A tall dark figure, less than a metre away, darts in the opposite direction. Without thinking, I sprint after it with all the energy I have left.

"I have my gun!" I lie, yelling in-between gasps for air. "Stop or I'll shoot!"

They continue running in a zig zag, ignoring my warning. I whip the crowbar as hard as I can toward them and it snaps against a tree a foot away from their head, making them trip forward. They jump back up and start running left, towards the headlights at the top of the hill. I'm getting closer and closer. The figure isn't very fast and I've always been a runner. I close the gap in no time, dropping my flashlight and thrusting myself in the air towards them, toppling us both to the ground.

I hit my face against their back on the way down and it leaves me momentarily blind. The person squirms under my weight and uses my hesitation to roll out from under me and start hailing down punches to my gut. My arms are protecting my face but they grab the hair on the top of my head and smash it on the ground with a thud. I throw up what's left in my stomach, choking on some of it until I lean my head to the side, spewing the rest out. My ears are ringing again. I'm in a vulnerable position. I resort to my training and start using my kicks and screaming as loud I can for Liam to hear me. I see an opening so I punch as hard as I can and my fist collides with what I believe is a rib. I hear a crunch. The person screams and falls back to the ground. I crawl on top of them, turning them over on their stomach in one quick exchange and they continue to scream in agony. The shrieking sounds familiar. I use my knees to hold down their hands. Just as I get them defenceless, Liam shows up completely out of breath and wide-eyed.

"What can I do?" he yells.

"Help me get them up standing," I say to him. "And *you*," I say to the hooded figure, "don't do anything stupid or I'll break another rib."

They murmur a fuck you and that's when I *know* I've placed the voice.

"No fucking way," I manage, as Liam pulls the small body up, and I rip the hood down.

Miranda stares back at me, anger radiating off of her. Her eyes are wild like a rabid animal, blood is seeping from her mouth down her pointy chin, and black tears are racing down her face.

"If we go down, you go down," she spits at me.

~~~

Bobby and Kenny arrive shortly after, with Jamieson and Francis in tow. Bobby does his best wobbly run over to me when he gets there and pulls me in for a soft but firm hug.

"For fuck's sake Jane, how many times do I have to tell you to go slow around those corners?" I wince at his yelling and he pulls me in for another hug.

They found Harrison's truck abandoned at the top of the hill and another set of tire tracks from another truck of similar size.

They've arrested Miranda and brought her to the hospital in a separate vehicle.

"You really know how to make the most of a leave of absence, I'll give you that." Jamieson says to me after getting my statement. I almost tell him to fuck off, but I believe he was just trying to lighten the mood.

I'm resting my head back on the seat of Liam's jeep as he drives me to the ER. I'm holding various gauze strips to my face where it won't stop bleeding.

The staff at the hospital are waiting for us with a wheelchair. I go ahead and take it. No sense in being proud when I could fall flat on my face.

Both nurses' eyes go wide as they take me in. Dr. Jenkins is inside, but instead of her usual clean-cut outfit, she's in ripped jeans and a plain white T-shirt. She has gorgeous red locks of curly hair, not in a tight bun this time but spread loose and reaching halfway down her back. She has piercing blue eyes beneath black-rimmed glasses and voluminous red lips pouted over straight white teeth. All of this, I realize, makes her look more like the world's next top model than a small-town doctor. She is 100 per cent what most men's fantasies are built upon and I'm immediately self-conscious having barely brushed my hair today.

A nurse hands her a lab coat which she shrugs on effortlessly.

"Hey Jane, we really have to stop meeting like this," she says lightheartedly, with a disarming smile that quickly turns serious when she gives me a proper onceover.

"Yeah, well, I know how to keep things exciting, don't I?"

"How are you feeling right now? Be honest with me." I tell her my list of immediate symptoms and she looks me over as the nurses help me into the hospital bed. Dr. Jenkins is in work-mode, completely plain-faced now, no emotion, just concentration. It's oddly comforting.

"Hey Liam, good to see you. Now, tell me the rest," she adds. I notice they're more than friendly with each other. They're *familiar*. Comfortable.

Liam fills in any other blanks that she needs. She shines a light in my eyes and I curse. She gives me a quick head exam, as the nurses wipe my arms and legs off and bandage me up. She tests my coordination and balance which are poor. They hook me up to an IV drip. She stitches a small cut on my head from when Miranda smashed my head into a branch. The other cut, from the crash itself, is easily bandaged up. The bleeding made it seem worse than it was.

"We should do coffee or something, sometime, so I'm not just seeing you in the ER," she says, giving me a warm smile. "We *outsiders* have to stick together, you know."

I wonder if she forgets our last exchange at the hospital or if this has something to do with Liam. Maybe she's just being the bigger person and understands I wasn't myself before.

But I take a minute too long to answer, and she switches back to her professional identity.

"I understand you've thrown up a few times as well, so I'm going to send you for another CT scan just to be safe. Okay?"

I give her a thumb's up.

"And I'm going to inject this into your arm. It will help with the nausea."

She pricks me with the needle and I pray the nausea will pass. Despite cutting parts of my shoulder on the broken window, my knee is actually my worst abrasion, and they coat it with that special paste. She tells me I have to stay for at least 48 hours, so they can evaluate my condition. It might take hours or days for more signs to appear. I groan as I pull on my hospital gown. I'm relieved that they now give you two gowns, one facing the right way, the other the wrong way. No accidental mooning for me.

"You can ask someone to bring you pyjamas if you prefer them over the hospital gowns," Dr Jenkins says, noticing my displeasure with them. "They just have to be loose fitting and easy to access if we need to inspect your wounds again."

I smile. "Thank you. And sorry about my attitude last time. Really. I wasn't being fair."

She waves me off. "No worries. I appreciate you saying that, though." She gives me a warm smile before leaving the room.

They give me the CT scan right away, then bring me back to bed.

I can hear one of the nurses outside of my room ask Dr Jenkins if she should suspend my visitors for the night to allow me to rest. I shout out to her. "No thank you! You need to send all visitors to me when they arrive."

The nurse pokes her head around the corner and gives me a disappointed look.

"It's police business." I add firmly.

Dr. Jenkins cuts in. "It's fine, but try to limit their time here. Jane, you need rest. Mentally and physically."

"I know. I promise to take it seriously."

She nods as she walks out of the room. "Goodnight Jane."

There's a gentle knock on the door a few minutes later and my eyes fly open. I'm surprised to see Liam in my room.

"Have you been here this whole time?" I ask.

He attempts a smile, but there's something dark behind his eyes. Worry, I think. "Yes. I wanted to make sure you had everything you needed and were okay."

I look over at the wall clock. "It's been over four hours since I was dropped off?"

He shrugs.

"You don't have to stay."

He waves me off. "I do. I spoke to Bobby and told him someone should probably stand guard in case whoever helped Miranda roll those tires comes to finish the job. He was easily convinced. But I would've stayed anyway."

"I think we can guess who helped her with that." My voice is hoarse and dry and doesn't sound like me. "I thought the guys were watching Harrison's house?"

"Bobby says he must've snuck out the back."

"Of course." I try to relax into the pillow haven that the grumpy nurse created for me and change the subject.

"I think I'm starting to grow on Dr. Jenkins." I say jokingly. "What is she like outside of this setting?"

"You two are a lot alike actually."

"Stubborn?"

He nods. "Stubborn, resilient and defensive. Brilliant and hard-working."

I take in his words and picture Dr. Jenkins with her messy red locks and her worn blue jeans. She probably got out of bed and changed before coming here, just to make sure I was well taken care of. I make a mental note to thank her properly when I see her again.

"I guess you have a type then." I say with what I hope is a charming but mischievous smile.

He tries to read my face as his brows knit together. "If that's your way of asking if there was ever anything going on between me and Kim, yes, we have some history. But we decided we were more compatible as friends."

This revelation makes my heart feel a bit heavy with what I can only guess is jealousy. I am so average compared to her.

I hesitate, about to try and restore this conversation when Bobby storms in the door and straight over to me. Worry is written all over his face. He puts the back of his palm on my head so I remind him that concussions don't usually provide fevers.

He calls me a smartass but I can hear the waver in his voice.

"What is it?"

"Well, there's bad news, then really bad news. Which one do you want first?"

I stare at him blankly. "Is there any type of other news in this town?"

He ignores my sarcasm and offers, "The bad news it is then."

He explains that Miranda is refusing to talk without her lawyer but is still sticking to her story of working alone and being at the wrong place at the wrong time. The rifle that was used to shoot at us was left at the scene, and after I hinted that Miranda was the one with hunting experience, not Harrison, Jamieson lied and told her we found her fingerprints on it. In reality, it would take weeks for us to get the rifle processed, but the lie worked. She was spooked enough to call a lawyer and ask for a deal. The fact she has been hiding from the police and not coming in for their interview doesn't bode well for her either.

"We returned to the forest to search for anything useful and found quite the scene."

"Go on..." I say, impatience settling in my bones.

"Well, the truck that was parked at the top of the hill, a bit into the forest, was left there. It's Harrison's truck. There are dirt marks in the bed of the truck that match the tractor tires. There were tracks from both falling out of the truck and one rolled down the hill and hit a tree. It looks like they brought it closer to the road and then pushed it with all their might into the direction of the highway. The other tire that hit your car gained momentum on the last stretch and that's what sent it flying in your direction. Unfortunately, you would've probably missed it if you sped up or slowed down instead of veering." He gives me a sympathetic but slightly judgmental look. "Also, if there was no spike strip."

"Obviously." I mumble.

Liam shakes his head. "Stupid assholes. Could've killed someone."

"I believe that was their intention," I point out.

"I want to push for attempted murder." Bobby says firmly.

I nod slowly. "Any sign of Harrison? Miranda couldn't have managed those 500-pound tires herself. She's a twig."

"Well, we have a few eyewitnesses reporting seeing a tractor tire in Harrison's truck...but no one could correctly identify the driver because they were apparently wearing a black hoodie and black sunglasses. No one could remember if there was anyone on the passenger side."

"Okay...well where is he now?"

"This is where it gets weird. There are tracks from a smaller car pulling up behind Harrison's." He stops, thinking things through. "It looks like he was dragged from the driver's side of his truck and possibly put into the trunk of this other car."

I feel my whole body go cold. "What are you implying?"

"We believe he was abducted. Or there was a third person involved in this and they made the scene look very convincing. There was even blood on the driver's side window of his truck."

"What the hell? Did you tell Miranda this?"

"I didn't. Jamieson is in there with her now. Or they're waiting for her lawyer. I wanted to come check on you and he insisted on carrying out the interrogation without me. I'm heading back there soon."

"Where would they have even gotten the tractor tires?" Liam asks.

"Miranda's family has a huge scrap yard at the edge of town. It wouldn't be hard to get their hands on them." Bobby says.

I start to feel my headache come back. My hands instinctively go to massage my temple and my eyebrows. "Is that all the bad news?" I ask, wanting this to be over and to sleep.

He sits on the edge of the bed and almost whispers to me, as if lowering his voice will soften the blow. "Your concussion means you *really* need to take it easy. You can't work the case on your own time like I know you want to. For the next two weeks at least. Mentally or physically straining yourself can make your symptoms worse, possibly even cause you serious brain injury."

"Bobby..." I plead.

"I'm sorry Jane. Take the two weeks and then we can talk about bringing you back in. I haven't got a good read on how Jamieson feels about you yet...but anyways, let's talk about this later." He leans down and kisses the top of my head. "So glad you're okay, kiddo. You're my priority. Not the case. OK?"

"Don't let the locals hear you say that, Bob."

He smiles mischievously. "Fuck 'em."

It's so absurd hearing that from him that it makes me laugh out loud. Liam laughs too. It hurts but it also feels good.

Before they leave, Liam tells me he will stop by tomorrow to drop me off some real food, if that's alright with me. Bobby's eyes dart between the two of us, reading the situation and making him smile slightly. I tell him that sounds good. They turn off the main light on their way out and I close my heavy lids, drifting into sleep, and being woken up every hour by a different nurse, one who treats me more like a test subject than a patient.

~~~

I wake up while it's still dark, this time not by the grumpy nurse. I notice all the lights are turned off, and although I find it odd, I close my eyes again and try to fall back asleep. But something keeps me awake. The hairs on the back of my neck prickle. I feel the eyes peering at me through the forest again. Paranoia gets the better of me so I open my eyes, and I catch a movement in the corner of the room. A shadow moves ever so slightly. I hold my breath and listen as best I can, but the ringing is still in my ears and I find it hard to see.

"Hello?" I think I hear a breath inhale sharply. I'm being nuts.

I close my eyes again but just as I'm losing consciousness, I think I hear the door close lightly.

CHAPTER 21 - JANE

Liam visits both days around noon, with some bakery sandwiches from Sara's. On the second day, there's a handwritten note from Sara in it, wishing me to feel better and that she will try to stop by and visit later today.

As I read it, Liam says, "Kinda weird of her not to be here. Did you two get into a fight or something?"

I shrug. "No. But it's fine. She has a business to run."

"She also has employees." He hints.

I smile and unwrap my sandwich, taking a big bite. "It's okay. Really. But thanks."

"So, this is it huh? A day in the life of Jane Beckett?"

"What do you mean?"

"I mean, bodies dropping everywhere, shooters in town, car crashes, concussions and broken noses?"

"Well... I think you have the order wrong. But yeah. I'm a real treat." I can't meet his eyes right now because I'm not sure if this is 100% playful or if he's realizing I am a mess of a person and not worth the trouble.

He seems to sense my discomfort. His voice gets a little softer. "I don't mind it, you know. I'm a first responder too. I signed up for this life." His smile is warm when I look up and then he bursts out laughing.

I'm startled out of my thoughts.

"You have some egg salad on your chin. Sort of looks like baby poop." He reaches over and hands me a napkin. I look back at my sandwich, considering. I shrug and take another large mouthful. Liam smirks.

"I have a tough stomach." I say with a smirk of my own. "So, tell me more about why you moved here?" I already know half of it but want to hear it from him this time.

"Well, I originally grew up in Toronto but we moved to B.C. when I was a teenager and I especially loved Vancouver. I had an aunt who lived there and she let me stay for a few years 'cause my home life wasn't that great and she had a soft spot for me."

He catches the slightest reaction in my eyebrows before I can tamp it down.

"Yeah, I know. It was a selfish move. I left my mom and my older sister Amy to deal with an abusive Dad. But my sister only had a year left before she was supposed to be off to college and at the time...I just felt like I needed to get out and set myself up in the world and that I would go back for my mom when I could." His face is flushed.

"It's okay Liam...I'm not–" He waves me off.

"Anyways, I finished high school, graduated college with honours. Worked really hard to become a paramedic. Then one day, my mom shows up with a big belly and tells me she's pregnant with Julia. That's when our lives changed." He fidgets with the wrapper of his sandwich and then gets up and throws it in the

246

trash. He slumps back in the chair and throws his hair back out of his face. "My mom and Julia, once she was born, bounced between Amy and I, but my dad would often show up and make a scene. We got into quite a few brawls on the lawn. Some of which, resulted in visits from the police. I'm not proud of it but I did what I had to, to protect my mother and my sisters."

My ears are ringing, I'm listening so hard. I wait until he feels comfortable to go on.

"We ended up moving to Isinbury 'cause it was far away..." he says, softer now. "Our father, like I said, was a violent man. He gambled and he drank and he ruined our lives."

I'd like to say something like, "That's horrible Liam," or "I'm so sorry you went through that," but I feel we are past the niceties now and I always find it insulting when people downplay my troubles with word vomit, so instead I say matter-of-factly, "So you moved up here for a fresh start."

He nods.

"And he didn't follow you up here and cause trouble for you guys?"

He gets quiet now, and I realize this might be a step too far, before he continues.

"He got involved with some bad people and ended up in jail for aggravated assault. It got him away from all of us, which was good, and then we decided to move anyway, for a fresh start, and everything turned around for the better. Well, mostly." He means until his mother got too sick. "Isinbury has been welcoming enough, but I still sometimes feel like an outcast, even though it's been a few years now."

I guess we have more in common than I thought.

He studies my face as I fidget with my hospital wristband.

"I don't have a cheery backstory but I figured it was better to be honest with you about it. I know how it looks."

I shrug and pretend not to know what he means.

"You have a terrible poker face for a cop, you know," he says, with a hint of teasing in his voice. It makes me smile, though awkwardly. I look up at him and his eyes soften a little. He's nervous, waiting for me to say something.

"I've heard that many times. My face is too readable."

"Well, now you know, I also have a past."

"You seem to deal with it well, though."

"Thanks. I try."

We hear people arguing down the hall then angry, hushed voices. "What's happening?" I ask.

Liam motions for me to lay back down. "I'll go take a look."

He peeks out the door and then his face changes from curious to angry in one second. "Hey, why don't you leave her the fuck alone."

I struggle out of bed into an upright position and make my way over to the door, dizziness making me go slower than I'd like. My hand is against the wall beside me for support. I can hear Liam arguing with another man and a woman's soft voice pleading.

I pull myself out of the room and notice Liam and Jake pushing each other aggressively like they are about to fight. Dr. Jenkins is trying to pull Liam back from Jake, her dainty arms wrapped around his strong chest.

"Jake? What's going on?" I shout. His head whips over to me and then he softens completely, his arms falling back to his sides like a kid caught with his hand in the cookie jar. He leans away from Liam and starts toward me, giving them a sideways glance.

"I heard you got into a car accident, but I figured you would call me if that was true." He reaches out to touch my arm but I flinch back. He notices and his hand falls back down. "Sorry about that...misunderstanding." He nods back towards where Liam and Kim are. They're walking down the hall together. Away from us.

"What kind of misunderstanding?" I ask sternly.

He shrugs. "Kim and I were sort of on and off dating. Nothing serious. But I left something at her house and she won't just give it back. Kind of annoying."

I arch an eyebrow. "*You* had a thing with Dr. Jenkins?"

He laughs easily. "Yes, except I didn't call her *Doctor Jenkins* when we were in bed together... Though maybe that was a missed opportunity."

I just shake my head. "Gross."

"Why do you think sex is gross?"

"I don't. I just don't want to hear about *you* having sex."

"Why not? You jealous?"

I sigh, exasperated. "No. You know it's not like that." Even I can hear the blush in my voice.

He pouts theatrically. "Oh, come on. There were definitely some times where we were not *just friends*." He wiggles an eyebrow, trying to read my face. I keep it blank but assertive. "And I'm definitely hotter now than I was back then."

"And a lot less humble I see."

He pulls me in for a side hug and I let him. "Let's get you back into bed Janey."

I give him my best unimpressed look.

"What? I didn't say I was going to join you in there! You just look a little pale."

"You are *so* ridiculous."

"Yes, but you missed me." He sits down in the visitor's chair and eyes my crusts from my sandwich on the wrapper beside the bed. "Are you gonna eat those? Or do you still not eat crusts?"

"Go ahead." I wave an invitation for him to eat. "But it has my germs all over it."

He reaches out and throws the crusts in his mouth in one big swoop, giving me a smile full of food. "Even better."

"I forgot you don't have a lot of boundaries."

"Why should the two of us have boundaries? We've known each other forever." He swings a long leg over the other, and relaxes back into the chair. He definitely has double the confidence than when I knew him as a lanky, acne-pocked teenager.

I adjust one of my pillows as a nurse comes in to check on me. She gives Jake a nervous look and writes a different name on the whiteboard before leaving the room.. It reminds me of earlier. I wonder if Liam is coming back.

"Why were you and Liam about to fight in the hallway? I know I have a concussion but none of this is making any sense."

He pats my hand. "You know he has a temper, right?"

I shrug. "So do I. So do you."

"I just mean he tends to get really protective and controlling of the women in his life. It's what I've heard around town. Kim herself told me that's why she broke things off with him."

"So what, Jake. Why does that matter to me?"

He eyes me seriously. "Just letting you know in case there's something going on there. I know you have *a type*."

"Actually Jake, I don't think you know me at all anymore or what kind of men I'm into."

He flinches a little at that. "You're still the same Jane. Just a little more guarded than before."

I lay back into my pillows and close my eyes. "I need to rest. You're giving me a headache."

When I open my eyes again, the chair is empty. His footsteps out of the room were so soft, it's as if he was never really here at all.

~~~

Dr. Jenkins comes in to see me before dinner time, wearing a black and bright pink floral dress under her lab coat.

"I like your dress."

She smiles warmly. "Thanks. We have a business casual dress code here and I find it relaxes the patients much more than just white and black dress clothes." She shrugs.

"I wanted to thank you for checking on me personally." I give her my best smile. "One of the nurses mentioned you came here on your day off."

"No problem. Us women have to look out for each other, especially right now." She eyes the door before continuing. "Plus, I don't get a lot of time off, so I'm here anyway." She checks my head and fixes my bandages again.

"I'm sure the nurses could do this part for you though." I pause. "I mean, to free up your time."

"Are you trying to get rid of me?" She asks, a serious tone in her voice, glancing at me sideways. I open my mouth to answer, but she speaks before I can find a response. "I wanted to make sure I saw you myself before I felt good about discharging you." Her bright blue eyes meet mine as she sees me perk up at that. "And yes, you're good to go. I'll give Bobby a call if you want?"

"Yes please. Thank you so much."

"I just ask that you take it easy for the next week at least. You'll probably want to limit activities that require thinking and mental concentration for the next few days as they can aggravate symptoms." She gives me a stern look. "This includes work, I'm afraid."

I don't mention that I'm officially on leave right now. "So, lay in a dark room and try not to think. Got it."

"Actually, that won't help either. Though I'm sure it will feel good for a bit. You want *some* stimulus so that it isn't a shock to your system when you reintroduce things like T.V. or reading." She takes out a notepad and pen and scribbles something on it. "Here's the name of the physiotherapist I recommend. She runs her practice here at the clinic, so just ask for directions to her office at the front desk. It sounds strange to see a physio for a head injury, but she works wonders. Her instructions will be able to help you recover quicker once you're ready."

She hands me the piece of paper. "Thanks Dr. Jenkins."

"You can call me Kim." She tucks the pen behind her ear rather than back in her coat.

"Alright, thanks. Wait–Kim, can I ask you something?"

She turns and smiles. "Of course, what's up?"

"What was that about in the hall earlier?"

"Jake and I've been seeing each other but it's not working out. And Liam and him have always butted heads for some reason." She shrugs. "Anyways, take care of yourself Jane." She turns and walks out of the room.

Bobby is waiting in the lobby for me 20 minutes later, looking nervous. It immediately makes me feel less relaxed.

He tells me they've reached out to law officers from neighbouring towns to help with a manhunt for Harrison, now a prime suspect in the murders of Lilyann, Megan and Brandi. They are trying to work out a deal with Miranda.

"I can't believe it." I say, quietly. "Bobby, are we really sure they're murderers?"

He rubs my shoulder. "Darlin', they almost killed you last night. And Miranda smashed your head into a rock after, when they didn't succeed the first time. I wouldn't put it past them. Jamieson wants to push for a deal, and then a trial. The evidence matches up."

"I guess so."

He hands me a copy of the preliminary report that Jamieson has thrown together for the Crown Attorney to support Harrison's arrest.

The theory is that drugs are involved: Miranda and Harrison's side business. Something went wrong. There was some sort of mistrust happening between Lilyann and Harrison, that made her either talk to someone about something he didn't want people to know, or try to blackmail him after they broke up. That is clear from their Facebook messages, although they never outright mentioned what Lilyann knew, other than something to do with the caves. He could have been hiding drugs in there and finding Abby's body was just a coincidence. I read that this is why they are leaving Abby's case separate for now.

I swallow loudly and Bobby interrupts my reading. "They're likely going to make it a cold case since it's over 10 years old and there's not a lot of evidence available. If you're at that part yet. I know it's not ideal, but if new evidence is found they'll make it active again." He watches for my reaction. I keep it neutral. "It also means that once you're healed up, you can probably come back to work." I give him a weak smile. We both know he needs to get approval from high above him. I keep reading.

Lilyann, Brandi and Harrison's bank statements show matching amounts of cash withdrawals and deposits, pointing to a motive. Lilyann likely told her best friend Brandi, who instead of going to the cops with her information, or at least her suspicions once Lilyann was murdered, pressed Harrison for the money in her place. Miranda knew Brandi's work schedule because they worked together. Their coworkers say they were never friendly. Harrison might have tried to get Brandi to accept money for keeping quiet, before they decided to cut their loose ends.

It seems a little too tidy for me, but sometimes the most obvious answer is the right one. Blackmail with a banking trail is pretty convincing. I shut the folder and hand it back to him.

I think about my experience in the city. Most of the time, the lawbreakers weren't psychopaths. It's not like T.V. Those people are usually the hardest to find in real life. No, the usual suspects? They were just regular people making mistakes, motivated by a number of things; usually love, sex, guilt, revenge, power, money, you name it. Their crimes can often be linked to self-preservation or protecting someone or something they love.

The boundaries aren't so clear when those things are involved.

The scary part is, most of the time, I understood the position the guilty were put in. I even empathized with a few of them, though I would never admit that out loud. I'm not sure I would've done anything different in their shoes and *I'm* the police officer. I'm supposed to have a moral compass of gold. But sometimes, it's not so black and white.

That makes me realize with a flip of my stomach, that of course Miranda and Harrison could do this. There were signs from the very first day I got here. I shake my head. Bobby grunts in response.

"What's on your mind kid?"

"Nothing." I say a little too quickly. "I'm glad it's coming to a close."

He hands me dark sunglasses and we walk outside. It's painfully bright. Bobby notices my wincing and he gives me the ball cap he's wearing.

"Wow, my head is pounding. I need a dark room and some TV to put me to sleep ASAP." I don't mention Kim's instructions. He doesn't seem to notice. "Are we headed straight home?" My eyes dart to the side of the hospital where an ambulance is pulling up. Liam hops out of it and waves. It takes me a second, but I wave back.

"Actually, I wondered if you wouldn't mind staying with Liam for a bit?"

My head turns back to Bobby. "What? Why?"

He notices the infliction in my voice. "Sorry. Did I misread the situation? I thought you two were close. If it's too weird, I'll tell him you're staying with someone else."

"Wait, you already asked him if I could stay over? That's why he's here?" He's walking over to us now. I give Bobby a grumpy look. "Why him?"

"I thought it would be safer. We haven't found Harrison yet and I'm still worried he's going to try something again. He'll be less likely to expect you at Liam's. Plus, he has a medical background and the very look of the guy is intimidating." He seems flustered. "I could ask Dr. Jenkins or Sara..."

I wave him off. "No. Sara's in la la land with Langdon right now, and Dr. Jenkins is right next door to Liam's, so his place makes sense, I guess." I whisper this, as Liam closes the gap between us and joins our conversation.

"Feeling any better?" He asks me.

"Like shit. Need darkness."

"Alrighty, follow me. Your hideaway hotel awaits." He smiles and grabs my backpack from Bobby. "In all seriousness, I'm glad you guys thought of me. It's a big house and I never mind visitors."

I hesitate, looking at Bobby. He pulls me in for a soft hug. "I'll send Judie over to drop off your stuff. We're staying at her place, by the way. Both my girls will be safe." He leans back and gives me a weak smile. "I'll try to drop off Bear later too."

"Oh, Liam, is that okay? I feel like we're taking advantage of your generosity."

Bobby makes an annoyed noise, pointed in my direction.

Liam smiles wide. "I love dogs. Plus, Bear has stayed with me before when Bobby goes out of town. We're buddies."

I feel my shoulders relax a little. "Well...I would *love* to have Bear with me. So, thank you."

Liam nods.

"As soon as Harrison is found, I'll come pick you up. Get some rest." Bobby says to me, before turning to Liam. "*Make her rest.*"

CHAPTER 22 - THE KILLER

I watch you sometimes when you don't know I'm there. Sometimes you can feel my presence and other times you don't. The forest is a good place to watch you from, but not always feasible. My tinted car windows work well, but I think you're starting to catch on. I can hardly breathe when your face turns in my direction. I feel like sprinting the other way but my knees keep me in place. Your blue eyes squint as you're trying to figure out if I'm actually here or if you're imagining me. I wonder if you see me even when I'm not there. That thought excites me.

You are so gorgeous I can't believe you're real. You don't look like a model, like Kim does, but I find your beauty more sincere. A plainer face but a stronger mind. I could pick you out from a crowd with my eyes closed.

I usually am so good at blending into the crowd, but I've almost been caught a few times by nosey neighbours who I would kill easily, just for stepping too close to me. No one has put two and two together yet. Not even you.

Your body has been close to mine a few times. When you ended up with that concussion, I visited you again after hours. You looked so sad, so broken in that hospital bed. It must have really knocked you out, because you didn't feel my fingers as they brushed against your bruised cheek. You didn't smell my cologne as I bent over and smelled your hair, fresh with shampoo.

I killed those girls for you Jane. I hope you'll understand when we see each other soon. This time I'll make sure you're awake.

CHAPTER 23 - JANE

We hop in Liam's navy jeep and make our way to his place, which is on the other side of town. His street has mostly log house bungalows with wide porches and big backyards. I know from memory that at the end of this road is Miranda's parents' house.

Liam's house is near the end, and looks a lot like Bobby's log home but this one has an upstairs. It's one of only two second storey houses on the street. The other belongs to Dr. Jenkins, his closest neighbour to the right.

"Nice to have a doctor next door, I bet."

He nods. "It was helpful when my mom lived here. Kim definitely took good care of us and she still sometimes watches Julia for me if I'm working late. She's been a lifesaver."

"That's nice." I try to keep my tone light but I want to know more. I'm a detective after all; nosiness is what we do. "If only we could all choose our neighbours. You really lucked out." I sneak a peek at his expression, which remains neutral.

He simply smiles and nods his head. He isn't giving me squat so I let it go.

Liam lets us inside and takes my bags. "Make yourself at home. Your room is up the stairs, second door to the left. The bathroom is just to your immediate left."

While I wait, I take a look around the quaint, two-storey home. Everything is neatly in its place. There are no dishes in the sink, or fluffs on the floor and even the blankets are folded neatly on the couch. I wonder if it's always like this or if he cleaned up just for me.

The first floor of his home is built similar to Bobby's, but has a different feel to it. There is evidence of a child's and a woman's touch, almost everywhere you look. Definitely an artistic family. Julia's artwork is framed around the house and there are small homemade cushions on the denim couches, lace curtains on the windows and colourful rugs throughout the home. I assume the homemade decor was likely made by his mother before she got sick and moved to the residence.

When I look a little closer, I also see evidence of Liam peeking out from the corners; a well-used fishing toolbox beside the back door, beer bottles in the recycling bin, some non-fiction novels stacked by a lonely-looking, worse-for-wear recliner. It instantly gives me a cottage-like feel.

There are copious amounts of intricate wooden shelving, drawers and side tables in each room. It takes me a few minutes to realize that they were probably all handmade by the same person; a unique but identical style evident in each design. I gasp as I run my hand over a majestic bookshelf in the centre of the living room. It's light brown mixed with a sea-teal colour on the inside shelves that make it look as if it was found in a magical sea cave somewhere; the wood is perfectly smooth with small, hand carved floral designs that run along the top.

I'm still in awe, looking it over, as I feel a prickle on the back of my neck and look up to see I'm not alone. Liam is standing at the bottom of the stairs, relaxing against the wall, smirking. I let out a light breath.

"Do you like it?" he says, his voice smoky.

"Yes, it's beautiful. Who's the artist?"

He chuckles. "It was possibly one of the hardest projects I ever took on. I'm really proud of it."

"You really made this?" I ask, intrigued.

"You seem surprised." He says, grinning. "After I decided to take some time off from being a paramedic, I made sure to find something to keep me busy in the meantime." I'm reminded of what Bobby told me, how Liam is also struggling with PTSD. I don't know how to bring that up, so I decide not to mention it for now.

I've never thought twice about furniture before, but knowing the person who created this with his bare hands makes me stop in amazement. I could never in a million years carve anything this magnificent.

"What made you get into woodworking?"

"My Uncle is into woodworking. I spent a year with him before we moved here...and he showed me the tricks of the trade. It started off as a hobby to get my mind off things but I ended up selling a few pieces." He smiles warmly, remembering a memory perhaps. "My mom is a huge fan of the antique look. So, when I moved out here to be with her and Julia, I started making this bookshelf and its carvings. I sanded the crap out of it, painted it this teal colour on the insides, waxed it, sanded some more, then applied the finish. There's a lot more to it than that, of course, but that's the simple version. But because of its sheer size and weight, it took me twice as long to make it. I also wanted the details and the colour to be perfect."

"I never knew furniture could be like a piece of artwork, Liam. Really, it's gorgeous."

He gives me a small smile, but stays silent, watching the bookshelf which was once a gift and is now collecting dust.

"Thanks. Do you have any hobbies?" He asks absent-mindedly, chauffeuring us to the kitchen as he grabs some glasses and takes out some snacks.

I give him a lifted brow because I honestly can't think of the last time I had a real hobby, that wasn't watching television or playing games on my phone.

"I used to love reading and being outside doing things, like hiking or camping. I was an outdoorsy kid once. Since I've been back here, I've actually had a taste of it again and I want to get back into it."

"You definitely should." He adds. "Water? Iced Tea? Sprite?" He holds out a glass.

"Water would be great. Extra ice if you have it."

"Coming right up." He fills my glass and hands it to me and I take a big sip. It's so cold it hurts my teeth but that's exactly how I like it. Liam continues to chop up veggies and cheese and make a sort of charcuterie veggie tray combo. I sit on one of the stools at his island counter and watch him work in silence. He looks up from his task and catches me staring and the crinkles around his eyes return.

"By the way, I hope it's not weird you staying here. Bobby was talking with Kenny about a safe place you could hunker down in, and of course Kenny offered to take you in, but their daughter is staying with them right now with their newborn so it would've been a bit chaotic, not exactly restful...and I figured you would go with Sara but..."

"She doesn't even have a couch to crash on?"

He chuckles. "Yeah, exactly."

I smirk. "I could've crashed on Judie's couch but I'm kind of worried about bringing something bad to her front door." He smirks and I catch it and my face goes red. "Not that I think you're dispensable or something. Of course not. I'm very grateful to you, I just feel like you're more capable of handling things if shit hits the fan. You know, more muscles and what not. And...I'm going to shut up now."

He just chuckles, shaking his head playfully and popping a cheese in his mouth. "I like when you're nervous."

"You know, I actually still own a house in town. Inherited my childhood home from my parents when they passed."

"Really?" He asks surprised. "I thought you hadn't come back here in like a decade?"

"I haven't. I've been leasing it out."

"You think you'll move back?"

It's my turn to laugh now. "Not a chance."

I instantly notice the shift of mood. His eyebrows are furrowed and he's more reserved. After a few beats of silence, he decides to put some easy soft rock music on in the background.

Killers don't intimidate me, and yet being alone with a man like this does.

Conversation was easier through dinner. We mostly talked about Julia, the best outdoorsy stuff to do in Isinbury, and what we miss about living in the city. Hands down, we agree it's the variety of the takeout options. You won't find any Mongolian Beef or Pad See Ew in Isinbury.

Before I know it, it's 9:30 p.m., and Liam brings our Sprites over to the couch and begins to make a fire. It isn't cold, but I'm appreciative of the gesture because it makes the night feel a little more relaxed. Even if it also makes me a bit more nervous.

"I love fires," I say under my breath. Liam looks up at me, expectantly. "I grew up with a real fireplace. It was our main source of heat and we always made one for special occasions. I never really noticed how much I loved them until I moved to the city where they became so rare. Now I love the calming sensation they provide. I could stare at them for hours."

"I would miss the smell the most I think," Liam adds.

He finishes the fire and takes a seat beside me, looking up from his glass at me as he takes a sip.

"I haven't done this a lot," I say a bit too abruptly, hoping he will understand my meaning. When he looks confused, I add, "You know, being one on one with a guy like this."

His lips curve up instantly. "Like a date?" He asks me, turning my cheeks hot.

"I just mean–"

He interrupts my mumbling with a wave of his hand. "I'm teasing. This is more of a friendly retreat for hideaways and misfits."

"Which one am I?" I ask, playfully insulted.

"Oh, you're the hideaway for sure. I'm the misfit." He grins mischievously and holds his glass up in a cheers motion. "To us." I mirror the gesture.

"Pretty sure if you're one, you're likely also the other. Especially in a small town like this."

"I don't mind being in the misfit club if you're in it with me."

"Whatever this is, it's a nice break." I pause, picking at my cuticles a little. "However, I have to admit I am a little intimidated that you seem to have a way of making me both nervous and relaxed at the same time."

Liam nods slowly, then grins. "Is it bad that I like that I have that effect on you?" His voice is smooth as velvet to my ears. He's so attractive. I'm having trouble making eye contact with him. I feel like his eyes have the ability to read my thoughts and strip away each piece of my clothing at the same time; revealing everything and anything that I try to hide; all the good and all the bad left out in the open for him to analyze and do with as he wishes.

He meets my eyes and smiles warmly. "I bet Sara told you I dated a lot when I first got here. It's true. I did."

I'm surprised by this change of subject. Unsure what to say.

"I'm not a player or anything. I was just looking for some lighthearted distraction from my mom's illness." He fidgets with his glass, in deep thought. "None of them were very serious. I only had one that I would've considered my girlfriend but it just didn't work out."

"Why's that? Stop me, if I'm being too nosey."

"No, it's okay. Most women I date don't like the fact that I'm a two-package deal. Julia stays with our sister full-time for school, but she's with me during the entire summer, most holidays and some weekends. If it wasn't that, then they just ended up losing interest in me or I worked too much or I didn't party enough. Dating sites really leave a lot to chance."

"Ah, yes. I do know a little something about that."

"As for the one who I thought was my girlfriend? We dated for about five months, but the flame just kind of burned out. Other than that, I haven't found a lady that understands me yet or who would put up with me, I guess." He shrugs.

"I've always found it hard to connect with people," I say. "Especially in a long-term relationship kind of way. It seems so hard. Scary, even, to open yourself up like that." I think it over, trying to sound more positive. "You're braver than me. That's for sure. And by the way, I think Julia is fantastic. She's a burst of positive energy and rainbows. Anyone who doesn't appreciate that isn't worth your time."

This makes him smile his timid smile, the one where he purses his lips to the side. It makes me smile in turn.

"Thanks. And I'm glad you ended up staying with me. It's sometimes been hard for me to connect with people around here."

"I felt the same when I lived here." I pause. "And I'm glad I ended up here too."

"Anyways, what about you? I shared my past. Any crazy boyfriends in yours?"

Yeah, actually. The one who we think murdered everyone...

I literally swallow those words and try to find an answer I can actually use.

"Nothing that lasted over three months, for me. Part of the problem, I suppose, is that I work too much and am sometimes not soft or ladylike enough."

He chuckles.

"No, seriously, it's a huge problem for women in my profession. I guess the fact we can usually beat them in a fight intimidates them."

Liam continues to laugh at this. "I think it's awesome. If I'm ever in need of a bodyguard, I'll let you know."

I throw back my head in a laugh, which feels good, so I stay in that position after, relaxing into the couch and bringing up my socked feet under my butt. I am so down to just forget about everything that's happened recently and all the mess that's in my head and enjoy something easy.

"Do you still think I could be the killer?" He asks. I'm startled at first by his outlandish directness, but when I look over at him, he's grinning ear to ear, obviously thinking this is hilarious.

"Haven't made up my mind yet," I reply. "But I figure if you are the killer, staying with you will only help me catch you when your guard is down." I smirk, playing along.

"Ah, I see. So this is your alternative reason for staying with me then. Well, I hope you sleep with one eye open."

"I hardly sleep, so that's pretty much guaranteed."

"I don't sleep well either, so if we're not having a big showdown in the middle of the night, let's meet in the kitchen and I'll make us some pancakes. Carbs always help me sleep."

"Sounds nice, Killer." I say, barely holding back a laugh.

The smile reaches his eyes, as he shakes his head.

We stare at the flames for a bit and enjoy the comfortable silence. We've become friends through the past two weeks, so it's not unusual for us to feel at ease. Only when I look up at him or remind myself of the feelings between us, do I feel my heart pick up its pace.

"Do you like hot-tubbing?" Liam says out of nowhere, eyeing me mischievously.

I eye him back, just as playfully. "I do. Why?" My tone goes up a pitch in excitement.

"I have one out back and the night is just perfect for it. The sky is clear and full of stars and it will help with any soreness you might have."

I smile to myself. Ever the gentleman.

"I don't have a bathing suit."

He nods once. He thinks for a moment, his fingers brushing the end of his jaw. "You can wear one of my T-shirts if you want? No pressure though if you don't want to."

I smile at him and nod. "You won't mind?" He shakes his head with a smirk.

He runs upstairs and grabs his things. When he returns, he passes me the shirt and he heads outside to ready the tub. He's already in his bathing suit, topless and looking more sculpted than I gave him credit for.

I take off my clothes, letting them fall to the floor, and quickly throw on his T-shirt over my bra and undies. Out of habit, I pick up my clothes and fold them.

Once a cadet, always a cadet.

I head outside, which is cold as shit. I shriek as I open the door and the wind hits my body, giving me goosebumps all over. I can feel my nipples poking through his shirt in response to the temperature change. Liam runs over to me and wraps a towel around my shoulders and guides me to the hot tub next to his woodworking shed. He holds out his hand and I take it as he carefully guides me into the hot tub. In his other hand, he offers me a hair elastic. This makes me smirk. I realize he's already wearing one, and I do the same. His hair is longer than any guy I've ever dated, but it's not as long as mine, and he wears it well.

He makes his way into the tub and I take in the gorgeous night sky. There's hardly any light pollution in Isinbury, so the star show is always the greatest. In the first few minutes, we spot a shooting star. I feel his toes brush against mine in the tub and I fight the automatic response to pull away. Instead, I push them closer to his, and as I sneak a look at him, I catch his approving smile and returning gaze.

We keep playing footsies and gazing at the stars and talking about the parts of our lives that are easy to talk about. We even broach some harder topics too, such as our mothers. I tell him more about my parents and how they've both passed away, because the topic came up that my mom used to live in the residence too, and well, I feel obligated to fill in the blanks after that. It's fine. I've told the story so many times, it's almost like I'm on autopilot. But instead of making me upset like it usually does, I feel sort of at peace for the first time about it. It must be the stars that are making me so sappy, but I think about how they're together somewhere in the afterlife. Mom and Dad. They finally found each other.

We talk a bit about Game of Thrones and The Walking Dead and how much we love them and how annoyed we are that they keep killing off our favourite characters. Every good show does, we agree.

Long after our fingers are bumpy, we decide to go back inside and run all the way there after closing the tub. I'm frozen solid again, shaking uncontrollably in my towel, his T-shirt sticking to my cold breasts. We automatically try to be quiet because it's way after midnight, but we can't help but giggle at how ridiculous I sound trying to whisper to him while my teeth are chattering. And he reminds me there's no one else home which makes us laugh further.

He moves me over next to the fire he just rekindled, massaging his hands up and down my shoulders hidden under the towel, extra gentle with my left one, trying to warm me up. I pause briefly, trying to gather my courage, before lifting his cold, wet shirt up above my head and hanging it on a chair near the fireplace. I wrap the towel against me again, and try to dry off. Liam does the same and continues to sneak glimpses at me in my underwear. He invites me to sit on the couch with him and warm up. I gladly accept, sliding in beside his already-warm, almost-naked body, his left arm wrapping around my shoulders which finally gives me enough warmth to stop the chattering. Something hot and electrical crackles unspoken between us.

I look up into his eyes which are deadly close. I notice for the first time that they aren't only hazel, but they also have a bright blue ring surrounding his irises.

"Are you finally warming up?" He whispers to me.

"Yes." I pause. "Please kiss me."

He waits a second, surprised, thinking he must've misheard before taking in my smile and my eyes that have become heavy with anticipation. He leans an inch short from me and brushes his hand against my cheek, my ear, then the back of my neck, holding my hair gently in his fist. It sends chills down my spine, before he closes the gap and softly touches his lips to mine. It's slow, open-mouthed and warm. His tongue touches mine briefly before retreating. Our hands are all over each other now, sliding against each other's bodies which are quickly warming up from the heat coursing through our veins. I push him down onto the couch and climb on top of him, my legs on either side of his hips. I lower myself down, and press against him and it almost makes me tear up. It feels so good. It's been a long time since I felt another human body against mine this way, and this time it feels heightened, because this time, feelings are behind it. The way we are kissing is intense and almost desperate. The passion is there every time we go in for the kiss, and every time we pull each other closer. All of our flirtatious stares and teasing have built up and we're finally letting it out. He carefully and easily flips me around so that I am on the bottom. He props up a pillow behind my head which I think is cute, before lowering his body to touch mine in a very seductive way. He moves his hand from my back to my abdomen, and slowly upwards where I push into him begging him with my body to touch me there. His hand slips upward and gives my breasts a soft but firm squeeze. I move my pelvis closer to him in response. He makes that low humming noise in his throat that lets me know he's enjoying himself. He kisses my neck, and slowly moves down my body, kissing all around, sending signals between my legs and making my eyes roll in the back of my head. All we've done is kiss each other and it's gotten me so hot.

I'm ready to go all the way with him, let him do delicious things to my body and make me feel amazing. But he stops suddenly, holding me against him tenderly. I grab hold of his head and bring him back up to my face to search his eyes.

"You need to rest a bit more..." He whispers. "It could make you feel worse if we continue. And...I want to take things slow with you."

I kiss him some more before whispering against his ear. "I don't want to move too fast either."

Our kisses get shorter and shorter before he reluctantly pulls himself off me. He squeezes in behind me, and wraps his arms around me in a spoon.

"That was...so hot," he says, a little out of breath. "Sorry about the..."

He's trying to cuddle me, but I can feel the bulge under his bathing suit pressing against my butt. It's turning me on, so I try to think of something else. Although it really is hard to think of anything else at the moment...

I lean back against him. "That was very sexy. Don't think that every muscle in my body is not trying to continue doing all of that with you. I would love to raincheck on that one."

"Of course." He pulls me tighter.

To be held like this, in a man's warm arms, with no pressure to have sex, not being used or judged, just held tenderly, is an intimacy I've never experienced before. I stare at the flames a bit longer and enjoy his warm body wrapped around mine.

A couple of hours later, we wake up. I had no clue that we had fallen asleep. The fire is out and it's about 5 a.m. according to my phone. I pull myself from his warm snuggle, waking him up as I do so. He gives me a sleepy smile.

I put the glasses in the sink as he throws our wet clothes in the wash.

Liam lets me take a hot shower then gives me a pair of his boxers and another shirt to sleep in and I appreciate their dryness. He brings me upstairs to his spare bedroom and tells me I can sleep here and he will be right next door, but when he sees I'm cold again, he jumps in. I have zero complaints. I'm wrapped up in his warm embrace yet again and for the first time in a long time, I feel my body relax and my heart rate slow. I feel at ease. Safe. Happy even. My eyes cannot stay open any longer.

CHAPTER 24 - JANE

I spend the rest of the week with Liam in his cozy log home. At first it was like I was tiptoeing around the house, but he called me out on it and we laughed it off, and now I'm pretty at ease. Having Bear here now also helps.

Despite being totally cared for, I still feel pretty nauseous for the first few days and can hardly keep anything down except ramen. I eat way too much ramen.

We spend most of our days snuggled up on opposite sides of the couch watching Netflix and spend the nights in separate bedrooms. I'm still not sure how I feel about all of this and I don't want to rush things.

One night in the middle of the week, from the other bedroom, I hear him grunting strangely. Bear is in bed with me and his ears shoot up at the sound. At first, I decide to ignore it but then I hear his noises turn into more of a whimpering sob. I tiptoe out of the room, the dog behind me as backup. My phone's flashlight is on and I open Liam's door slowly, pointing the light toward his bed. He's thrashing around in a real sweat. I walk over to the bed and my hand goes out to wake him but stops mid-air, listening to hear if I can make anything out. I'm not sure why I do it. It feels wrong and like I'm invading his privacy, but some sort of instinct of mine kicks in overriding my ethics.

"So much blood," he murmurs. I hold my breath. He continues on with incomprehensible mumbling until I give up, shaking his arm until he snaps awake in a panic.

"What," he says, "What's...Jane? What's wrong?"

"I think you were having a nightmare."

"Oh." He rubs some sleep from his eyes. "I thought you might be coming in for a booty call." His adorable sheepish grin spreads across his sleepy face. I'm finding it a sort of weakness of mine.

Concentrate Jane. Stop smiling like that.

As if reading my mind, he says, "I like when you smile like that."

My heart speeds up. Bear walks over to the side of his bed and Liam gives him some pats on the head.

I look down away from his prying eyes and notice the sheets are drenched with his sweat. "You're okay then? You were mumbling a little..."

"Sorry. What did I say?"

"I couldn't make it out." I lie. Then I look at his sad, sullen face and change my mind. I need to know. "I'm sorry. I did make out one thing." I hesitate, trying to gain more courage. "You were saying something about blood? A lot of blood?"

He laughs, breaking the silence of the night, and it startles me. He notices and gets quiet. "Sorry, it's just pretty funny 'cause you're trying to solve murders and here I am talking about blood in my sleep."

I nod, trying to make myself understand. The silence creeps further until he breaks it.

"I have PTSD." He says it matter-of-factly, then gets up out of bed and walks to the ensuite bathroom, grabbing a cloth and running cold water over it. Then he wipes himself down starting with the back of his neck. "I guess I should've mentioned this before, especially because you trusted me enough to tell me the complete story with Marcus. Once I heard your story, it of course only made me want to get to know you more...because I could relate to it, in a sense. My partner got seriously injured on the job and ended up in a coma."

I'm instantly shocked. Whatever it was I was expecting, it wasn't this.

"Her name is Hannah and we were paramedics together in Vancouver. We responded to a domestic violence dispute in East Hastings. You know how bad it can be down there. A guy shot his wife. The cops were trying to negotiate a surrender while we were on standby. Somehow the guy got past them and came up to us, waiting a block away outside the ambulance. He snuck up on us. Wanted to take the bus. I lunged for him, tried to take the gun, but he pulled the trigger and the bullet went straight into Hannah's spine. I froze. The guy slammed the rifle into my head and took the bus anyway. When I came to, there wasn't much I could do for Hannah but be there for her and keep her comfortable until another dispatch of EMTs arrived."

His head is down, eyes closed, but his face is pure sorrow.

"I am so sorry Liam."

"Yeah, me too. I've heard she's out of the coma now, but that she will never be the same. Wheelchair-bound for the rest of her life."

"She's very lucky to be alive."

"I don't think she feels that way, but yeah."

"It's not your fault, if that's what you're thinking."

The silence is deafening.

"Anyway," he says, putting the damp cloth in a laundry hamper and changing his shirt, "it's the reason I chose to step back from being a paramedic for now. I was foolish and put both of our lives in danger. My actions made it so she will never walk again." He takes a big breath. "I see a therapist every two weeks and she helps a lot. She's the one who thought I might benefit from woodworking again. And then she pushed me to sign up as a SAR volunteer. That only happened this year."

"Thank you for telling me." I sit on the bed and hold out my hand. He takes it. "I have nightmares too."

He nods.

"Can I tell you something I've never said out loud before?"

"Of course."

"Sometimes I think about quitting and never looking back. I never was one to look on the bright side, growing up in a family of cops. But I swear, the things I've seen...they've left a real scar. You can't unsee some stuff. I know you get that, having been a paramedic and struggling to go back to it. Just know that I understand how you feel."

"The worst ones always haunt you."

"I was never a worrier until the Marcus thing. Now it's like I can't escape my thoughts...or my doubts."

"It's nice, at least, to know someone who understands what I'm going through." He says it quietly. "Maybe we can work on it together?"

Bear walks out of the room, comforted now there's no danger, and I hear his nails clip-clapping it back into the spare bedroom.

"I'd like that." I look up at his sleepy face and smile. He too has a past that haunts him. Maybe that's why mine doesn't scare him off so easily. He sees the worst parts of me and I see the worst parts of him and we still want this. "How about you come sleep next to me in the spare room? These sheets need a good wash and it's..." I check the clock behind him, "it's 3a.m."

He squeezes my hand. "You had me at come sleep next to you."

~~~

I survive the rest of the week mostly in sweats and T-shirts, no makeup. He doesn't seem to notice or care. He's super sweet, making me light dinners, walking the dog and mostly letting me choose what we watch.

I learn that he likes reality T.V. and country music, two things that I despise. He chews with his mouth open more often than not, and he spills absolutely everything on himself. He's also best avoided until he's had at least two cups of coffee in the morning. And he likes ketchup on pretty much anything. That last one is almost unforgivable.

Still, I stick around, completely intrigued by him and his bad taste and his clumsiness, wondering if this is what it feels like to have a boyfriend or if this is just some phase that will wear off.

I spend a lot of time on Facebook, scrolling through the town's group page, looking at every comment on every post, and following up with any profile of a person that fits what we're looking for. I know Jamieson and Francis want to pursue Harrison as a lead suspect, but something about it just doesn't feel right to me. I write down a few names found on the social media site to ask Bobby about later, but I presume it won't lead to much. Whoever this is, is smart. Likely not even to be on Facebook, let alone posting in public forums. But you never know.

I get a few visitors that stop by. Judie drops off more clothes and some casseroles and groceries for us. She stays for a short visit but can tell I'm wiped out, so she gives me a kiss on the cheek and reminds me to let her know if I need anything at all.

Jake video chats with me for a bit, wanting to stop by before I tell him I'm not at Bobby's. He pressures me a bit to tell him where I am, until I agree to go out for dinner with him in a week when I'm better. Liam hollers at me from the kitchen, asking me if I'm hungry for dinner and Jake's face changes into something that looks like sadness. He tells me he has to go shortly after that. I swallow the urge to ask Liam what the beef is between them.

I take the short walk over to Kim's the next day, after she calls me to check in and I tell her my headaches are not getting any better. She offers to stop by, but I tell her I want some fresh air.

Her home is made of the same bones as Liam's but it's completely different inside. It's a lot more feminine, and has a light blue, coral and white colour scheme throughout that gives off a sort of beach house vibe, even though the house is surrounded by woods. She offers me some chocolate and light snacks, and iced tea.

Apparently, coffee is bad for concussions so this is my small caffeine fix, authorized by her. She believes the headaches are made worse by my caffeine withdrawal and suggests I try some tea in the meantime. I don't tell her I have a repulsion to tea like kids do to broccoli.

At first I think this is just a checkup, but Liam goes on an errand run (like he does a few times during the week), and I end up staying a few hours and we get to chatting. She tells me that her parents grew up in Isinbury but moved to the city when she was five, only coming back in the summer to visit family and friends. I don't mention that I know most of this from Bobby.

"Yes, I heard Laryssa is sort of like an aunt to you, is that right?"

She nods warmly in response. "Yes, like you and Bobby, I imagine."

"Can't always pick your family, but sometimes you get to." I shrug. "Must've been nice to know at least one person when you moved back here. Did you know anyone else?"

"Not really. But it didn't matter to me. All those summers boating and fishing and spelunking with Laryssa, ruined me for city life forever. I grew up in the city, but my heart has always been country. Those memories are part of the reason I came back here to Isinbury."

"Yeah, I didn't realize how much I missed the outdoors and the forests and the mountains 'til I came back." Even now, with the breeze coming through the window, I can smell the damp leaves and the cool air bringing with it the scents of spring.

"I should've searched harder for Abby," I say out loud before I realize I've said it. I look up to find her kind eyes on mine.

"Don't beat yourself up, Jane. She was over 18 years old. Plenty of young people her age simply up and leave. There was no reason to think something happened to her like that." She reaches out her hand and rubs my knee lightly. It's comforting; not like a doctor's hand, but a friend's. My head lays heavy in my hands. "I hope you can take comfort in knowing that her body has finally been laid to rest."

She changes the subject by telling me stories she's heard from her father about mine. I know they were close friends before they moved away.

My mother Liz and father Henry starred in many of Kim's father's fondest memories. She asks me more about them and I tell her about how hard-working my mother was and yet also a free-spirited, quick-to-laugh artist who loved creating things with her hands. I tell her my favourite stories about my dad. About him, a 6-foot beast of a man, being chased by a Canadian Goose once, swearing at the top of his lungs because he was scared of it. Or that time he came home from work, his uniform full of crap, because he chased someone through a barn and the two of them slipped in animal's feces before he got the cuffs on.

"He was a little rough around the edges, in the way that he always had emotional walls up." I explain. "But he was always so good to my mom and I, and he could be so damn funny when he didn't mean to be."

I feel a bit lighter. It feels good to talk about things with someone who genuinely seems interested and who could offer helpful advice. It's something I haven't experienced with Sara in a long time.

We finish the snacks and she gets up to put the dishes away in the kitchen. "We might have even met before, in passing when we were children," she says, calling out from the other room. "Our parents were so close, I'm sure we did, though I don't remember. Do you?"

I look towards the frames on her shelf above her couch. Family portraits, shots of her laughing with friends or artsy travel pictures.

I know we met. I just don't want to reveal this yet. "Not that I can recall," I holler back.

She comes back into the room and sees me looking at the photos. "That was a skiing trip in the Alps with my ex-girlfriend Haley a few years ago. Time of my life."

I get up to get a better look.

"This one brings back memories." She points to the frame a bit behind some of the others. A romantic shot of her laughing in the air, with a handsome man kissing her cheek with the Eiffel tower in the background.

"Wow. Is that actually Paris?"

"Yep. I did some travelling a few years ago, before settling here."

"You seem to have had a very exciting love life."

She laughs lightly. "Oh, just some past loves. Maybe part of me thinks it's not all in the past, especially when it comes to Haley..." She shrugs. "Love and life, you know? Sometimes it's so complicated."

I nod, smiling politely.

"This one is mostly a joke between my parents and I." She points to a professional baby photo, to the far left. It's a young baby with orange curls on top of their head, a gummy open mouthed grin, wearing a greenish brown wool top.

I've seen this photo before. I reach out and grab it, pulling it closer.

"My parents hated this photo for some reason, so as a joke, I display it here just to piss them off." She studies the photo. "Might be the ugly sweater, but why they chose that one for a photo to begin with I'm not sure. I think it sort of makes me look like a boy, don't you think?"

But I'm already deep inside my head. I've seen this photo before...inside my dad's favourite book.

Why did my dad have a photo of Kim inside one of his books? I suddenly feel a bit ill.

The pieces are starting to fall together.

"Were you adopted?" The words leave my mouth before I can think better of them.

She looks startled. "Yes, why? My parents couldn't have kids so they adopted me. It was a closed adoption."

The room starts to spin.

"Are you okay? You look sick." She helps me sit down. "You must have gotten up too fast." She feels my head with the back of her palm. "You're sweaty. Do you feel okay?"

"Fine. I'm fine. Just...my stomach is a bit off for some reason."

"How did you know I was adopted?" She asks, studying me.

"Must've heard it somewhere. I only remembered it now." I lie.

"That's one hell of a trick. Though, I guess Bobby must have told you. And, you know my father. I know I don't look anything like him. My mom, neither." She considers this, her bright blue eyes searching my face. "How about I walk you home?"

I think it, but I don't dare say it out loud: *You know who you do look a lot like, Kim? Laryssa.*

And my father.

~~~

I pour myself a small glass of wine, just as it starts to rain. I really want something stronger, but I better not push it with this concussion. I sit by the open window and take it all in.

Liam comes home shortly after with some Chinese Food in hand. He eyes my drink with an eyebrow, but doesn't give me grief about it. Instead, he pours himself a glass and lets me eat most of the chicken balls with the sweet and sour sauce because they're my favourite. We play a few games of cards outside in his gazebo, wrapped up in blankets with his electric fire pit on in the centre, and Bear cuddled up my feet. It's cozy. And it's a great distraction from my thoughts about Kim.

"Best wellness retreat ever." I say, meeting his eyes above my cards. "Thanks again."

He smiles. "Anytime."

At first, I want to laugh that we're playing *Go Fish* and *War*, but I'm relieved that I don't have to think too much and he kicks my ass almost every time anyway.

"I have an eleven-year-old sister," he says in his defense. "This isn't my first game. Or my last."

He tells me about Julia, and his mother, and his best moments in college studying to be a paramedic. He tells me about his trips around the world so far, and how he wants to visit Japan next. I tell him how I've never left the country but want to go everywhere. He makes me list the places I dream of visiting and tells me the best parts of each destination. He helps me note my top five places I want to visit someday. He asks me all sorts of strange questions like, "what quality do I appreciate most in a person," and "what new foods would I like to try and what ones would I never give a chance," and "what do I like best; fashion, architecture or art?"

We talk for hours, about everything and anything, temporarily making me forget my worrying thoughts tossing about in my head.

We don't talk about the hardest cases I've worked or the horrors he's seen on the job. We leave the dark stuff in the corner, untouched, and I forget about it for a while.

I like myself around him. And I don't like myself around a lot of people.

After the moon comes out, I get a chill I can't beat and we head inside.

My shoulder since the crash has been hurting like hell, and although the pain meds Dr. Jenkins gave me help the majority of my aches, the pain in my shoulder is different. It's chronic pain mixed with current injury and it never lets me forget it.

Liam notices me nursing it and asks me how it's feeling.

"Let's just say this shoulder will find any reason to be sore. At least I can always tell when I'm gonna need a rain jacket."

He shakes his head with a smile. "Would you be comfortable with me applying some massage therapy?"

My eyebrows raise up, as he gives me a sort of flirtatious smile. As if reading my thoughts, he says, "I'm not trying to flirt with you. I'm a medical professional and I believe I can help you with this little thing in your otherwise big to-do list."

"Well...I did always keep up with my massage therapy in the city. You're sure?"

"Yes of course. Just relax," he says, moving closer to me. "I mean...I'm trying to flirt with you a little bit, but I also know this will help."

A huge grin spreads on my face as I turn away from him and pull my shirt downwards so he can access my shoulder. He massages softly at first, applying pressure only at my direction. I resist the urge to make a comment about a "safe word."

"Kinda looks like a flower, your scar," he says quietly.

"Hmm. Never saw it that way before."

"Maybe now it won't be such a dark symbol." His eyes meet mine and I feel myself relax further.

"My mom loved flowers. She was a florist."

He just smiles and so do I. Bear flops down with a groan near the couch.

Liam's fingers work their way across my shoulder blade, the base of my neck, down my arm, across my skull. He's giving me shivers and I can tell he notices, even if he pretends not to.

"You should make a follow up appointment at the hospital to see what they can do for your pain management until you see that specialist," he says.

When I start to protest, he sighs heavily and accuses me of being a difficult patient. "Trust me it could help."

I listen to him speak his medical jargon out loud and enjoy his hands working through my most painful spots. Never knew such a big man could be so gentle. I try really hard not to make a noise even though it feels very good. I squeeze my thighs tightly together; an impulse. I hope he doesn't notice. He's still talking. "...have a really good physio and massage clinic, despite being such a small town."

When he's done, he tells me to drink lots of fluids and pours me a warm bath with Epsom salts; my go-to for pain relief. The bath works wonders. All my aches and pains subside for at least a few hours.

We fool around a bit after Netflix gets boring and his warm body against mine gets too distracting. This has happened a few times this week but I keep getting dizzy and he makes us stop. Today, the seventh day, I feel better.

"Wow I am feeling much better," I say in an exaggerated voice, teasingly, "I ate all my food and even went for a walk around the property today...plus that epsom salt bath...wow..."

He eyes me up and a smirk sneaks through as he catches my meaning. "I'm so glad you're feeling better," he says mockingly.

"Keep resting so that you continue to heal." His voice is monotone, strict almost, but I can see him trying to hide his amusement as he leans back on the couch, out of reach.

"Okay boss."

I can't help but frown but I love the playful back and forth. It's like an electric jolt through my body every time he comes home or I'm near him.

After another episode of some Netflix Original comes on, I get up to take my pain medication. I lay back down, comfortably stretched out, my head on a pillow and my feet in Liam's lap.

"Are your feet ticklish?"

The question itself makes me pull them closer to my body. "Nope." I'm hoping he doesn't test me on my answer, but then he asks me another question that makes my heart speed up again.

"Would it be okay with you if I gave you a foot massage?"

I smirk. "You just can't keep your hands off me today, huh."

His bellowing laugh splits the silence in the air and makes me jump.

"Let's just say, I saw the crash you walked away from. I know you're hurting, and I just want you to feel as comfortable as possible."

"Well, I'm not going to turn that down." I pause. "And thank you Liam. Really. For everything."

He waves me off.

Well, one thing leads to another, and a foot massage turns into another back massage, and that turns into heated kissing. He completely relaxes my body, still stiff and sore from the crash, somehow avoiding my bruises as if he's memorized each one.

I'm still craving him from a few days ago.

So, we make love.

We embrace each other on the couch, pulling each other closer and closer, until there is no more room between us. It's carefully sweet and passionate; a heated explosion rising in my head and spreading across my entire body, making it tingle. Then he carries me in his strong arms, my body wrapped around his torso as I kiss his shoulders, step by step, up to his bed, where we begin again. He stops several times to check with me on how I'm feeling, which at the time, is high on affection, lust and deep waves of pleasure.

We fall asleep in each other's arms.

In the morning, I turn my head and smile into his chest. I know this isn't going anywhere. It's just a hookup. Light, easy, fun. I have a life in Vancouver and he has one here.

"What are you thinking about so hard?" He asks, his voice still full of sleep, while his fingers twirl a strand of my hair and tuck it behind my ear.

"I'm wondering what you're going to make me for breakfast."

He chuckles, pulling me closer into his warmth and I feel myself relax, my shoulders falling and my jaw untightening.

He brings me breakfast in bed: eggs benny with fried potatoes, a big glass of orange juice and a black coffee just how I like it. I try to read his expression: peaceful, regretful, full of contemplation? Who am I kidding? Human beings are never that easy to read. Especially not ones like Liam. But I get my answer in a different way, because we do it all over again when he shows up early from his volunteer shift that day, still taking it very slow and careful.

"You're three hours early!" I say as he walks inside, his long strides bringing him to me in seconds.

"I couldn't stay away," he mumbles before kissing me, my fingers tugging his long hair loose and pulling him closer to me.

~~~

There have been no sightings of Harrison in over a week and the town has been searched top to bottom, so Jamieson and Francis decide to make him a wanted person and close the case.

Bear and I are back at Bobby's now. I'm in a hot Epsom salt bath, thinking over the last week and running it through my head. This is the closest I've felt to being happy for the first time in years.

Miranda made a deal with the Crown Attorney and confessed to knowing Harrison's involvement with the murders of Brandi, Megan and Lilyann. She's playing victim and saying he threatened her life if she didn't go along with the tire stunt. No one believes that part, but she's going to jail for two years with the chance of parole, for aggravated assault, rather than the possibility of life imprisonment for attempted murder. Maybe she'll straighten out a bit afterward, who knows?

A knock on the door distracts me from my thoughts.

"Hey kiddo, it's Bobby. How are you feeling?" His voice sounds hoarse and strange. Tired.

"I'm pretty much back to my new normal as far as I can tell." My hand glides over my body in the water, pausing at each bruise and cut, the only sign that the past two weeks actually happened.

His silence makes me weary. "What's up, Bobby?"

He clears his throat.

"You're going to want to get dressed and call your union rep again." Another pause. "We found Harrison in the trunk of his car at the edge of town. He's dead."

CHAPTER 25 - JANE

The moment I heard Harrison had died, my body went numb. I've been trained to understand the symptoms of shock, but moreover I have been burdened in knowing it like a familiar friend who stops by to surprise me every now and then. I can walk but it feels more like floating. My fingers move through my damp hair but it feels like someone else is moving them for me. The puppeteer behind the curtain of my existence, silently helping me get through the motions of life moving on, even after tragedy. There is a fire in my belly and it's moving through my veins reaching through to the tips of me.

I always knew he would die young. He was reckless that way. I thought it would be suicide, or drug overdose or maybe a car crash while intoxicated. But he was murdered.

Maybe it's the murder part that is making me so messed up. Or maybe it's all the feelings and emotions and memories that I worked so hard to hide for the past ten years flooding back all at once, coming up like bile, burning me from the inside out. Unable to stop it once I feel it in my throat.

I'm not relieved like I thought I would be, instead I feel crushed. Part of me is pissed because everyone on social media is focusing on the good parts of him: "He was always the life of the party" and "He was an older brother, those poor boys having to move on without him." All these stories from neighbours and buddies, about a man who was at the root good, not evil?

I realized long ago that in death we can finally escape all of our mistakes and the pain we caused people when we were alive...and leave a golden legacy, regardless of blind truth. Our guilt melts away, but only in death.

I go through the motions of getting dressed. One foot after the other. Clasp the bra. Shirt over head. A sock on each foot.

Why is it that he hurt me so bad back when I was at my weakest point, messed me up so completely, that I still flinch or have panic attacks with lovers in bed or when somebody grabs my wrist playfully, and yet here I am feeling bad for his mother and his younger brothers?

Death is such a permanent state. The person can no longer redeem himself of his sins or his bearings; he takes it with him to the grave and whatever is beyond. He's gone. I suppose being a cop means that despite what I see every day, I'm always looking for that redemption story; even when I don't realize I am, even in my own life story and in my own supervillain.

Does that make me weak or does it make me strong? I hear those words in my head, echoed like déjà vu. I remember my father saying those exact words before. I don't remember the context or to whom he was speaking, but it's his voice I hear when I think them.

Bobby snaps me out of my thoughts by knocking on the door again. He's worried about me. I pull the towel still hung loosely around my head and unlock the door to let him in. I sit down on the toilet and moisturize my face. There it goes again, fingers moving by themselves.

"You in shock?" He asks. "I know it's a lot to process."

"Yeah, I don't exactly feel like I always thought I would."

"I figured." He fiddles with his hands. "I don't exactly feel relieved either. I always thought I could kill him myself for what he did to you but I realize now that I couldn't."

I look up in surprise, then lower my eyes back down to my fidgeting hands. I take a big breath. "Is it fucked up that, now, more than ever, I'm second-guessing what happened, wondering if it was some miscommunication between us, that maybe I misinterpreted a signal? That I imagined it even?"

"You didn't imagine it, Jane," he says quickly, then softens his tone. "You know from your own experience as a police officer, victims are conditioned to second-guess their experiences and blame themselves or think they're at fault, even though they aren't." He places his hand gently on mine, which is gripping the edge of the sink. "I know his death brings up a lot of shit. But none of what happened is your fault, Jane. Then, or now."

"I know what you're saying is true, I just feel like I can't trust my gut anymore and I often wonder if I ever could."

"Come here," he says, pulling me into a hug. I feel myself shaking and realize I am sobbing. I let myself fall into his safe embrace.

"I thought my life was fucked up before, Bob." I say between sobs. "But it has gotten so much worse...since I... came back here."

"Hey now. It's not all bad." He rubs the top of my head, soothingly. "It's just a tough one. We'll get through it. We always do."

Abby. Harrison. A possible sister I never knew about. I don't say any of it out loud, I just let myself lean on Bobby and cry until my throat is sore.

"I'm here for you honey." Bobby says gently in my ear. "I will *always* be here."

When I get my breathing back under control, I pull away. "I'm just trying to come to terms with it all. Can I have a few days to process it?"

"Yes, of course. I just thought maybe you'd wanna stay in the loop," he stifles a cough. "Take whatever time you need. Kenny and I got this. Jamieson and Francis are still in town. Probably not leaving anytime soon, since this just got a whole lot more complicated. You can play catch up when you're ready to come back."

I see him turn to leave but he stops in the doorway. He turns to me and just holds my gaze.

"I know he meant something to you, even if it wasn't good. So, I'm sorry for what you're going through right now. I'm here if you need me."

I nod as tears fill up my eyes again. He leaves me alone to pick up the pieces of the mess that's circling in my head.

CHAPTER 26 - JANE

Kenny and I are washing the station's windows that were covered in spray paint last night by a couple of idiots. The words are bright blue: lazy pigs.

Everyone else is at Harrison's funeral. The town is pretty pissed because we told them Harrison was the killer and now he's turned up dead.

To be fair, Miranda had been a witness (albeit, unreliable, sure), and there was some pretty damning evidence to prove what she was saying was correct.

"Why would she lie?" Kenny says, between strokes.

"I've been wondering the same thing. Why lie and go to jail for two years anyway?"

"Jamieson and Francis are working an angle that still supports the theory that Harrison killed those women, and that someone else killed him." He hesitates, out of breath from washing the windows. "We all just want the pieces to fit. For this to go away."

I stay silent. It's an embarrassing moment for the police force here.

"The victims' parents...they have strong alibis for the time Harrison was missing? This isn't a revenge killing?"

"Yeah, I vetted them myself."

Jake comes around the corner then and his eyes go wide. "I saw the Facebook post and came right away."

"There's a Facebook post now?"

"Yeah, it's on the town's homepage." He eyes me.

I roll my eyes and keep washing. Jake comes over and grabs a soaking towel from the bucket. I look over at him as he helps.

"You're not at the funeral?" I ask.

He chuckles. "Why the hell would I do that? I'm glad the bastard is dead."

I inhale sharply. I stand still and study his facial expression as he washes. He's angry.

"Pretty soon to be talking ill of the dead," Kenny utters almost under his breath.

"Isn't anyone with half a brain thinking the same thing?" Jake says. "Not my fault they're too chickenshit to say it out loud." He laughs, easing up a bit. "The real people you have to watch out for are the silent and deadly types. At least with me, you know what you're getting into. I'm not hiding it."

The soap from the sponge is running down my right sleeve. "Uncontrolled anger in general is a recipe for disaster too." I adjust my hat with my left hand. "I'm not pointing the finger at anyone here. I struggle with it too."

"Which one is Liam?" Jake says, eyeing me from the side smirking.

"Not sure. I don't know him that well."

"Yeah right Jane. I know you've been staying at his place."

Kenny interrupts. "How did you know that? That's not common knowledge."

Jake laughs out loud. "If you think anything in this town stays a secret, you've been hiding under a rock."

"Fair." Kenny says. "I don't mind it under my rock, thank you very much. Less assholes there." The station's phone is ringing inside so he goes to grab it, leaving Jake and I alone.

Jake catches my eyes again.

"Why don't you like Liam?"

He looks surprised that I've asked, and his smile seems insincere.

"No, seriously, there has been some obvious beef between you guys. Just tell me."

His tongue presses against the inside of his cheek, a nervous habit of his that makes me think he's wondering whether to tell me the truth, or a lie.

"How's your head?" Jake asks me instead.

"It's fine. Now answer my question."

He laughs. "You're so stubborn." He reaches out to caress my chin but I jerk my head back to show him I'm not impressed. "Okay, I just don't like the guy. We've never gotten along."

"Any reason in particular?"

"Let's just say, we share the same taste in women..." He waits, enjoying my cheeks reddening as I catch his meaning. "And...I don't buy the whole hero complex persona. Have you ever stopped to wonder why he volunteers instead of working a real job? It's because he wants people to think of him as a hero who dedicates his free time for others. And why does he drive alone at night all the time? Don't you think it's weird he doesn't have a proper alibi for the night those women were murdered?"

"He had an alibi." I say defiantly.

"Had. Past tense." Jake says smugly, folding his arms.

I try to think back to what Liam's alibi was. I checked it on my first few days...

"I messed up my tenses. He still has an alibi. It was Kim."

He chuckles darkly. "Yeah, you should ask Kim about that one. She says he was out for a drive alone one of the nights at least, and he asked her to cover for him."

"You're just spreading rumours. Kim wouldn't lie about something like this."

"No? You don't know her like you think you do, then. And you don't know him well either, clearly."

"You sound jealous." My voice betrays my rising anger.

He shakes his head. "Nah, I just care about you. And like I said, it's the quiet types you have to watch for. And don't they say that people who involve themselves in the case are often the ones behind the crime?"

"Sometimes, not always. He's a SAR volunteer."

"Yeah...who has conveniently showed up a few minutes after every single bad thing that's happened to you so far since you've been here."

My face burns with embarrassment and doubt. He's not wrong.

"I worry about you around him."

"I can handle myself, Jake."

"I know that. But this town has always had it out for you. Your uneasiness and fear about it...it makes you vulnerable."

I realize I'm biting my lip just as his fingers come across and gently pull my bottom lip out from between my teeth. There's an intimacy between us that is still red hot intense, even after all this time.

I pull back quickly and continue cleaning the side of the building. I'm trying to play ignorant even though my face feels flushed, betraying me.

He seems surprised at first that I broke the spell, but then his smile breaks open across his face and there's a kindness to it: a sort of understanding reflected in his eyes, of who I am and who I've always been, and an acceptance of that too.

"You're not alone here, Jane. I'll always do anything I can for you, you know that right?"

"Thank you," I say softly, just as Kenny makes his way back outside.

"More useless tips," Kenny grumbles. "God, this town has really lost its mind."

"Anyway, follow up on those things I mentioned Jane. Take care of yourself." Jake says as he turns around and heads in the direction of the Raven.

"Oh? Something I said?" Kenny asks.

"Nah, he just came by to chat my ear off. I think he could tell I was done listening. Be right back."

I enter the station and use the public washroom. I scroll through my phone but I still haven't heard from Liam in a few days so I send him a quick text.

Want to have dinner tonight? Miss you.

I want to call him instead. He would be a help and a comfort. But I'm too proud.

~~~

We get a call later on from Laryssa who says she overheard some people in the bar talking about the vandalism at the station.

Megan (and Adam)'s mother is taking credit for the spray painting. She apparently has been causing the majority of our disturbances online and spreading rumours that are working against us. When Kenny relays the message, we aren't too surprised.

Bobby says we might not even do anything about it. We've earned some second-guessing lately and who wants to arrest a woman who just lost her daughter for something as small as police harassment or vandalism?

Although it makes me wonder how things are for Adam at home.

The guys get dispatched out for a wildlife vs. auto collision, involving a moose and a crashed SUV. The people are fine but the moose is injured. I ask to go with them, but Bobby tells me they've got it and that I don't have the stomach for it. He's right. I'm still reeling from everything else I've had to see and confront these last weeks. I'll take a back seat on this one.

I radio for Wildlife Management to meet them at the scene.

I'm not allowed to work or touch the case involving Harrison or Abby or the other victims. I'm back to patrol and reporting duty for now and it seriously sucks.

Before I leave, now that everyone is gone, I can't help but look up the autopsy and case file for Harrison in our computer system. They've moved the murder board into a locked incident room so this is the best I can access for now.

They've gotten nowhere with this case. No suspects, no leads on who might've killed Harrison. Whoever it was, disinfected, detailed and thoroughly cleaned Harrison's unregistered Honda beforehand. No stray hairs, blood or fingerprints.

Worse, the SAR forensics team reported a few missing protective suits from one of their trucks, which could explain the complete lack of evidence at the crime scenes.

Jamieson has interviewed all members of SAR, including Kenny and Liam, who would've had the opportunity to steal the suits. I'm denied access to those interviews, so I move on.

I'm trying not to focus on all the ways I'm doubting Liam right now but the coincidences are getting a little harder to ignore. I think about those errand runs that took longer than usual when I was at his house. What was he really doing?

The case file for Harrison's death pops up with only minimal, basic information. The only DNA in the vehicle found was Harrison's and a few of his close friends who have solid alibis. Typical if it's the same disciplined, methodical killer. And yet, to me, the kill seems so much more personal and extreme than the others. It also makes me wonder how lucky one careful person can be or if our killer has firsthand experience with DNA evidence. This lead has been mentioned before, but to me, this seems like an extremely valuable clue to follow up with.

Jamieson and Francis seem to think the killer has just evolved. Maybe they're right...but the kill itself was so much more gruesome and time-consuming, and that doesn't seem like a simple evolution to me.

Harrison died a slow and agonizing death according to the autopsy. His mouth was duct taped shut and his hands and feet were bound to a chair, as he was brutally beaten to death with a blunt force object–then five of his fingers were cut off using what the coroner guesses was an electric saw. I shiver thinking of it. He eventually bled out from his wounds, but it took several hours.

Why only half the fingers? I can only guess that the killer found out he didn't have the appetite for torture after all.

Harrison hurt me badly, so many times, but I can't help but feel my anger melt away like butter and understand for once, that while my life went on to bigger and better things, his never got better and he's dead now. Tortured and six feet in the ground.

His soul just vanished, never getting the chance to heal from its time spent here on Earth.

I know Harrison's mother was a docile defender of him when his father would abuse him, and later, when his stepdad would do the same. He was always a victim in his home, which is why he was the complete opposite everywhere else, where he felt he had some control.

He learned how love should be from his mother and the adult men in their lives; controlling, jealous, harsh and unforgiving. I was drawn to his damaged heart, because my own was the same, after losing my dad and Abby. We could share the burden, I thought, not knowing that two broken people usually make the wound bigger instead of whole.

I think of the night he almost took my virginity away, how I laid there in the long grass still as a statue in shock. Or even before that, our few months together dating. All the mind games he played with my head, the times I caught him cheating on me, or our screaming matches and the walls planted with fists.

Harrison's death made me angry at first. Angry that I never got an apology or even an acknowledgement of wrongdoing or a sign of remorse. Any chance at that had been taken away with his last breath.

Sometimes we see that we are only a small part of the broken puzzle of someone's life, even though their actions were a big part in how ours were created.

Now, I feel a mix of what could be closure or forgiveness, with confusion clouding both. The damning question of "why." I'm not making excuses for his behaviour. It's less about letting him off the hook, and more about *releasing myself* from the shame, the guilt, the endless questions and doubting of myself.

I log out of the computer system and lock up the station, feeling heavier than I did before I looked up the details of Harrison's death. My body is so stiff and painful, and I feel completely overwhelmed. My depression returns to the forefront, no longer accepting a backseat, and weighs me down so much that every step feels like I'm walking through quicksand.

CHAPTER 27 - JANE

I eat in my new rental car that is parked down the street from the Raven. I check my phone again but still no reply from Liam even though it has a read receipt. I try not to overthink this. He's probably out on the wildlife job. It's harder to remember when I'm not around him, but little by little I've learned to trust him.

The things Jake said probably aren't even true. He's just pushing my buttons like he loves to do.

I think about the spooky, dark drawings from Megan's notebook and it suddenly makes me feel as if I'm being watched.

I stop and look around, scanning the sidewalks, the trees and any windows from nearby houses. I don't see anyone except for a few stragglers smoking outside the bar.

~~~

I'm woken up by a vibration in my pocket. I'm confused because it's no longer dark outside. The sky is a dark blue blending into sapphire, with some light orange rising from the other side of main street. I've fallen asleep in the car, still a few blocks down from The Raven. It's freezing in here and my body is as stiff as a corpse. I sit up, my joints and muscles screaming in protest, and turn the key in the ignition, watching the car come to life. I put the heat to full blast. I take my phone out, expecting it to be Liam finally replying, but it's that same unknown number.

My mouth feels as dry as the desert as I click it open and there's no message. Just a picture, taken from far away. I zoom in to get a better look and see that it's Liam, walking with his arm around a brunette woman, down a side street at night. I can't see who he's with because they are faced away from the person taking the photo, but I recognize Liam's long blonde locks and silhouette immediately. I check the time stamp on the photo. This was taken last night.

I never saw them...but I did fall asleep at some point. What does it mean? I feel a tickle go up the back of my neck, and my eyes start to water before I push it all down to a dark place deep within me.

Focus Jane. This is a distraction. It's nothing.
Doesn't feel like nothing.
Whoever this is, they're trying to fuck with you.
Well, they're doing a damn good job of it, aren't they?

On my way back to the log home, I smell the smoke before I see it. I park the car and wander to the back of the house where Bobby is having a bonfire by himself. Leaves crunch under my boots and an owl hoots in the distance. When Bobby looks up and notices me, he doesn't smile or nod, rather his eyes return to the flames. He takes a swig of his coffee.

"Burning the evidence?" I joke. He gives me a weak, fake smile before it quickly disappears. He doesn't trust me right now.

Bobby brings me out of my thoughts with a cough. It seems like we both want to disappear inside our own heads for a little while, so even though we aren't saying much, the company is still reassuring. He hands me the lid of the thermos, wordlessly, and tops it off with still-hot coffee. I bring it to my lips and let the steam and smell comfort me.

Bobby stirs in his seat and finally breaks the silence.

"What are you hiding from me Jane?" He asks suddenly.

I feel my face get hot but know he can't notice it in the light of the fire.

"I'm not–"

"Tell me about that night." His voice is stern and low. "The God's honest truth."

"The night that Abby died, you mean?" I ask quietly. It hurts to say it out loud.

He nods and looks over at me, waiting.

I tell him what I do remember all those years ago, keeping my eyes on the fire rather than watching the disappointment and fear dance across his face in response to my words.

After what seems like forever, he speaks. "Does anyone else know?"

"I don't know."

"What about Miranda?"

"From what you've told me, she's still refusing to say anything about that night. She got her deal. I doubt she will say anything at all, unless it helps her in some way."

His eyes study me closely and I have to look away in shame. For the first time in my life, Bobby is second-guessing how much he knows me.

He gets up suddenly, grabs the pail of water next to him and douses the fire. The red and orange flames turn black and the smoke spits from the fire into my face. I get out of its way and catch my breath.

"I'm going to stay at Judie's for a few days. I need you at a distance right now so that I can see clearly." He says these words looking up at the clouds rather than facing me directly. "Please, Jane."

"Okay," I manage in a stutter. My heart is beating outside of my chest.

He turns on his heel and walks to the house, closing the door behind him.

I fall back into the wooden seat and my mind is racing with questions. Is he going to arrest me? Should I run? No I shouldn't run; I didn't do anything. Did I?

My thumb hovers over my text messages. I'm not exactly on speaking terms with either Liam or Sara right now. I sigh and put my phone back into my pocket. Then I think of Jake, and text him instead.

Hey, where are you staying again?

As I go to put my phone on the arm rest, it falls on the ground. Reaching over for it, I notice out of the corner of my eye, a white triangle in the coals of the pit. I look back at the house but the blinds are drawn. I grab a stick and fish it out carefully. I take a photo of it from my phone. It's part of a piece of paper, or rather, card stock. I can make out only one word: "cabin".

I bite my lip but the thoughts won't come together like a puzzle. I don't know what this is, but I scoop it up with a piece of leaf and bring it back to my car. I head back to town.

I check the Raven on my way in, not bothering to park at a distance. I enter and look around, but no Jake and no Liam. I'm getting back into my car when I notice someone suddenly standing there a foot away. I stumble back on the grass, pulling my pocket knife out as I catch my fall.

"Jane! It's me! It's Sara."

I lower it and go back to a neutral stance, though the adrenaline coursing through my body still makes me feel stiff. "What the fuck are you doing sneaking up on me? I could've stabbed you."

"I'm sorry," she whispers. "I need to talk to you but it can't be here."

She looks like she hasn't slept. "What's wrong Sar? I'm sorry I haven't stopped by to see you lately, I've just–"

"It's fine. Jane, please can we?" She motions to the car. I join her in the front, a little distracted by the few people walking the streets, still staring at us.

She locks the door, although no one is that close. And it's daytime.

"What's up? You're acting a little nutty." I try to make my words sound less condescending and more concerned.

"Langdon told me something that I need to tell you but you can't freak out," the words rush out of her mouth and she looks at me with a worried expression.

"Okay...go on."

"Langdon said he noticed Harrison's Honda cruising through town when he was missing...like the night before his body was found...and when he looked in the driver seat when the car passed, he saw someone in a cop's uniform, wearing a trapper's hat with the mask pulled up. Obviously he didn't get a great look at who it was...but he said he could definitely make out Bobby's Detachment Commander jacket..."

"I call bullshit."

"No, listen," she begs, "Langdon said it was like after the bar and mainstreet were closed and he was walking to my place when he saw the whole thing. He said at first he thought he imagined it...but then he had a really bad feeling and so he asked me what he should do and I told him I'd talk to you about it first."

I actually laugh. "This is Bobby we're talking about, Sara."

She stares at me blank-faced. "Yes...I know. But Langdon wouldn't lie about something like this."

I try to process what she's saying but my mind won't let me. I think back to the words Bobby spoke to me in the bathroom after he told me Harrison was dead. I can't remember exactly, but I think he said something like: *I thought I wanted to kill him myself for what he did to you...*

"You're saying...the night or so before Harrison was found dead, the night of April 4th, Langdon saw what looked to be Bobby in disguise, driving Harrison's car?"

She nods. "The same car they found his body in."

"You think Bobby killed him." It comes out more of a statement than a question.

"I don't know, maybe. Or moved his car at least. That's what Langdon says."

"Yeah, because Langdon is the *embodiment* of truth and good judgement." I shake my head. The anger is rising within me, about to burst through my chest.

She holds her hands out desperately. "I know, but if Langdon saw it and thinks it looks bad, don't you think that means something, Jane?"

"Not really. I don't trust your boyfriend, Sara."

"That's not fair," she says, irritated.

"I saw him the other night with a cute blonde on his lap. He was having one hell of a time at the Raven, until I walked in."

"You just want to change the subject because you know how it looks for Bobby. Not to mention your involvement in any of this. What are you guys hiding?"

She notices the panic in my face and smiles quickly as if she's won this argument, then lets it fade away. I try to let that go. "Well, if you're so worried, tell Langdon to go tell Jamieson at the station." They wouldn't take this seriously either. I'm pretty sure anyway...

"I wanted to come to you first." Her voice is softer, but I'm waiting for another blow. "But I guess I forgot who you've become."

She bursts out of the passenger side door. I jump out a second later and slide over the front of the car to her side in one leap.

"Sara! What the hell does that mean?"

"Oh, fuck off!" She screams back, as the passerby's turn in our direction again.

She turns to face me now, her body stiff and her eyes livid. "It's always been about you, Jane. You were always the centre of attention, the one who had it worse than everyone else."

"You know what I've been through. I didn't ask for any of that! It was never easy like your spoiled life!"

"You were always selfish. That's why your life turned out this way. Because you go through things and then collapse under them. Forgetting that everyone has problems that make them want to give up. The difference is that everyone else just does it in silence. They get through it."

I bite my tongue and try to hold it together. There's a crowd forming now, watching us.

"You never think about anyone but yourself!" She yells.

"If that was true, Sara, I wouldn't be in this job. All I do is think about other people and sacrifice my own life to help others."

"There we go again. The sacrifice, the hardships, the poor me I'm an orphan crap–"

Sara stops mid-sentence. She's taken it too far. We both know it. My voice feels stuck in my throat.

"Fuck you," I finally spit the words. "Langdon's alibi the night of the murders was another chick. Did you know that? They've been fucking each other behind your back. You two really *deserve* each other!"

I go around to the driver's side, hop in and slam the door. What I said was true, but I have been holding it in. It's supposed to be confidential but we can't help what comes out naturally. That definitely wasn't the time to tell her, but in that moment, it felt good to see the look on her face.

CHAPTER 28 - JANE

I get a reply from Jake reminding me he's renting one of the new homes downtown and that I'm welcome to drop by or stay over if I need. I wonder if he's spoken to Bobby or Sara, or if he's just putting two and two together from my cryptic text. I hold off replying for now.

After the whole afternoon spent inside my head and pouring over my notes, and against my better judgement, I called Kenny and told him to pick up Sara and bring her to the station for questioning. He seemed surprised until I explained to him that she came forward with a witness statement that could provide some insight to Harrison's murder. One that we simply could not ignore. He was equally surprised when I told him I wouldn't be joining them, but would come later with Kim who might have lied about Liam's alibi.

"What's going on?" He asked. "Should I be worried?"

"No." I lied, hoping my voice wouldn't give me away. "Just protect Sara and get her statement. I'll meet you guys at the station in a few hours. Something I have to do first."

We hung up and I knew I was in real shit after they spoke to her. I'd definitely be suspended and maybe I'd even go to jail if they pressed Bobby hard enough.

It feels like I'm ruthlessly throwing him under the bus, but I believe in his innocence and I don't want Langdon having some sort of blackmail to use against us. Which I know he will.

The roads are quiet tonight. It doesn't take me long to get there.

I arrive at his house unannounced, but the outside lights are on as if he's been expecting me.

How can you tell the difference between paranoia and healthy suspicion? After Marcus, I've lost my ability to tell.

I kill the engine and make long strides to the front of the house in no time, noticing immediately the eerily quiet outside. The wind is still and not a bat nor a cricket is disturbing the silence of the evening.

I pound the wooden door with my fist anyways. Keeping an eye on the tree line as I do so.

A sleepy Julia peeks her head out the side window, moving aside the curtain. My foot taps the porch impatiently.

The lock turns and she opens the door confused.

"Is Liam okay?" she asks, rubbing her eyes of sleep.

"What do you mean? Isn't he here?" I step inside, not waiting for my invitation.

"No. I thought he was with you. He got called out for an emergency yesterday and never came back or called."

"You've been on your own? This whole time? You're sure?"

She rolls her eyes at my question. "I'm not stupid."

"No that's not...he isn't here?" I ask again.

She studies my face and her arms drop to her sides. "What's going on?"

She might be ten, but she certainly isn't stupid. And she's not lying either. I still check the house and I call Liam's cell three times, but it immediately goes to voicemail. His phone is off. I don't have time to really think through what that means.

I call one last time, stepping outside of the house to leave a voicemail. "Liam, it's Jane. Call me as soon as you get this. It's about Julia, she's...been hurt and I've had to bring her somewhere safe." I wait a moment, feeling guilty I lied about Julia's well-being, but I know it's the one thing that would make him call me back. "I need to know where you are. Call me NOW."

I hang up and instantly feel uneasy. Why is his phone off?

I go back inside and hand my phone to Julia, who looks increasingly more worried. "I want you to please dial Kim's number. I want to speak with her."

She does as I tell her, and as soon as she picks up, I tell Kim I need an emergency babysitter for Julia.

"Where's Liam? Is something wrong?"

"I can't talk right now. Are you able to come watch her or not?" I'm trying to keep my voice level. I hear her tapping a pen on her end of the line.

"Right now?" she asks.

"Yes. There's a serious situation over here, Kim. I'll explain more when you get here. I don't want to worry anyone–" my eyes move to the young girl's face listening to my every word, me trying to read her expression,"–but I need you to come pick her up and bring her somewhere else. Not your house, it's too obvious. Do you have somewhere else you two can go?"

She waits a beat before answering. Probably coming to terms with what my words really imply. "Uh, yes, I'll be there in ten minutes." She hangs up without a goodbye.

I feel a heavy longing to protect Kim, to not have her involved in any of this, but I knew Julia would feel safest and happiest with her, while she stresses about her brother.

We wait in the living room for what seems like half an hour but the clock only says eight minutes have passed when Kim finally arrives at the front door. She bursts in, in a panic.

"What's going on?" Her eyes scan the house for signs of what is happening but the place is tidy as usual. She eyes Julia and embraces her against her waist in a hug. "Hey sweetie, go pack a sleepover bag for me, okay?"

Julia hesitates, staring from me to her.

"Go on, it'll be okay." Kim says, softening.

She runs up the stairs and darts to her room. I study Kim while we wait, trying to memorize every inch of her and store it away for later.

Finally, we can hear Julia shuffling about.

"Jane, how worried should I be? He's my friend. Is he in trouble?"

"I don't know. And keep your voice down." I say, flickering my eyes around the house as she starts to pace. "Tell me, is there an emergency in town that I don't know about, that would've taken Liam out of the house since yesterday and not call anyone to check in on Julia?"

"No. I would know." She rests her head in her hands, then looks up again. "Since *yesterday*?" Her blue eyes widen in horror and she reaches out for the closest chair to sit down.

"That's what Julia said." I lean back against the door frame and cross my arms in front of me. I need to focus but my mind feels like someone is shaking it violently.

"Liam would never leave Julia for more than a few hours."

"I know." I pause, choosing my next words carefully. "I didn't notice at first but yes, I haven't heard from him in a few days either. Have you?"

She shakes her head; perfectly curled, red locks of hair bouncing on her shoulders. "No, he's been extra quiet. I thought he'd just been spending more time with you."

My heart sinks. The last time Liam and I were together was unlike any other experience I've ever had with any man. I let myself get too hopeful.

I'm worried about him.

"Kim, did you lie for Liam when you were his alibi?"

She meets my eyes and her face darkens. She sighs. "Yes. I did. But before–"

"That is not okay!" I yell, interrupting her.

She shushes me and I try to calm down.

"He has PTSD so he goes out driving at night sometimes so he's tired enough to sleep and hopefully not have nightmares," she explains. "Sometimes he has nightmares first, then goes driving to clear his mind. He mentioned you already were looking into him the first day you got here because he was an outsider. I was helping out a friend. I know he's not involved with any of this."

Kim looks like she's going to cry. She cares about him too. More than I expected.

"How well do you know Liam?" I finally ask her.

Her face distorts into confusion, then a wall of defensiveness. "Pretty well. As you know, we dated first but found it easier to be friends. He's one of the best people I've ever met in my life." She hesitates. "He could be getting murdered right now and you're trying to pin everything on him!" She's starting to get hysterical. I hold out my hand to her in a calming gesture.

"Please lower your–"

"You know, I was one of your biggest advocates here Jane. Through everything everyone was saying about you, how the body count has only doubled since you got here and how you have a shady past...I stood up for you. But I have to admit maybe I was wrong to do that if you think there's any chance in hell Liam is involved in what's been happening here."

I strengthen my stance. Try to imagine her not having said the words she just said.

"I don't know what to believe, I'm just considering all–" I start but she cuts me off.

"Did you know my dad was convicted of forgery a few years ago? He was caught forging government documents."

I didn't know that. She's talking about Bruce. Her adoptive father. "Okay...what has that got to do with anything that's happening now?"

"It means I know that even the smallest of revelations can be damning to someone you love when they're put in front of a jury. I didn't know then what I know now, and that is to keep my mouth shut if I don't have anything helpful to say."

"Kim..."

She holds out her hands. "It's not Liam. Simple as that." Her face flushes red. She's visibly stressed.

This is not going how I planned. I swallow. Hard. "I just want to find him safe right now. That's all I want to do." I have to control my voice. My impatience is slipping through the cracks.

I check my phone and still no reply from anyone. I flip through the messages until I find the one I want. "Do you know who this is? Or why this would be sent to me?" I ask her, my hand extended to show her the photo in full screen mode, making certain that the threatening messages aren't also on full display.

She leans in and studies it. She looks as confused as I feel. She leans back again. "I'm not sure. Why do you have this?"

"An anonymous number sent it to me. It's from last night."

That surprises her.

"Isn't that when Julia said he left? It's not like him to leave her for a *booty call*."

I try to reel in the jealousy and anger I feel that comes rushing in like an avalanche. Suffocating.

"Are you sure you don't recognize the woman?"

She gives my phone another hard look but shakes her head. "This feels really off, Jane."

I take a seat on the edge of the couch now. "I know. That's what I've been trying to tell you. Something is wrong here, and I just want to get to the bottom of it."

She studies my face. I look away from her, her gaze too intense, as if she's reading my every thought.

I wonder for a moment about asking if she sees any resemblance there.

"Okay. I'm sorry I overreacted. I know you're just doing your best." She says the words softly, like she's surrendering.

Julia opens her door and makes her way down. My cell phone rings. It's Kenny. I press ignore for now and help them bring everything to Kim's car. Julia seems to sense the tension in the room.

I turn towards Kim who's sitting in the driver seat. "I'm just trying to follow leads and cross people off the list. I don't want this."

Her gaze stays straight ahead but she gives me one firm nod. "Find him please."

My phone rings again as she starts to back out of the driveway. I pick up this time.

"Damn it Jane!" Kenny roars. "Bobby's place has been ransacked and he's missing."

"What..." I barely get the words out. My mind starts to feel numb. I'm seeing black and white dots in front of me and I think I might pass out. "No...he's at Judie's for a few days..."

I feel, rather than hear, Kenny still talking in the receiver. Kim looks over to me and stops reversing the car. I dig my fingernails in my thigh as hard as I can, letting the pain focus me.

"...Come back to the house for something...Judie's at her place worried sick." He continues on. "Bear's here whimpering up a storm. He was locked in Bob's office when we found him. And something else..."

"Tell me," I whisper.

"There's a lot of blood. It looks like he was dragged out."

I feel the air get sucked from my lungs and I choke on it. Tears fall down my face. I'm terrified. I'm doubled over in shock. Kim gets out of the car and kneels down to my level. She's reading my face, hers changing from panic to pure fear. I assume it's mirroring my own.

She starts rubbing my back, trying to tell me to breathe in and out slowly. She's waiting for instructions.

"I'll be there as fast as I can. I'm coming with Kim. She can take Sara back to your place. We have Julia."

"Why do you have Julia?" he asks.

"Nevermind that. We'll be there soon." I hang up and jump in my car, motioning for Kim to follow me. I smash the palm of my hand on the dash hard in frustration. It burns like I just put it on a hot iron.

I floor it all the way to Bobby's.

~~~

The first thing I notice is the blood on the porch, leading a messy red trail through the gravel and then disappearing where Bobby's truck is usually parked.

I feel the panic rise in my throat and deafen my ears.

The porch light is off for some reason and Kenny has his truck's lights facing the house with all the lights on inside. He's on the phone with someone but he hangs up quickly when I arrive.

I jump out of the car.

"Is that...blood?" My voice cracks as I say it.

Kenny nods and hands me paper foot covers I slip on over my shoes. I glove up.

"Go ahead and check out the scene inside. Jamieson and Francis are on their way as well. Watch your step...the porch light...the bulb is missing."

"What?"

"The bulb has been taken out," he says quietly. We both know Bobby wouldn't have left it that way. Whoever was involved with this planned to make Bobby vulnerable as he answered the door.

"It looks to me like the bastard wounded Bobby and then dragged him in his truck to a separate location." Kenny says it angrily, then leaves my side to usher Kim to park on the grass away from all of this.

318

Sara doesn't say anything to me, just a quick worried glance in my direction, as she gets out of Kenny's truck and hops in with Kim and Julia and they head out, as instructed. I watch the horror on Julia's face from the car window as they pull out of the driveway.

I'm starting to feel dizzy. I can't feel my feet as they move, but they carry me carefully around the scene and through the house.

Kenny is saying something to me again but it feels like I've gone deaf. It's like I've taken drugs and am on a bad trip. Maybe I'm just having a nightmare.

There's broken glass and various objects thrown all over the floor: a vase, the coffee mug I got Bobby last Christmas, one of Judie's large glass container candles, a frying pan which was left in the sink from yesterday. The kitchen table has been knocked over and there's a knife missing from the block.

Bobby fought hard.

There's a small pool of blood in the living room, where it looks like someone was hurt badly enough for them to be dragged out and to leave a steady trail of blood all the way through the kitchen to the front door and down the steps. I shudder, wondering what part of Bobby might have been leaking blood this way. Leg? Head wound? Stomach?

Tears fill my eyes again and I brush them away with my sleeve. I try to focus.

The front door is unharmed. It looks as if Bobby knew whoever did this to him and let them inside himself, or because of the empty bulb, was rushed once he opened the door.

I feel ice cold.

I snap out of it once I reach the office where Bear is. He jumps up and I kneel to his level, catching him in my arms. I'm filled with relief, but it doesn't stay for long.

"...Don't you think?" Kenny has been talking to me this whole time but I haven't heard a word he's said.

"What?"

"He was just in here with the door closed. There are scratch marks on the door. But he's a beast of a dog. Don't you think he would've put up more of a fight if someone was trying to harm Bob?"

He's right. I look around the room confused. I feel a pang of betrayal.

"Why didn't you protect him Bear?" I say, my voice hoarse and frustrated, fighting off tears. I let myself fall to the ground in a heap. Bear is sulking in the corner. He knows something is wrong. He comes over to me a few times to touch my face with his nose, desperately wanting me to tell him it's okay. One of Bobby's photo frames has been knocked down, and Bear has obviously walked over it, leaving a small crack.

I look up at the wall of frames. Then I scan the rest of the room.

"This room has been left untouched. It's not messed up like the rest of the house." I say.

Kenny kneels down to me. "Yes...because Bear was shut in here. Probably by Bob. To keep him safe."

"For fuck's sake, Bear could've helped!" I notice Kenny flinch. "He could've at least provided a distraction."

"Darling, Bear doesn't have any training. He wouldn't have been of use. Bobby was just trying to protect him."

"Wait." I say, trying to work through my thoughts, pushing aside my feelings to get to the root of what's been bothering me. "This room. It was closed. With Bear inside."

Kenny stares at me. "Yeah, so?"

"Bobby opened the door to whoever did this to him. But first, he locked Bear in here..."

Kenny frowns. I feel a shiver take hold of me, from my lower back all the way up my spine.

"Jane. He...knew he was opening the door to someone capable of this."

"Looks that way to me." I respond numbly. "But why?"

Is this why he was going to stay at Judie's? Did he know this was about to happen?

Kenny slumps to the floor across from me. "What the fuck."

I crawl over to Bear, softening, and give him a pat, while I pick up the busted frame on the ground. It's the photo of Bobby and his fishing buddies at the cabin.

"What do you think it all means?" Kenny asks.

"I don't know." My mind jumps elsewhere. "Kenny, did Sara tell you what was going on?"

"No, she wouldn't say anything until you came and then this happened."

I'm not sure if it's loyalty or spitefulness that's made Sara keep her mouth shut, but for a second, I allow myself to be grateful.

"I think Liam is missing too," I add, almost in a whisper.

"Fuck!" Kenny yells this time.

I hear footsteps outside the room now. Someone else entering the house. Bear lets out a warning bark.

"It's Jamieson and Francis!" Jamieson yells. "You guys in here?"

I look up to Kenny who is already on his feet. He relaxes a bit. "I called them when I called you of course." He says, as if answering an unspoken question. "I guess if we're all dropping like flies, it's good to have extra help."

I feel broken inside.

He walks out of the room to update them on the situation. I pull myself up to standing. My legs feel like Jello.

Bear whines. I look down at him and rest my hand on his soft face. "I'm sorry I got mad at you. I know it's not your fault."

I put down the busted frame face up on Bobby's desk, with my other hand.

"I'm gonna take care of you until we find Bob, okay?" I say to him. I quickly inspect his paws for glass pieces and find none, thankfully.

I turn for the door, but something makes me stop and look back at the frame.

Cabin.

I feel for the plastic bag still in my pocket, holding the piece of paper from Bobby's bonfire, and pull it out. I rub my fingers over it to clear some of the remaining ash from the fire.

I can see it clearer now. It definitely says cabin. And now, a framed photo of my dad's old cabin is the only thing disrupted in this room. A room Bobby locked Bear away in, before answering the door to a possible murderer.

Did he throw the frame down in an attempt to send a message to me, in a quick panicked moment? I stare at the photo trying with all my might for it to tell me what Bobby meant by doing this, if he did it at all. Bear could've knocked it down when he heard Bobby in trouble.

But the piece of paper...

KILLER IN THE MIRROR

The photo is of Bobby, my dad, Kenny and Kim's dad Bruce Jenkins.

If he's trying to tell me one of these people are the murderer, that leaves Kenny or Bruce.

Fuck, fuck, fuck.

CHAPTER 29 - JANE

I stop by my room quickly and grab the gun in my suitcase under the bed. I check the safety is on, then tuck it in the back of my jeans and throw on a loose cardigan over top, seconds before Jamieson walks by the room and sees me there.

"Jane, are you okay?" He asks, sounding concerned. He flicks on the light which burns my eyes. I try to look natural but I know I'm failing. I go to sit on the bed but remember the gun wedged between my jeans and think better of it.

"No, I am not okay," I say instead, standing awkwardly in the centre of the room.

"Do you have any idea what went on here, or who would want to hurt Bob?" He asks, reading my face carefully.

"I'm assuming it's whoever killed our victims. Small town Detachment Commander seems to be the best target if he was getting close." Again, my voice cracks as I say it.

"Kenny told us he might have known he was opening the door to someone who would harm him. Did Bob share any of his ideas on suspects with you?"

I shake my head. "He wasn't sharing any of his thoughts with me."

I catch a slight reaction to that from Jamieson. "Really?"

"Yes. He wasn't sharing any information with me at all. He plays things by the book." As soon as I say it, I'm glad Sara hasn't shown anyone the video yet. I feel immensely guilty and regretful about sending her to the station and am sure Jamieson can read it on my face.

"Okay," he says cautiously, "stay put here. I might want to pick your brain a bit further on that but I wanted to check out his office and the back rooms first."

I'm starting to panic. "Sure, I just need to use the bathroom. I'm not feeling well."

He turns towards me and nods firmly once. "Understandable. See you in a few."

I make my way into the bathroom at the back of the house, attached to Bobby's bedroom and lock the door. I try to steady my breathing but I must act fast.

I pull the piece of paper that says "cabin" on it out of my pocket and lay it carefully on the sink. I know what they've always said about me–I don't play well with others–and sure, there's some truth to that, but I just need a head start.

I go to the far end of the bathroom and yank open the window and pull the screen free. I climb onto the toilet quietly and dangle my legs out first, one at a time. One big push off and I feel a small vibration in my ankles as I land feet first on the ground. I listen so hard it feels like my ears are burning. There's no noise from inside making me think they heard that.

I make my way around the house quickly and am thankful for the bulbs being out on all four sides. I feel guilty for feeling this way but swallow it and continue on to my car.

The wind howls, scraping my nerves like sandpaper.

Kenny's truck lights still illuminate the front door, but that's the only light pollution out here. It's a cloudy night, so the moon is tucked away, and the pitch-black helps shelter me from getting caught.

I slide into my driver's seat and with only a second's hesitation, bring the car to life. I say another thankful prayer that this car is an older model and doesn't have those automatic head lights for nighttime. I keep mine off and slowly back out of the driveway. My heart is beating out of my chest because I hear the gravel under my tires and it sounds *so loud*.

I can only hope that their ears aren't trained to it like mine are.

At last, I'm on the grassy part of the drive and I pick up the pace, still driving backwards. I feel the gun against the small of my back and I know my flashlight is in the glove compartment.

My phone is in the cup holder and it lights up now. A few text messages light up my home screen.

Laryssa: *I'm calling in that favour. I know you know.*

I roll my eyes at this. It's not all about you Laryssa, I think viciously.

Jake: *Where are you right now?!*

He must've heard about Bobby. I ignore him.

Adam: *Hey Jane, It's Adam again. I heard about Bobby and I might be able to help. I found a track...*the message is too long to show up on my lock screen.

My mind feels like it's going to explode. I ignore the texts for now, getting to the end of the drive and whipping the car around to face in the right direction. The cabin is about twenty-five minutes from here.

I floor it there.

Bobby, I'm on my way.

I might be walking into a trap. I try to make peace with it even though my heart is pounding out of my chest and all I want to do is scream at the top of my lungs.

Whoever has Bobby might think he has the upper hand here, but he obviously hasn't seen a feral animal backed into a corner defend itself.

He will soon.

CHAPTER 30 - JANE

So many have died because of me. At first, I thought it was my personal curse; one which followed me from town to town ripping out anything that was beautiful. It began when I lost my best friend and then my father in the span of one year when I was 17. Then a few months later, I learned what true evil was. I thought I had bounced back from this wretched town of hate and loneliness and loss; I made myself a new and better person since I left it all behind. But now that I'm back here, I realize that I never changed. My surroundings and my life did, but my soul didn't. It's in my blood. There's something evil in this town and whenever I am here, I feel it linger in me too. I heard a singer once describe the darkness inside her and how it originated from her small town's water supply. It ran through her veins forevermore, she said, regardless of where she fled to. I feel that the town of Isinbury has the same effect. There are people here who are truly good, don't get me wrong. Some I consider my only family left in the world. But those people have secrets too. And I have lost my ability to trust anything or anyone at all anymore. Including myself.

KILLER IN THE MIRROR

I stop these thoughts and focus on the task at hand. It's pitch black out here but I make my way to the cabin door. With my gun in one hand and my flashlight in the other, I turn the door knob. It's unlocked. I hesitate, knowing it isn't just my life that might be on the line here. I crouch and enter the place as quietly as possible. As I do, I hear a muffled sound to my left. Just as my flashlight turns to shine on a pale, wet, distorted face, I feel a hard thump on the back of my head. Did I hear the thump first or did I feel it smash into my head first? The delirium has started. I smell the iron of my bloodied head wound as I fall to my hands and knees and quickly lose the battle to fight for my life... My body drops to the cold wooden floor and my eyes close. The killer has me unconscious.

CHAPTER 31 - JANE

I wake up tied to a chair. My hands are bound behind me, but it feels like my feet are free. My gun is gone.

There's a light on somewhere now and it seers through my head.

What am I doing here again?

I look to my left and gasp. Bobby is beside me, lying down on a couch with his hands tied in front of him and a headwound trickling blood down his tired face. He's hardly conscious. He looks distraught and pale. I almost ask him if he's okay, before Liam walks in the room, holding ropes in his hands, his head hung low.

I almost swallow my tongue in shock. I close my eyes fast and pretend I haven't woken up yet as I try to steady myself for what this means.

I try to come up with a reason why he would do all of this but I can't. I'm so confused. Blindsided again. I'm such an idiot.

He doesn't seem the type to commit murder. But being a cop teaches you that everybody looks the part and nobody looks it.

It's a shock to my system that he's here right now, in front of me, involved in this. *The murderer.*

I peek through my eyelids and see him tying my feet together now, but he's doing a lousy job of it. I test the ropes on my hands carefully and notice they aren't tied tight either. I could kick him in the face right now and break free.

My head is pounding and I try to focus. I remember then that I was knocked on the head before passing out. I have definitely aggravated those concussion symptoms from two weeks ago.

I don't know how steady I will be on my feet, but I can do this. I have training and experience with these types of situations–okay, no that's a lie, this is pretty fucked up–but I *have* to do this.

He's kneeling and just as he's about to tighten the knot I swing both feet up and give him my best kick in the chest. He yells, falling back on his ass, and sprawls out on the floor.

I hurry to untie my hands behind my back as Bobby wakes fully and his eyes go wide taking in the scene.

"Bobby, it's okay! I'm almost out–"

I look back desperately at Liam on the floor, but instead of the sinister or angry look that I'm expecting, his face turns inward, shaking his head in defeat and looking at me as if I just killed his puppy.

I freeze too long, my thoughts jumbled, as another man walks in the room with a gun pointed at Liam's head. His towering presence commands the room instantly, even in comparison to Liam's large brawny figure.

It's then that I realize all three of us–Bobby, Liam and I–are held captive here.

My eyes narrow and I notice Liam's bruised knuckles, a dark purple shiner on his cheek and the way he's holding his ribcage protectively, as if he's hurt. My kick landed on his chest, so his ribcage would be from something else.

"Jane, I've waited so long for this moment. I've played it through my head countless times." The low hoarse voice comes from the man holding the gun. "You are even more beautiful and strong in person, up close, than I ever could have imagined."

I spit out the blood that has dripped in my mouth from my head wound and concentrate on the man's face.

I am expecting someone else. Anyone else.

My mind takes longer to register the thick grey beard now hanging down to his chest, the grey hair grown long and tied behind his head. Ungroomed and so much older than when I last saw him.

But it's those piercing blue eyes, as cold as ice, that are unmistakable.

I gasp a sob when those bright eyes, *my eyes*, look sorrowfully back at me.

"Dad?"

CHAPTER 32 - JANE

The man holding the gun to Liam's head is my father, Henry.

I stare at him for a long time before saying anything.

"Is this real?" I ask slowly, unsure of everything. I glance over at Bobby who gives me the tiniest of nods.

I immediately search for Henry's hands and he notices, giving me a small wave of his left hand with three missing fingers.

Henry motions with his other hand for Liam to sit next to Bobby on the couch and Liam does as he's told. Henry comes closer into the room. He's talking to Liam still. "I'm going to lower this gun, but like I said before, I'm a good shot and I wouldn't test me if I were you, son."

I'm still staring at my father. Unable to comprehend. He comes over to me and kneels down a few feet away. Out of reach.

"Nice kick, honey. But I'm going to stay right here until you have a moment to catch up, okay?" He says the words as if this is a normal conversation that we have all the time, and he isn't supposed to be deceased.

"You're...dead?"

He gives me a nervous smile. "I needed it to seem that way. I needed to disappear."

"Kim." I say it like a statement, not a question, and his face changes from seriousness to complete shock.

"I didn't know you worked that one out." He clenches his hands together, a nervous habit he used to have. "We can talk about that too, of course."

"She's my half-sister, isn't she?"

He closes his eyes slowly and nods. "Yes."

"How could you do that to Mom?"

"It wasn't planned. One bad decision. One night."

"I can't believe it...you left us with no goodbye, no explanation...just a slew of chaos afterward. We almost didn't get the pension payout because they argued your death could be ruled a suicide."

"My life insurance policy had coverage in case of suicide, I made sure. But I knew, of course, they would still put up a fight paying it out." He's talking so matter-of-factly. I'm starting to shake. I don't know if I'm cold or in shock or if this head injury is making me hallucinate. "I knew Bobby would fight for you and make sure you and Mom got what you needed."

Henry walks over to the corner of the room, picks up a wool blanket and drapes it around me. I stare at his maimed left hand as he does so. And even then, I get a wave of nostalgia. *Or is that nausea?*

I'm still bound to the chair. "Leaving everything I had behind and knowing the Northern Rockies like the back of my hand, was all I needed to disappear. Bruce Jenkins provided me with forged ID's and I had five thousand dollars cash in the safe in our home office, in case of an emergency. I hunkered down in a canyon for a few weeks then made it out on foot which took another few weeks. Hitchhiked it up to Alaska for a year and a half to wait until things blew over."

"But, why? Why did you do all of this? What the fuck is going on!" I yell the last part.

"I know it's a lot, just try to calm down and I will explain all of it. I promise."

"Why am I tied to this chair!" I scream now. I can't calm down. My mind and heart are racing and it fucking hurts so much, my head, I can hardly even focus.

"Sorry love, I need you to listen before you react. I know it's not your strong suit, and I know you get that from me." He's trying to be coy right now. *God help me!*

"You don't know anything about me! You left me all on my own!"

"I had to. But you were never alone. I've always been there, keeping an eye on you."

"That's such a fucking lie!"

"Jane, I did this all for you. What happened to Abby that night...Laryssa tried to warn me you were involved but I wouldn't believe her. Then Daniel Briggs tried to use it against me to let him go. He tried to blackmail me with it and..."

"You *did* kill him." I say, thick with accusation.

"You killed your friend, so don't point the finger at me."

I flinch back.

The words come out of his mouth so fast, he seems to only now realize what he's said. He back pedals. "I was protecting you."

"It never had to be like this, Dad. You shouldn't have tried to cover it up. Mom..." A sob escapes and I can't finish.

His hand moves to cradle his forehead, hiding his face from view. But I can hear it in his voice: shame, regret, self-loathing. "I know...that's on me too," he says quietly. He reaches out to grab a firm hold on the table next to him for support. "I'm so sorry, Jane."

It's not enough. I want him to feel it, the loss of her. What it did to me.

"She died from the stress of her grief over you...and you weren't even gone. You could've come back and she would still be alive."

The pain is obvious in his stricken eyes, the creases of his forehead, the bunched-up frown. "It wasn't that easy."

"She...couldn't deal...with you being gone...like that." I can hardly breathe trying to hold back these tears. "Why did you leave us like that? Her death...is on you. So much...is on you."

He walks over to me now, and softly takes my head in his hands and kisses my forehead. "I want to protect you. It's what I've always wanted. I'm so sorry it all got fucked up." Tears are crowding at the corner of his eyes and he wipes them away absentmindedly. "Not a day goes by without me torturing myself for what I've done to her. To you. You're a strong woman. A smart detective. You have persevered through so much and I'm so damn proud of you. I'm sorry I missed it all."

"Don't tell me all of these people died to cover up what happened to Abby." I look desperately to Bobby to back me up and notice for the first time that his leg is propped up on a pillow, a huge chunk of glass in his thigh.

"Fuck! Is he okay?" I scream.

Henry sighs. "This is a complete mess. I tried to talk to Bobby at the house. I knew he was on to me. But he freaked out. He was pissed that I had chosen to leave you and we had a bit of a fist fight, he was so very angry at me, and we both slipped and fell into a lamp and the shard went straight through his leg... he wouldn't calm the fuck down because he thought I was involved in these recent murders here and he–"

"What do you mean? Aren't you invol–"

"Well...no. It's a long story like I said, if you would just–"

"Bobby is bleeding from his leg right now. We need to get him to the hospital."

"It's not a main artery. I picked up Liam here to make sure of it. Though I have to say he hasn't been the easiest house guest either."

I look at each man in this room. I have a different sort of love for each one of them. They all mean so much to me. How can I get us all out of this situation in one piece?

"Fine. Explain it to me. But be fast because I want Bobby taken care of. He looks awful." Henry studies each of our faces. He softens a bit. Is that...guilt I'm sensing? "If anything happens to Bobby, I swear I'll fucking kill you myself. I don't care if you used to be my father in another life." I spit the words with as much venom as I can.

"Jane," Bobby speaks up now, the hoarseness clear in his voice, "Let's just listen to what he has to say. I'm fine for now."

Henry breathes deeply. He looks at Liam. "Is he still okay? Do you need anything else to keep him comfortable?"

"I'd like to clean this cut on his head a bit more, but we will need to have this piece of glass removed *at a hospital*." Liam says the last words slowly for emphasis. We all know the stakes right now.

Henry walks over to a medical kit on the ground, clearly there from before, and kicks it toward Liam. "Go ahead. And please take another look at her head." He looks at me wincing. His eyes darken. "I'm sorry about the head. I wasn't sure it was you and fuck, I almost threw up when I realized."

"And what happened to his head?" I ask without any tone at all. Henry stands up and leans against the wall, gun still in hand, but relaxed at his side now.

"I went to Bobby's to try to warn him that it was someone close to you committing these murders." He raises his hands in defense, "I know what you're thinking, but it's not me. Let's bring it back to the beginning. I found out you were involved in Abby's disappearance." I try to interrupt him but he holds up a hand. "Let me finish. I poisoned Briggs to shut him up. Okay? I did it. I panicked and didn't know what else to do. I knew Miranda and Harrison were involved and likely dragged you into it somehow. Briggs had shown up that night apparently for a "drop off" and Harrison had confessed that Abby was dead or had asked for his help–he wasn't very clear on that part other than he walked in on the whole thing. From my understanding, you guys were driving drunk in the junkyard behind Miranda's house and something happened that caused Abby's skull to be bashed in." He swallows and tries to read my expression. "Sounds about right?"

I shake my head slowly but I feel so drained. I keep working at freeing my hands, careful not to reveal that's what I'm doing. I'm almost there. "I don't remember. I blacked out."

He eyes me suspiciously then softens. "I'm not sure if you're telling me the truth because Briggs wouldn't tell me anything else because he wanted proof I was going to let him go first. Obviously, that didn't happen."

I steal a look at Liam and Bobby. They look scared. They're hearing all of this which makes us all wonder what Henry's plans are for us after he's done telling me his story.

Would he just simply let us go?

I doubt it.

I try to focus but I feel so tired. So nauseous.

"I've been keeping an eye on Harrison and Miranda over the years as well. I've been trying to think of a way to bring to light their involvement but not yours, or at the very least, make sure they keep their mouths shut. I've searched their houses several times but have never found anything on any of their devices or in any of their hidey holes. I sent Harrison a few threats via anonymous letters in his mailbox. It seemed to be working but, well, I guess he must have told Lilyann about that night because she ended up dead and then I overheard Brandi trying to blackmail Harrison with it later from behind his house."

"You killed them." I say, my voice betraying my defeat.

"No, Jane. It wasn't me."

"If not you, then who? Who else would want these women dead to keep this secret?" I sigh loudly. "Get to the point Henry."

"Lilyann's death took me by surprise. I thought it was Miranda at first—I didn't think Harrison had it in him—but I've since changed my mind. I was keeping an eye on Megan too, or so I thought, trying to keep her safe until I got a chance to talk with her about who she might have seen kill Lilyann. But I think Megan might've caught me watching her house and thought my intentions were evil instead of protective. All it did was scare her more and anyway, I was stretched thin, as I was also watching Miranda as best I could, and then Megan died and then I heard

Bobby telling Kenny he was going to bring *you* home in the middle of all of this and–"

He throws his hands in the air dramatically.

"I haven't been the only one watching and waiting, Jane. Someone close to you is doing this to protect you or to control you...and it's not me." He gulps loudly and looks over at Liam who is fidgeting uncomfortably on the couch. "That's what I was trying to tell Bobby tonight, and is the reason I am coming out of hiding now because you're in danger and your life is more important to me than anything. I am willing to go to jail if it means you will be safe." He looks at me sadly. "I know for certain it wasn't me, but I have my suspicions about Liam and that's why they're both here."

I look over to Bobby and Liam again and my dad watches me do so. Bobby is near passing out and Liam shakes his head, his long locks dangling in front of his face. "This is ridiculous! I didn't even know Jane before she came here."

"You were both in Vancouver and I looked it up. You only lived a block over from her before you moved to her hometown. How do you explain that?"

My eyebrows shoot up and I study Liam's face. It's beet red but he doesn't say anything, he just glares at Henry.

"What the fuck, Liam?" The words shoot out of me so fast. "There's so much you haven't told me that you really fucking should have."

He struggles for words, his mouth opening, then closing shut in defeat. He heaves a big sigh.

I can feel my own hot tears spilling from my eyes. I try with everything I have to get them to stop but they keep pouring out, betraying how vulnerable I feel.

All this time lost with my father...and for what? Someone covering for me when I didn't even do anything, why? What's Liam's involvement here, really? I don't need protection. Or maybe I do, but only from the people in this damn room!

I steady my voice. "If I was involved in Abby's murder, then I'm going to turn myself in." I say it with more courage than I feel. "For whatever reason or accident, I deserve to go away. I'll make peace with that and I hope you will too." I wipe my wet face on my shoulder, hands still tied behind me.

"Let's talk that over together first," Henry says, raising his hands in surrender, "there are still options for us, Jane. But what I really want to know is, Liam did you–"

There's a firm two knocks at the door. We all freeze.

CHAPTER 33 - JANE

"Did someone follow you?" Henry asks me in a loud whisper, stepping back from me in a readying position.

"Not that I know of." I say back. I hear myself say the words but it sounds like I'm underwater.

They knock again. Harder this time. Henry raises his gun toward the door and motions for Liam to answer it. I shake my head against that idea, but Dad ignores me.

He trains his gun on the door and I take my hands out from behind me slowly, letting the ropes fall to the floor. Henry notices I'm easily out of the chair and simply shakes his head.

I wipe my wet face with the back of my hands and ready my own stance in a crouch in front of the chair. I keep my eyes trained on Dad as I do so, almost asking permission, and notice he looks almost pleased. His reaction surprises me, and I smile mischievously without thinking, like a kid who just made their parent proud. As if we're both playing an innocent game of hide and seek or cops and robbers, rather than life or death.

Oh, what my life could've been.

Liam gets up slowly and walks shakily to the door. His eyes lock on mine and I wish it was me answering the door and not Liam. I push aside the fact I thought he was a killer two or three times in the last 12 hours and wish with all my might that he will be protected. That Liam, the first man I have actually opened up to, who is here *because of me*, will be kept safe.

"Be ready for anything." Henry whispers to him, encouragingly, as if he wasn't just holding him hostage. He seems to think better of it as he adds, "and if you do anything stupid, you'll get a bullet."

I glare at my dad but he ignores me. My heartbeat is pounding in my ears as I wait for the door to open. I look to my dad once more, worried, trying to read if this is part of his plan. I can tell by the blood drained from his face, that it's not.

Just as Liam makes his way to the door, a shotgun blast splits through the wooden panel, spraying wood everywhere. Liam jumps to the left but I can't tell if he's been hit. He's on the ground when what's remaining of the door swings open.

It's Jake.

Henry's gun goes off then and barely grazes Jake in the upper right arm. He flails backward as I scream. The shotgun falls to the ground.

"No! Hold your fire!" I'm yelling.

I run to Jake as my Dad tries to grab me, but as I make my way to him Jake catches his balance and twirls me around with his good arm, making me fall backwards into his strong embrace. He pulls a second gun, this time, a revolver, from his belt and points it to my head.

He's holding me in a chokehold, the perfect hostage grip.

"Jake! It's me. What are you—"

343

But it all makes sense now. My body suddenly goes cold.

"Henry, holy shit, I thought it was you I saw the other day. Damn you look...old." Jake says, malice and surprise in his voice.

"Let her go, Jake." My dad is using his policeman voice now. Strong, assertive, calming. His gun is raised towards us.

"Nah, she's coming with me." Jake says this matter of fact. "And you'd best drop your gun if you want her to come with me, *unharmed*."

Henry hesitates, but doesn't drop the gun. Jake presses it harder against my temple, making me wince involuntarily.

"Fine, fine. I know you don't want to hurt her. I'll put it down slowly." Henry says, his voice a little shaky. He leans over and puts the gun on a nearby side table. I'm pretty sure if he gets a chance, he can still grab it in time, but I don't think Jake has thought this through.

"Good thinking," Jake says, pausing to take in the scene. Shifting me around with him as he does. His body is too hot, sweaty even, though it smells like he recently showered. "Well shit, looks like you already mostly took care of Bobby for me." I look over to Bob. He's more alert now, reading the room as best he can, but he looks pale. He's hurting.

"Jake, why are you doing this?" I play dumb. "My dad already confessed to the murders. He's going to turn himself in." I can't see Jake's face as he has me turned toward the room, away from him, but his grasp on me tightens. He doesn't believe me.

"You're not a very good liar. Not to me." He whispers.

"You were shot. Let me look at it for you." I try instead.

"Oh Jane. You just don't know when to let me lead, do you?" He spits the words in my ear. I try to struggle from his grip but he's strong and he has my bad shoulder pinned under his bicep. "Stop moving or I'll shoot your Dad."

"You'll shoot us all anyway," I say between my teeth, pissed off.

"Eh, you're probably right. But it's up to you if I do it quickly or if I make them suffer."

An animal-like growl escapes me. He laughs.

"That's the Jane I know and love."

"How did you find us here?" Bobby interrupts, croakily. He's hoping someone else might know we are here.

"I turned on a tracking app I put on Jane's phone a year ago. But I've been following her for years."

I remember all of those times where I could feel eyes on me walking home at night or alone in my apartment, getting so paranoid that I often had the blinds closed, creating a dark and depressing atmosphere. I thought it was just my ghosts following me around. My parents, or Abby. But it was Jake all along.

He seems to read my mind when he says, "Yes, you weren't crazy. I have been following and studying you. I became so good at it, I even managed to make myself a spare key to your apartment in Vancouver."

The family photos that were just missing one day. Things I would find out of place. The fridge emptying quicker than I thought.

"And occasionally, taking some things to remember you by."

I remember all those things I thought I had misplaced: the single ruby necklace from my mom, a cashmere sweater I splurged on, my case notes sometimes...my favourite pair of lilac silk undies.

I shiver.

"How did you put something on my phone?"

"You're a heavy sleeper sometimes. Especially when you drink beer."

Henry moves closer. Jake raises the gun to Henry now which is what my dad wants. Jake seems to read his expression and brings the gun back to my temple.

"Alright, I have the gun here. So, we're all gonna listen to me right now. Okay?" Jake says, using his best authoritative tone. "I'm sorry Jane but these two have to die. Say your goodbyes."

"No!" I yell. "Don't touch them." Again, it comes out like a growl.

"We're going to make it look like Daddy # 1 did all the murders and have Daddy #2 die while confronting him. It won't be hard to string together considering the scene they left at Bobby's house. Thanks for that fellas; making my job easier."

"And then what's your plan?" I say urgently, trying to delay the inevitable. "What's your endgame here, Jake? We leave and ride into the sunset together? You know that's not realistic."

He laughs. "You killed my sister, Jane. I knew it then. And I still wanted to be with you. In fact, it made me love you even more."

His face is pressed against mine, and he's trying to look at my reaction. I try to keep it calm.

"I'm sorry it has to be this way, but after this is done, I'm going to drive you to a house I have up north and we'll see if you change your mind then. We can be ourselves up there, just the two of us, like old times. I've got enough funds to keep us comfortable for a long, long time."

I swallow hard, but my throat has become dry as cotton.

"What do you want me to say here? Thank you?"

"I mean...you killed my sister, then I killed those girls to keep you safe. You even killed your partner Marcus, *without hesitation!*" he says this last part, excitedly. "God, how can you not see it? We're both killers, Jane. We've always been dark souls, or have you forgotten how you once told me that I was the only one you ever met who seemed to understand you?"

I do remember saying that. And I had meant it at the time. I was always an unhappy kid as long as I can remember. Moody, frustrated, rebellious. Abby might have taken me under her wing, but she never understood me like Jake had. He had seen my inner self struggling just under the surface, and instead of telling me to lighten up or asking me what was wrong, he would meet me in that dark place as an equal. No questions, no accusations, he would just accept me as I was. It was a comfort.

But now I realize, when I left Isinbury, when I tried to smother that part of myself and never look back, I only ignited something in Jake that had laid dormant.

"...We belong together whether you want to admit that or not."

"Why did those women have to die if this is about us?"

"Aren't you listening? Harrison had confessed to Lilyann while he was inebriated, that he had killed Abby. Lilyann told Brandi, and they decided to blackmail him for it...until Lilyann saw me at a party and confessed to me what they were doing and what they knew, but that she was ready to come forward because the guilt was too much to bear. She's always had a thing for me, but more than that, she wanted my legal advice on how to go about it. Can you believe it?" He laughs in disbelief. "The nerve of her to come ask me about how to get out of a blackmailing charge if she came forward with info about my sister's death. She *had* to go.

Unfortunately, Megan saw me take out Lilyann that night. I was wearing a small body camera, you see, to re-watch it and learn from my mistakes–"

"–You mean to get off on it," I spit.

"No, not like that. Come on, I'm not *an animal*."

"You tore open Lilyann's shirt and left Megan naked."

"Oh come on, they deserved to be exposed. Exposed for what they truly were: blackmailing whores. I was trying to send you a message, Jane."

I shake my head. I don't even know who this person is behind me. It's not the Jake I knew at all.

"Anyway, I noticed Megan in the footage. So, I let myself into her place with the babysitter's key, got her while she was in bed, and returned the key no one the wiser."

"You left her kids to find her like that. You're a monster."

"There wasn't much I could do. Plus, those kids are better off now. Don't tell me you don't see that."

"They'd be better off with their mother."

"That's hilarious. She was a drug addict and could hardly afford to feed them. Now they live in a three-storey home with two sober grandparents who will give them everything their little hearts desire." He makes a sound that isn't quite a laugh and isn't quite a sigh. "Brandi wanted to get out of this town and was sucking Harrison dry to do it. The second he didn't give her what she wanted, she went to threaten you. But I had been watching her and I knew what she was going to do so I came prepared. Having her die in front of you like that, fuck! That was a rush. You almost caught me too that night, but I ducked into the dollar store on main street at the last minute." He licks his lips; I can hear the wetness of it inches away from my ear still pressed against him.

"And Harrison? Was that for me too?" I ask.

Jake chuckles. "He was the biggest liability of all. Wasn't he, Henry?"

My dad looks as angry as I've ever seen him. I can feel Jake grinning against my cheek.

As Jake is talking, I think I see a face in the window to my right. I try not to give it away. I take a chance and look at it again from the corner of my eye.

Is that...Adam? I never read his whole text.

No, no, no. He is too young. He's going to get himself killed. I mentally try to convey a message to him: *Call Kenny. Make the call and get as far away from here as you can. Do it Adam. Please.*

But I see it in his eyes. He might only be seventeen, but he's thinking of his sister. He's feeling the guilt of her death and her absence in his life, and somehow, maybe because he's too young to know better, he feels brave. I hold my breath and slowly shake my head from side to side. I hope he understands the message and that Jake just thinks I'm shaking it at something he's said.

I see his head disappear and I hope to God he's run for the woods. But I get myself ready. I can hear my heart hammering in my ears.

"Fine then let's be together." I say, interrupting him. "But leave them out of it."

"You don't mean that now, but that's fine. I'm patient. You'll come around." He thinks it over. "As for these two, I'm sorry Jane but they will never stop looking for you."

He points the gun to my dad. My heart pounds in my ears. I can feel Jake smile, his cheek pushing into my cheek as he does.

Then he slowly moves the gun left, toward Bobby. I feel my face flush with anger and I try to slam my body against his in a failed attempt to have him let go. But he's strong. And his hold over me stays. He's laughing now.

"Ding, ding, ding! Ladies and gents, I think we have a winner!" He says, sounding like the host of a reality show. "Sorry Henry, looks like she's chosen her favourite father."

Before I can even process the situation, Jake points the gun back at my dad. Henry's face softens as his gaze narrows at only me, and for a second, I feel it is only us here. It's completely silent, as if the room is holding its breath.

His eyes betray so much regret and a fatherly protectiveness. "I love you Jane," he whispers with a slight smile.

Just as Jake is about to pull the trigger, Liam comes from behind the door and tackles us all to the ground. A shot goes off to the right, and my body is slammed underneath the two men. The weight of them sends the breath right out of me. My chin hits the ground hard, a searing pain shooting through my body as my teeth slam together and my jaw vibrates from the impact. I'm sure I've bitten off a piece of my tongue.

The room is spinning, my eyes revealing black dots. I hear the men behind me wrestling, so I spit out some of the blood pooling in my mouth and struggle to my feet.

But Jake has been quick and recovered easily. Bobby is alert and hovering at the side of the room, but his leg makes him not of much use and his hands are still tied. He points toward the table where my dad left his gun.

I leap towards it and once it's in my hands I take aim at Jake's legs. It will stop him but not kill him. Seconds pass slowly. The safety's off.

The three of them are a jumbled, bouncing mess of fists and kicks and grunts, so I focus all my attention on aiming. Even just a few feet away, it can be easy to miss such small, moving targets. I don't want to hit Henry or Liam by mistake.

I breathe in deeply and hold it. Focus, aim, pull and...*release*.

I let go of the trigger.

I hear it go off and feel the small recoil, but nothing happens. I pull it again and again, to be sure.

This gun was never loaded.

I swear under my breath and throw the gun aside. It's useless.

Jake moves like someone who's taken some sort of hand-to-hand combat training, because he's successfully holding off both Liam and Henry from his own gun that lies on the floor beneath his feet. Henry probably hasn't fought in years and Liam has had no sort of formal training whatsoever. They hardly have time to throw their own punches, because they're catching blows from Jake at a relentless speed and needing a second to recover and re-strategize. Then Jake is back at them again. Hungry for blood.

Liam lunges for the gun but Jake crushes the fingers on Liam's right hand with his boot. The crunch of the small bones is loud, but Liam's scream is louder. In the same moment, Jake dodges a blow from Henry and stabs him with his elbow in one swift, angry shot. Henry stumbles back, clenching his chest.

Jake is the smallest out of the three of them and yet it works to his advantage; like a short boxer against a tall opponent, Jake is thriving in this close distance fighting. He's a smaller target and he has a devastating uppercut.

It's up to me.

Henry sees I'm ready; no time to wait for my head to catch up to the scene unfolding here or for the blood to stop pouring down my shirt. He steps back to catch his breath, but Jake pivots on his right foot, grabbing a rock figurine from the mantel beside us and launching it at Henry's head. Henry tries to avoid it by ducking to the right, but his delay in doing so actually helps the rock smash into the nape of his neck instead. A crack sounds off as it makes impact, Henry still spinning to the right then falling face down, motionless.

With this pause, the three of us all leap for the gun underfoot but Jake gets to it first and dives forward to stand beside Bobby, levelling it at his head.

I freeze. Liam raises his hands in surrender as Jake lets out a barking laugh. We're all panting heavily.

Henry is moaning on the floor but manages to turn himself around slowly and prop himself up in the corner facing us. His face is a deep shade of red and covered in sweat. He's exhausted and badly wounded.

I'm trying to think of something to say to make Jake leave here with me alone or to bide time for help to arrive, when he says suddenly, in-between gasps for breath, "I almost forgot you were here big guy…"

Liam is still as a statue.

"Can't have any competition." Jake sneers. "Plus, I just don't like you."

My heart sinks through my chest as I watch Jake pistol-whip Bobby in one sharp movement, Bobby sinking to the floor in a slump, then point the gun toward Liam, almost in slow motion. My body freezes with anticipation, the shock of it. He lets out a shot that goes right into Liam's mid-section, at the same time I fling myself downward in a slide that closes the five-foot gap between us and sends Jake falling forward above me. He catches himself on all fours, but I'm faster now, already on my feet again, my whole body alive with adrenaline. I kick a shocked Jake as hard as I can with my right leg directly into his kneecap, bursting it from its joint. He falls down into a lunge with an ear-piercing scream, gun still in hand. I throw a punch towards his face but miss as he dodges and lands his own uppercut punch to my stomach, winding me completely and pushing me onto my back.

All three men are either shot, passed out or hurt too badly to move.

I'm lying on my back, trying desperately to catch my breath when Jake slides over and lays his heavy weight on top of me. Half-straddling me; a very sexual position. I struggle to get out from under him before he points the gun against my chest and pins my good arm beneath his good knee. His face is so close I breathe in the smells of spearmint and cigarettes from his mouth but his body reeks of fresh sweat now and it surrounds me like a blanket. He's breathing heavily. I'm pretty sure I feel a lower extremity reaction from him and when he notices me taking note of it, he pushes himself further into my stomach where he's sitting.

I glare at him but he leans forward so that his face is just above mine. "You used to like that, remember?" he says, barely above a whisper.

I wiggle from under him but he presses the gun harder into my sternum and it feels like an electrical pain shoots through my chest.

"Leave with me right now, no more fighting, and I'll let them go." He pauses. "Come on Jane. You know it's always been us."

I stare into his green eyes to see if he's lying and weigh the consequences of doing what he says. He leans forward and breathes deeply in my neck, sending chills down my spine that I hate myself for. He plants a desperate, wet kiss there, then sucking on it until I'm sure he leaves a mark.

He pulls back for my reaction. I pretend it's not making me angry as fuck, but I don't know if I'm being convincing enough.

"Fine. Take me away. Leave them. I'm done fighting. I just...want to feel good. Happy." I try to stick as close to the truth as possible. Jake has always known when I'm lying. He's trying to read my eyes so I pull my head forward and open my mouth for him, licking my lips and drawing him in for a kiss. "Kiss me," I whisper urgently. "Convince me to go with you, Jake." He hesitates, trying to read me, before dipping his head forward and shoving his tongue in my mouth angrily. He kisses me open-mouthed and slow at first, and I can feel his eyes watching me intently so I keep mine closed shut but kiss him back passionately. He might be able to read my eyes but he can't read this. I've been playing this game a long time: faking intimacy to fill the void. The kiss tastes of iron and sweat, one of us must be bleeding, but it only adds to the frenzy. It becomes more desperate and he loosens his grip on the gun at my chest. I moan as if I'm enjoying it and he leans forward even further, unpinning my arm from his leg. My self-defense training is screaming at me and I take a second to prepare myself. I know that doing what I'm about to do could end up in him shooting me. Even by accident. But I have to try.

I trap his foot with mine and buck myself upward, spinning us in a roll to the side as fast as I can. He screams out in pain as I've twisted his knee further but the gun doesn't go off. He's surprised and livid when we're face to face again, me on top this time, and I bring both elbows downward into his crotch and he lets go of me with his legs.

Adam bursts through the door then. He provides just enough distraction that Jake leaps up, forgetting his busted knee and falling to the side. I leap for the metal fire poker beside me, grab it with both hands and swing it as hard as I can in a blow to Jake's head. But he moves out of its way and it lands more on his back. As he falls forward from that, a shot goes off, and I hear a thud and a howl. As much as I want to look, I force myself to focus and I finally manage to knock the gun out of Jake's hand with my left boot. It falls to the floor and another shot goes off, but I see Jake dive for the revolver and I do the same. He's closer to the ground so he gets to it first, but I'm hovering over him, both hands trying to grip it free. My left arm has lost so much muscle in it during the last few months and the pain is so intense that my arm keeps giving up without my permission. I might not be stronger than him but my boots send bone-crushing hits to his side to compensate for this weakness.

The adrenaline and will to survive burns through me. My strength is bolder, outlined by my fear. It steadies me, makes me alert.

We're wrestling with the gun, safety off, and again, for one clear moment I realize this will probably go off and one of us will be shot, whether we intend to or not. He must think the same thing, because I see the panic in his eyes. His goal so far has been to protect me, and to be with me. Will that change in this instant?

I hear shouting from the others in the room now but can't make it out. All my senses are locked on Jake. The gun goes off once more, and this time I feel the bullet buzz by my head. Jake lets go of it this time. Out of fear of killing me or killing himself, or just from the shock of the bullet coming so close to me, I can't tell. My shoulder and head injuries are making it hard to concentrate. The excruciating pain makes it hard to even see properly. But I have the gun now in my grasp, and I point it at him as he tries to crawl backward. I train it on his head and he stares me dead in the eyes.

We're both winded. I hear another whimper and I steal a quick glance to my right. Adam has been shot. In the stomach.

Fuck. I steal another glance and notice the blood spreading, just as Jake makes a move my way. I shoot the gun about a foot from his head, as a warning. He falls into a backward crouch, wincing as he does.

"On your stomach Jake."

"Jane...don't do anything rash. We can work this out."

"The last time I heard that from a criminal, I shot him in the head. And that man was my family. You? You're just a stranger to me now. So get on your stomach and *shut the fuck up*!"

"You don't mean that. I know you don't." He's catching his breath still. "That kiss meant something to you. I felt that."

He might be right. Maybe it was a goodbye. Even though he's a stranger to me now, there's a part of me that still knows him as my childhood friend. As Abby's little brother. I push those thoughts out of my head.

"You better not push me and find out if I mean it." I growl.

He rearranges himself slowly on his stomach, his hands going up behind his head. For the first time I notice the stickiness of my chin, my neck and my shirt. I wipe my chin with my good hand and it comes back bright red. I look down to see my shirt soaked with blood too. I must look like a vampire; pale, sickly and covered in red.

"All I wanted to do was protect you," he says, mumbling from the ground. "My reason for living."

"I don't need anyone's fucking protection!" I snarl.

Henry comes out from behind me then and gives a powerful kick right into Jake's face. Jake's head snaps back with the impact and he passes out immediately. Or is dead. I definitely heard a popping sound. Blood is pooling from Jake's face which is still face down on the ground. I think Henry's going to kill him in a blind rage.

I step in-between Henry and Jake, and he finally stops. He's panting, out of breath. Shaking with anger.

"We got him." I say sternly. "Now help the others."

Now that it's quiet, I start to hear the sirens. They're close. *About time.*

Liam drags himself forward, trying to make his way to Adam. It looks like Liam has been shot in the lower chest. My breath catches in my throat. The blood seems to have stopped, as he's made himself a tourniquet from his belt, but he's pale as a ghost.

The kid is barely conscious now. I feel tears in my eyes. Angry, broken tears.

Henry rushes to Liam's side. "Don't move, son. Looks like more of a flesh wound, you lucky bastard, but it could've punctured your stomach, we can't be sure..." Henry gently pulls Liam forward and inspects the wound from behind. "It might be clean through, but that doesn't mean you're in the clear."

Liam is glaring at Henry. And struggling to breathe.

Bobby gets himself up carefully, wobbling over to me and grabbing the gun from my hand. He aims it at a passed-out Jake.

I crouch over to Adam and Liam who are both near the door. Liam reaches out a hand to caress my chin, his paramedic eyes trying to assess me.

"I'm okay," I answer in response to his worried eyes. He's been shot, but of course he's more worried about me. *I might love this*

357

man. "I bit my tongue pretty bad in the fall." It still sounds like I'm talking funny. I can feel the pressure growing in my mouth. The kissing definitely didn't help. I feel my cheeks get hot, wondering who saw that embarrassing tactic, but quickly push it from my mind. I need to focus. "Tell me what to do for Adam." I say firmly, desperately. "I will be your hands right now. You're not up for it."

"Press down as hard as you can into the wound," he says, his voice betraying how much pain he's in.

I try, but my shoulder hurts so much I can hardly use it at all. Henry notices and rushes to take over.

Adam is coughing up blood now. He's trying to reach into his pocket. I do it for him and take out his phone.

"Do you want us to call someone for you?" Henry asks, shakily, as I try to scroll through his recent calls and find the contact information for his mother.

He shakes his head and whispers, "Kenny."

His phone log shows me Kenny was his last phone call. He must have called them as soon as he saw what was going on.

"They're so close, Adam. They'll be here any minute," Bobby says from above us.

"You saved us," I say. "You really did. Just hold on for me, okay?"

Henry continues pressing his hands into the kid's stomach. Everything is turning brownish red, leaking like a spilled can of paint.

"Adam, I'm so sorry. We're going to get you through this."

We all know that's not true. Henry gives me a worried look. Liam is shaking his head in defeat. I'm sitting up now, the pain making my head sizzle like a couple of fried eggs.

Focus Jane, focus.

Adam is struggling hard.

"They're going to arrest us both." Henry says under his breath now, catching my eyes. "There's no statute of limitations on murder in Canada, Jane."

"I know." The words come out as a mumble, my tongue swollen and painful.

Liam's face turns slightly in my direction. "Jane, maybe you should leave with him."

"What?"

"You're going to be arrested for Abby's murder and you don't even remember it. It was probably a wrong time, wrong place situation. To me, that's not justice."

"I can't do that."

"Why not?" This comes from Henry. "This is all my fault Jane. Let me help you."

"Because I'd be just like Marcus and all the other guys I've put away. Running away from my crimes. Benefiting off other people's pain and loss. I made a vow to serve and protect. I'll be turning myself in, and you should too Henry."

The room is silent, other than Adam's small moans.

"I never taught you how to deal with pain. Only how to run or hide from it. I'm taking your lead now, Jane." The words come out as a defeated whisper from Henry. He realizes everything he did was for nothing. And I'm forcing him to have to live with that. I won't carry that burden. I can't.

I crawl even closer to Adam, who is barely breathing now, and hold him in my lap as Henry tries to make him more comfortable.

"I finally did it," Adam whispers.

"Did what?" I ask, between quiet sobs.

"The shadow man in the woods." He's not speaking full sentences anymore.

Henry looks at me confused, and I just shake my head.

"Yeah, you did. You saved us all. He's gone now. He won't hurt anyone anymore. You did that."

The person his sister saw watching her house in the woods was probably Henry. The shadow man in her drawings was my father. But Henry was trying to *save* Adam's sister.

The one who killed his sister though...that was Jake. And because of Adam providing that distraction, Jake will be put away for his crimes. And the rest of us...we will likely live.

We have Adam to thank for that.

He mumbles something I can't quite hear. He reaches out to me now. Calling me by his sister's name.

"Megan?" He asks, while coughing up blood.

The tears are running down my face, uncontrolled. I start rocking him back and forth, holding him closer, shushing him and making him feel safe. What else can I do?

"I'm right here, Adam. Don't be scared."

I'm not sure how he takes my last words to him, but at that moment it's the only thing that feels right. Maybe he knows it's me, Jane, and it brings him comfort that I'm here with him. Maybe he thinks I'm his sister, coming to bring him home.

However he takes it, whether he understood or heard it at all, he dies after one last ragged breath.

CHAPTER 34 - JANE, ALMOST 2 WEEKS LATER

I'm sitting in the guest chair propped as close as it can go to where Liam is lying in the hospital bed. My right cheek is rested against his hand and I watch him as he sleeps peacefully.

Liam had to be airlifted to the nearest level-one trauma centre which was Vancouver. His injury ended up being more of a flesh wound, but he needed surgery of course which they performed in the city.

Between Dr. Kim Jenkins, RCMP Sergeant Jamieson and SAR leader Jimmy Slovak, favours were called in, and after a week of post-op care in Vancouver, Liam came back home to recover locally in the hospital closer to Julia and his mother. They transported him from Vancouver to the closest airport out here, Northern Rockies Regional Airport, only a ten-minute drive from Isinbury.

I've been back and forth from here and Bobby's room all week.

Liam has been hooked up to antibiotics and fluids all week, but he should be discharged in a few days if there's no complications. He's covered in yellowing bruises and has two broken fingers.

He'll need physiotherapy and he will continue his therapy for severe PTSD. He has qualified for long-term disability because his PTSD is so bad.

It could've been so much worse. The guilt is almost unbearable.

Bobby was finally discharged yesterday. He needed surgery to fix the damaged tissue and muscle in his leg from the glass, but Kim, his surgeon, said his life was likely saved by leaving it in until they could safely remove it. They kept him longer because he needed stitches to his head, and had concussion symptoms along with high blood pressure.

Many townsfolk have dropped off food or supplies, stopped by with coffee or treats or flowers. If they were hoping for some gossip or to get a good peek at us, they would've been greatly disappointed. Kim had reception accept gifts but not allow any visitors, other than the ones we gave special permission for. The hospital's security has seen to it that we haven't been bothered.

It's not like they all have ill-intent. In fact, it seems like the whole town has really pitched in to help us. Professional cleaners came to get the blood stains out of the floor and the house fixed up for Bobby's homecoming. The local physiotherapist has offered all of us an extreme discount if we need her. They must feel bad for all of the harassment they gave us when we were working the case. I'll take their help and well-wishes, but I still can't look some of them in the eye.

I sent Sara some flowers with a long-winded apology note. She stopped by after with some baked goods for us, and we spoke a little, but it was strained. She's decided to stay with Langdon, despite his infidelity.

Sara is all sweetness and pumpkin pie on the surface but she holds a grudge like no one I've ever met. I'm not sure this is something we will be able to mend. Maybe we've just grown into different people than we once were, and that's okay. I'll still have her back if she ever needs me. I owe her that.

Bobby is at home resting now, under Judie's care, and Kim checks in daily via Facetime to make sure he's managing. I'm so thankful for her, always going above and beyond. As the town's only general trauma surgeon, she's had her hands full with the rest of us.

Henry has a badly sprained neck, a broken finger on his good hand, and some bad abdominal bruising, but nothing some pain medication, a finger splint and a neck brace won't fix. After he was deemed fit to travel, he was sent to be detained in the city, awaiting trial for first degree murder of Daniel Briggs and criminal charges associated with *Pseudocide* (faking his own death) that mostly include obstruction of justice and public mischief. I will be helping him with his legal fees. After all, most of my money comes from my inheritance. He has one of the best lawyers in the country working for him. But he very likely could get life imprisonment with parole eligibility after 25 years.

I haven't allowed myself much time to think about how I feel about that. Or what our relationship will look like, beyond just helping him financially. I've had my own shit to deal with.

I have a badly sprained shoulder, a couple of bruised ribs and a severe concussion which has kept me in the hospital for close observation for a week and a half. Feels more like I'm being spanked for bad behaviour, but I've been happy to be so close to Liam and Bobby.

I also had a bit of dental surgery done. When Liam tackled Jake and took me down with them, I *did* chip my tooth. The front left one, to be precise. They fixed it and gave me some stitches for a 2 cm cut on my tongue. I didn't chop it off completely after all. But for the first few days, I couldn't talk because it was so swollen.

Unfortunately, because of the concussion, the pain meds they can safely give me are quite limited. To say I've been *suffering* is to put it mildly. I don't think there's a human word strong enough to explain the pain I've been in.

I shuffle myself into a more comfortable position now, adjusting the pillows I've surrounded my body with for support and lean back in the chair to stifle the pain radiating up my back and shoulder. Liam won't mind. He'd probably be pissed off to learn I'm even in this chair, instead of my own bed.

One of the regular nurses, Jill I think, walks in and adjusts his pain meds. She smiles at me as we make eye contact. "You seem more at ease around him, dear." I smile back at her in response as she leaves the room. I've been getting that a lot lately. And I feel the change inside, too.

Jamieson had stormed through the door with Kenny, Francis and some paramedics, minutes after Adam died. Kenny nearly passed out upon seeing Henry in the flesh. They rushed Bobby in the ambulance and called in an airlift for Liam, and arrested the three of us remaining. We all had to be sent to the hospital first, but they kept a close eye on us the entire time. Full security detail. Jamieson himself followed Henry around everywhere, not even leaving to go shower, as he deemed him a flight risk as soon as he realized the situation.

Francis was in charge of monitoring Jake, and lacking other options, they had trusted Kenny to watch me. Those first few days were a blur anyway. So much pain...dizziness...I wasn't myself. I'm glad it was Kenny who was there, and not some stranger. If I said anything incriminating at all, Kenny never repeated it.

If I thought our injuries were bad, they were nothing in comparison to Jake's in the end: dislocated knee with patella fracture, three broken ribs, severe concussion and numerous facial fractures as well, including eye socket, cheekbones and a shattered nose. Kenny told me his face looked like blackened, stitched hamburger meat.

We fought him with all we had.

I think of the rage and determination, but also the skill, of how he fought us off. Who knew one man could cause so much damage to the three of us? Especially considering two of us were in law enforcement. I wonder why he even got combat training in the first place? I suppose he thought he would be successful in holding me hostage and needed to be able to hold his own if I ever had the opportunity to challenge him. But the amount of training it would have taken to gain that level of skill...he has obviously been planning this for years.

An involuntary shiver runs up my spine.

Jake's also on remand, awaiting his sentencing hearing for five counts of First-Degree Murder for Lilyann, Megan, Brandi, Harrison and Adam. He'll go away for life, no doubt about it. I also heard the prosecution is arguing for parole ineligibility of 50 years or more. They seized video footage on his computer from a camera he wore attached to his jacket when he killed Lilyann. They also found the rifle that killed Brandi locked in his gun safe, and a page torn from Megan's sketch book of her artistic interpretation of Lilyann being killed that he took from the scene. They didn't need any of this evidence of course, as he pleaded guilty right away. I heard he provided his guilty statement with a grin on his face the entire time. Like he was proud of himself. But, maybe that was just a rumour...

After only two days of fixing him up, they had to wheel him out of Isinbury's hospital with cuffs wrapped around his wrists, attaching him to the wheelchair and into the transport for Vancouver Island Regional Correctional Centre. I walked down the hall to the other side of the building to watch him from the window. His leg was in a full cast and the top of his head bandaged up like a mummy, making him unrecognizable except for the small spaces allotted for his mouth and eyes. Still, right before they loaded him into the transport, as his wheelchair was slowly being lifted in, he turned his head upward in my exact direction and smiled.

He *smiled*.

He's long gone now, but I still can't get that image out of my mind. It replays over and over, along with his words from the cabin, "We're killers Jane, two dark souls."

~~~

The most surprising thing out of all of this chaos was when Jamieson came to see me yesterday to tell me Miranda provided a video of the night Abby died in exchange for a plea bargain.

"Sounds like her to keep that in her back pocket until the second she can use it," I quipped.

"Yes, I was quite surprised she came forward." He said, watching me closely. "Though her plea deal from before was revoked considering she lied about Harrison's involvement. This video gave her the full sweetheart deal she needed. Only two years and then she's free."

"She only gets two years and there's four...no, five bodies, from this? It's not right."

"No, it's not. But it's the justice system."

"And conveniently, Harrison isn't here to tell his side of the story."

"Well, the video pretty much sums things up. Not much more to tell."

"But did Jake really kill Harrison?"

"We have a written confession. You know this." He thought it over, trying to read my face. "Doesn't sit well with you?"

I shrugged and changed the subject, keeping my voice even. "Are you here to arrest me now that I'm well enough to travel?"

He considered this. "We'll see."

"What's on the video?"

"I'll show it to you if you want, but first, can you tell me your account of what really happened that night?" He said it like a challenge, setting us up for an informal interview with his recorder that he took out from his pocket. "Now that you've finally decided to be honest with us."

I decided to let that jab go. I deserved it, after all. I stated my name and position for the record. "Like I said before in my previous statement, we were partying at Miranda's that night. I blacked out sometime after we added marijuana on top of all the shots."

He let the silence creep up. His face was passive, but his eyes weren't. He knew more than I did. I decided to be as honest as I possibly could.

"What I didn't mention earlier...was that after that blackout I don't remember anything until waking up in front of the cave, the one where we found her body, the morning after." My cheeks became hot as fire, their redness betraying my guilt.

But instead of nodding, standing up, cuffing me and reading me my rights, he smiled and leaned back in his chair. "And that's it?"

Honesty, remember Jane?

"Do I need a lawyer?"

"I don't know. Do you?"

I sighed. "That's as much as I'm willing to comment without a lawyer, I'm afraid."

Again, he smiled back at me. "You know, you're quite fun to work with. Always keeping me on my toes."

I stared at him. Tried to read him. He was like a stone wall.

"Are you going to show me the video now?"

He laughed. "Yeah, alright."

CHAPTER 35 - JANE

The video is grainy and not well lit. You can hardly make out who people are, let alone any details.

As if reading my mind, Jamieson reminds me this was taken on a flip phone over 10 years ago.

"I'm going to fast forward a bit here, if you don't mind," Jamieson says to me now. I nod, but don't look up. I'm glued to the video. Waiting impatiently for the memories to come back, or the blanks to be filled. I catch glimpses of characters moving erratically on the screen as he fast forwards the video.

The footage shows fast forward flashes of the ground, presumably someone not paying attention to filming, then the yard, then the inside of the van. Jamieson presses play again.

The video shows Harrison basically throwing me in the back of the van. Abby sighs and pulls me deeper inside the back, then moves to take the middle seat. "She's *your* girlfriend." She looks embarrassed by me. The anger rises in my stomach again. *You were my friend. You were supposed to look out for me. Instead, you dragged me in over my head and laughed behind my back.* I know it's useless to be mad at her now. It obviously didn't work out for her either. But this night ruined my life. I can't help but feel mad at her still.

The phone is faced toward the ground again, and then it comes up showing Harrison now, as the driver. He must've just passed the phone to Miranda. She's filming him as he drives like a lunatic, then switching back to Abby who is dancing vigorously in the back to music blaring from the van's speakers, standing up even though there is no longer a door on the one side of the van. She hesitates, checking on me in the back as the van continues to do its spirals.

"Eww, she just vomited and now she's actually passed the fuck out! What a loser." Abby screams to the camera, laughing. Then she seems to think better of it. "Hey, if you're filming, don't post this."

And just then, the phone is pulled to the right and they all scream excitedly. "Hold on bitches!" Harrison yells. But the fuzzy shape that was Abby has clearly been yanked out of the screen. The phone is moving wildly in all directions.

"Oh shit." Harrison says. "What was that?"

"Oh my God!" Miranda yells, but there's still a lightness to her tone. She's laughing hysterically.

"Abby just flew out of the side like a twister!"

"What?" Harrison's voice is deadpan.

The phone drops to the floor of the van suddenly. The video is black.

Watching this video, I feel like I have been holding my breath for the last two minutes.

"What's wrong with you? You probably just gave me fucking whiplash." Miranda screams.

I hear a van door being opened and closed.

A few seconds of silence pass. Another door is opened but left open.

"Holy shit. Holy fucking shit." Harrison says.

"Oh my God. Is she…is she okay?" Miranda's voice is barely above a whisper.

"Fuck sakes!" Harrison screams then. "Her head is bashed in. It's actually bashed in. What the fuck are we going to do!"

"Hold on…oh fuck. That's…disgusting."

Someone sounds like they're vomiting.

"Come on. Throw her in the van." Harrison says.

"What? What are you talking about?" Miranda sounds properly hysterical now.

"I have a plan. Help me put her in."

"Why? We have to call someone. The cops or that drug dealer of yours. He'll know what to do right? It doesn't look like…I think she's dead."

"Fucking just help me."

A few minutes pass. The video is still black, presumably on the passenger side floor. My mouth has gone dry but I feel tears at the edge of my vision.

"Where are we going?" Miranda asks after a few minutes.

"The caves. We're gonna make it look like we had nothing to do with this."

The next few minutes of the video reveal their plan. They thought rubbing me with Abby's blood and putting me in front of the cave would make me look guilty as hell. They hoped if I woke up like that, I wouldn't say anything. They were right. For extra measures, they would go to her house and pack a bag and write a note.

Jamieson pauses the video. "The video goes on for another hour. We hear bits and pieces of their conversation and plans for the next while. But most of it is muffled. Miranda didn't dare touch the phone or remind him the video was still on. She said eventually she realized she could use this for security reasons and that she's had it stored away in a safe place if she ever needed it as a ticket out. Which of course she did. She claims she was scared for her life back then, just following orders, and again recently, once she realized it was all connected."

Miranda kept it for a ticket out. Of course she did.

He takes a deep breath and looks me square in the eyes.

I've been trying for the last several minutes to figure out what this means for me.

"I didn't kill her." I say, with a hint of surprise that I'm sure he notices. And Miranda turned this video in, knowing it would exonerate me when she could've just kept it hidden. Did she feel guilty and want to redeem herself of her sins? Or was it as simple as her using it as a bargaining chip for quicker freedom? I doubt I'll ever know for sure.

CHAPTER 36 - JANE, FIVE MONTHS LATER

I wake peacefully wrapped up in his warm arms, the soft morning light peeking through a slit in the curtain. I close my eyes again and listen to his gentle snoring. I shimmy back so I'm deeper in the cuddle. He wakes a little bit, nestling his chin on my shoulder.

Technically this used to be my parents' room, but that was too weird for me. Taking down the wall that separated the master bedroom and the guest bedroom was the first renovation to be undertaken. Now I have a giant master suite with a walk-in closet and a small balcony, mostly for my small vegetable garden. Helps to know some handymen around here willing to help make this place a home again.

It's been a busy few months. I haven't visited or spoken to Henry since he's been on remand, waiting for his trial. It's been a slow process but to my understanding he at least has a court date scheduled. I check in on him through an old contact there, but he doesn't need to know that. I'm not even sure I ever want to speak to him again.

I'm still working through my shit. Trying to "come to terms" with it all, and "find my peace" as my new therapist Lila says. Lila wears her hair down and doesn't bother with the fake smiling. I've always gotten along with women who skip past the pleasantries and get down to business. She's a local, and has a no-nonsense attitude that somehow translates as soft and understanding when she speaks to clients. I see her in-person once every two weeks and schedule video calls whenever I can't wait.

I like her much better than Teresa. I trust her. We fit well together.

My closet doors are open just a foot. They've been that way since I moved in. There's a small picture frame on the floor, slanted sideways. I always stare at it when I wake up. It's of Dad and I the day I caught my first fish.

So...I'm still working through it. I haven't let go of the person I thought Henry was. The person he could still be, under all the chaos.

Lila says it's possible, but not to get my hopes up.

Last night was a bit rough. Liam woke from another nightmare and instead of trying to sleep again he decided to read next to me while I slept lightly. I woke up a bit later myself, plagued with endless thoughts and questions keeping me wide-awake, but instead of reading, I guiltily woke him up and asked him to tire me out. He's never that deep of a sleeper and always seems more than pleased to be woken up that way. We sweat it out and the pulsing high relaxes us both back into a few hours of restful sleep. It's not perfect, but it's something close to it.

He must sense I'm awake now because I feel him stretch out his legs and then kiss my bare back. I turn my head to the side and sneak a peek at his sleepy, slept-on face. He peeks open an eyelid and when he sees me, he smiles.

"How long have you been up?" Liam whispers. His voice is hoarse from sleep.

"Just a few minutes." I tuck my arm under his grasp.

"*Liar*," he says playfully. He knows I'm still having trouble sleeping through the night. "Still thinking about whether to tell Kim you're her half-sister?"

"I don't have it in me to tell her just yet." I pause. "*Hey Kim, remember when we talked about you being adopted? Well, not only did I know then that we were half-sisters but it means the dad we share is actually that lying, cheating, murdering vigilante I sent to prison. Welcome to the family!*" My voice is thick with sarcasm.

He chuckles lightly. "Hey, it didn't scare me off. Give her more credit." His fingers graze my shoulder, drawing circles and giving me goosebumps.

"Trust may come easy to you in your warm ways, but for me it's like flexing a muscle I haven't used in years."

"She's mostly alone out here, Jane. She could really use more family."

"I know, I know. So could I. I'm talking through it with Lila. Trying to find the right time."

I don't owe Laryssa this extra time before Kim finds out the truth. And she knows it.

I'll tell Kim soon...just...not right now.

"I'm so proud of you for going to therapy." I roll over to meet his face and he kisses me softly.

"Yeah. Well, you led the way."

He smiles.

"It's chilly in here."

"I'll go close the window."

He makes it half way up until I pull him back down.

"Can you stay just a bit longer? I'm enjoying this."

"Who even are you?" he jokes. I shake my head and suppress a laugh.

"I guess your ways are rubbing off on me."

He gives me a squeeze.

"Once we're up, I'll go make some pancakes for us. I have to pick up Julia from Kim's and then go visit my mom. Do you want to tag along? Mom would love to see you again."

"Of course. I'll come with you. But I don't like pancakes."

He snorts. "How am I still learning these things about you?"

"To be fair, I don't even know your favourite colour."

I think about the long conversations we had once we were both out of the hospital. We laid it all out: all of our history, all of our secrets, all of our questions answered. It turned out to be a complete coincidence that we lived a block away from each other in Vancouver. We don't remember ever meeting but we probably crossed paths before; either on the sidewalk, in the grocery store, or on the job, him being a first responder and me being a cop. The blonde woman from the cryptic photo Jake had sent me from an unknown number? She drank too much at the Raven that night and Liam was walking her to his car to drive her to the ER. Henry had ambushed him coming back out of the hospital.

"It's grey."

"Grey? That's not even a colour."

He pinches my butt and I involuntarily squeal. He leaves me in the blankets as he gets up and closes the window. He pulls on a tight white shirt as I check him out from the safety of my blanket fort.

"I'll go make us some eggs and bacon then...unless you want me to help warm you up still?" The flirtatiousness of his facial expression gives my stomach butterflies, and I'm about to pull him back into the covers when my cell phone vibrates. It's Bobby. I expect it to be another *fine, you were right* or *thank you for pushing me* text, since he moved in with Judie a few months ago and they've never been happier. They're even planning a romantic trip to the Bahamas with some of the money Judie got for selling her house.

Instead, I look down and his text has one word: *incoming*.

It rings. It's a number I haven't seen in a very long time.

Liam senses this won't be an easy call, so he kisses my forehead and makes his way to the door.

"Omelette and fried potatoes then?"

I nod, but my eyes stay glued on the screen. I let myself meet his gaze for a comforting moment before answering on the last ring.

"Hello?"

A pause.

"Jane, is that you? It's Elena."

Elena and I used to be best friends at Depot together when we were both training to be RCMP officers. I'm pretty sure she filled my position at The Major Crime Unit in Vancouver when I was demoted.

A pause from me now. I sit up in bed and take a sip of water from my nightstand. It's stale and lukewarm but it wets the throat.

"What do you want?" I ask bluntly.

Maybe that was a little rude, but it was deserved.

"I already spoke with your RCMP station commander sergeant and he gave me your new number." Silence. "He thinks I could use your help."

"My help? With what? Last time we spoke, you told me my life was too dramatic and you didn't want to be seen with me anymore."

"Jane–"

"No. That was a real shit move Lena." I stutter ever so slightly. "Elena." Can't be using nicknames right now. Put your damn wall up Jane. "We were best friends since Depot and when I needed you the most, you just dropped me like I was–"

"Jane, I–"

"I had nobody left. I just lost someone who was like a brother to me and suddenly everyone hated me even though I wasn't the bad guy. I was in a dark place. You could've...you could've helped me then."

"Jane!" She nearly yells it into the phone. "I'm sorry, okay? I really am. I didn't have a strong enough backbone to withstand the scrutiny you were under. I took the easy way out and it was wrong. I'm sorry."

I sigh. Strangely her admitting that after a year and a half doesn't have the sweet ring to it like I thought it would.

"But we found a murder victim here and she's from your hometown. It's one of your residents."

Suddenly my mouth feels like the desert. I reach for more water, but there's none left. I cough.

"Who?"

"I can explain all of that when you get here."

"Who...Wait what do you mean?"

"We made a good team once, you and I. This case could use your expertise. And you sort of know the victim. All signs point to you." A sigh from her end. "Chief Henderson is on board with bringing you back. We wouldn't have to work in the station, we can have our own outpost if you're more comfortable with that. She's okayed it already."

"Well, I'm not sure I–"

"Regardless of what has happened between us, there are women in this city being hunted. A city you used to call home. Literally being hunted, only because of their gender and the fact that they are in powerful positions. If you don't come help, I'm going to have to team up with cocky Ulrich or dickhead McIntosh, and they won't care about it like you or I will. I don't trust them like I trust you."

I notice my body has gone still. I hear Liam call from downstairs then, announcing breakfast is almost ready. I think about the life I was going to set up here. The home I just renovated. The boyfriend I now have. This peaceful, no-stress life.

"When do you need me?"

I think about Liam's recent offer to take up his uncle's woodworking business in Vancouver that he didn't accept because he wanted to make this work with me. How he and Julia would see each other more than just on weekends if we moved, because her school is there.

I'm walking out of the darkness and into the light, and this time I have my loved ones surrounding me, thick as a shield, against whatever I face next.

"Can you be here in five days?"

"I'll see you in a week." I hang up and stare at the phone in my hand. It doesn't even seem real.

I'll be there in five days. I just want to make her sweat.

CHAPTER 37

Dear Jane,

I saw what happened that night. It was like I told you: Harrison and Miranda and even Abby, your bestest friend in the whole world, got you shit-faced on purpose, mostly to make fun of you. Their plan was to humiliate you later with videos leaked to the entire school. You were always Abby's plaything. Just like me, her younger brother. She used you to get what she wanted and made you feel special, and when she was done with you, she would throw you away like garbage and somehow make you think you deserved it.

Oh Jane.

You were bouncing around in the back seat, completely passed out. Abby flew out of the side of the open van door, her skull crushed by the van's tire. Later, I would imagine that you woke for a second and pushed her out of the door, before pretending to be asleep again. But that is all pretend. It used to comfort me though, believing we were the same, you and I.

I saw it all from the tree line of Miranda's property. They never even considered calling the police and saying it was an accident. They came up with the idea of the caves so fast. Even drunk, they were quick to hide what had happened. I watched them, hooked on the scene like I was in a trance. They made sure you were still unconscious and then drove you both to the caves. I had to bike like hell to keep up with you and I was 10 minutes late, but again, I watched and I followed. My heart was beating so fast. I watched you lying there on the ground, outside the caves, completely passed out. They were inside dropping my sister's body down the cave shaft, so I crept up beside you to make sure you were okay. You were breathing so deep. Snoring even. I was both excited and terrified you would wake any second but you didn't.

I crept down and touched your body briefly with my kisses, lovingly of course. I would never hurt you Jane. I just wanted your body to know I was near and that I loved you and wouldn't let any harm come to you. I heard them coming out, so I ran back to the tree line. They fought over what to do with you next. Miranda was whispering that they should bash your head in and throw you in beside Abby. By then, I had a heavy branch in my hands, I was ready to kill them if I needed to. Anything to protect you; to be your hero. But Harrison surprised me by ordering her to leave you out there. He believed you would be so terrified waking up like that, you wouldn't ask many questions once you learned Abby was missing. "Or maybe the wildlife will get her and solve this problem for us," he had laughed. I felt my fingers tighten around the branch. They left and I stayed up all night watching you, making sure nothing else happened to you. Just like I said Jane, I was your protector. I always have been. I watched you wake up scared and confused in the afternoon, and I followed you until you flagged down that car and were safe.

What I never told you, what I couldn't tell you, my sweet Jane, was that once you were safe, I went into the caves to see where my sister was kept. To say goodbye. What surprised me the most was that she was still alive. A barely-there pulse, but I could feel it through my frozen fingers. Her body was still warm. The idiots! They never even checked for a pulse! I would think about it for years later, how a quarter of your skull could be missing, crushed like the consistency of a juicy watermelon, but you could still be alive.

Her being alive and telling her version of events, whatever they would be, would ruin all of your big plans of being a police officer Jane. You could've even gone to jail for this. She would've loved to play the victim. To be the centre of attention, to be loved and cared for by all. And most importantly, to have us all kiss her feet in adoration and thankfulness that she was alive. There is so much power in being the victim, Jane. You know this now. I helped you become this person instead.

So when I found her there, I did not hesitate. I put my hand over her mouth and nose and waited for her pulse to stop and for her body to stop wriggling. I did it for you, my love. I know you will understand. Maybe you will even love me for it.

PS: I wish I killed Harrison, but it wasn't me. Think that one was your dad.

Acknowledgements

It took me 8 years from start to finish, but I finally did it. I started my chronic health journey unable to walk at all and the frustration of not being able to have control over my situation was what inspired me to write my first book.

To my readers, thank you for taking a chance on this book and on me. I hope you enjoyed all the twists and turns, and the excitement of watching Jane get a little beat up but overall, kick ass no matter what situation she faced. Please continue to support disabled and marginalized authors, as well as novels whose main character belongs to one of these groups. As a reminder, these groups include but are not limited to: BIPOC, women, LGBTQ+, low-income individuals, the disabled, senior citizens, and many more. We truly appreciate your support!

A sincere thanks to my Dad for everything you did for me to help this book make it into other people's hands. Sorry for sacrificing your ability to read this book for the first time in its polished, finished form, but you were the only one I trusted with this in its rough drafts to make it great. Your constructive criticism and plot-hole-finding-radar were invaluable. You passed on your love of reading to me, and that helped me become a better writer. Love you Dad.

To my beta-readers Emile, Nikki and Paula - you were all fantastic. I couldn't have done this without your feedback. Paula, I hope you never stop beta-reading, because I will need your services for every other book I write - it was so fun for me to read your comments because it felt like I could be a fly on the wall with my very first reader and watch all of their big reactions with the shocking parts of the book. Thank you all so very much from the bottom of my heart.

Mom, you were instrumental in the creation of this book, and I'm not sure you realize how much. You were my biggest supporter from the first time I mentioned I was even writing a book, and every little bit of writing I sent your way, you made me feel like I was the best writer ever. You truly are such a big support in my life: financially, emotionally, and so much more. Dropping off groceries, giving me time to write, taking me on adventures around the world - you're an awesome Mom and I love you with my whole heart.

To my friends who are as excited about this book coming out as I am: you mean the world to me. Christelle, Andrew, Nick, Sarah, Hannah, Roman and so many more I'm afraid to try to list them all and forget a name. Thanks for being in my corner and supporting me in all the ways I needed. Your friendships are what keeps me going every day.

Andrew, you were especially helpful in allowing me to learn from you after publishing your book, Dollhouse, and follow in your footsteps. Thanks for being so generous in your time and sharing all your great tips and information. I will never forget it.

To all the literary agents who passed on this book and especially the ones who were "almosts" - thank you for taking the time to read my submissions and to provide helpful feedback. I hope you will see how awesome this book is and reach out in the future. My next book, No Cure For This, will rock your socks off.

Thank you to my medical team for helping me get back to being more myself - there were countless doctors and specialists throughout the years, and the majority of you never gave up until we got real answers and tried all the solutions. You know who you are. Thank you for not giving up on me.

Last but certainly not least, Cody, my love, there are no words to explain how BIG a part you played in helping this book come to publication. All the times you would come home and find me hunched over my laptop, and you would silently bring me water and snacks and a kiss on my forehead, telling me you were proud of me. I don't know what I did to deserve a love like yours but I'm thankful every single day of my life that you're my husband and we are the best team. Thank you for supporting me in the million of small and big ways and for always being my biggest cheerleader from day 1 until now. I can't wait for you to finally read the book in its finished form, as a paperback in your hands, and for you to see how cool your wife is.

And thank you to everyone else! Lots of love for all those who supported me from start to finish. I hope you love this book as much I do.

About The Author

Now, let me tell you a little bit about where I am today, and how I got here.

Right now, I'm a part time writer, and I feel very lucky to be able to do what I love in my spare time. I have been chronically sick and disabled since 2016, although I have a great medical team who has finally found me a treatment plan that gives me a part of my   life back. My experience navigating a world with chronic illness at a young age has inspired my main characters to also face these challenges. I hope you enjoy their uniqueness, and their undeniable strength and resilience.

Not-for-profit work is very important to me. I work closely with my favourite local dog rescue, called Rocky Road Rescue. I'm on their social media and marketing team, I regularly volunteer for their fundraising events and I've adopted all my rescue dogs from them over the years. Joining their community of strong, resilient, funny dog-loving women was one of the best things that ever happened to me.

I have also collaborated with Lanark County Interval House, Elizabeth Fry Society, Hospice Care Ottawa, Maple Hope Foundation, Dress for Success Ottawa, Kidney 4 Craig, Project Tembo and more.

I always wanted to be a writer, right from when I was a little girl. I was always scribbling out little stories and finishing storylines of dreams I woke up too soon from, creating even better endings. Later, in elementary school, I was getting noticed for my poetry and essays, as well as getting nominated to represent my entire school at annual speech competitions (unfortunately my great fear of public speaking prevented me from accepting this honour). I won several monetary bursaries at my high school graduation, from essay competitions that my teachers entered me in without my knowledge, but which helped me afford college. I graduated with an Honours Certificate in Media and Communications and an Honours Diploma in Journalism. I was the Managing editor of Glue magazine and have published articles through British Columbia magazine, Canadian Traveller magazine, Pacific Yachting, explore magazine, Glue magazine, the Algonquin Times and Kanata-Kourier Standard for Metroland media.

When I was in my twenties, I represented Canadian Traveller on press trips around the globe. I've kissed giraffes in Nairobi, climbed mountains in the isolated Torngat Mountains in Labrador beside Margaret Atwood, done wine tours along the Amalfi Coast in Italy, kissed the Blarney Stone in Ireland, and almost gotten eaten by a hippo in Tsavo East National Park in Kenya.

Now I live outside of Ottawa with my husband and our rescue dogs. Our backyard faces the forest and you can see the River from our front lawn. We love to hike, kayak, camp and swim. The town we live in is very outdoorsy and has inspired my writing on more than one occasion. You'll often find me in my hammock facing the forest, disconnecting from technology and curling up with a great book.

Printed in Great Britain
by Amazon

45370893R00225